THE OBSESSION

By T. V. LoCicero

Also By T.V. LoCicero

NOVELS
The Disappearance (The Truth Beauty Trilogy, Book 2)
The Car Bomb (The *detroit im dyin* Trilogy, Book 1)
Admission of Guilt (The *detroit im dyin* Trilogy, Book 2)
Babytrick (The *detroit im dyin* Trilogy, Book 3)
When A Pretty Woman Smiles
Sicilian Quilt

NON-FICTION BOOKS
Murder in the Synagogue
Squelched: The Suppression of *Murder in the Synagogue*

COLLECTION
Coming Up Short

Praise for *The Obsession*

"...very exciting. I was hooked by the time I finished the first chapter. It is very well written, fast moving and suspenseful. A stalker who is truly deranged, a beautiful professor, lovers, and friends, what more could you ask for? Looking forward to reading the next book." — Barbara Juhl

"...a taut thriller allowing the reader to experience the feelings and behaviors of stalkers and those stalked...An added bonus is the beauty of Italy. What an excellent, unputdownable read!" — Fran Hoffman

"This novel is 'packed' with everything from international news...mystery twists, love and complication, death, a stalker, and my favorite...visuals and enjoyment reading about places in Italy. As for the ending...nope...I didn't figure it out!" — Elyse Walters

"This academic, psychological thriller is a page-turner. There is a touch of romance. The characters are fleshed-out, especially the heroine. The plot is suspenseful. The twist and turns of the plot and subplots keep the reader guessing what will happen next." — Candace Peterson

"...keeps the reader guessing on multiple accounts for most of the narrative. This book is much closer to the works of Patricia Highsmith, especially the Ripley novels. It is fascinating to see how the obsession is carried out and how the evil actions in the book are conceived. It was definitely a fun, stimulating and intellectually captivating tale." — Robert Blumenthal

"Alfred Hitchcock would have enjoyed directing this thriller about stalker Stan's psychopathy and victim Lina's plunge into fear, depression, and guilt. This is a novel that you either stay up all night to read or, like me, you'll have to walk away as the anxiety escalates, only to be called back by the need to know." — Irene Balassis

"...this book takes many of its cues from books like Kingsley Amis' *Lucky Jim*, Mary McCarthy's *The Groves of Academe*, and even Max

Beerbohm's *Zuleika Dobson*...the petty scholarly battles for which academia is justly famous, and which are thoughtfully represented in this book, pale in comparison to the acts of the novel's principal characters." —Mark Feltskog

"The characters in this story are brilliantly and believably drawn (some you will hope never to meet) and the story so vividly written, that although I was trying to ration myself to only read a chapter at a time, everything tiny part of this intense cat and mouse "game" stayed crystal clear in my mind...The is one of those rare books that can be read in sections, or devoured in a single sitting. Whatever your approach, it will be a book that will stay in your mind for a long, long time." —Rosemary Standeven

"A book full of intrigue with a surprise ending. T.V. LoCicero has outdone himself in the first of The Truth Beauty Trilogy. Great characters...A great mystery with surprising turns. Loved it!" —Cathy Morgan

"Lots of exciting scenarios, with several twists/turns & a huge set of unique characters to keep track of. This could also make another great romantic mystery movie, or better yet a mini TV series." —Tony Parsons

"This one has it all! Love, murder, horror, and travelogue all wrapped up into one...had me so entrapped that when I started reading it around 11:00 at night before going to sleep, I found that I did not stop till long after the sun came up the next morning. It will suck you in right quick and you won't be able to put it down." —Maggie Julia

"The setting was beautiful. The historical details fascinating. And the plot...a mystery/thriller of sorts, but it's more than just your average mystery due to skillful writing and exquisite detail." —Valencia Redd

T. V. LoCicero

T.V. LoCicero has been writing both fiction and non-fiction across five decades. He's the author of the true crime books *Murder in the Synagogue* (Prentice-Hall), on the assassination of Rabbi Morris Adler, and *Squelched: The Suppression of Murder in the Synagogue*. His novels include the romance *When A Pretty Woman Smiles,* the coming-of-age literary novel *Sicilian Quilt,* and the crime thrillers *The Car Bomb, Admission of Guilt* and *Babytrick* (The *Detroit im dyin* Trilogy), and *The Obsession* and *The Disappearance* (the first two books in The Truth Beauty Trilogy. Eight of his shorter works are now available as ebooks. They are available as well (along wih several other short pieces) in *Coming Up Short,* a collection of fiction and non-fiction. LoCicero has also published stories and essays in various periodicals, including Commentary, Ms. and The University Review, and in the hard-cover collections *Best Magazine Articles, The Norton Reader* and *The Third Coast*.

THE OBSESSION

By T. V. LoCicero

The Truth Beauty Trilogy
Book 1

TLC *Media*

The Obsession
by T. V. LoCicero
Copyright 2012 by T. V. LoCicero

Grateful acknowledgment to Patrick Frank and Leo McNamara for their enormously helpful reading of the work in progress, to David Womersley for his review of Saturday by Ian McEwan in The Social Affairs Unit, and to Jack Beatty for his essay "The Crooked Timber of Humanity" in The Atlantic.

For more information on this and other works by T.V. LoCicero please visit:

www.tvlocicero.com

For David

Chapter 1

Side by side they lean on the railing, gazing down five stories of darkness to the sidewalk below. For the past 10 minutes, first inside and then, when Hal said he needed some air, out here on the patio, he's been listening to the guy tell stories about the kindness of his grandmother. Most of them Stan has heard before. Yes, everyone needs to mourn, but enough of this. He glances at his Rolex. "Jesus, it's after one. I gotta go."

He heads for the patio's open door. Hal follows. "Hey, man, can I ask you something?"

Stan turns, and Hal ends up standing just a bit too close. This often happens when he wants to ask about something serious. As if there's some spatial adjustment mechanism that goes slightly haywire in his brain.

"Sure, ask away." Stan tries moving back a few inches. Hal leans forward.

"Well, here's the thing. I've been thinking a lot about Lina lately."

"Yeah?" This is not going where he expects, or wants.

"And the thing is, we always have these great conversations, and she's always so warm and friendly to me."

"Yeah?"

"So I'm thinking she's probably kind of lonely here, and maybe she'd like it if I asked her out."

Stan tries to stay calm. "If you asked her out."

"Yes, frankly, I think she really likes me."

Stan waits a beat, trying to control himself by keeping his head perfectly still. "You've got to be kidding."

For a second Hal seems flummoxed but plows ahead. "Well, no, I'm not kidding. Is it really so hard to imagine?"

Staring with scorn at those sappy brown eyes, Stan sees him finally begin to get it, inclining that big head slightly forward, as if trying to get a better angle on his friend's new contempt. This only stokes more anger. His body sets itself, and both hands fly up to land with force on Hal's breastbone, just as Stan utters, with a special rage,

1

his final word:

"Get off me, you stupid FUCK!"

As he delivers the blow, Stan blinks and then watches Hal, who's always seemed a bit top heavy, on the verge of imbalance, reeling silently backward. A second later the night is split with a cat's high-pitched scream. Now Hal is doing a weird, spastic dance, a desperate lift on his toes to save little Tess from additional pain. Just enough lift, as he continues to sail back, for the top of the patio railing to meet exactly the right spot on the small of Hal's back, to flip him, heels-over-head, in an arm-flailing arc into thin air.

There is no last second eye-contact. Hal simply disappears. Without a sound. Until some seconds later, when he lands below. That terrible thud slams Stan in the stomach and sends him to his knees, and, with a gasp and a shiver, to all fours. His vision blurs, and he wonders if he'll pass out. He has to focus. Listen and look. Despite the choking fear and despair, listen and look.

He doesn't know his ears are buzzing until they stop. And now, incredibly, the night is perfectly still. No rustle, no stirring, no shouts, no street noise, no birds, no insects. Nothing. He crawls on hands and knees to the patio wall and slowly hauls himself up just far enough to peer over the rail. It's a dark, overcast night, and this side of the old building has almost no lighting, but there's enough to see Hal, frozen in a hopeless sprawl, on the edge of the sidewalk, half on, half off. Stan looks left, then right. From the quiet street in front, to the abandoned softball field that borders the building, to the small parking lot at the back, he sees no one. On all the patios within his view no light comes on, no figure appears. Nothing moves. Dropping back to his hands and knees, he moves to the door, then pauses to listen for a distant siren responding to a call from some hidden witness in the building or shadowy passerby on the street. Silence.

On his feet inside, he closes the patio door, then opens it again. Tess is nowhere to be seen. His mind on the ragged edge of panic, he knows he must get out of this apartment now. But a glimpse of Hal's glowing laptop screen—a photo of Hal at age 8 arm-in-arm with grandma—stops him cold. At the keyboard he finds Word and clicks on it. How to write a suicide note in 30 seconds or less? Don't think, just type whatever pops into your head. A word, a phrase, a sentence. Forget caps or punctuation, there's no style sheet for this. The blank page is ready.

2

too much death

i cant take it anymore

please forgiv me

my live has no meaning

grandma I've coming to join you

sorry

I lost everyone I care about

goodby

Hal

Reading it back, he knows this is a mess, nothing the meticulous Hal would ever leave behind. He wants to fix the typos, cut and paste "please forgiv me" to the top. No fucking way, there's no damn time, just get out. But his prints! His fingerprints are all over these keys. He clicks back to that stupid desktop photo with grandma, pulls out his handkerchief and rubs it over all the keys. Now click back to the note and wipe off the mouse. Almost to the door, with Hal's key sitting there in the inside lock, he remembers his black leather binder. Jesus Christ! He finds it quickly on Hal's old steamer trunk coffee table. In the patio doorway Tess reappears. She meets his gaze with a baleful glare, then drops her back and slinks away. Back at the door, he tells himself again: no one can see or hear a trace of him, in the building or as he leaves.

* * *

An hour later, in his underwear, wrapped in a blanket, he sits in his dark apartment, a converted gatehouse four miles out of town. For some reason it seems important to fix in his memory all the moments in the last several hours that could just as easily have gone a different way. Often slight diversions would have changed everything.

Starting where? According to Hal, in Pittsburgh. After the late afternoon post-funeral dinner, his sister had begged him to stay the night. He'd been there five days. What was one more night? It would be midnight before he'd be back in Cedar Hill, and with all his lost sleep, he was already dead tired. But, no, Hal did not succumb. He really needed and wanted to get back. There were papers to be

3

graded. He was certain he'd feel better back at St. Thomas.

On the drive back he was so filled with reveries of a grandma who raised him like a mom that he only remembered when he left I-94, fifteen minutes from Cedar Hill, that Stan had the apartment key. When Stan got the call, he insisted on meeting Hal at the apartment.

"Hey, that's not necessary. I'll just swing by and pick it up."

"No way. You've been through a terrible ordeal, you've been on the road all night and I'm well out of your way. I'll meet you there and let you in."

"Stan, I don't…."

"It's nothing, buddy, see you in a few."

"Man, thank you. You're too much."

No, actually, he was an absent-minded dunce when it comes to that fucking leather folder. Not a half-hour earlier he had suddenly remembered leaving it at Hal's place when he stopped by to open a can for Tess. Along with a Taco Bell dinner, he had brought the damn thing in with him, in case a thought worth recording occurred to him while munching the burrito. When he opened the folder, he found the yellow legal pad inside covered with doodles and scribbles from almost a week ago, including a couple of versions of the note he had ended up printing out from his computer and leaving for Marissa on the windshield of her Volvo.

> Hey, check it out!
>
> Your husband's fucking a prominent campus
> whore.

That was the first iteration, but as he sat alone at the Bean, he decided it needed names.

> Hey, Marissa,
>
> Thought you should know: John's fucking Lina,
> the sexy new Italian prof. You're a lovely person
> and don't deserve this.
>
> Yours truly,
>
> A Friend

From her booth at Two last week she had snapped her undercover photos, but the tale they told might still leave room for doubt. He

4

needed to make damn sure Marissa was convinced.

Whatever. There was no way he could let Hal see that note. So he drove quickly back to Hal's and found the folder sitting right there on the kitchen counter. Ripping off the tell-tale yellow sheet, he crumpled and shoved it into his jeans pocket. And then he became aware of a stench in the apartment. The litter box. Hal had asked him to scoop it, but he hadn't bothered. To air the place out, he opened the door to the patio and felt the cool October breeze on his face. Large enough for a table and chairs and shielded from the neighbors with sidewalls, the patio was the apartment's only feature he liked. The building was ancient and decrepit, with tenants lured away to newer housing, now only half-occupied. Paint peeled, hallways smelled, and the buzzer system at the entry doors no longer worked. As Hal put it, the price was right.

When Hal pushed through the half-opened door and walked in with his duffle bag, Stan was surprised by a half-hug. "Man, thanks so much for doing this."

"No problem, buddy."

Hal fussed over Tess, turned on his computer, and sorted through the stack of new mail. Then picking up a batch of old mail, he was shocked to find it covering the second key he'd been searching for so frantically before he left five days ago. Taking it to the door and sliding it into the inside lock, he insisted that Stan just keep the key he had, so there'd always be someone who could come in and take care of Tess "in case of emergency."

Ready to leave, Stan made his biggest mistake. He asked how Hal was doing. Unlike most humans, for whom the question is rhetorical, Hal too often answered it. This time he moved almost non-stop through everything he'd been pondering about grandma on the way back from Pittsburgh. At one point, he paused and said, "Hey, I'm feeling a little light-headed. Let's go out here for a minute and get some air." As Hal walked onto the patio, Stan had missed his chance.

If he had just said, "Buddy, I really need to go...."

If Hal had lifted that pile of mail on his computer desk before leaving five days ago...

If he had listened to his sister...

If Stan had not forgotten that bloody leather folder...

If he had cleaned the litter box...

If Hal did not have that stupid habit of standing too close to you...

5

If the fucking cat hadn't been hanging around her owner's clumsy feet...

The hum of a car on the rural highway running past the gatehouse makes him feel his heart beat. The pitch of the hum says it's moving fast, like the other four that have zipped by since he got out of his clothes, pulled the blanket from the bed and camped himself on the couch. He needs to look like he's been asleep when the cops arrive to grill him for the rest of the night.

Not that his flight from Hal's building was, as far as he knows, anything but clean. He paused in the hall only to lock the door with his key. Of course, now it would appear locked from the inside. Then moving without a sound over the stained and frayed hallway carpet, he passed the noisy old elevator, hit the stairwell and stepped carefully down four flights to the backdoor, In the chilly night air he sprinted to the Beemer, and on his cautious drive back, he spotted one moving vehicle, a beer delivery truck. Yes, someone might have seen or heard something to report to the police, but, other than that one truck driver, he never saw a soul.

So why, upon his return, did he stick that key deep into the soil of his potted cactus? Why, every time a car passes, is he certain the cops have come for him? He has no guilt. He did nothing wrong. He shoved a guy in the chest. A guy who was being obnoxious. Well, maybe annoying. Was there any criminal intent? None at all. Then why flee? That one's easy. Because without question it's impossible to explain the truth in a way that will surely set him free.

He knows now what he'll do. In the morning when the horrible news of Hal's tragic fate reaches him in some fashion, he will go straight to the police in Cedar Hill, and, distraught, broken with grief, haunted by the knowledge that he should have noticed something in the demeanor of his good, dear friend, he will tell all the truth he can possibly tell. Right up to the moment when Hal arrived at the gatehouse to pick up his key.

Chapter 2

So, really, starting where? You'd have to go 4500 miles east of the gatehouse and back to his birthday in June, nearly four months ago now. The rarely casual Fr. Redding surprised him at breakfast with his greeting that morning in the hotel. "Stan, Stan, the birthday man."

"*Buon giorno*, Father."

"*Buon giorno*, Stanford. Sleep well?"

"Yes, and you?"

"Like a baby. So what is it, 29?"

Of course the priest knew it was his 29th, though Stan hadn't mentioned it, or that it was in fact his reason for this trip, a gift to himself that has turned out even better than he hoped. Bob Daddy, as he calls the priest behind his back, heads the department and, given the man's memory and inclination, probably has total recall on all of Stan's records.

The week has been everything promised by the website for the 2007 San Giulio Conference on Comparative Literature with its impressive list of scholars and perfect scenic photos. "Seven days of intellectual and aesthetic stimulation" in what has to be a candidate for the world's most beautiful place, the Italian lake district above Milan, exploring Como, Maggiore and the one he had never heard of, Orta, where their Hotel San Rocco is located. The description from Balzac clinched the deal: "A delicious little lake at the feet of the Rosa" — that would be Monte Rosa, the dominating gray peak looming above the surrounding green mountains — "a perfectly-placed island in calm waters, coquettish and simple."

The island is San Giulio, maybe 500 yards beyond the lakeside wall at the far end of this public garden where, among clusters of pink roses, about 75 folding chairs have been set for the mostly English-speaking academics waiting for the conference's final lecture. He and Redding visited the tiny island and its 11th century basilica earlier in the week, a few minutes on a small motor launch for a trip that, back in 390 AD, a Greek evangelist named Julius had made by floating on his cloak. It was a miracle, of course, but then Julius would turn out to be a saint—thus, San Giulio—who could manage many remarkable things. And having spotted the little island just off Lago d'Orta's eastern edge, he quickly decided it should be his.

Why the cloak? Because, when asked for their help in boating him there, the locals immediately knew he was out of his mind. The lake was full of monsters, the island crawling with snakes and guarded by a horrific dragon that devoured anything foolish enough to come near. Julius, of course, knew that, doing God's work, he had nothing to fear and so laid his cloak on the monster-infested waters of the beautiful lake and floated unscathed to the island. There he rid the place of its snakes and disposed of the dragon. Once ensconced on his little isle, he built his 100th church and in 400 AD passed from this vale of tears.

Thereafter, this serene and fetching place was fought over for some 15 centuries by the Germans, the French and, of course, the Papists, all of them, more often than not, power-hungry, greedy, deceitful and vicious. Yes, Stan thinks, there is enough history here to keep him reading for years. He already knows he'll return, probably sooner than later, and, in love now with all things Italian, he's even been fantasizing about spending the rest of his days here.

And now this woman. Stan knows her the moment he sees her. Lina Lentini, the professor of comp lit from the University of Bologna, about to deliver the conference's closing lecture on "The Sources of Good and Evil in the Novels of Ian McEwan and Philip Roth." Even though he's never seen a picture, and to this moment she's simply been a name and a 100-word reputation. Even though in his mind's eye she's either been close to anorexic with a pinched face and anxious little gestures, or pear-shaped, substantial through the hips and thighs in a way that seems inevitable for some women in their late 30's. In either case, he pictured an overly serious, slightly judgmental gaze. A woman, in short, anything but hot. Now he sees the only thing he was close on is the age.

The bio in the conference literature said she's published one book based on her doctoral dissertation (*Nord e Sud: Guilt and Redemption in the Post-War Italian Novel*) and another, seven years later, that takes a broader view of the literary landscape (*Rational Morality: British and*

American Novelists at the Close of the 20th Century). With many essays in prestigious reviews and journals, her work has been widely acclaimed for its keen moral insight, her ability to isolate and analyze "the ethical dilemmas that define our time," and her "daring in taking up the largest themes with which our most important practitioners are engaged."

Now he sees a redhead, the hair up in a clip but sparkling in the warm sun. The face is calm, self-possessed and heart-wrenchingly attractive, the eyes large and expressive and the mouth sensual. The yellow sundress — inappropriate yet wonderful for the occasion — is cut above slim pretty knees and scooped low over remarkable curves. Christ, is she even wearing a bra? The stork-like fellow on her left — lank blond hair over his collar and his mouth hanging open as he stares down her chest — can certainly tell. And the bald little guy on her right, short hairy arms gesturing often as they chat, can surely testify to the charm in that smile as it turns from one to the other. Stan hasn't seen her move, yet knows the body is extraordinary.

With his gaze elsewhere, the redhead and her sundress must have walked in with these two characters, one of whom will no doubt introduce her in a couple of minutes. Most of the lectures and seminars have been held in the San Rocco's meeting and conference rooms, but a few were scheduled for nearby locations like this garden behind a classic 3-story palazzo. Now she's moving a few steps forward, a large straw bag over her shoulder, following the tall guy who's heading to the lectern. Has Redding noticed her? A quick side-glance at the priest's ruddy face confirms those clear blue eyes are trained on the redhead. Stan gazes down at the man's black slacks and shiny black loafers, then slowly up past the light blue short-sleeved shirt and the white collar to check out the pink, clear-skinned face again. Just as Redding turns slightly to catch him and, of all things, give him a wink. As if to say, "Yes, she's lovely."

So the priest has noticed. Not surprising with this 70-year-old man of the cloth, vigorous, always walking at a pace Stan finds uncomfortably swift, good-looking with that unruly shock of white hair, intellectually curious and energetic, a touch vain — he obviously loves the looks he gets when quoting those long patches of *Paradise Lost* — and no doubt propositioned by more than one adventurous coed over the years. Has the old guy ever fallen prey to that temptation?

9

As the woman nears the lectern, she pulls typescript out of her straw bag. The dirty-blond stork steps to the microphone, unfolding notes. He's a Brit, Mark Leander, one of the conference organizers, and he quickly intros his American counterpart now sitting in the front row, the little guy with the hairy arms, Silverman from Rutgers. After the speaker's bio from the conference pamphlet, he turns to a crumpled, hand-written sheet.

"Now I thought you might like to know a bit more about this extraordinary woman and scholar, and Professor Lentini was gracious enough to share a few personal details."

Stan thinks the "woman and scholar" line is strange, but personal details would be good.

"Lina—she asked that I call her Lina—was born and raised in Catania on the eastern coast of Sicily. A passionate reader as a child, she knew from the age of five that she wanted to be a professor like her father, whose field was anthropology. Like many bright, creative children she had imaginary friends, but she also fashioned imaginary classrooms filled with students listening to her lecture. Her mother was from a well-to-do family who owned a series of boutique hotels from Barcelona to Prague, and Lina often traveled with her mother, who oversaw the business. Thus, from an early age Lina became especially attuned to differences in language, culture and customs. She studied French from elementary school on, added English in secondary school, with intensives in the summer months in England, and mastered Spanish in her undergraduate years. If she was going to be a professor of comparative literature, she felt it was imperative that she be able to read in the original. 'There is no substitute for the original,' she told me. 'No way to really understand the appeal, meaning and value of a book without being able to read in the original.' And so, with no further ado, Professor Lina Lentini."

Stan adds to hearty applause. While interesting, those were not the personal details for which he was hoping. Smiling brightly, the woman places her typescript on the lectern.

"Thank you so much, Professor Leander." Eyes glinting, she pauses for a split second. "He asked me to call him Professor Leander." Amid the laughter she quickly adds, with an even broader smile at the guy now sitting next to Silverman, "Sorry, Mark, I could not resist." Even more laughter as the stork gives her a wave that Stan sees as, "Honey, you can call me anything you wish, as long as I get to look down your dress."

The voice is captivating. Her English comes with a British twist and an Italian lilt almost too light to call an accent, a warm tone and great poise. After a few moments he finds himself simply enjoying the sound and the way she holds herself—shoulders back, bosom high, with calm though animated gestures. No scholar's slouch for this gal.

"Near the end of *Black Dogs*, published in 1992, the British novelist Ian McEwan grapples with the pervasive fact of evil in our world. The book's climactic episode occurs in 1946 in the south of France where a woman named June encounters two black dogs. The dogs attack her, but somehow she manages to fight them off. Later she learns they had belonged to the Gestapo and had escaped into the countryside when the German troops were called back to Normandy after D-Day. A rumor has it that the dogs had been trained to rape women."

As the redhead quotes McEwan's character, Stan wonders if any man in this garden is hearing a word she's saying, or simply feasting on her looks? Maybe her beauty is gluing them to every syllable, every nuance of every phrase loaded with "acute insight and a special sense for the moral issues with which we all wrestle." Whatever, this is clearly a woman who knows the power of her animal presence and has not the slightest compunction about using it.

Now having paused for effect, she reads, "So this is June's insight: Acts of human kindness, however seemingly insignificant, may accrue to actually counter the massive accumulation of evil we humans continue to inflict on each other. This is humanistic atonement as McEwan sees it."

Stan's glance at Redding, who seems totally engrossed, notes the hint of a smile at the corners of the mouth. A sign the priest is impressed, and disagrees. Again Stan forces himself to concentrate on what the woman is saying.

"In the trilogy he presented as we advanced on a new century— *American Pastoral* in 1997, *I Married a Communist* in 1998, and *The Human Stain* in 2000—American novelist Philip Roth gives us both the story inside—what happens between our ears, in our heart, and of course in our genitals—and the story outside—a large-scale perspective on America since the end of World War II."

Sometimes he really wonders. Here's this brilliant woman talking about old Roth's important contribution, and all he's thinking about is wanting to slip that sundress off her shoulder, cup a full, probably freckled tit and feel the nipple firm up under his finger. Maybe it's because the only thing of Roth's he's read so far is *Portnoy's Complaint,* an embarrassing fact he's managed to keep from his department colleagues.

He's never had a redhead. They're supposed to be different—a little strange, maybe, a little wild, perhaps in touch with the body in some special way that could make them terrific in bed. His favorite Hollywood actress, at least one of his favorites, is a redhead, Julianne Moore. There was that story, maybe in the Times, about Robert Altman deciding he wanted her in his movie version of "Short Cuts," the Raymond Carver short stories, calling her up and saying she'd need to do full frontal. Her unhesitating response was, "Well, what you see is what you'll get, because I'm a real redhead." As it turned out, the scene had her stalking around the house naked from the waist down, that little red bush confronting her jealous husband.

Later, after a long Q and A, and even before the burst of applause begins to fade, Redding leans close to his ear and says, "Would you like to meet her?" To the right of the lectern five men and a couple of women are already lining up to greet and chat with the professor, who is putting the typescript back into the straw purse and turning to them. Stan immediately moves but finds it difficult to get past several people standing in their row, apparently so stirred by the experience they simply want to stare at her. By the time they reach the end of the line, it stretches past the third row of chairs.

Stan wants to ask Redding first, but the priest beats him to it. "So what did you think?"

"She's extraordinary. How about you? Did I catch a few moments of disagreement?"

"Yes, you know me. I have my quibbles with everybody. But I thought she was brilliant, especially on Roth. I'd love to have her on campus."

That thought is so stunning that Stan smiles, turns away and counts 14 people in the line ahead of them, some with books they probably want her to sign. Taking her time with each, she is smiling, nodding, occasionally laughing, responding at length to certain comments, and finally actually hugging two of the women and even

12

a bent old guy with lots of white hair.

Ten minutes later there are still eight ahead of them. Most of the garden has cleared, and workmen are quickly collecting the folding chairs. One of them glares at Stan and snarls to another, "*Subito! Il matrimonio alle sedici.*"

Redding seems intent on overhearing the professor's response to a fortunate fellow at the head of the line. Stan says, "There's a wedding here at 4. They're going to want us out shortly."

Redding nods and looks at his watch. "I'd love to meet her, but I really need to check my e-mail while there's still time to send one back tonight. Why don't you stay?"

He thinks about approaching this woman alone. "No, I should check mine also."

"She's probably staying at the hotel. Maybe we can catch her later."

"Maybe. I know I haven't seen her there."

"Yes," says the priest, "that's a face you won't forget."

Chapter 3

The baroque lobby of the Hotel San Rocco, its elaborate cornices framing a celestial scene on the ceiling, holds a dark-hued portrait that always grabs him: the stern-eyed face of Anna Theodora Silana, noted in the hotel literature as the first Mother Superior who ruled the girls school and convent that operated in this building from 1647. For centuries the sisters ran things here until the place was finally turned into a four-star hotel and spa in the 1960s. But for 300 years this was home to a procession of tingly young women and horny nuns, most of them, he figures, longing to be ravished by some angelic stud with silver wings and a golden dick.

As he moves past the carved wood doors of the lobby, the implacable Anna again holds his gaze, as if to say, "A filthy mind in this hallowed place. You will burn in hell." Alone in the elevator on the way to his room, he wonders if all the sexual tension still trapped in these ancient walls is filling his head with these obscene images of the redheaded professor. Sliding the plastic card into his door, he's again getting hard.

Inside the modern guest room, his glance from the bed to the lake's warm afternoon colors beyond the window somehow prompts the idea of a massage before dinner. Scanning the San Rocco's brochure for the "Body Harmony Centre," he's surprised at the many different types of "Manual Massotherapy": Draining Massage, Reducing Massage, Remodeling Massage, Firming Massage, Anti-stress Massage, and Lympho-draining. He looks at himself naked in the full-length bathroom mirror, and the damn thing is pointing almost straight up. A Draining Massage sounds good, but a stiff dick during a spa treatment might be awkward.

Finally he showers, dresses and goes down to the lobby to have a drink, thinking maybe she'll be there with a glass of wine. No such luck. Now on their last night in Italy, he knows he should have stayed in the garden this afternoon to meet her. He blew it. He was

14

unsure of himself and, unlike his usual attitude with women, intimidated. The fact is he was a frightened little piss-ant. He has to start asserting himself.

When Redding comes down to the lobby, Stan suggests they try the nearby restaurant whose posted menu was so intriguing the other day. The priest says he'd love to, but he needs to have this last dinner with their colleagues at the hotel. He'll be networking diligently now, since he just picked up an e-mail saying Mendoza, with profuse apologies, has pulled out of the visiting lecturer position in September. Something about his wife's mother falling ill and needing constant care. They'll have to remain in Mexico City.

"But listen, go out and enjoy yourself. You've been saddled with an old fogy all week."

"Father, you're hardly a fogy, old or otherwise. It's been my pleasure. No, I'll be happy to join you. And I suppose there's a chance that Professor Lentini might show up for dinner."

"Maybe, but she's not staying at the hotel. I checked."

* * *

Afterward, at Redding's suggestion, they head out for a stroll and a nightcap. In a small funk, Stan thinks a walk might help. With no sign of her, the dinner took forever, and he was trapped next to an overweight broad from Marquette, whose most apt and interesting comment was how all this great Italian cuisine was going straight to her hips.

On cobbled streets the priest for once moves at a reasonable pace, past four-hundred-year-old houses and palazzos with galleries, granite columns and wrought iron balconies covered with flowers. Stan has fallen hard for the charm of these narrow, ancient streets. He loves their silence at this hour, but Redding is spoiling that now as he rattles on about the potential candidates whose names he collected at dinner. Hardly listening, Stan perks up only when the priest mentions that Silverman from Rutgers promised to send him Professor Lentini's address in Bologna. "She's worth a try," he said, when Redding asked if she might be available.

In the Piazza Motta, the small, lively town square, people are enjoying the evening breeze off the lake. Some are strolling, many sit at the tables in front of restaurants and cafes in the medieval buildings lining the square. Along the lakefront, small motorboats rest quietly at their docks, and San Giulio twinkles in the distance.

15

Trying to decide on a café, he and the priest pause in the center of the stone-covered square. In a fresco on a wall above a souvenir shop, Christ bare to the waist shows his wounds, and Stan thinks how much he hates the ugly, gruesome story of the Passion. Redding says, "Well, there she is."

The priest is gazing at a table in front of the café next to the souvenir shop. Smiling straight at them, the redhead turns to say something to the young man sitting next to her. Redding is already moving for their table, and following a few steps behind, Stan tries to sort out the group around her. There are six of them, mostly younger and mostly good-looking. The fellow she turned to looks more like he's with the dark-haired girl on his left.

"Professor Lentini," says Redding, "please forgive the intrusion, but I must tell you how much we enjoyed your presentation this afternoon. We thought you were brilliant."

The woman offers her full-wattage smile and surprisingly gets to her feet. She's in a snug black cashmere that shows off her tits and slacks that emphasize the slim waist and hips.

"Thank you, Father, you are very kind. From the audience this afternoon I recognize you and your friend." She turns the smile on Stan, who feels lost in her bright green eyes.

"Forgive me again. I'm Father Robert Redding, dean of the comparative literature department at St. Thomas University in Michigan." She offers her hand, and he holds it briefly. "And this is Stanford Lyle, who's working on his doctorate in our department."

She takes Stan's hand with a touch so feathery yet firm, so soft, tender and sensuous that he's certain he's never experienced anything like it. That subtle, amazing feeling in his hand flows through him so swiftly that he fears he won't be able to speak. And yet out tumbles Italian. "*È il mio piacere grande e honore, professore.*" He is pleased and honored.

"*Ah, parla Italiano.*" So he speaks Italian.

"*Si, un po. Sto studiando la vostra lingua per scrivere la mia dissertazione sul meraviglioso Primo Levi.*" He's studying the language for his dissertation on Primo Levi.

"*Si, Levi. Questo è molto impressionante.*" Very impressive.

A few seconds into this and he's boasting. She asks if they would like to join the group.

Redding says, "Yes, of course, as long as it's not an imposition."

16

"Wonderful." She looks to a tall blond fellow sitting next to an empty table. "Hans, could we get two of those chairs for Father and Stanford here?"

"Professor, please call me Stan."

"Only if you and Father call me Lina." Those green eyes sparkle with interest.

Hans places the chairs across from Lina. Stan can't take his eyes off her. There are women whose beauty fades in a close up. Not this one. As she carefully introduces everyone in the group, he notes again the beautifully modulated voice, and he's still marveling at that touch, the incredibly tender, delicate handshake he already knows will haunt him. He tries to concentrate on the names in this group. Most are Italian, though there's Hans and a girl named Marta. Most are in their twenties, though Aldo and his wife, a black woman named Rena, are in their forties. Edgardo, the group's best looking male has a long, possessive arm around a pretty girl named Bella. They are colleagues, students, ex-students, all superb friends, she says, and staying in a villa owned by Marta's parents, just down the lake. They all seem to have an easy give and take with her, clearly a kind of retinue or entourage attached to this rock star professor.

She asks if they've had a chance to explore the beauty of the other lakes, Como and Maggiore. Redding goes on a bit about the palace and gardens on Isola Bella, and Stan adds that they spent a day at Como, walking the grounds of the famed Villa D'Este and checking out George Clooney's pad. Did they know the Hollywood film star has a villa on Como?

Lina smiles at him. "Si, Villa Oleandra."

Rena says, "Actually he owns two now. The Villa Margherita also.

Hans adds, "And the beach between the two, which the town is up in arms about."

Rena again: "Well, he says he's going to clean it up and then keep it open for everybody to use, so they're letting him have it."

Stan glances at Redding whose pink face is beaming. All this interest in an American bodes well, even if he's a tinsel celebrity — one of the priest's favorite phrases.

"Clearly," Stan says, "you all know more about our American movie stars than we do."

Marta says, "Professore Lentini has dated Mr. George Clooney."

"Please! He asked me to his villa to view Syriana. Along with his girlfriend."

Marta: "For me that is a date. I am sure he wanted a three-some."

"Marta, *maletesta*! He was a perfect gentleman. Unfortunately."

After the laughter settles down, she turns to Redding. "Forgive them, Father. They are young, foolish and like to tease."

"And I think you like to tease them back." More laughter.

"It's true. But, Father, how wonderful that you and Stan have come to our beautiful country to share your erudition."

"You're very kind, but the pleasure has been ours. And I'd like to take advantage of our good fortune here to invite you to *our* beautiful country. If you'll permit me, St. Thomas is a highly regarded private university, our department has one of the finest reputations in the country, and our campus is one of the most beautiful in the Midwest. As it happens, our visiting lecturer position is open in the fall, and we would be deeply gratified if you would consider spending the semester with us and filling the position."

Lina sweeps the group with that dazzling smile. "Father, I am honored and grateful for such a wonderful offer."

The priest hasn't finished. "And let me just say, not that any of us do anything for purely financial reasons…" His wink is obvious. "…but the position is very generously endowed, and as we say in the states, we could definitely make it worth your while."

"So, Father, clearly you are a man of persuasive skill."

"Yes, if only that were so. But please promise me this: that you will do us the honor of at least reading the e-mail I will send shortly with details about the position and its amenities."

She turns to Stan and suddenly affects a droll American accent. "Is he always this good?"

Stan widens his eyes and shakes his head. "You ain't seen nothin' yet."

Chapter 4

On the terrace of her 4th floor apartment, she reads the morning edition of the Corriere della Sera on her Dell. Occasionally she looks out at the sunlight bathing the red brick buildings and their red tile roofs as far as she can see. *La Citta Rossa*. From her glass top table, she finds the roof of the central train station, about which she was writing last night.

When she finally stopped, after 2, she just crawled into bed, too exhausted for the usual rituals with toothbrush and face cream. It was a night filled with coffee-fueled dreams — most of them unpleasant, some obviously related to feeling behind schedule on her book as she dealt with the emotional scatter from the break up with Paolo back in April. Deadline dramas is what she calls these anxiety dreams, and she has had them often since her teens. But some of the nocturnal discomfort was probably also generated by the horror of the event she was describing last night, the bombing of Bologna's Stazione Centrale on August 2, 1980. Eighty-five people killed and more than 200 others wounded — men, women and children.

At 10:25 on that morning more than a quarter century ago, a timed improvised explosive device, made of TNT and T4 in an unattended suitcase, detonated inside a crowded air-conditioned waiting room. The explosion destroyed most of the main building and damaged the Ancona-Chiasso train waiting at the first platform. The blast was heard for miles.

The Prime Minister quickly blamed the extreme right: "Unlike leftish terrorism, which strikes at the heart of the state through its representatives, black terrorism prefers the massacre because it promotes panic and impulsive reactions." In fact, it was soon clear the perpetrators came from a neo-fascist terrorist group, but the investigation, arrests, trials and appeals extended almost to the present day. The second of August became designated as a memorial day for all Italian massacres. The station's main clock was left forever stopped at exactly 10:25.

Her writing flowed like blood last night. Until she got to the part that involved Paolo. The 40-year-old trial attorney from Milan usually represents those accused of high-end white-collar crime, often with a political dimension. In 2004 he defended a man in his 40s who, at the time of the Bologna bombing, was a 17-year-old member of that far-right group. Despite Paolo's efforts, the man got 30 years for his role in the bombing, a sentence upheld on appeal just two months ago. It did not help that while free on bond the fellow was arrested for robbing a bank.

She met Paolo through friends when he was in Bologna for the trial. That first night they talked for four hours straight about what he called "the exquisite moral dilemmas" his work often presented. Their sex was just as passionate as their talk, but their busy schedules didn't mesh well. For his cases he was always flying off to Kenya or Brazil. He always wanted her to come along on a safari or a rainforest trek. It was interesting and exciting for a time, but she too often found herself distracted and vaguely unhappy. And so she ended it seven weeks ago. She knew she had done the right thing when he reacted like a little boy punished. Still, he writes or calls her occasionally wanting to meet, and she, in spite of everything, is too often tempted. There are times when being someplace where she might not be available does not seem like a bad idea.

A click on International News gives her a weekly round up on Iraq: explosions in Samarra destroy the twin golden minarets at the Askariya mosque, a suicide truck bomber in Baghdad kills 87 — more of the god-awful same. A visit to Juan Cole's blog at the University of Michigan — her favorite on Iraq — is overdue. Instead she clicks into her e-mail and re-reads part of Fr. Redding's invitation. He quotes lines from the St. Thomas University web site, making the place sound like it's devoted to excellence, committed to the honored tradition of open and free inquiry and proud of its reputation for tolerance and understanding for all points of view. The mission statement includes this: "Our goal is to educate students to be morally responsible leaders who think critically, act wisely and work skillfully to advance the common good."

Other lines from Redding: "I know you'd be coming to us from the 'world's oldest university' to lecture at one of the youngest. Yes, we are one of many scholastic institutions the world over named after the redoubtable Aquinas, who, in his hay day in the 1300s, often lectured at your remarkable institution. And yes, the great University of Bologna has working relations with many wonderful American universities, including Brown, the University of California, Indiana U. and Johns Hopkins, and of course you could have your choice. But if you really want to explore and understand the heart of America, what makes it tick and what life is truly like here, you would do well to consider St. Thomas in the lovely mid-Michigan city of Cedar Hill."

The priest is either shrewd or lucky, or maybe both. The money he mentions is more than she expected, even with his line about the position being well-endowed. Not that she has to worry much about money. An only child, with her well-to-do parents gone, she is set quite comfortably. More important, given the book she is working on, she would be lecturing only once or twice a week, with limited contact with students and no papers or test essays to read.

The new book is on the writing of fiction in an age of terror. How is the novel influenced by the anxieties, fears and moral uncertainties so often intensified in a society plagued with acts of terror? How do novelists deal with this kind of reality? Does their writing reflect the moral ambiguities of their time and place, the insecurities, suspicions and shifting attitudes toward religion and secularism? Her hypothesis going in was that novelists are often attuned to the moral tenor of the times, and that the themes informing their work can be traced in many ways to the new, altered reality of a world beset with terror.

In the foreword she finds the graphs she keeps working over:

> When those motivated by staunch religious belief and a sense of political victimization perform murderous acts in the name of their God against thousands of innocents, when they do so with no sense of guilt, while expressing ultimate devotion to their cause and to their religion by forfeiting their own lives in committing mass murder as an act of love for the Divine, then many may be prompted to question the very basis of all religious belief, the existence of God. That may be one reason for the current glut of bestsellers that make enthusiastic

arguments for atheism.

> Yet living constantly with the fear that the world
> is beset with terrorists who want to kill us, who
> are scheming to slaughter us in large numbers
> with random acts of violence, many others turn
> with even greater fervor to their faith, and so
> Christian fundamentalists see wide-spread acts
> of terror as a sure sign of the coming Rapture,
> when those forlorn and wretched unbelievers
> Left Behind will soon be suffering the horrors of
> our world's catastrophic end.

Instead of fussing further with these lines, she clicks on an e-mail from Paolo: "Because God (having consulted with Cheney) has told W to bomb the shit out of Iran, we should have no doubt he will do it sometime before his term ends. Let's not forget the poet: 'Gather ye rosebuds while ye may, Old Time is still a-flying; And this same flower that smiles today Tomorrow will be dying.' Keats is it?" No, Paolo, it's Herrick. But Paolo, like everybody she knows, seems obsessed with the Americans, their culture, their stupidity, their madness and their power.

Feeling strangely scattered and distracted, she finally gives in to the urge to follow any whim or thought line that grabs her. For a few warm minutes she dips into a website with photos from her favorite nude beach on the Croatian coast, wondering if she could simply plop down on the sand with the Dell and work there on the book for a while. Clicking back to the priest's e-mail, she again checks out the St. Thomas University website, gazing at photos and reading their captions. An expansive aerial shot: "Two hundred eighty-two acres of sheltering forest, rolling green hills with the peaceful Green River meandering through, our beautiful campus resides on the city's northern edge." A candid shot of a clearly fulfilled professor chatting calmly under a tree with eager, attentive students in three different skin colors: "We respect the dignity of each person and value the unique contributions that each brings to the greater mosaic of the university community."

As always at this time of the morning, the sun is moving up and to her left. She is having a hard time with its sheen on the Dell's screen and, knowing, without giving it a thought, exactly how to move it, she reaches up to twist the umbrella until it again casts its shadow. And now as she thinks about that move, it feels as if she has just made a decision.

Chapter 5

The Airbus behemoth lumbers, settles, then, engines rushing, strains to slow down. Passengers close by in coach pull out mobiles and start dialing. Powering the Nokia, she presses 7, the speed dial slot filled until yesterday with Paolo's number. Now it holds one included in Fr. Redding's last e-mail, the priest announcing that he himself refuses to carry "one of those infernal little pests."

A voice says, "Hello, this is Stan."

"Good day, Stan. It is Lina. We just landed."

"Ah, Lina, welcome to America!" His voice tinged with excitement, Stan says it should take about 30 minutes for her to arrive at the gate, get through passport control, claim her baggage and clear customs. So the timing is perfect. Father will not have to break any laws to get there in time. As usual, every detail seems carefully planned for her comfort and convenience.

Now, a half-hour later than expected, Lina finally emerges from customs in the McNamara Terminal at Detroit's Metro Airport, moving slowly through sliding glass doors, pushing a luggage cart loaded with two big bags, a large carry-on, and in the basket her ample leather purse. Riding atop of the carry-on is the September issue of Vanity Fair.

Sweeping the few faces still waiting, she quickly spots the huge welcoming smiles of the priest and the grad student. Her first urge is a light hug for each with a brush of the lips on both cheeks. They have been so kind and thoughtful in all the phone calls and e-mails over the past two months. Still, they are Americans on their own turf, Fr. Redding already extending a hand, the younger man, again, as in Italy, seeming so anxious to touch her. She offers her hand.

The priest, his blue eyes piercing: "Lina, welcome. It's so good to have you with us."

"My pleasure, Father. Thank you so much for meeting me here. You have made everything so easy."

24

"We aim to please."

With a slight bow Stan says, "*Buon pomeriggio, Lina. Benvenuto a Michigan. Tu ci onora con la tua presenza.*" Welcome. She honors them with her presence.

"Ah, Stan, *grazie.*" He takes her hand and holds it as if he might bring it to his lips. Her eyes dart to Redding's for a second. "A real Italian greeting." She looks back into Stan's smile and notes the eyes. Not really brown, but lighter...hazel? And deeply eager.

He's still holding her hand but releases it just as the moment becomes awkward. "*Com'era il tuo volo?*"

Again a quick glance at Redding. "The flight was good. Very smooth, right on time.

But I am sorry to keep you waiting here so long. Everything was good until I got to customs, and then for some reason they took a special interest in me."

Stan says with a smile, "I wonder why."

Redding says, "We're just sorry you were inconvenienced."

"It was nothing really. They took me off to the side, and three inspectors came to go through my luggage. I just waited, reading my magazine while they combed through everything, but for some reason they seemed very concerned about my underwear. They handled every little piece. What they thought might be there I do not know."

Stan says, "All guys, I bet. They all wanted a good look at our beautiful Italian visitor."

"And her underwear?"

"Especially her underwear."

Redding says, "In any case, we're just so pleased you're with us now, safe and sound."

While she takes a restroom stop, Redding goes for the car and Stan watches her luggage. In the stall she opens the leather bag and fishes for tampons between the laptop and the new Hitchens book. Knowing she was about to start, she used one in Rome, and then another five hours into the flight. As it has been lately, her flow is already heavy. There is supposed to be a two-hour drive ahead, so she changes again. At the mirror her hair needs brushing...the eyes are still okay...just a touch of lip gloss. Both men seem taken by her looks. Was her reference to the underwear for the priest? It would not be like her. Redding is well-preserved for his age, good-looking

25

and seemingly straight, but offering no sexual vibe. Maybe for Stan, who seems a bit like an adoring puppy. In the long run he might turn out to be endearing or annoying. When she emerges from the restroom, he is paging through the Vanity Fair.

He looks up and says, "So the American edition."

"Yes, the Italian one had a more modest cover, so I bought this one. It is fantastic, no?"

He flips back to glance at the cover. Some model named Gisele in a silver micro mini.

"*Incredibile.* So you bought the magazines for this?" He points to a cover tease: Lake Como... The Russians are coming. "It's probably got a photo of your friend Clooney's pad."

"It does. But I really bought it for the Christopher Hitchens column on touring this country for his new book. The arrogant atheist in America. Very amusing. Actually, I love Hitchens, except on Iraq, about which he is crazed."

"Interesting. You might not want to mention Hitchens to Bob Daddy. That's our pet name for Redding, though not to his face. He thinks Hitchens is crazed about everything *except* Iraq."

"Truly? He supports this catastrophe?"

"Well, he's like all of them now—it's been bungled badly, but McCain's his guy now."

In the priest's spotless late-model black Cadillac the ride is quiet and smooth. Stan shares the back seat with her carryon. In the chatter as they leave the airport and head west, she learns they have found her a furnished apartment with two bedrooms, one for an office, on the edge of campus. The complex borders a large wooded area offering lots of peace and quiet, a great place for long, contemplative walks. And she'll also have a car, nothing special, says Redding, a little Ford Focus owned by the university, but it should do her just fine. Actually, Stan has arranged everything, making sure that Lina's four and a half months at the university will be pleasant, comfortable and productive. With a week still left in August, she'll have the better part of two weeks before the start of classes.

With a kind of hunger, she takes in the late afternoon landscape— two broad concrete strips with a wide grassy median rolling through low hills, clumps of forest, small farms, billboards, apartment complexes, small industrial plants, large petrol stations with tall signs you can see from a distance, all of it baked by the sun ahead of them, but with no vistas of towns or cities, nothing particularly beautiful or charming or impressive.

Feeling Stan's eyes on the back of her head, she turns. "I see this sign that says that Ann Arbor is next? Home of the University of Michigan and the excellent Juan Cole."

"You know Cole?" asks Redding.

"I know his blog. I think it is the best on Iraq and the region."

Redding says pleasantly, "I find him rather biased. There are a couple of political scientists on our campus I much prefer."

Lina glances back at Stan, who raises an eyebrow with an "I told you so." She says, "Well, I'll be anxious to meet them. But I would like to visit with Professor Cole."

Minutes later, apropos of nothing, Redding asks, "Are you interested in sports, Lina?"

"I follow it very little. Football, or you call it soccer, when there is the World Cup. And basketball. The players are so beautiful, and you can truly see them without all the heavy clothing and the big helmets, like in your American football."

An awkward pause, and back of her head feels Stan's gaze again. Redding says, "Still, our college football can be an incredible spectacle. We'll have to take you to a game in Ann Arbor this fall...110,000 people in that stadium is an amazing sight."

She would like that, she says and then for a time there is only silence. Finally Redding asks if she would mind the radio. Not at all, she says. The priest pushes a button on the dash and the Cadillac is filled with the close of a Bach partita. Then a woman reads the news: "In a speech to the Veterans of Foreign Wars today, President Bush warned that a quick pullout from Iraq would result in a heavy loss of civilian life, which he said was the case when the United States left Vietnam in the 1970s."

She cannot resist and finds Stan reading the Vanity Fair. "Stan, please explain. Does Bush not have anyone to tell him that if he says the lesson of Vietnam is that the U.S. pulled out too soon, most Americans will think he is an idiot? Or do they think that most Americans already know he is an idiot? Or do his advisors live with him in his alternate universe?"

She watches his eyes flick up at the rear view mirror to check Redding's gaze. Then he stammers: "Wow...well...there's, I mean, that's a lot of questions. If you ask me, I think the answer to all of them is. . . yes. But what do you think, Father?"

The priest turns off the radio and says, "I think the analogy is ill-advised."

She winks at Stan and asks what he's reading. The Hitchens piece, he says.

She asks, "Have you read it, Father? So many fans are showing up on his book tour."

"No, not that piece. But I do keep tabs on Hitchens, and I know he loves the anecdotal. I'm sure if he comes here to mid-Michigan, he won't find many folks okay with atheism."

Looking at Stan, she says, "Yes, you are right Father, but it is interesting that he seems to encounter so many questioning Americans and real, live atheists in the places he visits."

Redding cocks his head at her for a second. "I think, Lina, you may find here that many Americans love to question. But you may also learn there's a reason that not one of all these politicians, from both parties, running for the presidency, would ever dream of renouncing a belief in God. In any case, I don't find Hitchens very reliable in recounting the theological positions of others, so I don't exactly trust his reports of the attitudes he's encountered."

Again with a glance at Stan: "Yes, Father, I understand." But after a pause she asks, "And what is this place I see now with the sign that says, 'Lion's Den. Adult Superstore'?"

Dead silence. Finally, Stan says, "It's a chain of pornography emporiums."

"Oh, of course. And the one I saw a few minutes ago: 'The Velvet Touch. Live Girls'?"

Stan says, "Strip tease."

"Ah, yes, a strange phrase, 'Live Girls,' no?"

Redding finally says, "Yes. Unfortunately, Lina, the devil's playground has no borders."

Chapter 6

With Redding and his Caddy dispatched and her bags in the foyer, the old guy clearly happy about not having to lug anything up, this moment is exactly as he planned. No, actually, it's better. Their arrival at the apartment later than expected, his calculations are off a bit in terms of the angle of the sun lancing through the wooded area in front of these new-fashioned row-house apartments. So as they walk into the living room, that broad front window facing west gleams with even more warmth and color because of the lower slant of that blazing orb sitting atop the trees, poised to burn its way to the bottom. A quick side-glance at Lina finds glints in her red curls. The smile seems lit from within.

"Ah, yes, a beautiful welcome." She gazes through the window.

In last night's daydream, it was this moment that launched the grateful touch of her lips on his. As the two of them slid into an exquisite passion, the fantasy that followed quickly left him tense with excitement. Now he turns to her more than half expecting the kiss, but getting instead a large, pleasant smile and the words that will have to do for now: "Stan, what a marvelous choice you made." And she's already moving, turning into the kitchen, finding the milk, grapes, cheese and eggs in the fridge, the loaf of French bread and the Café Verona from Starbucks on the counter. "How thoughtful you are."

Before he can tell her it's nothing, she's moving again, stashing the big purse on the dining table, and, as his heart quickens, heading for the bedroom. Their bedroom? He flicks on lights, including one in the adjoining bath, and a queen-sized bed gleams with that huge white quilt ready to envelop them. He finally manages to say, "I hope you like it."

"No, I love it! This is more than I imagined. I must call Father to thank him."

"Well, I don't think he'll answer now. This is usually his hour for evening prayers." That line has popped out of nowhere. He has no idea if the priest has a prayer schedule.

As she turns to leave the room he shoots a glance at the vase filled with assorted cut flowers. He spent 10 minutes last night trying to decide where to place them. In the living room next to the sofa, or here on the bedroom dresser along with that thick red candle, standing like a proud prick ready to be lit. Maybe they should be where she'd see them as soon as she walked in the front door. No, too obvious. He'd show her the bedroom and then gauge their impact. And now she's leaving the room, without even seeing them. Until a glance at a mirror shows her the flowers on her right, and she stops. "How beautiful, Stan," she says, fingering a petal.

The line he prepared about how they paled in comparison now seems too over the top. He says only, "It's nothing." And a second later: "Here, let's have a look at your office."

In the next room he clicks on a lamp next to a comfortable armchair and pushes a button to start the desktop. "You're all set with the basics here. Word, a pretty decent broadband connection. You just tell me what else you'll need, and I'll get it for you. And here's a cell phone with a new account I opened for you with a thousand minutes. I figured it would be a lot cheaper for you than the international roaming charges you'd probably have with the one you brought."

Back in the living room he demos the flat panel TV with the top end cable package and "tons of movies." He grabs the car keys from a decorative dish on the coffee table and leads her back to the office window from where she can see the white Focus parked under the carport.

"It's an automatic, easy to drive." He pushes a button on the key fob, and the tail lights flash. "You can even lock or open it from up here." Buzzed with energy, he feels like he's been talking non-stop. Now silent, standing inches from her, he's ready to make the move he's been dreaming about. Raise the left hand behind that beautiful red hair, turn her gently, then kiss softly that remarkable mouth. Is she feeling what he is?

She turns away, saying, "I am sure it will be perfect." She moves back toward the front of the apartment. "Stan, you are so thoughtful about everything. I cannot thank you enough."

He thinks she certainly can but says, "It's nothing. Now how about dinner? Are you hungry? I've got reservations at the one really good Italian place in town."

She smiles, shakes her head and walks toward the front door. "No, actually, thank you, but I am more sleepy than hungry." She glances at a gold watch. "My body is telling me it is 3 in the morning, and I slept on the plane almost not at all."

"Oh, of course. I'm sorry."

"No, you are being a sweetheart. But I will nibble on the bread and cheese, have a glass of wine and a nice warm shower, and that will be all for me."

"Well, then let me take you for breakfast in the morning"

She looks at him quizzically and then says, "How about lunch? Call me about noon?"

He nods. "*Mezzogiorno.*"

As she turns to open the front door, he feels the buzz begin to drain. Through the open door he sees soft, fading light on the silver BMW Z4 Roadster parked in front. As he's about to move, she surprises him: a hug, brief but firm enough to feel those amazing tits, and a kiss, also brief but on the lips, light but with sufficient tenderness to immediately feel unforgettable.

He stares into her smiling green eyes for a moment, his lips still savoring her taste. He should seize this moment, grab her and do it right. But there's something in the eyes that says don't, not now. He grins, trying for gallant, and moves past her to the front porch. "Sleep well."

"It will not be a problem." She looks down at the street. "But can I drive you someplace?

"No thanks. That's my little Beamer down there."

She looks past him at the $50,000 car. "So, yes? How beautiful." The surprised lilt in her voice says she suddenly knows he's not your typically impoverished grad student.

* * *

Lunch is at Melody, his favorite campus diner, with large papier-mâché musical notes hanging everywhere. Their talk at first feels stilted, at least compared to those intimate moments at the apartment last night. They've crowded his thoughts for half the morning. This feels more like a first date, with tentative forays into the trivial and the already established. How did she sleep last night? Fine, but not until staying up long enough to switch between Leno and Letterman

31

for a while. Finally, he thinks of something he's been meaning to ask. Why she really chose to leave Italy for this extended stay in the States. In Orta-San Giulio, surrounded by all her friends and colleagues, she seemed so happy, so comfortable.

Certainly, she says, there were good reasons to work on this new book here in the U.S. But there was also a personal factor. She tells him about a sunny morning in Bologna where she was taking coffee on her patio and using her laptop. A moment like a million others when she was reading something on line and caught herself moving her large umbrella to shield the computer screen and doing it without even thinking. A moment in which she thought perhaps her life in Italy had become just too predictable, too comfortable. Maybe she should think about pushing herself, stretching beyond comfort, challenging herself and her ideas. Looking back she thinks that moment might have carried the day.

Stan says he thought maybe a tragic love affair was part of the story.

She laughs and says she has not been involved with anyone for a while. Besides, none of her love affairs have been tragic. Not that there really have been that many!

He says that's hard to believe. Everybody in Italy seemed to be in love with her.

She gives him that amazing smile and reaches across the table to cover his hand so softly with hers. The electricity and warmth of that touch again.

She says, "You are so sweet!"

Another haunting moment. Yes, he knows there's a cultural difference here, that she likes to touch and is earthy in a way for which European women are famous. But this is different. And coupled with that amazing hug and kiss last night and the way she opened herself to him just now, revealing an intensely personal moment, with her self-doubts and intimate thoughts in its wake, all of it certainly means he can stop feeling intimidated by this woman. She's beginning to want him every bit as much as he wants her. It's just a matter of time.

Chapter 7

She wakes, sprawled in darkness, at an angle across a large bed, everything strange, unfamiliar. A faint light seeps from blinds covering a window. Where is she? Why so disoriented? A dream seems to be scurrying away like a small animal. She rises slightly from a damp pillow and turns her face the other way. Now she can barely make out something that helps, something she recognizes, flowers in a vase, flowers she knows, despite the darkness, are wilting. Flowers that Stan placed in the bedroom for her welcome nearly a week ago.

Without stirring, she thinks about Stan. Has she seen him every day? No, yesterday he called to invite her to a movie, "your friend Clooney's Good Night and Good Luck with a discussion after at the campus film club. She surprised him by saying she already had a date.

He sounded so close to hurt that she followed quickly with, "Redding and your president Fr. Hagen are taking me to a steakhouse called Marble's?"

"Yes, it's good. But you didn't tell me you were meeting with our eminent Fr. Hagen." As if she needed to clear her social calendar with him.

"Redding called two days ago. I neglected to mention it."

"No, of course, you'll like Hagen. He's erudite and charming."

"And his field?"

"Poli sci. I think he also has an eye for the ladies."

"Well, then dinner should be interesting."

And it was, though a bit exhausting. Later she felt as if she had lectured off the cuff for more than two hours as the priests pressed for her views of present day Italian culture, politics and socio-economic trends. From the garbage crisis in Naples, to the new Mafia, to immigration, to the new favorites at La Scala, and whether anybody but Berlusconi could hold things together. Hoping to talk

American politics, she got off on the wrong foot by asking their view of Senator Craig and his men's room misadventures in Minneapolis. After a couple of strained minutes, during which each priest used the words "sad," "unfortunate" and "American media circus," the conversation crossed the sea and remained there for the rest of the evening.

Hagen *was* charming, a vigorous, dark-haired, well-tanned man about 60, who every so often seemed to stop just short of flirting. He was effusive in his praise of her work, delighted with her presence on campus and confident about the bright course ahead for his university when so many other private institutions are suffering fiscal blight and uncertain futures.

Does he dye the hair? Probably, but it looks natural. And does he have an eye for the ladies? Certainly, there is a kind of potency about the priest and a gleam in the eye that tells a woman he is interested. Something just a bit different in Hagen than, say, in Redding. The older man seems just as vigorous, mentally and even physically, but there is something about Hagen that suggests he might go further. Or come closer. Of course, over the years she has met many a priest with sex appeal and many who clearly enjoyed being around women, while giving off that aura, that mystique of the sexy celibate that often intrigues and sometimes befuddles the opposite sex, wondering without sufficient clue whether this virile, attractive man of the cloth really wants you to make the first move and rip off the cloth.

One of the more esoteric mysteries of human attraction. What about Stan? Does she find Stan attractive? Many women probably would. Just under six feet, trim, perhaps too thin and fine-boned for some (but in these matters there really is no accounting for taste), active, energetic, athletic enough to be a runner—long distance, he says, in high school. Clearly he stays in shape and, from what she has seen, watches his diet. Sandy hair, cut short but not severe. Fair skinned, but with a healthy pallor, not a stranger to sun and fresh air. The face well-shaped, the nose a bit sharp but, combined with the high cheek bones, it adds to the intense, inquisitive look he usually carries. She asked about his ethnic background, and he answered quickly, "I'm a mongrel. Some Eastern Europe, some Scottish, a little French."

Will she try an affair with this bright young man who is so clearly primed and ready? It would be easy, perhaps interesting and maybe surprising. Probably nothing more than a semester fling, a few pleasant memories. But as an outsider on this campus, she has already seen that quarters can be close indeed. Things could easily get awkward and unpleasant. And then what? Yes, she finds him attractive but the eagerness in those light-colored eyes gives her pause. Is it just the eyes? There was a moment a few days back when they walked to campus, and he took her to Markham Hall to the office that would be hers for the semester. The key was already on the ring along with those for the Focus and the apartment.

"A quarter turn to the right." As usual, helpful, precise instructions. Markham was an older building, and the dark wood door creaked a bit when it opened to reveal a small, pleasant looking office with a window, a desk, an armchair and, on one narrow wall, floor-to-ceiling book shelves. And there on the middle two shelves were her books, shipped ahead three weeks ago.

"Oh, my books." Next to the surprise in her voice was a hint of dismay. He must have caught it, quickly explaining that, because the box was boldly marked "*Solo Libri*," he had "taken the liberty" of opening it and putting them on the shelves for her. The box was right here in the closet, he said, opening the door to show her. As if saving the box somehow made up for the invasion of her private things. She was about to say something to underscore the importance to her of certain limits, when he gave her what seemed like a slightly embarrassed smile and said, "I hope you don't mind, Lina. Actually, I was hoping there would be copies of your own two books, which I'm dying to read. I've tried to find them everywhere on line without success."

"*Non problema*," she said in spite of herself. "I will make sure you have copies."

"*Ah, grazie, grazie.*"

On their way out of the building, at the opposite end of the hall from her office, they passed an open door. Stan paused, peered in and said with pleasant surprise, "John!"

The man inside looked up from a computer screen. "Stan, how goes it?" The voice was low, friendly. The fellow's eyes moved to hers, and he smiled quickly. He tapped the keyboard, got to his feet and moved to the door. He was taller than Stan by a couple of inches, and his face seemed so sad that it verged on homely. Tousled brown hair, rapidly turning gray. But the eyes, when he came close, were striking, a deep blue, and despite the sadness, somehow held a glint.

"John Martens, meet Lina Lentini, our new visiting lecturer." Stan gestured broadly.

"Ah, professor," said Martens. "Stan has told me so much about you. It's a pleasure."

He offered his hand, and she took it, felt the electricity now and watched as the blue eyes dropped to their hands. Maybe he felt it as well. John Martens was Stan's dissertation advisor.

She said, "Stan has gone on about you as well. Congratulations on the new book."

The eyes seemed to show strength, compassion. Or was she simply projecting Stan's flowing admiration: "My academic angel," he had said. "I don't know where I'd be without John. Certainly not in this program, that's for sure." She had heard about the man's insight, "both literary and life-based," his nerve in facing down cancer, and his patience in dealing with a difficult family situation. She had not asked for details then. Now she was curious.

Martens was saying, "Very kind of you, but my thing is pretty passé compared to what you're doing. Hardly anyone reads Lawrence anymore."

"That is their loss. Lawrence should never be passé."

He nodded with that sad smile. "In any case, professor, I hope your stay with us will be as pleasant for you as it will be for St. Thomas."

"Lina, please, and I am sure it will."

Martens nodded. "Lina then."

There was an awkward pause. Stan moved an escorting arm around Lina's waist and headed them for the door well a few steps away. "See you soon, John."

On Markham's front steps they encountered two more of her new department colleagues. Angela Boch carried a look of perpetual suspicion on her plain, middle-aged face, and Richard Roy was a thin, nervous black man who exclaimed, "Wonderful, we'll be there!" when Stan, in his proprietary way, as if he were functioning as Lina's agent, said, "We'll be announcing a schedule of Professor Lentini's lectures very shortly."

Later as they walked back through the woods to her apartment, Stan chattered on about how Boch and Roy were known on campus as "Witchy" and "Twitchy" and how he thought they would make "a perfect pair, though each of them is married to some other unfortunate." Lina almost asked about John Martens but instead thought back to her box of books and how close she had come to packing her personal notebook in it. In Bologna she had been taping the box closed when she decided she might want the notebook with her on the plane. It was very personal, filled with hand-written musings about her life and herself.

* * *

A few days later the campus seems nearly deserted, just a few solitary walkers as she leaves Markham Hall with McKewan's *Saturday* and Roth's *The Dying Animal* in her bag. A week before classes begin, and she thinks the books will help get her back into the manuscript. Until it is flowing again, she will not feel good, and in less than two weeks she will read from it in her lectures scheduled on campus. Leaving the silent building, she even paused at John Martens' closed door, wondering if his keyboard might be clicking. Nothing.

Now heading back toward the woods, she passes the campus chapel, the university's oldest building. Built with fieldstone, cedar-shake, and a plain iron cross, it had originally occupied the edge of a wide meadow outside of town on a dirt road running past a few large farms. Decades later the campus had been built around it. "A hundred twenty-five years-old," Stan said. "I know that's nothing to you. Around here it's something."

To see for herself, she heads up low stone steps, through double doors each carved with a simple cross. The doors do not creak, closing quietly behind as she moves into the cool sanctuary with its lingering scent of incense. In soft filtered light from stained glass windows, a lone worshipper, an older woman, a kerchief pinned to her gray hair, sits half-way up on the left, head bowed low. On the back wall is a large photograph under glass, an exterior of the chapel, very old in fuzzy black and white, with a caption that says St. Aloysius Catholic Church, 1882. The sanctuary's back row still has the original rough-hewn benches, but the rest is filled with neat oak pews with padded kneelers, a metal and wood communion rail and a plain marble altar.

By walking up the right side all the way to the front pew, she lets the woman know she is not alone now, making less likely some moment of small embarrassment. As she sits next to a small bank of votive candles, several lit and flickering, something makes her think of a series of scenes from earlier this week, all involving the mobile Stan secured for her.

First, picking up messages from her apartment in Bologna brought surprises: Paolo back from Algeria and wanting to see her, a hint of pleading in his smooth lawyer's voice; Guido, her mother's old attorney in Catania, as usual maintaining the polite fiction that Lina cares about the details of the hotel business he oversees; and her friend Lilli, with that cool Brit lilt, inviting her to an opening at the gallery this Friday, voicing, as always, quiet excitement over this new artist's importance and charm (was she sleeping with this one already?). Each is a reminder of how quickly this American venture came together. She was sure she had told everyone about her stay in the States, but obviously some had fallen through the cracks.

Then on Sunday Fr. Redding called to say he would be going to Chicago for a visit with his brother who's battling cancer. Of course, if she needed anything, Stan was there to help.

Of course. Stan has called everyday this week, inviting her to dinner, or a drink, or a movie, or just a cup of coffee, and she has put him off each time. Carefully she explained she was concentrating on her manuscript. With the move and its distractions, getting back into her writing was proving more difficult than she expected. He completely understood and then offered to bring her lunch or dinner. "As my mother used to say, 'You have to eat.'"

"Well, your mother was very wise, but thanks to our trip to the *supermercato*, I have everything I need. Actually, I am putting on pounds here and feeling fat." If she wanted to put him off, why refer to her body?

"Lina, your figure is perfect! But if you're concerned, come running with me."

"Just let me get this manuscript going again, and then we will get together."

Something prompts her to turn now with a glance at the woman behind, and she glimpses Stan backing slowly into the sanctuary, closing the door carefully without a sound. She turns back quickly before his head comes around, reasonably certain he did not see her seeing him.

How strange his arrival now, as if her thoughts have drawn him.

In any case, coincidence seems far-fetched. He must have seen her enter the chapel and followed. She waits without moving, not turning her head, not even looking away from the altar except for a brief glance down at the leather bag next to her on the bench. She thinks about pulling out one of the books to read but wonders what he will do now? Let her know of his presence, as she just did with the old woman praying, or remain silent behind her, no doubt watching her every move? Sensing his gaze on her back, she feels the tension rising in her shoulders and neck. Is there something troubling about his being here? Is he secretly observing, waiting to see her do something revealing, or simply respecting her privacy?

Still, the fact is he is back there watching and does not know she knows. Which gives her power. She can do, or not do, anything that might lead, or mislead, that can tell him something true about her or something false. She can pull out the Roth and start reading, thus saying this sanctuary holds little or no meaning for her as a sacred place. Or she can light a votive candle, knowing that he will likely see it as a religious gesture, when in fact she has done the same thing for years in churches all over Europe, with no special meaning to it, beyond a simple moment of solidarity with all those who have come with pain, hope, longing and despair.

Of course irrational, but it has always warmed her heart and, along with a long fascination with religious architecture, prompted most of the brief visits she has made to cathedrals and churches over the years. No, the old woman behind her is fervently requesting some kind of divine intercession that Lina firmly believes can never happen.

"*Ma, Rossa...*" But, Red... There was always affection and soft mockery in Paolo's voice as he used his pet name for her in bed back in the days when they were happy. "*Tutto succede secondo un progetto divino.*" Everything happens according to a divine plan.

One hopes not. For what it would say about your Divine Planner? The two-headed kitten? The baby with both penis and vagina? She always loved their little post-coital squabbles, amazed and confounded that this smart, clever, sophisticated lawyer was still a believer.

She would ask, so what is God for you? God is what we call the force that created the universe and keeps it spinning. And who or what created God? By definition God is the force before which there is no force. He simply is and always has been. "I am who am." He? Okay, She. This is a concept we can grasp and understand in any real way? Of course not. For our limited intellects it must remain a mystery.

So ultimately you have to take on faith that such an inexplicable primal force exists. But to cede the possibility that some power created and evolved the universe is one thing. The concept of a personal God, who cares about what happens to each of us, is quite another.

Given the evidence everywhere that life in its broadest scope makes no sense, the personal God thing was settled for her a long time back. A caring creator is so clearly a human creation, a concept born of the struggle to confront and live with the absurd cruelty of life, that she long ago stopped thinking about it in any systematic way. A caring God, who monitors with omniscient concern the plight of mankind, the fate of nations, the transgressions of man against man, the starvation of a child and, yes, even the fall of a sparrow, who is omnipotent, open and at least occasionally responsive to our pleas and prayers, is an idea so beyond the improbable that to give it serious consideration requires the abandonment of one of our defining attributes as human beings: the ability to use reason on the world around us.

She decides to do nothing. To simply sit in this pew until she is ready to leave. To do anything else would risk sending something less than the truth to the young man behind her, and truth telling is a value she feels at the core of her being. And yet, why should she limit her actions based on a possible misinterpretation by a fellow with a meager connection to her? What then to do with the need to be true to herself, to act in a way that is authentic? If she functions honestly, she will light a candle. If he has questions, she will answer with candor.

She gets to her feet and moves to the bank of candles. A small, hand-printed card says: "Votive offering: $2.00." Digging in her bag, she glimpses Stan standing in the back. Without looking at him, she slips the bills in the slot of a locked metal box and takes a thin wax taper. The faintly vanilla scent of the candles grows as she leans over them to dip the taper into a flame and move it to an unlit candle. With the new flame glowing, she turns back to the old woman whose face is now buried in her hands. Finally, she turns again and heads

40

back up the side aisle, lifting her gaze to find Stan with a cocked smile. She offers him an ambiguous one of her own, eyebrows raised to register either mild surprise or complicity in the knowledge that he has been there all along. Nearing him, she drops her gaze and moves past to the doors. A push and she is back in the bright morning sun.

She knows he is right there behind her and says, "So now you are spying on me?"

"Spying?" His voice is incredulous as is his look when she finally turns to confront him at the bottom of the chapel's stone steps.

He seems reassured by her smile. He says, "Of course. I've been following your every step for the past four days. You had no idea?"

"Ah, yes, I sensed your powerful presence." He obviously wants a hug. She is not in the mood. "But seriously, did you just stop to say a prayer for me, or did you know I was in there?"

He grins easily. "No, I was heading for Markham and saw you coming in here. I was delighted by my good fortune and rushed over, and then I said, 'Wait a minute, you should not be intruding on Lina's private moment of peace or prayer or whatever.' And so I just thought I'd wait until you left. Which is what I did. So where are you headed?"

"Back to the apartment to write. I needed some books from Markham."

"How about a cup of coffee first? I'm meeting Hal at the Bean. You know, the shop I showed you with the nice place to sit outside."

"Not Starbucks?"

"He says it feels like sipping a marketing phenomenon there. But you know Hal…"

"Well, I do not know Hal. I met him that once with you for two minutes. I would like to know Hal, but I really need to get back to my writing."

"Just one cup. And then I'll drive you back. It'll take less time than if you walk."

"No, I want to walk. I need the exercise." She does not like the way this feels...as if she is an ingrate and always so negative with him lately. "But, okay, one cup."

"Great!"

On the way to his little BMW in a nearby lot, they pass two coeds cycling and shouting a conversation between them.

41

"Ah, girls in skirts on bikes," says Stan. "I love girls in skirts on bikes."

"Oh?"

"The way their tits press against their tops as they lean on the handlebars. The way their skirts ride up as they peddle. With the right angle, you think you'll see all the way to heaven."

She nods with a smile. "So, Stanford, you have what they call a dirty mind?"

"No, I'm just honest. It's what most guys think."

She wonders what John Martens would think if he saw her in a skirt on a bike.

Chapter 8

As they walk to the Bean's patio, off a small parking lot and ringed with boxes banked with petunias still lush and overflowing as September begins, he spots Hal's big head of scruffy dark hair. How can such an infallible proof reader be so oblivious to his personal appearance?

With the prominent, to be charitable, nose and the Adam's apple accenting a narrow face, he's intent on the book he's reading and sitting at a small, two-top table. That's modest, good-hearted old Hal for you, always taking no more space than necessary. He should have called the guy to say Lina was coming too.

"Hey, buddy, look who I brought along."

Hal looks around with a gawky twist and gets awkwardly to his feet. Skinny at 6'3", he offers that shit-eating grin and extends his bony hand. "Ah, professor, good to see you again."

Lina takes the geek's hand with a smile. "A pleasure as well. What are you reading?"

What the hell is he reading? A slim volume with a black dust jacket. Oh, great, Roth.

"Ah, *Everyman*. Published last year? Roth's working so fast, I keep losing track."

Lina says, "Yes. So what do you think?"

Hoping to disrupt, Stan begins to push two tables together. Hal and Lina move to get out of the way. Hal says, "I'm just starting it, but generally with Roth I think he's so, so ruthless." As he swallows nervously, that apple bumps in his neck. "I mean he's so clear-eyed, so insistently honest. He's always staring at things that most of us are likely to turn away from, analyzing, picking apart things that are ugly, disturbing, not the way we'd like life to be. His novels read to me sometimes like horror stories. You just can't look away. It's funny, I hate horror stories, but I love Roth. I mean he's what, in his 70s now? And he's always been prolific, but lately he's been writing

43

like a madman, like a guy possessed and staring straight at his own mortality."

Inside, waiting for his order, the question is how to steer this conversation away from that fucking Roth. Back outside, with a cup of black in each hand, he watches them sitting across from each other, Hal reading to her from the novel and then closing it on his finger. Planting her cup on the table, he sits next to her.

"So, buddy, did Lina tell you she dates George Clooney?"

"Who?"

"George Clooney. You know, 'ER', 'Syrianna,' 'Good Night and Good Luck'?"

Finally, the light of recognition. "Really? You're dating George Clooney?"

Lina shakes her head, shooting a look at Stan. "Your buddy, is, as you say, pulling your leg? I have met the man twice. I am not dating George Clooney."

Hal still seems impressed. "But you met him? I read something about him the other day. He and some of his friends threw a party in Cannes and raised like five million bucks for Darfur. And some woman paid 350,000 to give him a kiss."

"Sounds like something he would do," says Lina.

Stan wants to keep this going. "I think my favorite line from old George was something like, 'But, really, who wants 70 virgins? I want 8 pros.'"

"That too sounds like George."

Hal says, "So, Lina, how's your social life going so far here in sleepy Cedar Hill?"

"Quiet so far, but good for me as I settle in. Last weekend I had dinner with Fathers Redding and Hagan, and, of course, your friend here introduced me to you last week, and on campus we met John Martens and two other professors..." She pauses, searching for the names.

"Witchy and Twitchy," says Stan.

Lina shakes her head. "Professors Boch and Roy. But, you know, sometimes I think Stanford here just likes keeping me to himself."

"Lina, now that's totally unfair. I've been inviting you all week to places where you might meet some folks you'd like to know. And you've just said, no and no."

Lina smiles at Hal. "True, he is right. I said no, I need to stay in

44

and work on my book."

Hal says, "Surely you've been invited to John Martens' big end-of-summer party this Saturday? It always kicks off the fall semester."

Stan says, "No, I haven't asked her yet. She's just been so negative. It's for everybody in the department, and it's always a great party, good food, good drinks, good people."

She turns a big smile on both of them. "If you two will take me, I will be delighted."

* * *

He's in a small funk in the midst of this party. There are times when his slightly anxious, pissed-off, free-floating mopes are difficult to trace. This one's easy. Having maneuvered Hal into meeting them at the Martens' old Victorian, he pulled up with Lina in the Beemer only to find the guy with his bad hair and that ancient Hyundai rattletrap parking next to them. There was no way to avoid walking in with him. She hooked arms with both of them, and there they stood at the open front door, as he tried to find a way to walk in first with Lina.

Suddenly the blond, beautiful, fucked-up Marissa appeared at the screen door, popped it open, and trilled, "Well, this must be the brilliant Professor Lina, with not one but two dashing escorts." As the three of them filed in still linked, she announced with manic volume, "Folks, we already have a ménage going here!"

"Marissa the Tross," short for what she is around John's good-natured neck, still seems reasonably straight, though, of course, it's early, folks. Pressing one of her substantial tits against his arm, she leans in to kiss his cheek and nearly catches his mouth. He knows already there will be flirting later, but first she clearly wants to present the new arrivals as a trio.

In the large living room with it's mostly older crowd, Marissa does her short-hand intros: "Professor Thomas McGraw, Victorian novel, and his wife Esther"—the wives or significant others almost always get short shrift, even with significant academic or professional credentials, as in Esther's case, one of the stars of the astronomy department. "Sister Gertrude Weeks, the German poets, and our resident French lit specialist, George Rolande." "Gert the Flirt" and "George the Pink" are Stan's pet names for the stolid-faced nun and the undercover flamer. For tonight's festivities, the old fag's in black gabardine slacks and a drab gray sport shirt. Not for nothing has this obviously gay man, with the round face and reddish complexion, managed to remain successfully closeted on this Catholic campus for nearly 30 years.

Nicknames are Stan's special province. He has a knack, almost, he would argue, a genius for them. The proof is in how often they stick, how often others end up using them. At times he feels uninspired, as with "T-Mac for that stick-up-his-ass old fart McGraw, or stymied, as with Hal, who's been "Buddy" since the day after they met, the only secret significance residing in the fact that the guy thinks they're fast friends when they're not. But Stan so values nicknames that he considers W's reputed fondness for them the presidential disaster's only redeeming quality.

With the oldsters in the living room is the middle-aged department secretary Elena Plouff, who missed her calling as warden of the state's maximum security facility at Jackson...Stan had tried "Malena" for awhile but finally settled for simply pronouncing her family name in an absurdly high-pitched and airy fashion, as if it were Poof! In the adjoining dining room were the youngsters, the new grad assistants: the smoldering Susanna Paul ("Sexanna"), the sad, plain-jane Becki Warshovsky (simply "Jane") and the constantly attached newly-weds Tim and Pamela Minor ("Beady" and "Big" for their eyes).

On the patio there's a mix of folks, including the popular "Witchy" and "Twitchy" with their lugubrious spouses, Marcus Boch and Amanda Roy. With the young Chinese lit expert Sam Waylon— his mom gave him the slit eyes—Stan started out with "Chink" but quickly decided it was too over the top and settled on "Wong." He's chatting with Charles Sarkevich, Latin American lit, and Cissie, his significant other. "Sark the Shark" for Charles has less to do with personality or proclivity than to prominent teeth, and "Mouse" for Cissie is unfortunately obvious. Sister Martha Cox ("Tayser"), the African-American Bob Bourne ("Jason") and Audrey O'Dowd ("Dowdy") have a small Circle of the Unattached going off to the side.

The intros complete, Marissa excuses herself "to find that elusive husband of mine," spinning into a near collision with the man himself, who makes a deft maneuver to keep from dumping a tray filled with glasses of red wine into the laps of the Circle of the Unattached.

46

"Whoa, honey, careful!" says John.

"You be careful! You're the one with the wine." Marissa, the soul of unassailable logic.

Why has he never come up with something for John? He thought about "Pop" for about ten seconds because of the mentoring qualities but dropped it for no real reason. The host greets him and Hal with his casual "Hey, guys," but those sad blue eyes are already locked on Lina in that amazing black sweater first seen that fateful evening in Orta-San Giulio. "You look marvelous this evening, Professor. I was so pleased when Stan told me you were coming."

"*Grazie*! I would not miss the social event of the season. But, John, it is Lina."

"Yes, sorry. Lina."

The wine is a Nero d'Avola from Sicily, says John. "One of our favorites, 4.99 at Trader Joe's." It's quickly in the hands of Stan, Lina, Bourne and O'Dowd. Thankfully, the host heads off with Hal to the kitchen for some white. Finally, Lina to himself.

"You know this?" Stan raises his glass a few inches after they've each sipped.

"Yes, certainly, it is good. From my old neighborhood. I am surprised he has it here."

"That's John. I'm sure he got something Sicilian just in your honor."

Lina cocks her head with a quizzical smile. "She is the family problem?"

He says, "*La moglie*?" The wife?

Lina nods, and they drift to a corner by themselves. "Yes, she is. But how'd you know?"

"Just a guess. She seems a bit less than stable."

"Really?" Her instantaneous insight is a bit unnerving. "Seriously, how could you tell?"

"I do not know. Maybe there is something about the eyes. The mouth perhaps?"

"Really?" He needs to stop saying really! "Her eyes and her mouth are her best features, I think. Actually, I think she's quite beautiful." Of course this is not the point, but he's surprised at how good it feels to praise the beauty of another to this woman who so dominates his dreams.

"Ah, *si, e vero*. Beautiful. Maybe I am wrong then?"

"No, no, you're not wrong. John never talks about her, but the word is she's bi-polar, you know, manic-depressive. And I don't think there's any question she's an alcoholic."

"You have seen her like that?"

"What, drunk? Yeah, a few times at the least. And somebody I know at St. Joe's, the hospital, says she's been in there for an overdose. Maybe more than once."

"Suicide attempt?"

"I guess, but maybe not a serious one. Although with the level of alcohol she had in her system, it could have been fatal."

"So you know a lot about this, Stan."

"Well, you know, some people like to talk."

"Yes, I have noticed." She seems ready to move away.

He says, "In any case, I'm sure it's all been very difficult for John. But as I say, he never says a word. Never complains. Just soldiers on, past his difficult wife, past prostate cancer."

"So it was prostate. You said he had cancer."

"Yes, and beat it. But he didn't have the surgery. It was some kind of chemo, I guess. And he keeps turning out books. The new one on Lawrence is his third. He just never seems to let anything get to him. Always upbeat in class, and the same way in one-on-ones, but then I've told you how I feel about him. He's the reason I'm in this program."

"Yes, you told me. But he has a very sad face." She's gazing at him across the patio as he carries a large tray of cheese, olives, dip and veggies to the Circle of the Unattached.

"Other people have said that, but I don't see it. To me there's always a kind of gleam in his eye."

And he's never seen the gleam quite so bright as when those blue eyes are fixed, as they are right now, on Lina Lentini.

Chapter 9

The evening has quickly become more than a little frustrating. All he really wants to do is head for that corner of the patio where smitten Stan is drooling over "*la professore.*" Not that he blames him. Catching those green eyes just now and the dazzling smile that followed, John actually felt his stomach flip. When's the last time a woman's look hit him in the stomach? But then every guy in the house, and a few of the gals, have eyes for her. Even sweet old Rolande, who can't move a little finger without giving it all away, and who knows that John knows and has known ever since that timid pass and polite rejection more than a decade ago—even sweet old George leaned in *sotto voce* with "My God, John, what a magnificent piece of ass!"

How pleasant it would be to spend some portion of this busy, littered evening just chatting with the woman, getting to know her a bit and puzzling out what Stan has told her about him. But in that direction lies chaos and recrimination. As usual, the evening, the party, the care and feeding of guests, the whole kit and caboodle, are entirely his responsibility. As always, Mar phoned in the order to the caterer, and that was it for her. She will spend the night circulating her beauty, charm and artsy bent until the up-front wine and secret vodka finally catch up with her. Then it will be some nasty narcissistic scene or a silent slipping away, whichever happens first will not matter. With little help from the inept 16-year-old girl sent along by the caterer, it's up to him to give everyone a good time.

And afterward, the usual drill, with Mar sprawled across their bed in her coma-like sleep, and with minimal assistance from the caterer's girl, he'll sweep through the house to get it back to something like normal, then concentrate on the massively cluttered kitchen, until the dishwasher has run at least one crammed load, send the girl on her way, and finally drop into bed in the guest room. Then lying in the dark, he'll look with new eyes—those penetrating green eyes — at his home, his wife, his life, his own ugly mug.

What does she see as she looks around this place? An eccentric, eclectic mess? Or a crafty, attractive, unique expression of the woman who authored it all? Maybe a little of both, but in either case this is Mar's creation. He's always maintained a limited veto, used only to avoid the most far-out, awkward, or impractical of her whims and fancies. A collection of antiques from different eras, along with comfy modern sofas and chairs, the walls packed with her own photographs, collages and paintings in various styles, a sampling of her ceramics. Yes, she's become less and less productive, and most of the arts and crafts stuff is from years ago. But this place, every inch of it, is nothing if not personal.

What does Lina see looking at Mar? A still-attractive blond, with a touch of the cool Deneuve around the eyes and mouth, or a face verging on flaccid. The body still curvy, or too much so, heftier by fifteen pounds than when they wed? Time, trouble and booze have taken their toll, but is that really so evident on a social occasion that fuels enough energy and animation to mask a thousand flaws? Does Lina, at the moment surrounded by half the males at the party, see Mar now with an obvious buzz, blatantly flirting with both Stan and Hal?

He has managed to catch only a few snippets of Lina's conversations as he passes or pauses nearby. Angela Boch's dour little husband Marcus, an attorney with some small firm in town, asks if Lina saw a report in the Times the other day about a police crackdown on rival Mafia clans in San Luca. "That's a town right in the toe of the boot and the base for a syndicate that is now more powerful than the Sicilian Mafia, because it controls the cocaine market in Europe. I'm wondering if that's the group the Sopranos tapped into in the old country. When they needed something really vicious done, you know, they'd send over for a couple of these thugs who seem to have no conscience at all."

Lina with an amused smile, with all the guys hanging on every word: "Yes, I have not seen The Sopranos, but I doubt they would have to go back to the 'old country,' as you say, to find someone sufficiently lacking in conscience."

Once dapper Dan Hagen arrives — as is his practice, the priest comes late and will leave early — he chats with the younger crowd about what General Petraeus will be saying shortly before congress about the true state of things in Iraq. Lina, impeccably polite: "But, Father, the consensus seems to be that we already know the general's take, since it could not possibly differ from the oft-stated position of your Commander-in-chief."

John's only personal exchange comes as Lina is leaving. After a brief awkward pause at the door, she's standing close to him and says, "John, you have a beautiful, fascinating home."

"Well, thank you. It's really, totally my wife's doing. People seem to love it or hate it or throw up their hands in total confusion."

"Really? Well, I like it."

"Thank you. And thanks again for coming. I wish we'd had more time to chat."

"Perhaps sometime soon."

"I'm sure. I look forward to it."

With a smile and that soft touch, she's gone. Again on Stan's proud, possessive arm.

* * *

"American readers are certainly more accustomed to thinking about ideological coercion and terror in the iron fists of Old World and Third World totalitarianism. But with this remarkable trilogy, Roth brings ideology and terror home to his own shores."

The place is packed. John has rarely seen the old Markham Lecture Hall so jammed, the steeply banked wooden seats all filled, several fellow faculty members standing in the back, late-arriving students lounging on the steps of the side aisles. From his seat at the top of the rim, Stan watches with rapt attention, taking laptop notes.

"In *American Pastoral* the antiwar violence of the '60s devastates a seemingly normal American family. *I Married a Communist* presents a man who embraces communist ideology as destiny. And with *The Human Stain,* Roth drops the massive weight of racial identity on the selfhood of a man who's driven to forge his own definition."

Stan certainly got the word out. A story in the campus paper, those flyers pinned to bulletin boards and stuffed in mail slots, email blasts, and incessant word of mouth. At least five students asked if John planned to be here. "Stan's indefatigable promoting," she told him with that sly smile as she started down to the seat reserved in the front row. Fr. Redding proudly did the honors and called her up to the lectern in the middle of the small stage.

"To this moral history of post-World War II America, Roth brings a passionate dialectical intelligence."

Now, with seeming ease, she commands a room he's always found a bit daunting and uncomfortable, having to look so far up, stretching the neck and, at the same time, speaking without a sound system and having to remember the need to project and maintain volume. None of it seems a problem for this woman. Does the knowledge of just how attractive she is help with the poise and the presence? It can't hurt.

"In the world created by these three books, Roth tells us that the source of evil is the urge to purify, to undo the loss of Paradise, and to wipe away the human stain."

Earlier, in the corridor Stan confided, "You'll see, she's not just sexy, she's brilliant." At the conference he attended in Italy in June, he already heard this lecture. "She thinks it's the foundation, the best way to start the intellectual journey she's embarking on here with these lectures and seminars."

A long Q and A holds even the standing-room-only people and is marked by her patience with a number of awkward student questions and a few self-aggrandizing queries from faculty members. She makes even simple-minded comments seem profound. The heady event finally breaks up, and while a large group crowds around her on stage and small groups debate what they've just heard, Stan stands beaming at the top of the rim, nodding to himself with some special pleasure in the scene. When he notes John's gaze, the nod turns into a wondering shake, as if to say, "Isn't she incredible?"

John leaves the hall and then flinches at his image of Stan and this woman in a sexual clinch. But they're both unattached. What's wrong with the guy trying to make it with her? A little jealousy here? John can still feel that touch of her hand.

Chapter 10

Four days after her first lecture, Lina enters Room 201 for her first seminar. A dozen selected students are waiting around a large table along with Stan, Hal and a few others she met at John's party. She comes ready to listen and respond, and the discussion soon turns to various theories of the origin and nature of evil. Hal starts it by noting that her lecture included several references, and he wonders if she could suggest a reading list on the subject. A helpful request, and she starts with the Old Testament account of Original Sin: Adam and Eve, tempted by Lucifer, give into pride and a lust for knowledge and finally succumb to disobedience. God says do not eat the apple. The serpent says do not listen to God, "*Mangia!*"

In the Judeo-Christian view, disobedience is the original manifestation of evil. Yes, there would seem to be more dramatic options out there — murder, torture, rape, enslavement. But, remember, this concept is promoted by a new religion trying to generate believers and perpetuate itself. Thus, obedience to its belief system is framed as the central issue.

What else to read? Certainly Augustine. As created, human nature was wholly good. But with Original Sin we suffered a constitutional corruption that makes evil inevitable. Whether or not we take the Garden tale seriously, at some specific point in the past, the ancestors of humanity misused their freedom, producing an inherited, congenital flaw in all of their descendants. So there is a universal tendency toward evil among human beings, and this is not (repeat, not) due to changeable social conditions.

Opposing views? Try the libertarianism of Pelagius, a contemporary of Augustine, and, of course, Sartre. Human beings have no fixed or determinate nature. We are free to make of ourselves whatever we will. Evil is an unavoidable by-product of this radical freedom.

For a sociological perspective, read people like Rousseau, Marx, and Freud. For them, evil is the result of a specific set of social conditions arising in the course of human history: the formation of society, the organization of religion, feudalism, capitalism, etc. Inevitably there is a failure to mesh the natural needs of human beings with the artificial needs and desires produced by society. The result: crime, vice, misery.

Also, check out the evolutionary or developmental perspective of Hegel and others. Evil is a necessary and inevitable phase in the evolution and development of the human personality. It represents a step up from the innocence of nature and a prelude to the achievement of virtue and wisdom. Sin results from the assertion of the individual against the universality of morality.

So far Stan has said nothing. Propped against a wall and tapping notes into his laptop, he is so riveted to her she feels a slight discomfort. Finally, he raises a hand and says, "Lina, may I ask if you'd be willing to share with us which of these perspectives is the closest to your own."

He is the first to address her as anything but "professor." His "Lina" is not offensive, but his claim to a special connection is annoying. "Yes, of course, Stan, you may ask, but no, it is not my role to tell you what I think about such large questions. I hope what happens here will encourage all of you to think more, not less. More thinking, more questions, more searching and ultimately more personally meaningful answers."

Stan smiles. "But wouldn't it help us better understand your take on the literature you so beautifully analyze, if you let us know where you're coming from on such basic questions?"

She smiles back. "Thank you, Stan, for the kind words, but my answer is the same. What is important is not what I think, but what you think, or rather the process that each of you engages in to arrive at your own personal understanding."

She turns away, but he continues to press. "Lina, in the spirit of that process then, and that quest, may I ask about the basis for your own personal moral compass? Each of those perspectives on the origin of evil might suggest a different conception of morality. So..."

She cuts him off. "Stan, I appreciate your interest, but I think my position is clear."

In the hall later, she talks with Hal and a good-looking undergraduate with a full blond beard. Stan hangs back, positioned

54

down the hall to pick her up on the way to her office. She smiles often at these two, and proudly reciting from memory, the bearded fellow wonders if she knows this quote from Camus: "The evil that is in the world almost always comes of ignorance, and good intentions may do as much harm as malevolence if they lack understanding."

Yes, indeed, she says, though it could use a better translation. When he is not sure how to take her response, she holds his hand for a moment and encourages him to laugh with her. A few seconds later she does the same with Hal, even gives him a quick hug, before urging the two of them to walk with her. As they pass Stan, she gives him a smiling nod, as if to say, yes, the affectionate gestures she gave him in the past are just a common occurrence.

* * *

A warm, pleasant evening and after dinner, as if she were in Bologna, she walks four blocks to a small store for a few breakfast things. Milk, eggs, a new dry cereal called Go Lean something. Two lectures behind her now, one seminar, and another tomorrow afternoon. She is settling in. Finding a rhythm, as Stan put it the other day.

"A rhythm?"

"Yes, are you finding some comfortable patterns for your new life here?"

"*Ah, si, grazie,...*I am definitely more comfortable now." Why does she often slip into an Italian response with him, then catch herself and finish in English? Especially when he asked her more than once to use Italian so he can "practice." A marker of her own ambivalence toward him, of how her feelings have shifted and hardened in the four weeks since her arrival. Was there really a time, not long ago, when she actually considered sleeping with this man?

Patterns, yes, but often not American patterns. She sees almost no one in this neighborhood walking to the store. Only the tiny woman with the crooked back who drags an aluminum carrier on wheels. Four blocks, or seven to the supermarket. Unlike in Bologna, which was made for walking, everyone here gets in the car and drives everywhere, presumably to save time. Americans seem obsessed with saving time.

Maybe she is thinking about these things because she received two emails from home this morning. Sweet Hans wrote asking about her American adventure and to let her know that, thanks to their

55

talk, he was no longer troubled by that disturbing fantasy. A week before she left Bologna she had found him reading *Crime and Punishment* outside a café just down Via San Vitale from her apartment. In their long discussion as they walked and talked, she had told him that reading Dostoyevsky had given her guilt pangs as well. Dear Rena's note reassured that Lina's plants were thriving: "I water, and then I sit and read them my new poems."

When did she see Stan last? Three days ago, showing up on her doorstep unannounced, carrying a white plastic bag containing a dinner for two, personally prepared, he said.

"But, Stan, if you had called first, I could have told you I am meeting friends for dinner."

He said nothing for a moment, starring blankly. Would he ask which friends and where? Would he pump her for details? He finally smiled with disappointment and explained that she could simply "put it in the fridge" and have it another night. If she liked, he would join her.

Why the made-up story? Why not simply tell this man the truth? She was not about to reward a presumptive, intrusive act: he could not simply show up at her apartment and walk in to a warm welcome. And then she made herself feel worse with the sudden thought that he might later lurk in the shadows outside her apartment, waiting to see if she in fact would leave.

The question about her finding a rhythm was part of an effort to extend that conversation, as he stood without moving on her doorstep. Trying to put an end to it, she said it was time to get ready for her dinner engagement. The dinner in the bag, he explained, was an apology for his recent "boorish behavior." This she already knew. "Stan, there is nothing to apologize for." Again the truth avoided, even while her rules to live by were fashioned, in part, from Keats:

"Beauty is truth, truth beauty,--that is all
Ye know on earth, and all ye need to know."

Later she thought about leaving the apartment and, if he followed, driving around long enough to lose him. But that would only compound the lie. She wrote late in her spare room office with the lights off in the rest of the apartment. The dinner turned out to be a decent spaghetti in a pesto sauce. Also a couple of cannoli that no doubt came from the Italian restaurant he had taken her to in her first week in Cedar Hill.

She blames herself. Early on she flirted a bit, enjoyed his intense attention. She should have responded professionally from the start, making it clear their connection would include no personal dimension. For some reason, an image of John Martens pops into her head. Those sad lines etched into a face that is, yes, homely, but somehow attractive when animated and focused, those blue eyes deep and knowing. The way he looked last week when she attended his lecture on Lawrence's *The Rainbow*, one of her favorites. He was casual and relaxed in the classroom, yet incisive and surprising, offering insights that seemed fresh and original.

Afterward she walked with John back to his cluttered office, and when she asked where she could find his new book, he said, "Right here," pulling a copy from under a pile of papers.

She read the cover: *The Human Touch...To Be Male and Female in the Major Novels of D.H. Lawrence.*

"Here, may I?" he said, scribbling inside the cover, then handing it to her.

His inscription read, "To Lina, with gratitude and affection." She looked up and found him gazing at her. "How kind," she said, "but gratitude for what?"

"For your interest, of course. I'm very flattered."

She felt herself blushing and paged ahead to the Introduction, prefaced with a quote from Lawrence's own *Studies in Classic American Literature*: "Never trust the artist. Trust the tale." She said, "I love that quote," but soon left, their parting feeling surprisingly awkward. The first three chapters confirmed a first-class critical intelligence and a passion for the power of art.

The grocery's automated doors swing open for her. It was after leaving John's office that she came upon her own office door, just as she left it, wide open. She had departed in a rush, not wanting to walk in late on John's lecture. But as she approached her office, a strange foreboding made her come up off her clicking heels on that hard, polished hallway floor and take the last few steps, almost silent, on the balls of her feet.

And there he sat, as in a nightmare, at her desk, pushing back into its place on a shelf the old blue-covered spiral notebook that serves as her personal diary.

"Stan! What are you doing?" Her voice sounded loud and shrill.

He stood quickly with a stiff grin and said, "Oh, Lina, sorry. The door was open, and I wanted to speak with you. Just thought I'd look through some of your books while I waited."

"Stan." Her voice this time is under better control. "My books, my notebooks, are private property. Looking through any of them, unbidden, is an invasion of my privacy."

He moved away from the desk, looking pale, almost stricken. "Lina, I'm sorry. I'm so impressed, so eager to learn from you. I'm afraid I wasn't thinking."

"What you were doing is inappropriate. Beyond acceptable limits."

He backed toward the door. "But really, Lina, I meant no harm. Just the opposite. I think your work is so important."

She glared at him, placing her purse on the desk, as if to reclaim it. She looked at the notebook, then shoved it further into place. "Stan, we will just forget it."

"Lina, I really hope…"

She stopped him with a flick of her hand. "No, we will leave it there."

He stared, nodded and moved out the door.

* * *

It is Crunch. Go Lean Crunch! is the one she likes. As she reaches for it, a male voice, deep and friendly, says, "So you like that too?"

Box in hand, she turns to find John Martens' sad smile. "John, what a surprise."

"Pleasant, I hope."

"Of course, pleasant. How are you? Do you come here often?"

"Oh, yes, quite often. We're only three blocks away, and I like to walk."

"Yes, I do too. But I almost never see anyone else walking."

"Yeah, except for Beulah Baine. She's the little old woman with the bad back?"

"Yes, I saw her today."

"She's always walking, but it doesn't do much for her mood. She's pretty cranky."

Lina says nothing, and a strained silence follows. He's in his uniform: a baggy old sweater, this one purple, and faded black corduroys. He has an arm through the handle of a red plastic basket with a few items in it. She too holds a basket and is suddenly aware of her drab and shapeless gray sweatshirt.

He says, "So, Go Lean Crunch! I have that stuff every morning."

She nods and says finally, "Well, it was great seeing you John."

"You too, Lina." He looks into his basket. "I'm almost finished. Just some half-and-half for my wife. She can't drink coffee without it. Me, I could care less. But then I have no taste. I can drink 2-day-old coffee, and it makes no difference."

She wants to say, "If you tried my coffee, you would know the difference." But the mention of his wife has suddenly explained their conversation's strained pauses. She smiles, nods, says, "Take care, John," and moves away. When she checks out at the cash register a few minutes later, he is already gone.

Once through the automated doors, she finds him waiting on the sidewalk. "Listen, may I walk you home?"

"Oh, no, it must be out of your way."

"No it's really not that much farther. It's a beautiful evening and I need a good walk. Besides, that way I can feel gallant and carry your groceries."

"Carry my groceries. Do I seem that helpless to you?" She cocks her head just enough to tell him she is teasing...and, yes, flirting a bit.

"Helpless," he says taking her bag, "is the last thing you seem."

"Well, then, thank you, kind sir." And as they walk, she says, "So tell me about Stan."

"You mean beyond the fact that he's nuts about you?"

"Oh, please."

"It's obvious, but what do you want to know?"

"Well, he told me he is 29, that he is writing about Primo Levi, and that he credits you with getting him to this point. But I am curious about his earlier academic career."

"Yes, it's a bit checkered. As an undergrad in Ann Arbor he was in a special program that allowed him to fashion his own course of study. So he took classes combining science and the arts. In grad school at U of M he concentrated on both chemistry and literature."

"Unusual."

"Stan's an unusual guy. But in his first year in grad school—he was maybe 23—his mother was diagnosed with cervical cancer, and he dropped out to care for her because there was no one else. He was raised by his mother after his father left them when Stan was eight. He says caring for his mom and watching her die was so devastating that he lost his equilibrium for a while and could not bring himself to return to his studies. His record for that year shows a couple of D's, but mostly incompletes. For a while he worked on a memoir based on a diary he kept as his mom lost her battle, but he says the memoir was so depressing that he finally burned it."

"Sounds like a terrible time."

"Yes."

"And money? I mean, he drives an expensive car, travels abroad, dresses well."

"No, not your usual starving grad student. His mother struggled to support them after his father split, working two and three jobs to make ends meet and send him to college. When she became ill, she had no resources and, as I said, no one but Stan to care for her. He said he began dabbling in the market, you know, day trading, to keep his mind off what was happening. I suppose his facility with science and math came in handy, and he became very successful at it. Of course, the market was soaring at the time, but finally, at some point after his mom passed, he became bored with it. By then he had enough in the bank not to worry about money."

John stopped for a moment and gazed off. "I asked for some stock tips once, and he said, 'Oh, god, no, I never feel comfortable giving tips.'"

"So how did he get together with you?"

"He literally knocked on my office door one day. Said he'd heard great things about me. How or from whom I have no idea. But he'd read both my books at the time, and he said he wanted to study with me. Stan can be very flattering."

"Yes, I know." She gives him a sidelong smile as they walk.

"Anyway, he offered to buy me a cup of coffee and then told me some of his history, the stuff I've just recounted, and said that since his mother's death he'd been kind of lost, just floating, he said. And then one day he was just aimlessly tooling around the Web and decided to google "chemistry and literature." And so he discovered the literary work of a chemist named Primo Levi. The more he read Levi, the more fascinated he became, and now he knew what he wanted—return to grad school and eventually pursue a Ph.D. in literature. He even had a plan for his dissertation. Analyze Levi's work and decide whether his death at 67 was a suicide or an accident. He knew he'd be almost starting over, that he had a long road ahead before he could even think about starting on the dissertation, and that he'd need to learn Italian. But he was determined to do this. He said his grades weren't always the best, but if he were given the chance, his commitment would be absolute. That was his word, absolute."

"So you were impressed."

"I was. It's not often I find a student with such clearly drawn, ambitious plans. But I was a little concerned about his grades. They were in fact quite mediocre, so I suggested he write me a paper on Levi, any topic he wished. And that paper was what really made the difference in getting him into the program."

They walk in silence for a while, and then she stops in front of her apartment and proceeds to give her own brief history with Stan. She starts in Orta-San Giulio and ends with the other night when he arrived unannounced with a home-made dinner. For some reason she leaves out finding him in her office, going through her notebook. The fact is she is afraid he may have misperceived a personal interest on her part, and she is struggling with how to be straight-forward and honest with him while not hurting his feelings.

"I guess what I am wondering, John, is how do I let him down easy."

He gazes at her for a second, then looks away and shifts the grocery bags in his arms. "Gosh, Lina, I would think you have, without doubt, a wealth of experience doing just that."

She smiles at him and shakes her head. "You would be surprised, John. But American men especially I do not know well at all."

"Yes, well, I have to say, you certainly seem to know the male of the species very well indeed, and when it comes to a woman with your extraordinary...assets, American men are certainly no different. I'm sure you'll do the right thing and handle it well."

Chapter 11

He slows the Beemer nearly to a stop before a right turn on her street for the one drive-by he's decided to allow himself. All afternoon, holed up in his apartment, he's been chasing his tail, arguing one side and then the other. Half the time he was sure the whole thing was a trap, a setup, that she left the door open just to lure him in and then returned to catch him in the act. Really, all he was doing was paying homage to her and her extraordinary work.

And then for a time he was just as certain he'd totally blown it. Sitting at her desk without an invitation, violating her in a sense that was actually palpable, starting to get a hard-on as he opened the blue notebook, a kind of diary with several recent entries. And then he found not a single reference to himself. In his quick nervous scan of page after page of her shapely cursive — until those heels approached in the hall — not one reference to the man who has spent the past month trying to please, delight and satisfy her in every way. True, no one else on campus had apparently merited a mention. The only guy he noted was somebody named Paolo, whose attention she didn't seem to appreciate. But the effect of not finding his own name was like a bitter cold rain that left him damp and shriveled.

For most of the afternoon he was swinging between recrimination and rage, between self-loathing and self-justification. Then slowly he began to realize that his own desperation and lack of control were the problem. He was pressing too hard, being too aggressive and pressuring her in ways that were only counter-productive. Really, he knew better. You can't force a woman into wanting you. Lure, entice, even act as if you don't really care. Be helpful, but laidback. Be kind, cordial and courtly again. But presume nothing. Start fresh.

So why is he allowing himself this drive-by? Almost stalking behavior. It's simply a small gift to the aggressive side that has often served him well in the past and that he might need again at any time. Except that, as he's about to turn the corner, he spots them in front of the apartment a half-block down, Lina in gray sweats he's never seen before, and, leaning close to her, holding two paper grocery bags, none other than his own esteemed mentor, John Martens. With a sinking feeling, he knows that letting them see him here (doing what, a coincidental pass by her apartment?) is unthinkable. He turns left instead of right and notes in the mirror as he drives away that neither seems to have noticed him.

Two minutes later he's parked on her street a hundred yards away, behind a car that blocks their view while his line of sight is relatively unobstructed. After a few minutes they move toward her front steps, then he loses them but knows they've entered her apartment. He should end this absurd vigil now. He knows he won't.

Thinking again about her diary has dredged up his own, something he hasn't thought about in years. Out of sight, out of mind, not surprising, since it represents, more or less abject failure. Literary fame and glory had been the goal. Instead, it was a bold shortcut to nowhere.

It really started that ugly January day in Ann Arbor, when the call came from Joleen. Heavy sobs at first with few words. Finally, his mother coughed out the news: she had cancer of the cervix. Dr. McIntosh said she had less than a year. She needed Stan now, desperately needed him, to come back to Murphysboro. "Asap," said Joleen, "because there is no one here for me, and Dr. Mac says there will soon be many things I won't be able to do for myself." The sobs swelled again. "I know it's not fair, sweetheart, but there's no other way."

In the car he drove straight through, a little over eight hours with a stop for gas, and pulled up in front of the Liquor Mart on 12th in Murphysboro. He grabbed a Southern Illinoisan from the stand and back in the heated car found the want ads. Marvella Goins said she was "available for homecare and everyday household duties." On his cell he arranged to meet her at the house the next morning, 9 o'clock sharp.

As expected, Joleen's protestations were loud and tear-filled, the red-veined blue eyes wide with betrayal, the flushed face—looking remarkably healthy for someone with a death sentence—fraught with self-pity. Of course she understood the importance of his schoolwork—she still called it schoolwork! But SIU was a fine school and just seven miles away, seven miles! He could probably still enroll for the new semester in Carbondale without missing a beat. It's where he should have been all along. He had heard all this many times before. He just let her go on and on and really didn't argue. When Marvella seemed competent and reliable, she was hired on the spot. And by one in the afternoon he was on the road again heading north.

On that trip back up I-57, through the world's most boring landscape, flat, endless Illinois farmland in winter, everything came together for him. Yes, continue with the astonishingly detailed account of his sex adventures, writing that began consuming him in the fall as he simultaneously found his grad studies becoming a pointless bore. He limped through two classes, dropped three others and by Christmas knew he would dump the whole thing.

Now with Joleen on her deathbed, or close to it, it was as if he'd been set free. His mind raced over the possibilities, a way to pull it all together for an astounding, shocking, best-selling saga. Novel or memoir? TBD, though as the true story of his incredible life, it was certainly more likely to make a big commercial splash. Yes, memoir was the way to go, if at all possible. Yes, the truth might be bent, broken or mangled at times, but, without Joleen to contradict or cry liar, who would raise questions about his clear-eyed report of a father absconding with millions in other people's funds, vanishing with his "sexpot assistant," according to Joleen, into the wilds of South America. Or his earnest boy's account of sleeping with his mother from the age of 9 to 15.

It would have to begin in Chicago, of course, where his parents first raised him, his father off each day to his job as an investment broker, his mother mostly at home with little Stanford, though teaching an occasional class in business skills at a local community college, just because she enjoyed it, she said. The neighborhood in Evanston was pleasant, comfortable and filled with schoolmates. Were his parents happy? Who knew what adults felt? Certainly there was never a fight, hardly a cross word. Then suddenly his world collapsed.

Knowing there were many in Chicago, victims of her husband's criminal machinations, including best friends and social acquaintances, whom she would never wish to encounter again, Joleen packed up and moved them to her quiet little home town of Murphysboro at the other end of the state. She still had friends and family there. But within three years her parents were dead in a plane crash and her two closest girlfriends had moved away. As for little Stan, he'd been ripped out of his perfectly happy little life with his pals and favorite places to play, his fantasies filled with Bears, Cubs, Bulls and Blackhawks, and dropped abruptly into a lousy boyhood in small-town southern Illinois, lonely, empty and devoid of heroes. There wasn't a single kid from his class who lived within two miles of their home.

Though often in the dumps, Joleen tried occasionally. On their trip to St. Louis when he was 10, his Cubbies battled the Cards, the one team he hated most in this world. Naturally the Cards won in the 10th, a walk off homer by someone he'd never heard of. And in the eighth grade, when a local gun club offered after-school classes in hunting safety, she finally said yes to his pleadings, entirely against her "better judgment," and drove him to and from the club's shooting range where she cheered on his sharp-shooting, calling him "Sweetshot Stan."

There were no financial concerns. Joleen did not need to work. But they were probably both clinically depressed, often lonely and painfully unhappy. There were times when neither of them could sleep much, and that's when she brought him into her bed, to share warmth and find some way to solace. So how would he would write that part? He knew already it would need to be explicit, the story of how he learned to please a woman in so many different ways.

What happened exactly as it all unraveled after age 15 was still not really clear. Her health began to break, and she was too weak to do much of anything. He began to bring home girls from high school. But when the question of college came up, the battle was on. She wanted desperately to hold him close, but he knew one thing for sure: he was getting out of southern Illinois. Ann Arbor's world-class U of M became a beacon, and it was never out of his sight.

"I don't want another knock-down, drag-out," she'd always say, just before she'd start one. "Southern Illinois University is nothing to sneeze at!" He couldn't believe he had a mother who could use a phrase like that and so responded with a kind of ironic mockery she could never even recognize. "To be a Saluki, Mom, will never be my destiny."

Finally, one thing became crystal clear: his father had planned his own escape with patience, care and shrewdness. Affecting a lifestyle and persona that were nothing but beige and boring, he had chosen victims who mostly invested money they wanted to keep secret, and he had structured trusts for the little family left behind that were both generous and well-protected. He had even looked forward a decade to give Stan full-access to one account to cover college costs, knowing apparently there might well be differences between mother and son at that point. Ultimately Stan had what he needed to go where he wanted. And that was that.

Ideas were flying at him as he headed back to Ann Arbor, his foot pressing the gas in his car back then, the black Thunderbird, until it was topping 90 in areas where the state cops patrolled with wolf-like focus. He set the cruise control for six over the limit and tried to relax. But before he hit the outskirts of Chicago his mind was already racing ahead to the call he would get from Marvella some months hence with the news that it was time to come home and say goodbye. And now he already knew how all this would play out and how his sensational book would end. Finding Joleen suffering with excruciating pain, deep despair and only occasional lucidity, he would send Marvella away for a well-deserved respite, and in the dark of the night, with bitter tears and one final kiss, he would pull the plug.

Would there be legal consequences for such a stunning admission? Probably not, but if so, and if serious enough, he could always fall back to plan "B," a deeply contrite admission that he'd made up the whole fucking thing.

Thirty-four agents and thirteen publishers were each sent an irresistible two-graph pitch, a roller coaster three-page summary and a shock-and-awe first three chapters. In response he received nothing but brutal silence from several recipients, a number of standard-form rejection slips, and seven personalized notes. These last included two from agents and one from a publisher who all asked to see the full manuscript. Of the other four, all from agents, he tried to find something positive in two. One said, "You have an interesting style, but the subject matter is a turn off here. Good luck elsewhere." And the other: "With all the questionable and problematic memoirs lately, we are hesitant to take this on. But my guess is you'll probably find somebody who is willing to try." The other two offered nothing to chew on but razor blades: "The writing is just not up to handling the off-putting nature of your content." And "I don't normally render such judgments, but I quite frankly found this truly disgusting."

But it only takes one, he told himself, as he sent copies of the manuscript off to the three who had requested it. In two weeks he heard from one agent who said the lists were full and his work would unfortunately not get the attention and support it deserved. And a month later, another agent gave him four words: "Sorry, not for us." After three months he was sure he would never hear from the one publisher who still had the full manuscript. But ten days later it came back, looking untouched, with a note: "Thanks for letting us see your novel. After a careful reading, and given the difficulty in selling fiction these days, we've decided to pass."

"It's a fucking memoir, you stupid fuck!" he screamed at the note. And then he wondered whether this was simply a mistake by some incompetent hack, or a flat-out statement of disbelief in his work's veracity. Ultimately he decided it didn't matter. He was done. This process was too humiliating. He would burn the manuscript copies he had left, hide it away in a corner of his computer, and someday write something else that would take the literary world by storm. And then with his readers agog and wondering who this wonder Stanford Lyle really was, he would pull out his memoir and further astound the world.

After this fiasco he floundered, lost in a suffocating realm of pointlessness and deep-running angst. He moved to Chicago on a sudden whim, and after a few weeks decided he was maybe on a quest for his father. A few years earlier word had filtered back to Joleen in Murphysboro that the woman who had disappeared with her husband might have returned to Chicago. Someone had talked to someone who was sure they had seen her in a North Side tavern. If the sexpot had actually resurfaced and could be found, there might be a chance to realize his sad boyhood fantasy of finding his runaway father and joining him in some Chilean beachtown or exotic city in Peru. With little more than a name he searched for the woman but soon ran out of leads and gave up. This quest was crazy. He needed to look forward, not back.

But how to grab hold of himself? He knew almost nobody in Chicago. So to meet people and because he'd always been intrigued with acting, he took a class with a small theater group near the U of C campus. Taking on the persona of another and, with shrewd deceit, convincing people of its truth seemed right up his alley. It also turned out to be good way to meet women. He actually auditioned for a number of roles, but after a half-dozen tries, all futile, he gave up. And then his idle googling one day led to a piece on Primo Levi by of all people Phillip Roth.

Three days later he was browsing in a U of C campus bookstore, when a professor from a Michigan college began speaking to a small group about his new book on the literature of the Holocaust. There was something about the man, his presentation, or the serendipity of his subject that captured Stan. He felt a deep appeal in the man's manner, and though he did not stand in line to meet him later, he bought his book.

And the rest is history, he thinks, as he watches John, still carrying a grocery bag, emerge from Lina's place forty minutes later and walk away in the opposite direction. How about knocking on her door now and letting her know that he knows about her visitor? What about his vow to step back and keep his distance? Besides, face it, he doesn't really know what's going on here. The visit could have been pure chance, the activity inside nothing more than professional conversation, or, even if personal, perfectly innocent.

But he now has something new to watch for, and over the next several days, there are a few moments to note in Markham Hall: the two of them so engrossed in each other as they walk and talk in an empty hallway that they barely acknowledge his presence as they pass; Lina carrying the new book on Lawrence into the seminar room; John leaning casually against her office door jam, nodding with a smile as she talks from her desk chair.

His drive-bys increase but turn up nothing, no sign of John's Saab, nothing he can see through her windows from the street. Maybe he should "accidentally" run into nutty Marissa and chat her up about the new rock star professor. But then one sunny, early October day he walks in for lunch at Two, a campus place with a softly lit interior and large windows on a popular outdoor patio where he's surprised to find Lina and Hal sitting together. He takes a booth inside, a dark back corner with a clear view of their table. Hal, dressed as usual in his nerdy red flannel shirt, with an old Pirates baseball hat covering that awful hair, is talking with his hands as Lina smiles indulgently. Stan watches as the two seem be having a marvelous time, until John arrives.

Immediately on his feet, Hal shakes hands with John and

promptly moves away, while they obviously urge him to stay. Thanks, but no thanks, and Hal disappears. John leans down to kiss Lina on the cheek, and then on the other, already doing that Euro thing. Stan takes a quick look around the restaurant interior. It's crowded, but there, alone in a booth, with a closer, even better view of that patio table, sits Marissa. Those careless blond curls seem more fetching than usual on a head that is clearly locked on her husband and his lunch date.

Stan picks at his Cobb Salad and watches. Will there be some kind of confrontation or awkward encounter? What if one of them comes inside to use the john and spots her there? But only a few minutes pass before Marissa pulls a phone from her purse and holds it in front of her face toward the windows. She's snapping photos. The first one just misses Lina leaning toward John and covering his hand with the trademark gesture of warmth and affection that Stan knows so well. But there are soon more opportunities for telling candids, from a touch on his arm, to big mutual smiles, to an intense leaning together. And after 40 minutes, the grand denouement: the two of them on their feet taking leave, a full hug that lasts maybe a second too long, followed by that two-kiss rigmarole. Marissa seems to get it all.

Starting that evening he ditches the drive-bys. They're both too risky and unproductive. If he were John, living only four blocks from her, his usual after-dinner walk would be the best way to see her without raising suspicion at home. He tries parking on campus, walks through the woods and finds a perfect vantage point in a thicket that allows him to monitor unseen Lina's front door. The first night is a fruitless, 2-hour bitch, mosquitoes biting like crazy, his back going into spasms, no sign of either love bird. After the first hour he's already thinking he needs to find a way to break this stupid fucking obsession.

The next night it rains, and he's not about to soak in it. But the third evening he's back and hardly there 10 minutes before John shows up with a small bouquet of grocery store flowers. When the door opens, there's no kiss-kiss fandango. It's full on the mouth.

Chapter 12

How can her hand touching his possibly seem more erotic than the first meeting of their lips minutes ago at the door? When those brilliant green eyes offered their jolt, he was ready to do the cheek thing, but then they dipped to his handful of cheap red carnations, and before he could move, her mouth was on his, her lips so wonderfully pliant and soft.

So much about her seems an exquisite turn-on. How about every facet of her being? Her subtle scent, just a whiff of some natural essence that works like a powerful magnet. Every amazing line of a body that so often grabs his breath. That slight hint of an accent, tinted with shades of British/American/Italian. Closed in his office the other day he sounded like an idiot, trying aloud to match the utterly charming way she speaks his name. Not Jawn, not Jon, not Joan, but some sweet blend of all three. Her mind, unique, extraordinary, fecund with laser perceptions and original takes on the intricate, trivial, mundane, and profound. The wise, warm, empathetic heart, with a kind of non-stop understanding that makes his own heart hum.

Her perfect pink-nailed index finger caressing the web between the thumb and the rest of his right hand, he regrets for the fourth time in ten minutes not taking one of his magic blue pills, ordered in bulk from a lab in Thailand and mailed to his office in Markham. For all Mar knows, he's been impotent ever since the brachyotherapy almost five years ago, unable to make any good use of what she calls his "sad ding dong."

"Look," he says finally, "I'm pushing 53. There's no way I'm going to…"

"So? I am pushing 40, and you know all that matters is how you feel."

He gazes at her for a few seconds, then says, "Okay, fine. I'm dying to fuck you."

"Good," she says, tilting her face to be kissed. "Because I am dying for you to fuck me."

He kisses her mouth with all the sweetness he can summon. She responds in kind for a time, but suddenly, with a moan, presses her open mouth on his, inviting his tongue and something much deeper. He starts to give it, then stops, even while he feels something rare down below, a serious stirring that almost never happens without the pill.

"Please," he says, "I need to tell you some things."

"Okay." She gives him one little nod. "Tell me."

Feeling too solemn, he says, "Five years ago I was diagnosed with prostate cancer."

"Yes, I know."

"Stan?"

"Yes, but maybe everyone knows."

"Probably. It's a long story, but the main thing is I was fortunate. I've been in remission for almost five years, and that's a kind of milestone the docs care about. In terms of side effects, which can be pretty nasty, especially with the surgery, I was also lucky. I have no incontinence. And impotence, which is common, is no problem as long as I use the little blue pill."

"Viagra."

"Yeah, thank god for Viagra."

"Do you?"

"No, I don't think she cares." He watches her smile and says, "When I left the house tonight for my walk, I actually debated taking a pill. But I didn't know if you were home, and I also didn't want to be presumptuous." She shakes her head, "I thought maybe it would be crossing a line that I needed to think about more carefully, no matter what you might say. In any case, it's a decision I've regretted several times since you kissed me at the door."

With a warm smile, she gives his hand a small squeeze.

"And there's another thing. I have a troubled and difficult wife."

"Yes, I know about that too."

"Stan again." He shakes his head glumly. "Yeah, I walk through my life everyday thinking it's my little secret, but probably lots of people know."

"Probably."

"Well, she's bi-polar and an alcoholic. Not an uncommon combo,

71

because they often use the booze to self-medicate, and the problems have gone on for a long time. Nearly every day she drinks a fifth of vodka and some wine, and by nine in the evening she's usually gone. I won't bore you with the details, but she's dried out and gone through recovery three or four times, and nothing has helped. AA worked the first time for three months, two months the second time, and now she has no use for it at all. The marriage is damaged goods, but I can't really imagine leaving her. I'd feel like I was writing her death sentence."

"I am so sorry, John."

"Thanks, but because she's like many people with these problems, a narcissist and locked into herself, and also because she so often sees life as a blur, normally she's not really all that aware of what I'm doing or feeling. I've had a few affairs over the years, and I tell myself they're the only reason I've been able to get through all this. I was with one woman for more than five years, until she finally got fed up and left town. And Mar never had any idea of what was going on. Totally oblivious. Yes, we were very careful, but still..."

"Why not just tell her the truth?"

"The truth?"

"Yes, if she is so dependent on you, and I am sure she is, why not just tell her that you will never leave her, but that you need the freedom to find a little peace and satisfaction in your life. Okay, she needs to drink, well, you need a lover. There are marriages like that, John."

"I imagine there are. But I know it won't work for mine. Yesterday I worked late at the office and brought home a pizza for dinner. She never cooks, never cleans house, almost never even does laundry. I do everything. I mean that's just the way it is. But anyway, I bring the pizza and she complains—bitterly—that I've been too damn selfish to get the kind she prefers, with a thin crust. So later, even though it's raining, I go out for my walk. I put on a slicker, and I walk more than two hours. Actually I spent most of the time thinking about you and resisting the urge to call and ask if I could stop by. But when I finally get back, expecting her to be in bed or passed out on the couch, she's waiting to jump all over me with accusations about how I've spent the evening with you and that we're having this raging affair."

Her lovely lips pursed, Lina says, "John, tell me more about you.

Where is your family from? Where did you grow up and go to school? Those kinds of things."

He is happy to leave the subject of Mar's rage. "I'll give you the short version." So his family is Dutch and British, his father a physician, a general practitioner, his mother a jazz pianist who taught improvisation at Cleveland State. They married in their late 20's. John came quickly and was an only child. He grew up in a Cleveland suburb called Shaker Heights, in a home where organized religion was not important but where respecting everyone's faith or beliefs was. He was studious in school and lost in books much of the time. At Ohio State University in Columbus he got his bachelor's, master's and Ph.D.

"Ah, where Phillip Roth went to university."

"Yes, of course long before I was there."

His wrote his dissertation on Dostoyevsky, then for seven years taught in Columbus. But without tenure and wanting more time and energy to write, he looked for options elsewhere. Redding back then had just taken over the department here and was building it, with what he called "top new talent." So it was on to St. Thomas, and it's been sixteen years now.

"Women?" asked Lina.

"Women. Well, in Columbus I was with a woman for nearly five years. She was in the music department. Very beautiful and very unstable. She used to cut herself."

"Cut?" Lina dragged a fingernail across her forearm.

"Yes, cut."

She shook her head sadly and looked away.

"And so she was another reason for my leaving Columbus. Here in Cedar Hill, after a year or so, I met Mar, one of my students, and a year after she graduated we were married."

She looks at him. "John, why this need to rescue beautiful and crazy young women?"

"It does look that way, doesn't it?"

"Yes, darling. So what exactly did Marissa say the other night?"

"Say?"

"Yes, when she accused you of being with me."

"Ah, yes, well, I don't even remember, but there was a lot of crazy rage. She'd been drinking, of course, but the adrenalin was pumping or something, and she was way more focused than usual. The thing

73

is, I just don't understand where or how she got the idea."

But, of course, he does remember their exchange, almost word for word, and later, on his walk home, he goes back over their confrontation. Because he'd done nothing more than think about Lina at that point, he's sure he sounded as convincing as possible. But he also knows that she certainly had the last word as she glared at him in a fashion he knew all too well.

"You keep on with her, Johnny boy, and you won't believe how fucking awful and miserable I'm going to make both your lives. But especially hers. She's an ego-maniacal, predatory bitch, and I knew it the first second I laid eyes on her, waltzing into this house with those two boys on her arm. They're moonstruck little puppies. What's your excuse?"

"Mar..."

"I'm telling you, John, you'll rue the day."

Chapter 13

Nerves on edge, he comes late to Van Heulen's, the funeral home chosen by the Minors, Tim and Pamela, and Hal's sister Hannah for the memorial service. With the body already autopsied and shipped to a funeral home in Pittsburgh, there was really no need for Van Heulen's. But the campus chapel, often used for such services, was reportedly ruled out by Fr. Redding because of the Church's implacable stance on suicide. And while there were other options, Hannah's emotional state was fragile, and the matter was quickly settled when she said finally, "Please, can we just do it at the funeral home?"

With the rosary set for 7 pm, his plan to walk in at about 7:20 is well-calculated. Redding has just started his eulogy when Stan nods to John and Marissa sitting on one side of the aisle. Lina's supportive smile comes from the other side. He takes a seat near the back. The priest appears drawn and pale as he thanks everyone for coming. The large room is filled with the whole department, plus spouses, mates and friends, along with assorted deans, administrators and about two dozen young people who must be Hal's former students in freshman English.

Redding tells the group, "Each of us comes here this evening from a different place, but all of us share common bonds: our admiration and love for our brilliant and gifted young Hal, our grief for his family, particularly his dear sister Hannah who is with us tonight, and our heartbreak over the loss of this very special young man with all of his bright shining promise."

Lifting in his seat, Stan looks for a woman near the front who might be sister Hannah. A tall woman in her early 30's? Maybe frumpy hair the color of Hal's and the upright stance of an elementary school principal. There's a woman with the right hair on the left side of the first row, but her head is so bowed that her height and posture are uncertain.

"Now so many questions have been asked," says Redding, "so many thoughts and feelings expressed about what has not yet been made official, but which sadly seems to be the case — that our beloved young Hal took his own life. There's been so much misinformation, that I thought it might be helpful to outline briefly the Church's position on the subject of suicide. Let me start by quoting from the Catechism of the Catholic Church: 'Suicide contradicts the natural inclination of the human being to preserve and perpetuate his life. It is gravely contrary to the just love of self. It likewise offends love of neighbor because it unjustly breaks the ties of solidarity with family, nation, and other human societies to which we continue to have obligations. Suicide is contrary to love for the living God.'"

The priest raises one bent finger and says, "But there's also this: 'Grave psychological disturbances, anguish, or grave fear of hardship, suffering, or torture can diminish the responsibility of the one committing suicide.' And finally, and again I'm quoting: 'We should not despair of the eternal salvation of persons who have taken their own lives. By ways known to Him alone, God can provide the opportunity for salutary repentance. The Church prays for persons who have taken their own lives.'"

Redding looks up from the lectern. "Now Hal was raised a Catholic, attended fine Catholic schools in Pittsburgh and received a first-rate Catholic education during his undergraduate years here at St. Thomas. Did he continue to practice his faith? In my perception he did, and he was a regular, if not daily, communicant at the campus chapel. In my office we had a number of discussions over the past year or so on the subject of faith — its rigors and demands in our modern age — and, yes, the doubts that many young people experience, especially those with a strong, inquiring intellect, and perhaps a certain restless quality to the soul. Nonetheless, I was left with a powerful sense that Hal's faith continued to be a matter of deep importance to him. Which makes what has happened both more confusing to some of us and perhaps in a way a little less troubling. The questions are obvious: How could someone with such an informed and abiding concern for faith do such a thing? And yet does it not also speak powerfully to our shared conviction that our sweet young Hal will ultimately be judged only with the infinite wisdom and mercy of almighty God?"

With Redding rolling now, the color is rising in his face, and his gestures are more animated. It came early, but there is only one line that sticks with Stan: "...our beloved young Hal took his own life." That and all the Catholic doctrinal bullshit that followed mean only one thing: at least for now he's off the hook.

The first call came at 9:35 that morning four days ago. It was Tim Minor, and he sounded stricken. The story came out jumbled, ass-backward, but shortly after 5 am, the body had been discovered, and by 7 police were calling an emergency number in Hal's wallet for sister Hannah. They finally reached her at 8:30, and, crushed by the news, she could only come up with the name of one of Hal's friends, his former roommate Tim. When the cops called, he gave them several names and numbers of people he thought were close to Hal, including Stan. They had already called Fr. Redding, he said, and then blurted, "I absolutely cannot believe this, Stan, but they're thinking right now that Hal killed himself!" At that point his only thought was to get sniveling Tim off the phone so he could call the police before they called him.

The rest of the morning went so smoothly it seemed almost unreal, as if he had written the script and, with few exceptions, everybody's lines. It helped that the two cops who debriefed him seemed more nervous than he felt. The lead guy, Sam Marbow, late fifties, with a lazy eye, was a fat chain-smoker, who quickly became "Marlboro." "Junior," across the table, was James Hoekstra, a blond with a slight build, who looked like he was 18. At one point Stan even asked if he could see the suicide note, and Marlboro said, "Not at this time."

Junior added, "Out of respect for the family. You understand."

Stan said of course and soon left, thinking, so far, so good, though not yet entirely out of the woods. Over the next couple of days these jokers would be canvassing the building and the neighborhood for someone who might have seen or heard anything.

Unlike Redding, who spoke without notes except for the catechism quotes, John reads his eulogy. He's obviously spent time on it, pouring his heart into the personal stuff—the quality of the mind, the eye for the tiny but telling detail, the exquisite, almost poetic care he took with his writing, the simple kindness he offered everyone, from close friend to perfect stranger—all of it replete with examples that have many in his audience nodding heads and brushing cheeks.

John's homestretch is full of thoughts Stan has heard before, most of them in a barrage of phone calls after he met with the cops that first day. First Redding, then John, then Tim Minor, then Susanna Paul, then Sister Martha, then Lina wondering if he might want to meet for coffee and a bite in the morning. Amazed, he said of course. Then John called again saying he and Mar wanted him to join them for dinner at the house. He begged off, but it took some doing. Apparently everyone in the department had heard that he was, most likely, the last to see Hal alive, and that he was blaming himself bitterly for not seeing something, anything, that might have hinted at the tragedy ahead. To each of his callers, he offered the same grief-stricken lines. Even if the poor guy had just looked sleepy, he would have insisted he spend the night on the convertible couch. Instead Hal seemed fine for someone who had spent the last 6 hours driving. He even refused a cup of coffee. Yes, he talked a lot about his grandmother but in a way that seemed normal, even healthy. And yet he just can't forgive himself for missing something in Hal that must have been obvious to anyone with eyes to see.

John speaks of how difficult it can be to read others, especially with Hal, who was so selfless and caring for others that he often made a point of keeping any troubled feelings strictly to himself. He simply did not want to inflict them, or himself, on those close to him. And John also puts a finer touch on Redding's thought that we cannot judge because, unlike the Almighty, we can never know exactly what goes on in another mind.

"Despite that reputed suicide note, none of us knows what really happened in those final crucial moments. Is it possible that, as he climbed to that precarious spot on his patio, he had a change of heart, deciding in that last second or two to choose life? And is it possible that in that moment—fatigued, frightened and alone—he simply lost his balance? So that in fact the awful thing that finally happened was not his intention, but, instead, a horrible accident? Not one of us can say what was truly going on in the mind of this beautiful young man we all loved so much."

Something, perhaps the fact that John is so utterly wrong about what actually happened, prompts the image that drives Stan nuts, the image he barred from crossing his mind as he walked into this room, but which now makes his teeth grind, his cheeks puff and his breath escape. John touching, kissing Lina in places that should not belong to him. A glance at Lina finds her gazing intently at John returning to his seat.

At their breakfast at the Bean he even tried to convince himself that she was, suddenly again, looking at *him* that way. She was friendly, supportive, understanding. She talked about how she herself had totally misread poor Hal the last time she saw him, the day he left for Pittsburgh. A chance encounter at the restaurant called Two, and he seemed so up, so pleased about his progress on the thesis, so excited that a new one from Roth, *Exit Ghost*, was due in just a week or two. He had already found a couple of rave reviews on line. All that must have been the flip side, the manic side, of the black depressions he must have battled.

But when Stan tried to caress her hand on the table, she moved it away, and then it was clear that all this concern, all this encouragement in his struggles with self-doubt, guilt and remorse over Hal, was only the result of her long, intimate conversations with John. The two of them in bed, perhaps, even playing with each other as they talked about poor Stan.

The call that shook him to the core came late in the afternoon on the day he and Lina met at the Bean. The Marlboro Man wanted to know if he could stop by headquarters in about 45 minutes. They had more questions for him. Fighting the panic in his throat that made his voice sound thin, he bought himself an extra fifteen minutes, saying he could be there at 5, if that would be okay. Marlboro said it would but sounded pissed.

"Is everything okay, detective?" A stupid question he immediately regretted.

"Look, we just need to talk to you about some things."

He tried to sound chipper. "Well, alright then. See you at 5."

Chapter 14

Tim Minor is up there now talking about how Hal would do anything for you, a literally shirt-off-his-back kind of guy. Small smiles greet Minor's brief anecdotes, culled from their two years as roommates, "ending this past summer when, as most of you know, Pamie and I were married."

Before leaving for police headquarters, Stan had called the Minors. They seemed to know more, sooner than anyone, because they were staying close to Hannah. The woman was near full melt-down and in need of around the clock care. Pam was spending the nights with her in a suite at the Cedar Hill Inn. Tim stayed with her during the day, driving her wherever needed, even, at the cops' request, remaining in the room when they spoke with her. On the phone Tim gave him a detailed account, saying Hannah had so stubbornly insisted that her brother would never, under any circumstances, harm himself, that the police finally showed her the note. Things only got worse. There was not a chance in this world, she told them with a burst of strident new energy, that Hal had authored this note. They brought in a female officer.

Hannah screamed at her. "This is absurd! My brother would never leave that thing—so many typos, no punctuation—it's barely literate, and Hal was supremely literate, obsessively meticulous about his writing."

The woman said, "Of course, Ms. Stroheim, we completely understand how you feel, but in our experience, people, in the grip of the kind of depression that can lead to suicide, often leave behind notes that don't seem to reflect their personalities or accomplishments."

Hannah screamed again. "Don't tell me about my own brother! He would never say this!" She slapped the paper on the table. "Look at this! 'Too much death.' What does that mean? Beyond our grandmother passing this week at 84, the only other person close to

Hal that he's lost was a high school English teacher who died of breast cancer 4 years ago."

The officer tried one more time on a different tack, asking if Hal had a girlfriend.

Suddenly calm, Hannah explained that until a year ago Hal had a steady girlfriend named Vickie, who then graduated from St. Thomas and took a teaching job in Las Vegas. They parted amicably and went their separate ways. She wasn't the one for Hal, and he knew it. Hannah finished and looked as if she wouldn't speak again. But after a minute or so when the female officer had left the room, she asked the detectives about "the guy with the key."

That was Stan, said Tim.

The fat detective was losing patience. "What about him, Ms. Stroheim? You'll recall we've talked about this."

"Stan had the key. Maybe he was there. Maybe Stan pushed Hal off the balcony."

"Ms. Stroheim, we've been over all this. We've interrogated Stan. We've talked to everyone we can find in the building and in the surrounding homes, and nobody heard a thing or saw anyone entering or leaving the building. I take that back. One woman said she thought she heard a cat scream out in that field next to the building sometime after midnight, but she rolled over and went back to sleep. Besides, Ms. Stroheim, you yourself told us that your brother called Stan one of his best friends and said he trusted him like the brother he never had."

Hannah thought for a moment and said that was true.

The detective tried to wrap this up. "I'll tell you what, Ms. Stroheim, we'll bring Stan back in and talk to him again. Just see, maybe we missed something."

Hannah was again sunk in hopelessness and offered a barely audible thank you.

Despite Minor's thorough recounting, Stan entered headquarters still thinking someone might have placed him in or near Hal's building. And the fact that Hannah, albeit in her crazed fashion, had accurately described what happened that night, made him feel queasy at the sight of detectives Marlboro and Junior.

They started with the note, saying they'd like to get his read on it. Obviously, he figured, they were reading him as he read. He moved through it slowly, twice, trying hard to produce a tear and shaking his head in anguish a few times. He had learned a few things during his time in this room. On his first visit, they printed him, just to eliminate and account for his prints in the apartment, they said. But he knew they were watching him closely for any signs of guilty discomfort. Thank the fucking lord he had wiped off that keyboard.

"Does it look like something your friend Hal would write?" asked Junior.

Stan stared at him. "No."

"Why not?"

"Because Hal was the best proof reader I knew. He caught everything. This just doesn't look like him. But then again, in a psych class once I saw writing done by people who were seriously depressed and it looked something like this."

Marlboro with a glance at Junior: "What do you make of that line there, 'too much death'?"

Stan shook his head again. "I don't know what to make of it. Of course, he had just lost his grandma, but I don't know enough about his personal life to say if there's been anyone else."

He paused, then started again. "Still, now that I think about it, Hal was deeply upset, really anguished about Iraq, all the killing there, especially all the civilian casualties. He was really outraged about this story in the news about these guys from Blackwater mowing down all these civilians. It kind of tore him up."

Marlboro changed the subject with a bang. "Stan, what would you say if I told you we have someone who puts you near Hal's apartment after midnight?"

"Well..." he paused. "If I believed you..." He paused again to look the fat man straight in his one good eye. "...I'd say they're mistaken."

"Now don't be too clever there, Stanley. It won't serve you well."

"It's Stanford. And when you're honest, detective, you don't have to be clever."

"Yeah, ain't that the truth."

Marlboro's look away makes Stan want to push. "So do you?"

"Do I what?"

"Do you have someone who makes such a false claim?"

Trying to look disgusted, the man actually shakes his head no. "Look, pal, we're out there doing what we do. Checking all the angles, talking to all kinda people maybe can help us. And we don't move 'til we have good reason."

"Which means, I guess, if you do have someone, you don't necessarily believe 'em."

The detective's voice gets louder. "We don't believe 'em, we don't *not* believe 'em. At this point it's a process."

Stan nodded emphatically. "Gotcha. A process."

And with that the cop seemed just as happy as he was to wind this chat to a close.

One of Hal's students follows Tim Minor to the lectern to share meager memories of the young instructor's generosity, and the service limps to a close. With many mourners seeking each other out, hugging and chatting quietly, he finds a small display of photos: Hal at the Minors' wedding, at John's party last month and at a department picnic two years ago. There are a few family photos that include grandma and Hal, and a wallet-size of what must be his high school graduation photo. That unruly hair somehow tamed into a kind of pompadour makes him look like an utter doofus. In all, an appropriate collection for a sadly truncated life.

"Is there someone I could talk to about using a few of these for the piece I'm writing?"

The voice is low and mellow, and belongs, he notes, turning, to an exotically attractive young woman, staring at him with large dark eyes. The hair is long, black and shiny, the complexion a glowing ivory, the dress a flowery print and very short to show off sleek and shapely legs, the chest significant under a deeply scooped neckline. There's a silver ring through a pretty left nostril, another at the corner of her right eyebrow, four more through the right ear, and two ruby studs in the left. An adder's head peeks around the right side of her throat, and part of a vivid red rose adorns what he can see of her left breast.

He says, "The Rose Tattoo. I loved that movie."

"Yeah, me too. Anna Magnani!"

"You bet! So you're writing something about poor Hal?"

"Yes, for the Sun. Do you read it?"

"Only the personals. They're hilarious."

"Yeah, well I write most of them."

"You write them?"

"No, I'm kidding. I'm Becca Popp. I write about culture and the arts, but that lets me deal with just about anything."

"So you're doing what, a profile?"

"Well, it's part of a larger thing I'm doing on campus crime."

His stomach twists. "Campus crime?"

"Yes, I mean I know they haven't officially called this a suicide yet, but they will very soon. There are only two things worse than suicide on a university campus...rape and murder. Screaming headlines, frightened parents, nervous deans. It's a mess, and they'll try to wrap it up asap. Anything to get it out of the papers and off TV."

"Really. By the way I'm Stan Lyle."

"I know, the last one to see Hal alive."

"Well now, you work fast."

"Life is short. Anyway, pleased to meetcha."

She offers her hand, and when he takes it, shakes his firmly. She says, "Hey, I'd love to talk with you about all this. How about coffee tomorrow at the Bean?"

"Well..." He's not at all sure he should talk to this woman.

"Or not. It's totally up to you. But if you're wondering, I don't bite. I don't scratch. I won't hurt you with what I write, and I think you'll end up really digging me." From a small black purse she hands him a card that says POPP in large letters and everything else in small. "Call me if you'd like to talk. I hope you do."

"All right then. And the person you want to talk to about these photos is Tim..."

"I know. That was just a pick up line. I've already talked to him."

He smiles and nods. "It was a pleasure, Becca."

"Same here."

He turns away to find Minor standing next to the woman Stan noticed before and now knows is Hannah. Tall, ungainly, she looks abject and defeated after the last couple in the condolence line has moved on. Minor has spotted him already, so it's too late to turn away. In the last two days Minor passed along two requests from Hannah, both of which he turned down. Would he speak at the service? No, he didn't need that. "Please tell her I'm afraid I'd fall apart." And the cat, Jesus, she wanted him to take the cat. Of course, he fucking loathes cats, especially this one. He said his landlord allows no pets. Later Minor told him Pam suffers with allergies, so the cat is going back with Hannah to Pittsburgh.

He shakes hands with Minor. "Beautiful job, Tim. Your words will

84

help a lot of people deal with a very tough time."

"Thanks, Stan. Hannah, this is Stan Lyle."

He turns to her and finds the small brown eyes glassy and red-rimmed, the mouth slack, hanging slightly open. She looks drugged for the occasion. Despite rounded shoulders and low heels, she's about his height. He tries a sympathetic smile and takes her hand in both of his.

"Hannah, please forgive me. I've wanted to come and talk with you, but the timing just hasn't been right." He has no idea what he means by this. He's never told Minor he wanted to see her. It was the last thing he wanted. In any case, it doesn't matter. She looks away and says dully, "Yes, thank you."

He nods once, then shakes his head slowly for sincerity, saying, "I'm so sorry about Hal. We all loved him so much."

She says, "Thank you," then looks to someone who's lined up behind him, and it's over. He moves on and with a backward glance sees Gert the Flirt take her hand. Minor is saying, "Hannah, this is Sister Gertrude Weeks."

In a back corner, all three with smiles about something, he spots a surprising triangle formed by the homely, blue-eyed guy, the redhead and the blond. His instinct is to flee, but Marissa is already waving him over. On the approach he wonders where these two women would prefer to be. Probably at each other's beautiful throats. Amazing, the constraints supplied by the right social occasion.

Marissa, the only one he hasn't seen or spoken to since that night, gets him first. Wrapping him in her arms and hugging him close, she says in his ear, "Darling, I'm just so sorry for you. This whole thing must be such a nightmare."

She continues to hug, and he's forced to say with his mouth in her hair, "Thanks, Marissa, that's very kind. But really I think I'm doing okay."

She holds him at arms length, her eyes watery. There's alcohol in the air. "Of course you're okay. You're a strong guy, darling, and you're gonna be just fine."

Finally, the release. He moves to a brief, gruff hug from John. "You doing okay?"

He nods. "I'm okay. Great job up there."

On to Lina, and unlike the light hug and quick peck on the cheek he got at the Bean a few days ago, she gives him a long, seemingly warm-hearted embrace, the first from her in a very long time. He can feel his heart pounding.

The green eyes find his. "You look good."

As if the other two aren't even there, he says, "You look incredible." Of course she does in his favorite black sweater and slacks.

There's an awkward pause, until John asks, "How's Hannah holding up?"

"Okay, I guess. Actually, she seems pretty out of it."

Marissa says, "Yeah, the poor thing. I heard Dr. Ring saw her and prescribed a tranq. A pretty hefty dose."

Another awkward pause. This time Lina ends it. "So who's your attractive friend?"

"Who?"

"Yes, the lovely young woman you were talking to a few minutes ago." She already seems happy for him, instead of the jealousy he was looking for.

"I just met her. She's some kind of reporter for the Sun. Name's Becca Popp."

Marissa chimes, "Oh, *that's* Becca Popp. I read her all the time. She's quite good."

"Well," says Lina brightly, "I like her name and her style. Very…alluring."

His annoyance swells. "Yeah, if you like piercing and tats."

"You don't?"

"Not my thing."

Marissa takes his arm as if she's about to walk out with him. "You should see what I've got. You might change your mind!"

With an amused grin, John says, "Mar, your body is pristine, absolutely unmarked."

"Yeah, but I'm thinking about a tat. And maybe a clit ring. Do they do clit rings?" He shrugs, and she tugs at his arm. "Honey, tomorrow can you find me a tattoo parlor in this town?"

Later in the parking lot, after Marissa and John are in their Saab, he tries Lina again, the feel of that firm embrace still vivid. "So, can I buy you a drink?"

Tilting her head, she gives him a sad smile. "Thanks, but I've got a date with a book."

"Too bad," he says, turning before his face gives him away. "I'll see you later."

By the time he reaches the Beemer on the street he's beginning to understand just how much he hates her, and that fucking John. If anyone deserves blame for Hal's stupid death, it's this self-centered cunt and the arrogant asshole who's fucking her.

Chapter 15

"You like that?"

"Yes, *si, incredibile.* I love it!"

His question, of course, is rhetorical, already answered by her eloquent body. The beautiful head flung back, red curls tossed on light blue sheets, the skin a rosy sheen in the bedroom's afternoon light, her cunt, totally naked except for one small red curl. She lifts against his busy hand—one finger pleasing her swollen clit, another massaging her vagina's moist ceiling, the third tucked deep in the smooth channel of her bottom—and he revels in the ripples and spasms coursing through her.

"I love it too," he says. Doing this for her, feeling her pleasure, her ecstasy, brings its own reward.

"Ah, John, my god, I just keep coming..."

"Good, sweetheart, good."

"But how do you know to do such things."

"You teach me. Your incredible body...*la professore.*"

Yes, it's true...and not true. But it's not a time for historical explanations. He will keep to himself how much he learned from being mostly limp after the prostate was zapped, how necessity taught him to use his hands and mouth to please...until Gabi, sweet, practical, matter-of-fact Gabi, said after their first time, "So we'll just have to get you some of those pills."

His free hand cups her lovely, freckled breast and serves her perfect nipple, pink and hard, to his eager mouth. He savors, then sucks, then sucks hard, and hard again, and again, until those sounds he loves start coming, those small cries, moans and gasps that stir him to even more fervid efforts to give her even more pleasure and joy.

He leaves the nipple to look at her face, flushed with passion, the eyes shut tight. When they open wide, her excited green gaze locks on him, her mouth soft, swollen and hungry for his. He gives it to her, his tongue finding hers in some absolutely essential way that makes her cry softly from high in her chest.

For a moment his hand on her cunt backs off. Then he moves just the tip of his index finger to her clit, massaging slowly, gently, tenderly, softly, only the clit. Until she whispers, "Oh my god, please do not stop."

"Don't worry."

Later she whispers again, "You do not know how incredible it is for me."

"Yes, I do…it's the same for me."

And still later when she says she can take no more for now, he lays back, his cock full and hard and thrusting to her incredible touch, soft, feathery, tender, her thumb and forefinger in a delicate circle, just barely brushing the top inch or two until his tremors and twinges are coming strong and fast. Then she takes the shaft full in her hand and firmly pumps him full of shuddering excitement. And when the explosion seems inevitable she leaves the shaft for his balls, caressing again with that light and tender touch, which soon includes a delicate foray to his bottom, playing with the edges of his anus in a way no one's ever come close to before.

"You like this?"

"Amazing, yes, incredible."

She does all this for a long time, obviously enjoying, exciting herself, at times using both hands and seeming to do everything at once.

Then leaning over him, she takes it in her warm mouth and seems to savor every second.

"You like this too?"

"You're unbelievable."

Eventually, of course, they fuck. He wants her on top first, to see and play with those perfect tits, to watch her eyes roll as she cries and comes again and that gorgeous face shows him the full measure of her joy. And he still doesn't come, so he turns her on her back and plunges deep, saying, "Sweetheart, I'll fuck you now."

"Yes, please, now. I want you now."

And finally he comes, in a way that transports, taking him both farther out of himself than he ever thought possible and deeper into himself than he ever thought he wanted to go. The climax comes quickly but lasts longer than he can ever remember, so utterly complete and satisfying, so totally engrossing that he has no idea if she has come again as well.

Laying next to her, still breathing heavily, he laughs softly and says, "If I never have sex again, it'll be okay. I'll always have this."

"Yes, darling. But this is three times, and each is better. So *qui sa?* Who knows?"

Curious...when they're making love, little bits and pieces of Italian, a few words here and there, tumble out, and the accent becomes slightly more pronounced. No doubt the excitement and emotion. For that matter, they render him nearly inarticulate.

The way he felt after the memorial service with Lina and Mar in close proximity. Mar was in tears. She'd been drinking, of course, before leaving home, and, as usual, he could sense her volatility. Offering his handkerchief, he held her as Lina approached. What would happen between these two he had no idea—the first time they'd met since the party at the house and since Mar had begun flinging threats. Now they were surrounded by friends and acquaintances.

He nodded and said, "Professor," when Lina arrived. Mar turned from his shoulder, tears glistening on her cheeks, and surprised him by moving straight into Lina's arms.

"Oh, Lina, how awful is this?" Her voice cracked. "We've lost this beautiful boy."

Lina glanced over Mar's shoulder and raised an eyebrow at John. She said, "I am so sorry, dear, I know he was so close to you."

"And to you," said Mar, raising her head almost defiantly. "You should have heard how that boy talked about you. Right, John."

The two women ended the embrace but continued to hold hands. Catching just a hint of accusation in that "Right, John," he said, "We were all close to him." Then as he watched Mar dab at her eyes and cheeks with the handkerchief, he sensed a shift.

"So Lina," she said, "how goes it? I take it you've settled in? I was hoping we'd become fast friends, but I haven't even seen you since the party at our house over a month ago. Where've you been keeping yourself?" The tears were gone now, and the edgy tone was building.

Lina flicked her eyes toward him and rambled a bit. "I have been so busy, and I know you have been too. We all are. Really, I have been a hermit, too anti-social for my own good. Writing a lot and seeing almost no one."

"Almost?" Mar glared at him.

"Yes, well, of course, I lecture and do a seminar every week, but other than that…"

"So no time to fuck around?"

Lina smiled with seeming calm. "I wish, but no such luck."

Under the blue sheet, her cheek on his chest, she asks, "So where are you now?"

"Where am I? I'd say lost somewhere in the rippling circles of pleasure you give me."

"Good, darling, but I mean, what do you tell your wife about where you are these days?"

"I don't tell her anything. Don't have to now that I don't do my evening walk. She knows I keep a bag at Markham with stuff I need for a jog. So I'm getting my exercise, but now I'm staying in after dinner and working late at home."

No doubt Mar still suspects, but now it can happen almost anytime…morning, afternoon, even late in the evening. Two nights ago, the last time they made love, he waited until close to midnight, working in "the hole," as she calls his office above the garage. Then knowing she was long gone from the booze, he walked the four blocks to Lina's arms.

She lifts her head from his chest. "So tell me about falling in love with your wife."

"Falling in love?"

"Yes, darling, I think you would not marry a woman and not be in love."

"Yes, I suppose that's true."

"*Si.*"

"Well, I told you she was one of my students and that she was very beautiful. And that I was coming off a difficult relationship with a troubled woman in Columbus."

"*Si.*"

"So I knew from her papers for me that she had an unusual mind. She was funny."

"Funny."

"Yes, she was majoring in design and fine arts, but her writing was clever and even made me laugh at times. We started dating the

91

semester after she took my class, and just before she graduated."

He stops, thinking about one early moment that should have raised a flag. "I suppose there were warning signs back then. I remember I met her for brunch one morning and surprised us both by greeting her with a kiss. And there was alcohol on her breath. But instead of thinking this young woman has a booze problem, I told myself, well, this beautiful creature is so taken with me, she steadied her nerves with a drink. Like an idiot I flattered myself. Anyway, we started living together that summer, and by the fall she had taken a job with an ad agency outside Detroit. So I had my house here, a small one back then, and she had an apartment there, and we had a commuter relationship. She'd be there during the week and then come here for the weekend. And every Wednesday, usually, I'd drive to Detroit and stay the night at her place. And even after we were married, we continued that way for four years."

"And you were in love."

"Yes, I guess in love. Ironically, given what's happened since, I liked how independent she seemed. After the clinging, neurotically dependent gal in Columbus, that was great. I even liked that she wasn't an academic. I saw her as my window on the big bad world beyond the university. Living apart and seeing each other only a few times a week, we were always on our best behavior, always sweet and considerate with each other. And the sex was pretty good. We were able to travel a little...Italy, Paris, the Caribbean, so we shared some good times.

"But, really, I hate to say it, I think I fell in love with how beautiful she was. Her ad agency took photos, head shots, I guess for publicity purposes, and I framed one and put it in my office. I thought she looked so calm, so kind and, of course, so beautiful. But she also had this look, a touch ironic, as if she were saying, yes, I'm beautiful, but that's not what's important. I'm also bright, warm, honest and caring. Really, to me she looked so poised, so completely self-possessed. But there's a fine line—sometimes no line—between self-possessed and self-centered. I don't know. It sounds so shallow, but maybe I really fell in love with her because of that photograph. I've never been able to make any sense of that."

"I think if you want to fall in love, the right photo can be a potent visual aid."

"Yeah, maybe, but how can a photograph hold that kind of power.

If you think about it, it seems like indisputable documentary evidence of the essence of this person. But of course it's evidence only that this is exactly what she looked like from that camera angle, in that light, at that split-second moment in time."

"*Si*, of course."

"And as often as a photograph tells the truth, it also lies."

The doorbell rings. For a second they both freeze. She says, "Who can this be?"

"Maybe we don't want to know."

She looks at him.

"I mean, just don't answer."

"Yes, but I can see who is there. The door has a spy hole."

Chapter 16

She grabs her thin white robe from the back of the bedroom door and loves that his eyes follow her every naked move. With a mocking, wide-eyed look, she dons the robe.

Through the front window she sees a uniformed fellow climbing into his small white van. "The postal service," she calls back to John. Through the eyehole she sees no one and, closing the robe, opens the door to find a cardboard box about the size of a ream of paper on the mat.

"No return address," she says, walking with it into the bedroom.

"Let's see." She hands him the box, and he takes a Swiss Army knife from his corduroys.

"Local postal mark," she says, sitting next to him as he slits the tape.

With the box open, he says, "What the hell?" Inside are religious items — a brown scapular, two holy cards, a small silvery cross, a cheap black-bead rosary — on top of a type-written note and several printed pages. He pulls out the note and reads to her.

"'Our dear fallen and disgraced Lina.'" His puzzled, unhappy gaze meets hers, then returns to the note. "'By your disgusting mortal sin of fornication with a married man, you allow the Devil to triumph over God's Sacred Will. To fornicate is to take one of God's greatest gifts — the pleasure of union that brings new life — and use it as an outhouse for our fears, insecurities and issues. The Evil One knows if he can succeed in making us love his barren, dead and twisted view of life, then we will end up as channels of sterility, instead of vessels of life.'"

"Outhouse?" she asks.

He nods. "Wait, all is not lost." He reads again. "'But it is not too late, dear Lina. If you will pray the Rosary, wear the Scapular and offer to God the prayers and alms that are His due (as outlined in the enclosed tract), you can surely avoid the eternal and excruciating

94

flames of Hell. May God bless you, dear Lina.'"

"Jesus Christ, " he says, "What century are we in?" He hands her the note.

The hand-printed message feels like a dead weight in her hand. Someone in her new American corner of the world has a personal animus toward her that amounts to an ugly threat. From the box he digs out two stapled batches of several pages each and gives her one.

"This one," he says, flipping through, "is addressed 'To Our Dear Brothers and Sisters in the Faith of Our Lord Jesus Christ.' And it's from some bishop of the 'Christ Charismatic Liturgical Recovery Church.' It's all marked up, with things circled and starred...like this:

"'The more God cries out for purity, the more people run to sin under the guise of civil rights; and open living.'"

He glances at her again. "Civil rights and open living!"

She nods without a smile.

"'Excess is worshipped in the place of Almighty God and our children past, present and future will be sacrificed on its altar.'" He flips a page. "And here's how you can save your soul:

"'1) Pray the Rosary every day for our people to turn in disgust from sins of the flesh to purity of heart.

"'2) Wear the Brown Scapular as a sign of our consecration to the Precious Blood of Jesus for purity of heart, psyche and body.

"'3) Offer up to God, in the view of the Cross, all of our sufferings no matter how large or small. We are especially called to do this through fasting and alms at least twice a week.'"

"Only twice a week?" she says and searches through the other tract. "This is on adultery from the Catechism of the Catholic Church. What Redding quoted from at the memorial service. "'*Lust* is disordered desire for inordinate enjoyment of sexual pleasure. Sexual pleasure is morally disordered when sought for itself, isolated from its procreative and unitive purposes.'"

"Sounds good to me."

She says, "Ah, the Sermon on the Mount: 'But I say to you that every one who looks at a woman lustfully has already committed adultery with her in his heart.'"

She gives him a glum look. "I can't recall the church having anything to say about a woman lusting in her heart after a man."

"I'm sure it's covered," he says. "Do you think Redding could have sent this?"

"Maybe this..." She raises what she's been reading and drops it on the bed. "...but not what you have there. He is too sophisticated for that." Picking the gilt-edged holy cards out of the box, she holds up one with a haloed young girl. "St. Maria Goretti."

"Who's she?"

She smiles. "As young girls in Italy we all learned about Maria. When she was 12, an 18-year-old neighbor boy started to rape her. She told him she would prefer that he kill her than rape her. So he stabbed her to death."

"Nice story."

"*Si*, but before she died she forgave him."

"Well, she was a saint. So who's the other one?"

She shows him a plump-looking, balding fellow with a fringe of gray. "Our own St. Thomas. In addition to being one of the giant intellects of all time, he was famously chaste. One night when he was 18, two of his brothers tried to tempt him with a wanton young woman they sent to his room."

"Why would they do that?"

"It is a long story. His family wanted him to switch allegiance from the Dominicans to the Benedictines. But he chased the woman out of his chambers with a torch, and that very night, two angels appeared while he slept and strengthened his will to remain celibate."

"See, that's what I think is so unfair. Here's this 18-year-old at the peak of his sexual powers, and he drives away this alluring young morsel. And then this amazingly saintly kid gets a visit from God's angels to strengthen his already incredible resolve. Now how many of us weak, lowly, unsaintly folks get a visit like that to help us do the right thing? It's just not fair."

"God never says the life he gives us will be fair." She knows why they are doing this, making light of the trouble in this box. For a moment at least they do not have to think about what this really means: someone close to them seems fully aware of what goes on here in her own bedroom. She grins. "There is a funny line about Aquinas in the new Hitchens book."

"Yeah?"

"A good bathroom read, full of amusing stories and anecdotes. But he has one about Aquinas leaving his treatise on the Trinity spread out on the altar at the Notre Dame in Paris. He thought perhaps God himself would look it over and offer His opinion. And Hitchens writes that Aquinas learned later that God had indeed given him a good review, and some suitably awed monks and novices found him blissfully levitating about inside the cathedral."

John with a sour smile: "Wonderful."

Silent for a while, they stare at the items spread on the bed between them. His lean torso naked, John sits cross-legged on the bed, the sheet covering to the waist. Her robe has fallen open, but she does nothing to close it and asks, "So what do we have here?"

"You mean besides a problem?"

"I mean who would do such a thing?"

"Someone who knows us. Someone who thinks they know what we're doing. And someone who's gone to some effort to put this together. Those tracts would be easy to find with Google, but someone probably went to a religious goods store to get the cards and the other things, then packaged it all up and mailed it from a post office."

"But perhaps it is also someone who thinks I am religious. So someone then who does not know me well. Or someone who has misperceived something basic about me."

"Yeah, I guess."

"But who could it be except your wife? Would she do this?"

"Maybe, because it's both cruel and funny, but she could have also shared her suspicions with someone else."

"Still, if we are looking for one with the motivation to do this, who but your wife?"

He says nothing for a while. "Yes, but I would not rule out Stan."

"He has said something to you?"

"No, but we both know he has a major crush."

"But Stan should know about my view of religion. Although..."

"Although what?"

"One day, soon after I arrived, he found me at the campus chapel. Maybe he got the wrong idea." She closes the robe. "No, I still think your wife is our number one suspect."

Chapter 17

Play the lotto, he thinks as he finds her office door open. It's a lucky day with everything falling into place. As he stops to rap on the jam, she's starting to swing the door closed.

"Oh, Lina, hi! Just thought I'd say hello."

"Hello, Stan." The voice is friendly enough, but she looks and sounds troubled.

"I'm sorry, are you busy?"

"No, just closing the door, but come in if you like."

"Sure. How've you been? You look a little distracted." He settles into a chair near her desk, his briefcase on his knees.

With the door closed, she sits at her desk. "Distracted, yes. I am fine, but I have just taken some annoying phone calls, actually, and I need to call that newspaper, the Sun?"

"Yes, the Sun. But what's going on? Annoying how?"

"There were three of them in the past half-hour. All strange sounding men, no one I know, and they are all asking about the same thing. They want to set up an appointment."

He gives her a look of puzzled concern. "An appointment for what?"

She stares at him for a second. "They want me to come to them and wear sexy lingerie. The sexier the better, one of them said. And another one said he would rather that I wore nothing at all. They all sound very strange."

"And that's it, just model lingerie?"

"No, and then give them a massage."

He shakes his head in disgust. "And the Sun's involved?"

"Yes. The first two said they had seen my ad in the Sun. With the third, I just hung up."

He opens his leather satchel. "You know, I just grabbed a copy of the Sun this morning. I wanted to see if it had the article that tattooed woman was writing on Hal."

"Does it?"

"No, maybe next week. Let's see, the ads and the personals are in the back." Opening the tabloid-style paper, he searches up and down columns. "Yep, here it is, in the personals. I can't believe this." He looks at her, finds the green eyes staring hard at him and begins reading.

"'Hi, I'm Lina. I'll model lingerie and give you a massage in the privacy of your own home. Call me.' And then it has your number here in the office."

He looks up. She is still staring at him. "Lina, this is unbelievably disgusting."

"Yes," she says and looks as if she's almost daring him to glance away. He doesn't. "Stan, you must tell me. Who would do such a heartless thing?"

His eyes don't waver. "You're right, it is heartless, but I have no idea. I can't imagine why anyone would do this to you. Has anything else happened like this?"

She pauses, thinking about something, but says, "No, nothing."

"Well, I'll tell you what. Let me make the first call." He's already pulling out his cell. "I'll talk to my new friend, the reporter. She gave me her card at the memorial, and I stuffed it in here somewhere." He quickly comes out with the card. "Yes, here it is, Becca Popp."

"Stan, I can do this."

"Please, let me try first. I want her to trace this back and see who placed it." He's already punching his cell. After several seconds, he says, "She's not answering. I'll leave a message." After a pause: "Hey, Becca Popp, it's Stan Lyle. We met at the memorial for Hal Stroheim. I'd like to talk with you about Hal, and, more importantly, a close, dear friend of mine has been victimized by one of your personals this week. I want to make sure a retraction or correction is published asap, and I need you to put a trace on who placed this thing. It's truly disgusting."

As he finishes his message, there's a knock on the door. Lina looks at him and moves to open it. Standing there is a pudgy kid with a buzz cut, black-rimmed glasses and a plastic pocket protector stuffed with four different colored pens. He's carrying what looks to be a freshman engineering text and a small paperback.

"Professor Lentini?"

"Yes?"

The kid's eyes dart to Stan and then back to Lina. "Should I come back later?"

"No, this is fine. How can I help you?"

The kid hesitates, but then holds up the paperback chest high. "Well, I found this book."

Stan can see the book's cover clearly. No illustration, just the title, black on white, the words arranged in the shape of a limp phallus: *The Very Long Dong of Samuel P.*"

Lina says, "You found it."

The kid nods. "Yeah, this morning. It was just sitting by itself on one of the benches on the quad, right near the chapel."

She swings a look at Stan and then back to the book. "And you brought it here because?"

"Because I...it says that it belongs to you."

"To me?"

"Yes. And that if it's lost and someone returns it to you, you'll pay them ten dollars."

"It says that."

"Yes, right on the inside cover." The kid offers the book to Lina, and she takes it. Stan moves to her side as she opens it. There glued to the inside of the wrinkled cover is a new bookplate, with a green vine border. In typeset it says, "If this book is lost, and you return it, I will pay you $10." Hand printed below are Lina's name and office address.

The kid gives his hefty shoulders a small shrug. "My professor said he thought maybe you were teaching a course in popular pornography. No, I mean culture, popular culture."

Lina frowns. "No, I am not teaching such a course. I have never seen this book before."

The kid nods. "So this isn't your book then."

"Correct," says Stan.

"And you're probably not going to pay the ten dollars to get it back then."

"Correct again. This is somebody's idea of a nasty practical joke."

"Well, I just found it." The kid sounds defensive.

Lina says, "Yes, and I appreciate you going to this trouble. Somebody is apparently doing some kind of mischief. The book is yours, if you want it."

"Oh, it's not the kind of thing I read. No way."

"Actually, Lina, I think you should keep it. We need to get to the bottom of this."

Lina nods slightly. "Maybe you are right. But I…"

Stan is pulling out a wad of cash. "Look, here's five bucks for your trouble."

The kid promptly takes the bill. "Hey, thanks. It really wasn't much trouble."

* * *

When Becca Popp called back about one, she announced she was "already on the case," and would soon have "the goods." "How about I buy you a pop at Melody around 5?"

Now as they sit in a booth in the bar his gaze is busy, moving from her bright brown eyes, to the rose and the adder's head, to the full tits showing considerable cleavage and no evidence of a bra beneath the beige peasant blouse she's wearing off the shoulder. He knows now, having watched her turn while slipping off her black leather jacket with all the buckles, that most of the small, striped snake is coiled on the back of her pretty neck. There is so much to look at with this girl, between the considerable natural assets and all the tats, rings and things.

"So I have to ask…"

"Yes, they hurt a bit for a few seconds, but not as much as the one through my nipple."

He shakes his head with a smile. "Good to know, but I'm also wondering how this phony personal could have happened. The paper must have some safeguards."

"Yes, well, normally our policy is that anyone who places a personal must provide a verifiable name and street address. You have to show your driver's license or whatever, but what happened this time was — and this needs to be strictly off the record, just between me and you, because I suppose we could be sued — it was the first day on the job for this kid taking the personals. Actually he was filling in for the regular gal, who was out with chlamydia. He's a pimply little jerk who is lazy as shit. And when this ad came in with cash that day and no return address, he simply called the number and when the voice said, 'Hello, this is Lina, please leave a message,' he decided that was enough verification. As I said, he's a lazy jerk. And he's been sacked. No longer works at the Sun."

"So what exactly will the paper print next week?"

101

She reaches into a green backpack and pulls out a reporter's notebook. Flipping it open, she says, "This note will be placed at the head of our personals in next week's edition: 'We at the Sun make every effort to insure the integrity of each one of our personal listings. But unfortunately, on occasion, and despite our vigilance, a misleading message does slip through. We deeply regret that personal 1756 in our 10/15/07 issue contained false information, and our deep apologies go to those who were thereby inconvenienced.'"

"Inconvenienced. Sounds kind of soft for what my friend's been going through."

"What do you want...*traumatized*? In my experience, the less said, the better with something like this. You draw attention to it, and frequently you just give it more life."

"Okay. Inconvenienced. But please do me one more favor. Call my friend Lina tonight, and give her an apology. You don't have to mention the pimply kid; just say someone made a careless mistake, and now it can't be traced. Tell her about the correction next week and apologize profusely, and I'm sure everything will be all right."

"Okie Dokie, but who's this Lina, and why would somebody do this to her?"

"I have no idea. She's this brilliant, gorgeous professor of comparative lit from the University of Bologna, and she's here for the semester as a guest lecturer."

"Wow, sounds like a great profile."

"Yeah, you have no idea, but right now is not a good time. Leave it alone for a while, and I'll fix you up with her near the end of the term."

"Okay then, but I'm gonna hold you to it."

"Fine. Speaking of profiles, what's happened to the thing you were doing on poor Hal?"

She pulls a face and sends her eyes to the ceiling. "Yeah, well, it'll have to be strictly off the record again. I'm serious." She waits for him to nod and then starts again. "I told you this university is hinky big time on the subject of suicide on campus. Rape and murder too. My editor was cool with what I was doing, but I probably made a mistake when I asked for a comment from that Fr. Redding at the memorial. My guess, he went straight to your prez, Fr. Hagen, who happens to be an old drinking buddy of my editor's boss. So Hagen drops a word to his buddy, and that's that. Story's dead."

102

Stan thinks, Play the lotto. He says, "That's too bad. I was looking forward to it."

"Yeah, well, now I'm working on a book review. Maybe you know the author."

"Who's that?"

"John Martens, and his new one on Lawrence. I just started reading it, but I'm a huge Lawrencian. *Chatterley* is like my favorite all-time tome."

"Really. What do you like about it?"

She licks her cupid's bow lips and says, "The sex."

Chapter 18

The third time she catches Elena Plouff frowning at her past the edge of the computer screen, Lina says, "This must be a very busy time for you, Elena, with Father away so much."

The frown is frozen as she types. "It's always busy in here. No difference for me."

Their first words since her chilly greeting: "If you'll take a seat, professor, Father's on the phone with Chicago. He should be with you shortly."

Sitting next to the priest's open office door, she listens to him talk with someone about morphine dosage. "With Chicago" was shorthand for Redding's brother, dying of colon cancer in a hospice center. How to keep the poor man somewhere between pain-free and lucid.

This morning she picked up Redding's voice mail: "Lina, Father Redding. A couple of troubling things have come up, and I'm sure they're troubling for you as well. I think it would be a good idea to meet and see if we can get to the bottom of this. Around 4 in my office?"

Earlier, she had opened her e-mail to find a surprising note sent apparently from Hal's computer to a list of what looked like everyone in the department and signed by none other than Lina herself. The latest of what John now refers to as "The Plagues." This one opened with: "Dear Colleague," and went on to explain that she was urgently facing the need for an abortion, and since she was "currently short on cash," she wondered if any of "you good, kind and generous people could help provide funding in this time of emergency."

She was dialing John when he called. He still suspected Stan despite the great help he provided on the Sun personal and on the "Dirty Book Assault," as she calls it.

"I suppose you think he is behind this as well," she said.

He surprised her. "He certainly could be, but I've been thinking this smacks of Mar."

"Really. Mar? She has the kind of computer knowledge to do something like this?"

"No, but her little techie guru does. Name's Billy Jeffer, and a year ago he was in high school when he set up a web site for her to sell her arts and crafts stuff. He's a strange little tech geek, but she flirts with him outrageously. He's a freshman on campus now, and I think he'd do anything for her and keep his mouth shut about it."

"Including getting into Hal's computer?"

"Oh, yeah, piece of cake. And I'm starting to think this is the kind of thing Mar would dream up. I never told you, but when we first started living together, Mar got pregnant and had an abortion. It was really her decision, but I backed her on it. At that point and for years thereafter she was remarkably clear that having kids was not a good idea for her. Especially, after she was diagnosed bi-polar. But lately she's been bringing up the abortion with great regret and blaming me for it. And she's actually been talking about wanting to adopt, and, of course, since I'd be the one doing everything to raise the child, I've said absolutely not."

She hears Redding hang up in the office. "Lina, please come in."

As she enters, he's moving to meet her half-way. He gives her a quick handshake and motions her to one of the chairs in front of his desk, which he then sits behind. Those blue eyes, lighter than John's, look tired. That perpetually flushed face shows signs of strain.

"So, Father, how is your brother."

"Oh, thanks for asking. It's very kind of you. He's not doing well. I think we're in the final stages, and he'll be with God soon."

"I am sorry, Father. This must be an ordeal, with some wrenching decisions to make."

As the priest talks about his brother—also a priest, who accepts God's will and, thus, makes this easier—she glances around the office. Everything is polished and in its place, spotless as his Cadillac, a large collection of books shelved in perfect order, grouped, as near as she can tell, by author and the language in which they were written, the desk pristine except for the book opened face down on top of what looks to be a folded over section of the Times. To change the subject yet still avoid this meeting's purpose, she asks, "So what are you reading, Father?"

He picks up the book and reads the title with a touch of mock bombast: "*Toward a New Catholic Church: The Promise of Reform*. It's by James Carrol, published five years ago, so obviously I'm getting to it rather late. But some people on this campus—and some of them wear the cloth—think this fellow has all the answers. For me he doesn't even ask the right questions, but then, everybody knows I'm a hopeless old fogy, locked deep in the past."

"Father, please."

"No, actually, I know Carrol, met him a few times at conferences, and we started out basically in the same place, that early 1940s working-class Irish Catholic world in Chicago. He joined the Paulists and was a priest for about five years in the late '60s and '70s. Then he left the priesthood, married and became a lay Catholic writer. So obviously we parted ways a long time ago. Of course, I find his liberalism bankrupt, his critique of the clergy mean-spirited, and his thoughts on the hierarchy terribly short-sighted."

She teases him. "Sounds like my kind of man. Maybe I should read him."

He smiles. "Maybe you should." Then the smile vanishes. "Lina, thank you very much for coming on short notice. I thought it important to nip this thing, whatever it is, in the bud."

"Yes, I agree we should move quickly."

"So what is going on? Like everybody this morning I got the e-mail blast. But I've only heard rumors about other things that may have happened."

The obvious place to start is the box, but she and John are clear that talking about it would only mean more purple rumors and hot talk about illicit sex, betrayal and mortal sin. At least with the other Plagues, there has been no linking of their names, or bodies. She begins by saying she is unsure what rumors might be out there, but the facts start with the personal in the Sun. Redding has heard nothing of this and seems appalled by the story. As he shakes his head in disgust, she moves on to the "Dirty Book Assault." About that the priest has heard only that a "pornographic book" with her name on the inside cover had been "returned" to her by a student demanding a reward. Correcting the facts, she explains that she is now in possession of 8 different books with titles like *Naked Vixens in Space, How to Get and Give the Best Oral Sex, The Priest and the Harlot, The Joy of Anal Sex, Orgy in the Cathedral, Father Flanagan Has a*

106

Boyfriend and *Confessions of a Porn Star Mother*. Stan, she says, has been a wonderful help on this as well, following up each time to see if anyone noticed who left these books in the wide variety of places on campus, from a cafeteria table to a bench in the chapel.

As for the e-mail blast this morning, she says it is perhaps the most painful. "Of course I am not pregnant. The reality is that I was born with an anomaly that means I cannot conceive. And this is a deep regret I will always live with."

"Lina, I'm so sorry...and so completely dumbfounded by all this. I just can't imagine anyone on this campus doing these things. It's just a complete mystery to me."

"And to...me." She nearly slipped and said "us."

"And this morning," he says, opening a small drawer in the desk, "I received this in the mail." He slides a card across his desktop. It's a magazine subscription card, mailed to Redding's Markham Hall address. Turning it over, she reads to herself: "Congratulations! You've just received a one-year subscription to Twat Magazine! For the connoisseur of all the finer things female! Thanks to..." Here someone had printed her name as Dr. Lina Lentini. "Each month you will receive a new issue in the mail filled with erotic photos and exciting articles about what every man wants...Twat!"

She looks up to find the priest staring at her. "I am sorry, Father. What is this Twat?"

"Again, I apologize. It's an obscenity for the female genitalia, and the magazine is pornographic. I've never seen it, but poor Elena looked mortified when she handed me the mail."

She puts the card back on the desk. "I feel terrible for her and for you."

"Well, of course, I've already called and cancelled the subscription. Naturally they couldn't tell me anything about who placed the order."

"Naturally."

"But on the e-mail blast, I checked with the police, and the laptop Hal had in his apartment was confiscated and is not online. I'm afraid we forgot about the university-supplied desktop in his cube. It's just been sitting there, easy to access or hack into by anyone who knows what they're doing. Now it's been taken out of service, so at least that can't happen again."

"Thank you, Father."

"The question is who's doing this and why? I mentioned it to the police, and they said this kind of harassment can be very difficult to trace. They said they'd come out, but I said no, we'd take care of it ourselves."

"Yes."

"Obviously, the one common factor is sexual sleaze. So that would suggest someone unbalanced in that particular way. But how we move beyond that, I have no idea. Just hope, I guess, that he makes some kind of false move and tips his hand."

"Or her hand."

He moves his handsome gray head a bit to the side. "I suppose it could be a woman."

"Yes."

"But, as I'm sure you've noted, this is a quiet, well-mannered campus. Lots of tolerance and mutual respect. You have people like Tom Friedman in the Times" — he lifts the paper a few inches off the desk, then drops it — "who decry how quiet our campuses are. He wants protests and agitation. But to me that's foolish, and, in any case, it certainly won't happen here."

"Yes, Father."

"You don't agree?"

"No, I absolutely agree."

"Here's the thing, Lina. What I think we need on this campus is a broader recognition of what a lovely, dignified and friendly person you really are. The problem is that almost no one knows you. Oh, maybe they've seen you lecture, but they don't know you as a person."

She is nodding, not sure where this is going.

"Now in a way, I blame myself. Normally our department has a reception and afternoon tea the second week of each month, and it's always very popular, well-attended. But because I've been away so much with my brother, we haven't been doing them."

"Father, everyone understands what you're going through."

"But I'd like to see you being more sociable, Lina, and giving people a better chance to get to know you. Then if absurd and disgusting things like these do happen, people will simply dismiss them out of hand, because they know you'd never be involved."

Clearly he has something in mind. "What would you suggest, Father?"

He nods. "George Rolande is retiring this term, 30 years of dedication and achievement on this campus. I don't know if you've met George."

"Oh, yes, at John Martens' party before the term started."

"So then you know what a beautiful person George is and how devoted he's been to his students. So to celebrate his 30 years, we're throwing a big party for him in two weeks. We're behind on the planning, again because of me, and we could use some help. We want drinks and hors d'oeuvres, and some live music. And it needs to come together quickly. Now Stan can certainly help you with all this, but if you could step up and oversee it, a lot more people would have a great chance to see that you're so much more than just some academic star."

She meets the priest's re-energized blue eyes. This is the last thing she wants to do.

Chapter 19

On the 10 minute walk over the woodchip path through the woods from the campus edge, she gazes at the late October colors, fiery red and orange, and thinks this American sojourn may well have been a mistake.

About John's marriage she knows two things: his life would vastly improve the moment he stepped out of his wife's life; and beyond any persuasion, he is certain that if he did, he would seal a tragic fate for Marissa. They told each other this could be nothing more than a 3-month affair, and back in Bologna by Christmas, she would not likely see him again. But if she chose not to follow what seems a vital urge, she could be asking for life-long regret. No strings. Just give and take everything she can, and know they have pushed possibility to its limit.

Yet this love affair—and she has to admit now what it is—has given her a shock. On a bone-chilled face a strong, warm, sensual breeze. Her response has been something she no longer thought possible, the kind of consuming passion usually found only in the over-heated pages of commercial fiction. Yes, sex with Paolo was good. With John it is profoundly beyond compare. But the connection runs so deep, is so encompassing beyond the physical, that she knows now it would take forever to explore. An exciting but clear-eyed 12-week affair, one that each acknowledges can last only as long as her stay at St. Thomas, that takes absolutely for granted John's deeply regretted but total commitment to Marissa as someone who could not, or would not live without him, this certain, constricted, fully knowable thing has somehow transformed itself into the ultimate mystery.

When they come together their talk is non-stop, eager, stirring, illuminating and somehow calming, words flowing quickly with care and precision that prompt a quiet joy of respect, empathy and understanding. There are silent moments also when they share music, films, lectures, the simple beauty of a sunset, the endless variety of the human face as people go about their daily lives, all of it a wordless communion she feels deep in the heart.

She tells herself she takes nothing from Marissa. The woman is throwing away her life, forfeiting her marriage. John has detailed the progress of her manic-depression; the descent into alcoholism; the periods of almost nightly suicide threats; the three actual attempts with their EMS calls and ER scenes—the charcoal cocktails, gurney restraints and irritated staffers; the brandishing of kitchen knives and the fortunately ineffectual violence; the midnight calls to the police with made-up charges of physical abuse; the drunk driving conviction that put her in the county jail for two months; the three serious attempts at drying out and recovery at three different hospitals; the months of AA sobriety and hope, and the crushing disappointment of relapse after relapse; the absurd games of hide-and-seek with her wine and vodka bottles; the lab scans that show cirrhosis and low blood count; the days of abject depression; the stretches of rapid cycling when vicious rage, desperate pleas for forgiveness and protestations of love and gratitude chase each other through day after day; the manic flight that took off from one of her recoveries and resulted in a small crafts shop in Cedar Hill that lasted all of three weeks after she relapsed on the champagne purchased for the opening; the only-when-she's-drunk interest in sex with her husband, a condition he calls a total turn off.

With John Lina has been honest about this wreck of a marriage and his sad sense of obligation. Without question he is wrapped in delusion if he does not see himself as a classic enabler. Everything he does for her—all his self-conscious efforts, from doing the housework to grabbing her back from the brink—only allows her to continue the process of destroying herself. Not to mention his life. Only if Marissa is forced to care for herself will she truly assume responsibility for her life, or her death. And certainly this can only happen if he leaves her. Then if her choice is in fact for death, whether fast or slow, he must fully prepare to accept it, and not eat himself alive with guilt or remorse. No one, least of all Lina, can help him with that.

All she can do is be honest about her feelings, to express without reservation and in every way she knows how the depth of her passion and love. On all of this she has been candid, to John and to herself. The regret that often stabs her with alarm, and that surely grinds away almost constantly below the surface, is that she is complicit in every facet of their ongoing deception, to keep this loving, consummated appetite for each other, known only to themselves. Yes, she can argue that John should consider being open with Marissa, no matter how dependent or unbalanced the woman might be. But how would Stan take the news, or Redding? And what would life be like in this conservative little place if they tossed caution away?

John would say, not a pretty picture, and he would be correct. But is this relationship, as wondrous as it is, really worth all the dissembling and deception? Especially to someone who has fashioned her own personal code on the immutable value of telling the truth? Now she finds herself withholding, misleading or outright lying at practically every turn. And what about all the harassment of the Plagues? Some of it, perhaps much of it, she actually finds amusing. That absurd, right-wing Catholic, anti-sexual rant, the nervous or presumptuous voices of unknown men on the phone, the often comic titles of the Dirty Book Attack. But occasionally, of course, there is ache, discomfort and anger when she allows herself to think about someone out there actually going to the trouble of making these ugly things happen. And there is always the distraction, the frequent interruptions and, perhaps worse, the constant, low-grade awareness that some terrible new thing may come at any time. Is it worth all this?

She is almost out of the woods when her mobile rings in her bag. John wonders how it went with Redding, and she gives him a short recap. She will have to work closely with the sour and suspicious Elena on planning the party and sending out e-mail invitations, and with Stan the Stalker on finding live music.

"Well, you know what Michael says in The Godfather."

She smiles. "'Keep your friends close and your enemies closer.' I think Sun-tzu wrote it first in the Art of War."

"I thought it was Machiavelli. But why doesn't Redding just throw you a party?"

"He said he wants people to see me not as an 'academic star,' as he put it, but as a friendly, regular person not afraid to roll up her sleeves and do something nice for others." Then she tells him about the Twat subscription.

"Actually that's pretty funny," he says.

"Yes, a lot of this is funny. But also, at the very least, it is a big distraction, and I've been thinking, darling, maybe the cost is just too high. Maybe we need to step back and stop seeing each other, at least for a while."

After a pause, his voice sounds concerned. "Is the cost too high for you, sweetheart?"

"I am asking. I want to know how you feel about this. Certainly it must be difficult for you. Perhaps much more difficult. In a few months I will not be here. But you will be, and people have long memories about such things."

"So what do we do? Make a public announcement—an e-mail blast or handbills on trees—that we're no long fucking?"

"It is not everyone who knows or cares, darling. It is Marissa or Stan."

"It's Marissa and/or Stan, and/or god knows who else they've told. Remember, this is the campus that time forgot."

"I want to see you."

"I thought we were breaking up."

"No, darling, we are not breaking up."

* * *

She licks then kisses the tip, runs her lips around the glans. She loves playing this way, feeling it stir and harden while her fingers caress the soft sac below. Her mouth takes it all now, as much as she knows she can, her tongue sliding gently down the smooth slick shaft and then up as she moves on it and listens to him hum his pleasure.

She loves the feel, the taste, the smell, the very idea of this powerful way of giving him pleasure. She wants to make him come this way. It would be especially exciting and satisfying because it would be the first time with him, and because he has spent the past half-hour making her come repeatedly, incredibly, wildly, doing things with his mouth on her clit she has never experienced before. And by the way his body stiffens now and the sac tightens under her touch, it won't take much of this to make him explode.

On the desk at the foot of the bed her mobile calls. Given the Plagues, why not turn the thing off when they walked into this room? She keeps her mouth firmly on his penis and sucks.

"Please, sweetheart," he says with a groan, "don't answer."

She stops long enough to say, "Of course, darling. You would like to come this way?"

His sensation must be intense. His speech is halting. "Oh, yes. But maybe, sweetheart, sometime later."

"Not now? You are sure?"

"You like it?"

"I love it."

"Then later sometime. Now I want you on top."

"Yes?

"You've made it so hard, you deserve to use it."

She takes her mouth away to smile at him in the soft gray light from the motel room window. Then gazing back at the bulbous, circumcised head, she says, "*Si, e bello, caro.*"

"That old thing is beautiful?"

"*Si*, very beautiful."

"Well, I want you to use it to make yourself happy again."

"I am very happy, *caro*, and I am not sure I can come again."

"I bet you can. You know just how to move to make it happen. No?"

"*Si*, maybe."

"Then give it one more little suck and get on top."

She does as he says and, with a small gasp, guides it easily inside.

* * *

Heads propped on pillows, they lie naked in the bed, glancing occasionally through the wide, uncovered window at the cold gray late-afternoon sky. I-94 is beyond view, but she can hear its travelers on their way to Chicago, Detroit and points in between.

"So why," she asks after a long silence, "were the varieties of orgasm so important to Lawrence?"

"Who?"

Obviously his mind has been someplace else. "David Herbert."

"Oh, Lawrence, yes, why did he make so much of coming together?"

"Yes."

"Sweetheart, I know you know the answer."

"Yes, you talk so beautifully about Lawrence, that I fall in love with you all over again."

"You are *pazzo*."

"Yes, crazy for you. So tell me about Lawrence."

114

He feigns exasperation. "So like any person of brilliance or genius, he was a very complicated fellow, but confronting a sexually stymied society, confused by its horrid split between the spiritual and the physical, the mental/emotional and the sexual, his attempt at a simple, powerful, healing answer was simultaneous orgasm. No artifice, no calculation. No working on each other, even to please. No manipulation. Just 'warm-hearted fucking,' as Mellors puts it. And so the ultimate expression of that, for Lawrence, in its simplest terms, is the bonding experience of mutuality, tenderness and love when two very separate humans come together at the same time and lose themselves in an ecstasy that is both physical and spiritual."

"See, darling, when you say it, even I, who knows better, believe it."

"Yes, but having moved well beyond that old Victorian split, you also know that, with understanding and trust, lovers can satisfy and bond with each other in any kind of orgasm."

"Yes, I know that too."

Her mobile beeps once on the desk. He asks, "The voice mail from that call?"

"No, I think it is a text message." She is up quickly to get the phone, pushes a couple of buttons and stares at the read-out.

"What is it?"

"A poem."

"A poem? From whom?"

"I don't know. There is no name or number or it was blocked." She heads back to the bed and reads:

> "Enjoy your stay
> At Motel 6
> A place to fuck
> But you need to pay."

He shakes his head. "I swear, nobody followed us here."

"Yes, but there are other ways to follow or know where we are. Not difficult these days to put a device on the car and then know its location."

"Or maybe it's your phone. They can add a program that tells others with the same service where you are at all times. Students use it a lot to keep track of their friends."

"I suppose it is possible. Stan got me the phone."

"We need to have it checked. How about the call? Is there a voice mail?"

She looks at the phone. "Yes, but I don't know if I want to hear it now."

"Lina, we need to know. I'll listen if you want."

"No, I will do it." She pushes a buttons. After a second a young man's casually confident voice says, "Hey, is this the Lina that loves to suck cock? If so, I've got one you're really going to have fun with. Call me…" She drops the phone on the bed.

"What is it?" he asks.

"Another plague."

"A new one?"

She hands him the mobile. "Push 4."

He sits forward, and she watches as he listens, finally making a face.

"I'll return the call," he says, pushing a button. "You should not talk to anyone like this."

She can feel his body tense just slightly next to her. He says calmly, "Yes, on that cock-sucking you called about earlier?" Pause. "No, I am not her pimp. Just a friend wondering where you got such a stupid fucking idea." Pause. "Well, let me tell you, pal. You ever call this number again, I'll have the cops squeeze you so hard your balls will pop."

He waits for a moment, then ends the call and looks at her grim-faced. "The guy says he found graffiti in three different men's room stalls on campus saying, 'Lina loves to suck cock,' with your cell number."

"What did he say when you mentioned the police?"

"He laughed and told me to go fuck myself."

Chapter 20

So how would he describe this girl's physical presentation beyond the eye-catching trifles you note when she has her clothes on? Well, the tits are nicely curved and hefty compared to the tiny waist and narrow hips, and, now that he can see all of her left breast, there is, in addition to the rose with thorns dripping blood, a small gold loop through the nipple. A diamond and silver clip decorates her navel, a phoenix rises above the crack of her ass and an orange day-lily sprouts from where her pubic hair would be if she had any. Bald down there seems to be the style these days, and a good thing indeed if he were forced to bring his mouth there for any length of time. So far, he's felt no such imperative with Becca Popp, even though she spent so much time servicing his dick that he was put in mind of Willie Nelson's famous line about "girls that can suck the chrome off a trailer hitch."

The sex was okay. She was properly enthusiastic, and he came when he, not she, wanted. But now in his bed in the gatehouse, instead of enjoying the afterglow and thinking, "Hey, this could really be the start of something," his mind is wandering back to how they got here.

It started with a phone call this morning, the second woman in a week to call and invite herself into his life. This one suggested he take her to see "'Michael Clayton' at the plex, because it's supposed to be great, not good, but great." And after, they could just talk, grab a bite or "do whatever" — that last word delivered with a little erotic innuendo. In the theater, when the car exploded while Lina's friend Clooney was fortunate enough to be admiring those horses, she grabbed his hand and wouldn't let go, whispering, "Stan, this stuff scares the shit out of me." Walking out she winked at him and said, "Thanks for helping me feel safe in there."

"No problem," he said, "my pleasure."

"I don't know what it is. I'm like a little kid at movies. Sometimes

I want to put my head under the seat. It's embarrassing." Then she decided they should "grab a pizza and take it back to your place, if that's okay with you."

At the gatehouse she loved his "crib." He said it had once been part of an estate owned by an eccentric old widow, who eventually burned through her entire fortune, giving much of it away to animal rights groups, until she died in near-poverty and without a single heir.

"Wow, what an awesome story!"

He wanted to ask what was awesome about it but explained instead that the county had taken over the place except for the gatehouse, which the widow had sold to a history professor at the university, whose family years later began renting it to grad students.

"Well, lucky you," she said, and then browsing through his books and things, while he cleaned up after the pizza, she found his Patsy Cline's Greatest Hits CD. Well, it wasn't really his. He had found it under the couch when he moved in a year ago.

"Holy shit, you like Patsy Cline?"

"Well, yeah?" He wasn't sure if she thought this was a good thing.

"I love Patsy Cline! A seamstress's daughter, Grand Ole Opry superstar, dead at 30 in one of those Country-Western plane crashes along with Cowboy Copas and Hawkshaw Hawkins! And look at this, you've got her singing two of the greatest songs ever written right here, 'Crazy' and 'I Fall to Pieces.' Can we play this?" And before he could say "Sure," she had his system figured out, and Pasty was blasting away with the volume set too high because that's the way he'd been listening to those two songs over and over and over for the past four days.

""Wow, you like it loud! Just like me."

They sat on the couch, listening to Patsy wail about how she falls to pieces "each time I see you again." And later when "Crazy" came up, the excitable Becca Popp announced over the intro that, as he probably knows, this one was written by Willie (he assumed the one with the line about the trailer hitch) and that Patsy at first thought it impossible to sing.

"Crazy...I'm crazy for feelin' so lonely," she warbled. And for feeling so blue. She knew he'd love her as long as he wanted, and then someday leave her for somebody new.

When Patsy finished, Becca was up to turn off the system. Then standing in front of him, she said, "So would you like to see my nipple ring?" His answer was, yes, very much, and that's how she ended up here in his bed, the second woman in a week, after one hell of a long dry spell.

Six days ago at mid-afternoon, when Marissa called his cell, she asked if he were home.

"I will be shortly. What's up?"

"Good. Give me directions, and I'll be there in about a half-hour. I made you something, and I want to see how it looks on your wall."

She greeted him with a hug and one of her collages, maybe a hundred "clips and snips," she called them, from magazines ranging from Newsweek and the New Yorker to GQ and Vogue to supermarket tabs and Playboy. He actually liked it, and they found a good place in the kitchen where it hangs now. He offered to open a bottle of Chardonnay, and she said, "Oh, no, I can't." And then said, well, maybe just one small glass, otherwise he'd have to drive her home.

He had not seen or spoken to her since their tattoo parlor conversation at Hal's memorial. She looked good, with her shaggy blond curls, just enough make-up, and a smiling energetic air. Once her beige suede coat was off, she was very sexy in jeans and a thin flower-print blouse with a couple of buttons unused to show cleavage and the lacy edge of a pretty green bra. A lot had happened since the service. He assumed that from one gossipy source or another, most probably from John himself, she knew about all the harassment. He asked what John was up to.

"You mean besides fucking our luscious Lina?"

"What?"

"Don't tell me you don't know what's going on."

"Okay, I won't, because I don't."

"Really, I thought sure you'd know."

"Nope. I mean I know they're friendly, and I see them hanging out together some and talking away. But beyond that, I know nothing."

"Well, they're friendly all right."

"You *know* this is going on?"

"A woman knows, sweetie. But what about all this harassing stuff that's going on, all these plagues, as John calls them. Who do you think is behind all that?"

"I have no idea. I was going to ask you."

"Why me? I don't have a clue."

"Well, I figure if you think John and Lina are screwing, you'd have a motive."

On his couch, he looked her in the eye. She didn't blink. "No, sweetie, not my style."

Whose style it might be they talked about for a while. He suggested it was clearly someone who had fixated on Lina and become obsessed. If Hal hadn't offed himself before all this stuff started, he'd be a prime suspect.

"Hal?"

"Oh, yeah, he was totally nuts about her. The night he killed himself, when he came here to pick up the key, he told me he had asked her out a couple of times, and she had turned him down. He was pretty devastated."

"Maybe that had something to do with what happened."

"Who knows, but really it could be anyone on this campus, guy or gal, for that matter, who's been like totally smitten, become obsessed and probably got flat out rejected by her. Then there's stalking, pranks and all kinds of harassment because they've like totally fixed on her as the only one in the world who can give meaning and satisfaction to their pathetic little lives."

"Actually, sweetie, I thought you might be involved. Not that you fit that profile, but I know you've really been taken by her."

"No, not really, she's not my type. Yeah, I think she's bright and interesting, but I usually find her rather cold and standoffish. You know, European women have this reputation for being warm and sexy, but I don't see her that way at all. Maybe it's because she' a redhead."

"What's wrong with redheads?"

"Nothing, but I've never been partial to them. They've always seemed kind of strange and eccentric to me, and that's been a turnoff."

Marissa shrugged. "Well, you could have fooled me, sweetie. And John thinks so too."

"He thinks I'm stuck on Lina?"

"Oh, yeah, big time. He says, 'That boy looks like a sick dog around her.'"

"A sick dog." He tried to dampen the anger beating up in his chest. "No," he said, taking her warm right hand from where she'd kept it waiting for him on the denim covering her thigh. "Give me a warm, sexy American gal every time."

Her pretty blond head, pressed back against the cushion of his couch, was turned to him with a smile that said kiss me. And so he did, as John's one piece of advice on women repeated in his head: "Never sleep with someone who's crazier than you are."

When he was finished with the kiss, which included a little tongue action, she was smiling. "Well, it's about time, young man. I thought you were never going to make your move."

"I'm sorry. You're so beautiful, I was a little intimidated."

"You very sweet boy," she said drawing him back for more.

In contrast to the anxious-to-please Becca, she was quite passive, lying there apparently expecting him to do most of the work and wanting a good deal of reassurance about her body.

"You like them?" she asked.

In fact he didn't really care for her tits all that much. They were big but kind of blockish.

"You bet. You're beautiful."

She was definitely thicker through the waist and hips than he preferred, but when she wondered if he thought her "a little too fat," he, of course, lied again. She seemed to want a lot of sucking from him, first the nipples, to the point of boredom actually. And then she moved his head down to her well-tended box, perfectly shaved and, it seemed, applied with something that tasted vaguely like strawberries. Throughout the process, she offered a variety of noises and exhortations and flipped around a bit, but he was pretty damn sure she hadn't come.

On the other hand, his hard-on had been forced to endure so long, he thought he'd lose it before he ever got the damn thing into her. Finally, she grabbed it, pronounced it "a nice big boy," and shoved it in. He came so quickly, that afterward she said, with a touch of pique, "Well, that was expeditious." And a few seconds later: "We'll just have to keep doing this until we're both having fun."

That, he was already quite certain, was not going to happen.

With the decorated Becca, beside him now, he can see maybe trying again sometime, but he already knows enough to forget his hope that one or both of these women will somehow snap the taut wire of his obsession.

Before dropping her back at the Sun to pick up her old Aztech—she called it "the world's ugliest car...that's why I love it"—he extends an invitation to the party for George Rolande. He makes George and his career at St. Thomas sound interesting enough for one of her profiles. With her usual gusto, she promises not to miss it.

The party. Planning for it has brought him back in closer touch with Lina, and, for the most part, that's gone pretty well. Recommending a new caterer in town instead of the one Elena always uses, he brought Lina to the shop where they sampled the Teriyaki Chicken Skewers and Shrimp Scampi and pronounced them *dilizioso*. Then it was on to Trader Joe's to pick out the wine for a very good price and to meet Muriel Markova at the Music School who gave them a CD with a sampling from her innovative jazz ensemble—flute, guitar, violin and Muriel's harp making popular standards sound fresh and new.

Lina actually seemed to be enjoying herself with him. And as thanks for all his help she invited him for dinner one night half-way between Marissa and Becca, Tagliatelli with a tasty Bolognese she made herself from scratch. Later, as they moved into her living room, he even allowed himself to think maybe she was tiring of John, or maybe the old guy wasn't getting it up all that well, given the prostate thing, and maybe he was filling John's very spot on this sofa. And then the conversation, pleasant through dinner, turned south.

Yes, she appreciated all his efforts to make her comfortable and to find the source of all the *merda* descending on her life lately. But one thing he has done she has found disturbing.

"Jesus, Lina, what are we talking about?"

"You know what Loopt is."

"Looped...like drunk?"

"No, you have it on your phone."

"Oh, Loopt. Yes, I have it on my cell. I don't use it, but a lot of students I know do. They like to keep track of each other, and it puts a little dot on a map on your phone."

"Yes, I read about it somewhere, and when I called Sprint, they told me that I have Loopt on the mobile you set up for me."

"Oh, Christ! And with everything that's been going on, all this *merda*, you think somebody could be keeping track of where you are.

You know you can block access any time?"

"Yes, Sprint told me that. But how does it happen that I have this on my phone?"

"Look, Lina, I know this is horrible for you, but when Fr. Redding asked me to get you a phone and set up an account, I didn't even think. I just said, 'Make it the same deal I have, the same plan. I just forgot I had Loopt on mine."

"So that is your answer. You forgot?"

"Of course, that's my answer. That's what happened. Listen, I'll call right now and have it removed from your phone."

"I have already done that."

"Okay, good. That's one less thing you have to worry about."

"Stan, I am grateful for your help, but this is not right, and it makes me distrust you."

"Lina, please, I understand. But there was no malicious intent here. None. It costs like three bucks a month, I think, and I don't use it, so it wasn't even on my radar."

Unsmiling, she nodded at him. "And I too do not wish to be on your radar."

Chapter 21

She even purchased a new outfit for the occasion, driving herself under a leaden November sky to a mall on I-94 where she found the blouse/sweater/slacks ensemble in muted fall colors, reds and browns. Now she is pleased with her new look and with how the party is unfolding. The praise for her started soon after the 3 to 5 pm affair began with Redding's greeting. As he over-stated her role and underplayed what Elena and Stan contributed, a round of applause extended for several seconds and included a few shouts of "Yes!" and "Lina!"

The second-floor banquet room in the Student Center was a good choice. Stan said, "Students never turn down a free lunch." In fact, most of them seem to have starved themselves all day and made lunch and dinner out of the hors d'oeuvres, wine, cheese and a large flat cake covered with a congratulatory message in blue-on-white frosting.

Looking pinker than ever, George Rolande opened his remarks with a reference to the cake. "Well, I hope you all have a look before most of it gets eaten. I read it—'Prof. George Rolande, St. Thomas University, 1988-2007'—and thought I was dead."

George rode the wave of laughter, even the usually grim-faced Elena showing a smile. Redding had joked that the delicate-featured little man with the snow-white hair had taken his Ph.D. at Tulane "just a year or so after Gutenberg invented moveable type" and praised his extraordinary love for his students and dedication to his calling as an "inspiration to all of us." George thanked many people for many things, including, near the end, "the brilliant and beautiful Prof. Lina Lentini, who came all the way from Bologna to throw me this party."

Later he thanked her personally and became the first of only a few to mention her recent litany of woes, calling them "disgusting beyond words. You deserve an apology from this entire campus."

And when he said his plan was to finally do the writing and traveling he has always dreamed of, she invited him to visit her in Bologna. Touched, he said he would love to.

Actually more people have come up to chat with her in the first 90 minutes of this affair than in her first seven weeks on campus. Maybe Redding was right: someone who is willing to order hors d'oeuvres and book a band seems more approachable. With the quartet swinging through standards, there is a pleasant mix of students, department colleagues and George's campus friends and well-wishers. Everyone has no doubt heard something about her recent tribulations, but most keep their conversations casual and friendly. Patti Pierce, a little mini-skirted undergrad, tells her "'Michael Clayton' is a must see" and asks if it's true that Lina was once engaged to George Clooney. When Charlie Spence, the blond, bearded kid who quoted Camus to her weeks back, says he can't wait for her analysis of Roth's new one, *Exit Ghost*, the thought occurs that maybe this American visit will turn out okay after all. Ten days have passed since a new plague surfaced, and almost a week since the last male caller, sounding like a frightened 15-year-old, asked about arranging to have his cock sucked.

Elena Plouff pauses only long enough to congratulate her on a "successful event." John stops by to whisper she looks "good enough to ravish" and points out Marissa with her "little techie, Billy Jeffer, to whom I put the screws and who insists he knows nothing." Stan, stiff and awkward since their talk about her mobile, seems looser as he passes, saying, "Hey, Lina, you throw a hell of a party." A minute later he's laughing with the exotic Becca Popp, and a minute after that, the girl introduces herself.

Lina says, "You are friends with Stan I think?"

"Oh, yeah, Stan's great. He said something about us?"

"No, I just saw you talking with him."

"Yeah, we were talking about you. He thinks you'd make a great profile for the Sun."

"A profile. Readers of the Sun would be interested in such a thing?"

"Oh, I can assure you. From what Stan's told me, you're awesome. So maybe we could arrange an interview some time soon? Actually, I'm doing a piece on a colleague of yours, Prof. John Martens and his new book on D.H. Lawrence? Maybe I could also talk to you about him?"

A red flag suddenly flashes over this eccentric young woman's head, and Lina says only, "Well, that is interesting."

After a beat, Becca asks, "So, what do you think of Stan?"

"Ah. I think he is bright and impressive. What do you think?"

"Yes, definitely, I agree. And I think we make the perfect pair, really. I mean, I drive the world's ugliest car, and he drives the world's most beautiful. Perfect! I mean, have you seen his car, that sweet little Beemer roadster?"

A few minutes later, Marissa's approach comes from behind. As she did at the memorial, she begins with a commiserating tone about Hal. There have been no references to Hal and his awful fate in any of her conversations today, until she hears Marissa's alcohol-fueled voice behind her say, "Lina, dear, it just doesn't seem right, does it?" By now the woman, holding a half-filled glass of red wine, has moved around to stop in front of her. "To have something like this, and poor, darling Hal's not with us. I mean, it almost seems heartless."

The last word is an accusation. Lina smiles with sympathy. "Yes, in a way it does."

Marissa is holding that glass of wine as if she might toss it in Lina's face. Instead she moves it aside and gives her a brief embrace. Then the woman stares at her for a moment with what feels like a dangerous air and says, "Love your outfit. Is it new?"

"Thank you, Marissa. As a matter of fact, it is."

"Where'd you find it?"

"At a store called Chico's."

"Oh, I love Chico's. We'll have to go shopping sometime and have a little lunch."

"That sounds nice."

"Yeah. So poor Hal is gone." She suddenly looks and sounds completely scattered. "It just seems, the way I see it, that transgression demands punishment, or atonement, or reparation, or at least an acknowledgment of the evil performed."

She has no idea how to respond, but Marissa never gives her a chance.

"Actually, you look fabulous in that outfit."

"Well, thank you."

"But then you look fabulous in anything, or I'm sure in nothing at all, for that matter."

Arriving for a rescue, John takes his wife's arm, announcing that he needs to introduce her to someone interested in buying a collage. Lina watches as he walks her away and gets halfway across the room before Marissa pushes his arm away and heads in her own direction.

With the Markova Quartet well into their set with a sprightly version of Brubeck's "Take Five," Redding stops next to her and takes in the scene. "Beautiful, says the priest. You've done a marvelous job, Lina. Usually at these things, most of the people have gone by now. But everybody's having such a good time."

For George Roland and some of his older guests someone has brought in several straight-back chairs and placed them in a semi-circle against the wall not far from a double-door entrance. George sits in the middle flanked by a contingent of nuns. Sisters Gertrude and Martha no longer wear the habit, but three very old sisters still do, and two others who appear to be in their early 20s are wearing the veil as well. They are all laughing and shaking their heads at something George has just said.

Redding says, "George and his girlfriends seem to be having more fun than anyone."

She wonders if this means the priest knows about that 30-year-old secret in the closet but says, "As it turns out, you were right, Father, and I want to thank you again."

"No. I'm just sorry for what you've been through. Maybe now the worst is over."

But just now, things take a sudden new turn. She hears it before she sees it. Something with cheap audio speakers bursts into song, the Village People doing "YMCA." The quartet has just finished its set, and this has obviously been timed to follow that. The new music comes from a large silver boom box set on the floor not far from George Rolande and the nuns, placed there, she knows immediately, by a good-looking young man with curly black hair and dressed in a white shirt, black bow tie and slacks. He's already dancing.

Staring at the young man, Redding says, "Well, now, what's this? More entertainment?"

She wants to say she has no idea but is struck dumb. This is surely unmitigated disaster. The young fellow with the box is already cutting loose, moving frantically to the beat and yelling to what is quickly becoming his rapt audience, "Com'on, everybody, let's show

George how much we love him!"

With shouts from the crowd, more than a few students begin dancing out the letters, forming them with their arms and torsos. But now with several sexy moves, the young man turns to face George and his girlfriends and, with one quick two-handed tug, neatly rips off his shirt, somehow leaving only the collar and bowtie in place. Twirling it three times over his head, he throws the shirt at one of the young nuns who catches it and smiles. And then, with only the slightest pause, he grabs those slacks below the hips and rips them off as well, only this time there is nothing at all left behind. He is stark naked except for the collar, tie and black dancing shoes. About being in this condition at this time and place, and with a body he has obviously worked on diligently in a weight room, he seems ecstatic, and so does his penis, bobbing and weaving with his frenzied moves and getting bigger by the second.

Shouts and screams come now from different parts of the room. Astonishment, fear, confusion and delight all vie with the silly, joyful song that continues to pound on the boom box. As she searches frantically for John or Stan, she spots Marissa standing in the middle of the room with a strange smile. Others are also standing still, some are cringing back toward the rear of the room or heading for exits, and many are edging forward presumably for a better view. When she turns back to Marissa, the woman has disappeared.

The dancer is clearly giving his best to the party's honoree and his special guests. Sisters Gertrude and Martha are leaving their seats now for safer ground, and two of the older nuns are gathering their habits to follow. The third, clearly the oldest, just sits there as if she is having a beatific vision. Of the two younger sisters, one continues to smile and hold the dancer's white shirt in her lap, and the other sits next to her with her hands firmly covering her eyes.

As for George, he is stock-still in his chair, a startled look frozen on that pink face, as if the door of that closet he has been in for thirty years has just been ripped off its hinges, leaving him suddenly blinded by the sunlight blasting in. Finally, she spots John. Apparently he was at the back of the room, but he is moving as quickly as he can now through the obstacle course of people rooted in place or heading in several directions. He is mouthing words she cannot hear over the Village People to get past those who shift in exactly the wrong way to let him pass.

Then behind her she hears a familiar male voice shout, "Okay, pal, you're done!"

Turning, she finds that Stan has appeared out of nowhere, and, thank the gods, he is carrying a trench coat. It is frayed and soiled but will certainly do the trick if Stan can find a way to corral this well-built whirling dervish. As the dancer spins, his penis waves what she hopes will be a final goodbye to the crowd. Matching the song, he thrusts his arms into a "Y" and then an "M," and as he gets to "C," Stan, with the coat fully unfurled now, literally jumps on him, throwing the long garment on the fellow's broad shoulders and wrestling with him to close it in front. Finally, Stan puts him into something of a headlock, shoves his fist into the small of his back and says something into the fellow's ear. Though a few inches shorter than Stan, the dancer showed in his performance enough musculature to toss Stan easily aside, but now he spreads his hands near his sides in submission and moves quickly in Stan's clutches out the nearby double doors currently held open by Elena and Fr. Dan Hagen, the always-late-arriving university president, who no doubt made it in time to observe this whole bloody mess.

At the boom box she punches the off button, ending the song on "M" and wondering why neither she nor anyone else had tried to terminate the disaster by doing this first. John arrives looking furious and says under his breath, "Jesus F Christ!" He grabs the box and, with the dancer's discarded slacks already in tow, takes the white shirt from the young nun's lap and heads out the double doors. She follows far enough to see him cross the hall to a men's room door. Then, not wanting to catch Hagen's eye just now, she turns back to find Redding hustling Muriel Markova and friends back to their instruments, urging them to somehow restore the party's former ambience, now shattered like broken crystal on the banquet room floor.

Chapter 22

Sitting in his office with Becca Popp, he finds the tiny eyes of the snake on her neck staring at him with an intensity matched by her own dark gaze when he glances up from the student essay she just handed him. He's feeling a rage that's been building almost from the moment she walked in and sat down. Rage has become a frequent visitor over the past few days, but there's been nothing quite like what he's feeling right now.

He was furious at the close to George Rolande's party, when he pushed through the men's room door with the shirt, pants and boom box and found Stan shoving the trench-coated dancer against a wall, a forearm to the throat, growling, "Okay, so who paid you for this?"

"That's confidential," the guy croaked.

"Look, pal, how about an indecent exposure charge?"

The dancer glanced at him and then looked at Stan for a couple of seconds, then managed to reach into a pocket of the trench coat and come out with what looked like a personal check. Taking it, Stan released the dancer and gazed at the check, shaking his head. As John moved closer to have a look, the dancer grabbed the box from him, snatched the break-away shirt and pants and ran for a door at the far end of the large men's room.

"Hey wait!" shouted Stan, but the guy was gone. John didn't even look up, his eyes riveted to the check, made out to one Frank E. Foxxx for the sum of $200, drawn on the personal account of Marissa Martens, and signed with what certainly looked like his wife's hand.

"Sorry, John," said Stan. "You keep it, and I'll take the blame for letting him get away."

Before he could answer, Fr. Hagen walked in, and John shoved the check into a pocket.

"Campus security should be here in a minute," said the priest.

"I'm afraid, Father, the guy got away. He had no personal ID on him at all."

"Stan, you were the hero out there. I don't know how you did it."

"Well, I just told him I had a gun, and I was dying to use it. I probably sounded crazy."

And that was that. A check made out from his wife's account to a fellow using a "stage name," and one that turned out to be untraceable. Could Stan have set the whole thing up to make himself look great? Yes, but for now he was grateful that Stan gave him Mar's check and kept it from Hagen. And then, headed home, he was smoldering again, convinced that over the past three weeks she had made good on her promise to make him "rue the day." When he got home he could not believe his senses. As he walked in there was something baking, in their own kitchen. He found Mar using hot pads to remove a metal sheet from the oven.

"What in Christ's name are you doing?" He asked in the broader sense of how she could be doing this homey thing in the midst of her efforts to wreak havoc on other people's lives.

She took a more restricted meaning. "Your favorite, chocolate chip cookies!"

There on the counter was the packaging for a ready-to-bake Pillsbury product, and here she was, acting as if this were a common occurrence, when it had not happened since two months into their marriage. "No," he said, taking the check from his pocket and holding it up, "I'm talking about this."

"About what? A check?" She leaned forward, as if trying to read it from across the room. "What are you talking about, John?"

"I'm talking about this check written to that fucking lowlife to ruin George's party. How could you do that? I thought you loved George. How could you do something so ugly?"

Her voice rose. "You think I did that? What happened today made me sick to my stomach. Literally. As soon as I saw what was happening, I went straight to the john and puked. And then I came home and to get that awful image out of my mind—that little asshole waving his prick around at poor George and those nuns—I decided to bake you cookies."

"This check was in the little asshole's pocket. It's one of yours. It has your signature."

She glared at him. "Anybody can forge a signature, John. Let me see that check. Wait, I bet I know which one it is." She went to her purse on the counter, pulled out her checkbook and leafed quickly through. "Yeah, I bet it's check number 2552." Eyes wide, inquiring, she looked sure of herself.

He glanced at the check, then back at her. "And that proves what exactly?"

"It proves, that's a check I've been missing, and looking for, all week."

"Mar, for chrissake."

"No, its true, look for yourself!" She threw the checkbook at him, and he caught it. "Go ahead, look at the slip for 2552. It's blank!"

"Jesus, that proves nothing. So you ripped out the check before you wrote it."

"No! Somebody stole it. Took it right out of my checkbook. I thought maybe I had ripped it out myself for some reason and forgot about it. I was blaming myself for being careless, but now it's obvious. Somebody stole that check!"

It went on this way a while longer, Mar screaming that if she had really wanted to do something like this, she would have paid the little prick in cash. He said that of all her stunts over the past few weeks, this was absolutely the worst, causing pain and discomfort for so many others. She said, look who was talking, when he and his fucking wop girlfriend inflicted so much vicious pain she could hardly breathe when he was off screwing the slut.

He said, "Mar, I've told you…"

She took the tray cooling on a rack and slammed it cookies-down on the kitchen floor. She followed that by grabbing a large ceramic plate — one of her own creations and set to receive the cookies — and raising it high, threw it down hard enough to create a thousand pieces.

"Happy?" she asked and stalked out of the room, leaving the mess for him to clean up. Which, of course, he did.

The next day the anger quotient was up again with word from a student that the world had been gifted with a cell phone video of the dance exhibition on YouTube. On the computer in his office he found it quickly. A small blur placed strategically, but the event was there for all to see under the title, "Stripper Does His Thing For Nuns." Already 7414 views so far.

And now this. A budding nightmare brought to him by the same pierced and tattooed young woman he found so pleasant and likeable last week when she sat in this office and they spoke for close to an hour, the small digital audio recorder working between them, for the profile she was writing on the occasion of his "marvelous and important new book."

This time, arriving for "just a few follow-up questions," she was again friendly but moved quickly to the real point of her visit. Yesterday she had received a message purportedly sent from the computer of the recently deceased Hal Stroheim. The note said the sender thought she might be interested in the attached document found on Hal's "school computer," a paper written apparently by Hal for a course on D.H. Lawrence taught by Prof. John Martens in the fall semester of 2005. "You might want to compare," said the note, "pages 2 through 14 of the paper and Chapter 2 of Martens' recently published book on Lawrence."

Knowing exactly what was going on here, he was boiling even before he took the printed-out class paper from her, with Hal's name and address on the cover sheet along with the title: "A Mother's Son in D.H. Lawrence's *Sons and Lovers*." Now he forces himself to read the first two paragraphs before trusting his voice with this girl. "Who gave you this, Ms. Popp?"

She stirred with a nervous, defensive gesture, a small half-circle with her right hand before replacing it on her blue-jeaned thigh. "I told you, it came attached to an e-mail from a guy who's dead. And I would not have even bothered you with this, except that I did in fact find much of it, word for word in your new book."

"No, really, Ms. Popp, who gave you this? Surely you agree that I have a right to face my accuser in something as serious as this. I mean, this is something, as I'm certain you understand, that, if true, would destroy my career."

"Yes, of course. That's why I'm here. To give you every opportunity to explain, rebut, or offer a response to what is alleged here. And, yes, I take this very seriously indeed."

He is already on his feet and digging through a drawer in his large metal filing cabinet near the office's one narrow window. He comes out with a stack of literary journals, and back in his chair he sorts through the staid-looking periodicals, until he finds the one he wants. "This is the Spring 2003 issue of the American Literary Review." He hands it to her.

She opens the cover and says, "Okay."

"In the table of contents there you'll find my essay on *Sons and*

Lovers, and, if you check it out, I think you'll find that most of it, verbatim, is in Chapter 2 of my book."

She flips through the journal, finds the essay and begins reading.

He says, "Just to help you with the math...that was published about two-and-a-half years before Hal supposedly wrote the paper that I supposedly plagiarized from."

Finally, she looks up at him, the sun from the window glinting on the ring through her eyebrow. "I'm sorry, Professor Martens, so who is it that hates you so much?"

"Yeah, I was hoping you could tell me."

"Well, this has the feel of that thing that was done to the gal from Italy, you know, that phony personal placed in the Sun for your colleague Prof. Lentini? Stan told me about all the harassment that's been focused on her. And now it looks like you've become a target."

"Maybe."

"Yeah, I've been thinking I should write about what's been going on. It sounds like some pretty bogue stuff, and somebody should put a stop to it."

"I'm afraid, Becca," he said, using her first name again to sound more friendly, "writing about it would only encourage these people. I would think that's exactly what they want."

"You think there's more than one person behind all this?"

"I have no idea. I'm just sure whoever it is would welcome publicity. I trust you'll consider that carefully before writing something."

"Well, I don't know it'll make any difference. I wrote a great piece about that stripper at the party the other day, and it got chopped. Second one of mine in the last three weeks. Really, it's getting to the point where I'm seriously thinking of starting my own blog, where I can write all the hard-hitting stuff the Sun won't let me print. Of course, I could kiss my ass goodbye at the Sun, but maybe that would be good thing. Get myself out of this provincial little Hickville and move on to Chicago or someplace that can really appreciate what I do."

Only minutes after Becca Popp leaves his office, Lina calls his cell. There's more concern in her voice than he has ever heard before.

"John, where are you?"

"At my office in Markham."

"I need to see you now. Somebody got into my computer here."

"What do you mean?"

"I am not sure what I mean. Whether somebody was in this apartment and got into my computer, or whether they got in electronically somehow, hacking in. Either way they found the chapter files from my new book and destroyed them."

"Jesus Christ."

"So, John, please, I need to see you as soon as possible."

"Wait, sweetheart, what do you mean destroyed them."

"They're blank, John. They're all blank, except for one line. Whoever did this left the same line in each blank chapter file: 'Because you are an evil liar.'"

"Lina, please tell me you have back up."

"I think so, but I cannot be certain. All of it should be on the laptop I brought from Italy that I keep at the office there where you are."

"Thank goodness."

"Yes, but I am concerned that they may have gotten into that one too."

Chapter 23

At a weathered picnic table they sit looking out over a small, sparkling blue lake surrounded by wooded hills that still hold shades of red, orange and gold. Until they arrived a few minutes ago, she did not know this place existed, fifteen minutes from Cedar Hill. What other pretty spots close by has she missed out on so far? A chill in the air despite the late afternoon sun, they are both bundled in sweaters and jackets. John's hands reach across the old table to keep hers warm.

Once she checked out the Dell in her office and found it apparently untouched, the chapter files all intact, she unplugged the web connection, and locked the door behind her. Inside John's office with the door closed, he held her in his arms, and she felt herself close to tears, something uncommon for her. In a way, this was the worst, most troubling of the plagues, inflicting a sense that someone has tried to kill off an essential part of her, to destroy something she has created and values deeply because it took the best from her. As he held her without words, she knew he understood completely. She kissed his tender mouth, then asked if he could take her to some quiet place, with no one around, where they could talk in peace for a while.

In the Saab he did most of the talking. The plagues had suddenly taken a literary turn, he said, and then described his meeting earlier in the afternoon with Becca Popp.

"Plagiarism," she said, the word hanging in the stuffy air inside his car. She lowered her window an inch and added, "So this is something new...you also as the target."

"Yes, I guess so."

He explained that while he was waiting for her, he phoned his friend Marcus Bolger in the computer science department. "Marcus said, basically, a savvy hacker can do stuff you can't even imagine. He said if I got him the desktop, he would have it checked out and de-bugged. They'd be looking for a "Trojan," meaning a Trojan Horse, I guess, which, if someone can get it on your computer, they have complete access to what you've got there."

"Charming," she said, feeling sullen. But once she saw the lake and sat there at the table knowing they were alone, she felt her spirits and energy lift a bit.

"Darling, we have to consider," she says, "the possibility that Stan, or Marissa, or someone, has found a way to get into my apartment. That makes me nervous. Really, since Stan rented the apartment, it is certainly possible he kept a key for himself."

"Yes, indeed."

"So what do I do? Confront Stan directly, as I did about the GPS program on my mobile?

" I wouldn't think so. That confrontation basically came to nothing. And with the key, it's worse. He'll certainly deny he ever kept one for himself, and he'll probably point out that someone could certainly hack in from outside. Look, I'll call a locksmith, and we'll have the lock changed, so you can feel safe in your own apartment."

"I think I should call the police."

"The police."

"Yes, John, this is a serious breech."

"Of course it is, darling. But you call in the police, and they start digging, and you'll have to be talking about all these things that have been happening."

"Maybe that would be a good thing. I know Redding did not want to call them in, advised against it. He said the police find a personal vendetta difficult to trace. But maybe we should have called them in right from the start."

"And tell them what when they ask if you have any enemies, or people who might want to do you harm? Will you give them our two obvious names? Or maybe just one? Which would it be, and what reason would you give for suspecting either of them?"

She gazed away from him and beyond the lake to the brightly colored leaves thinning on the trees. "Maybe I give them just Stan, and say he has been more than normally interested in me despite my attempts to discourage him over the past two months. Give them a few examples, and they go to him and warn him, tell him they will be watching him. And then if it stops, good, it stops, and we know it was probably Stan. And if it does not stop, then we know it is probably Marissa, or at least we know more than we do now."

He squeezes her hands and reclaims her eyes. "Sweetheart, do you really want the police poking around in our personal business?"

"It does not have to be our personal business I talk about. Only about who has been doing these awful things. There is nothing so far in all of this that puts us together."

"Yes, darling, but you put this out there with the cops, and we've given up control. There is no telling where this might go."

* * *

In Italy she would not think twice about walking ten minutes through the woods in front of her apartment. Even though it is 7:15, with the evening darkness already descended. The path, after all, is lit with several lampposts along the way and seems perfectly safe. As she turns the white Focus onto the street that will take her around the woods to the campus, she wonders if she has finally succumbed to the small, annoying fears she has fought for several days now. They stem, she is certain, from a sense that an unrelenting malevolence has fixed on her, that any moment may bring a sudden new affliction.

To quiet the low-grade dread, she has used the thought that this is exactly what her nemesis wants her to feel, and to not feel it is a kind of triumph. But the only sustained respite has come from her writing. Consumed with finding the apt word and crafting the cogent thought, she has worked for hours with her phone off, her e-mail unmonitored, with Word the only program open. Until this morning. In the wake of the cyber attack, with the locksmith's work already accomplished, her university-supplied desktop delivered to Marcus Bolger, and the decision about going to the police put off for now, she did her writing the old-fashioned way, in long hand on a yellow legal pad with a ballpoint pen.

They have decided to say nothing for now about the "plagiarism scam," since it would only join them as victims. As for mentioning the attack on her book, John said, "Let's play it by ear and see what this meeting with the good father is about."

As she walks up the steps of Markham Hall, her watch says 7:26. Right on time. John should already be in Redding's office. Instead he is suddenly there beside her.

"John, you frightened me."

He opens the heavy door for her. "Sorry, sweetheart," he says, "I was watching you from behind as I caught up, feasting on that strong, confident stride of yours."

"Please, darling, do not go crazy on me also."

"Mar was on the nut, and it took me forever to get her to take an Ativan. Let's forget about arriving separately. We walk in together, so what?"

And so they do. Redding is behind his desk and Hagen, a surprise, to one side facing the two chairs, set for them in front of the desk. Does Hagen's presence warn of something unpleasant ahead? The priests get to their feet with smiles that seem perfunctory. John must be thinking something similar; as they shake hands, his face is somewhere between grim and angry. On the desk are two large manila envelopes.

Once they are seated, Redding says, "Thanks for coming after hours, so to speak. Father Hagen and I thought it best, given the sensitive nature of what we need to talk about."

John says, "Sensitive, Father?"

Redding picks up the envelopes. "Probably the easiest way to do this is to have you look at these. The contents are identical, and they were waiting for us on arrival this morning."

John takes the envelopes and hands one to her. Addressed simply to "Fr. Robert Redding," it was opened with a neat slit. Inside are three 8-by-10 photographs and a letter printed on one piece of comparative lit department stationery. She can tell without a glance to the side that John is looking first at the photos, and she does as well.

The one on top shows the two of them holding hands, each looking in a different direction, as they walk away from what a sign says is a Motel 6. The searching gaze on each face makes it appear they are looking for someone who might be watching them, which, in her case at least, was exactly the fact.

The second is a slightly fuzzy view of the two of them greeting each other at her front door. Her face is visible, with him only the back of his head. The hair and the baggy black sweater are pretty obviously his. It must have been taken by someone in the woods.

In the third photo they are on the patio at the Bean. This must have been several weeks back. The petunias still fill the boxes that ring the place. Her right hand covers his left, as they smile at each other with a warmth that feels distant now. Also on the black metal table is her left hand extended a bit awkwardly, it seems.

John is already reading the letter. She does the same.

Dear Fathers Hagen and Redding,

Scandalized, disheartened, dismayed. That's how so many of us here on the campus of St. Thomas University feel about the selfish and disgusting behavior of two people we formerly held in high regard. As the accompanying, un-retouched photographs attest, Prof. John Martens and Prof. Lina Lentini, both of our esteemed Comparative Literature Department, have been carrying on a torrid and very public illicit romance and sexual affair that offends our deepest sensibilities and scoffs at our most sacred values. Please put a stop to this repulsive moral blight on our pristine and beautiful campus.

Very Truly Yours,

A Concerned Colleague

As she finishes, John says, his voice loud and forceful, "Okay, let's start with the letter. There's only one phrase worth considering in this piece of tripe...'un-retouched photographs.' Why even use a phrase like that unless they have in fact been re-touched? And I can absolutely assure you that they've been doctored."

Redding says quietly, "How can you be so certain, John?"

He hardly lets the priest finish. "Almost anyone these days with a little experience with PhotoShop can do this, Father. I mean, I've watched Marissa, for pete's sake, do incredible things manipulating her photographs, and she just picked it up herself, no classes, no training, just playing around with it."

There is silence in the room for a couple of seconds, probably, she thinks, because of Marissa's name. She glances briefly at John as he shuffles through the photos and forges ahead: "And beyond that, I can flat-out tell you I have never been at a Motel 6 in my life. Nor have I ever been to Prof. Lentini's apartment." He turns quickly to her. "I assume that's your place?"

She nods.

"You can barely see her face, and the guy could be anybody, a

140

delivery man, for godsake!" He takes the photo at the Bean and holds it up for the priests. "And this one. There's just one small problem with this one. I remember that day at the Bean. Do you, Professor?"

She nods again, trying to smile but wondering if it is appropriate.

"Yes," says John quickly. "It was a nice day, we had a nice chat, and, yes, she did reach out at one point and touch my hand, a perfectly innocent, perfectly natural expression of delightful human warmth. But as I say, there's just one problem here. You see the Professor's other hand?" Again he holds up the photo and this time taps it hard with an index finger. "That hand was offering the same kind of innocent touch to a hand that belonged to Hal Stroheim. Only our poor Hal is no longer in the picture. He's been PhotoShopped out."

She watches the priests glance at each other, and John is at it again. "As for this horrid letter full of god-awful, redundant purple prose..."

Redding interrupts. "John, I'm sure you realize that none of us here are looking for linguistic analysis."

"Well, I'm not at all sure what the hell you *are* looking for, Father. Surely both you and Fr. Hagen are smart enough to see this for what it is, part and parcel of the vicious and disgusting attack on this perfectly innocent woman, this brilliant scholar you personally invited to be our guest on this campus. It's been going on for weeks now, and as far as I can see, you've done absolutely nothing to put a stop to it."

Redding tries to interrupt again. "John..."

"No, you call us in here as if this were some dark tribunal or inquisition, Father, and you're going to hear what we have to say. First, let me fill you in on the latest of the plagues. As I learned a few minutes ago, Prof. Lentini's computer, the university owned desktop that Stan secured for her at the beginning of the term, suffered some kind of cyber attack in which all the chapter files of her book in progress were erased. Nothing but blank files."

The two priests again glance at each other, and Hagen says, "This is true, Lina?"

She says, "Unfortunately, yes. But in each empty file, there was one phrase placed, which said, 'Because you are an evil liar.' Fortunately I have back up files on another computer. But it was still terribly unnerving."

141

Hagen and Redding can say nothing before John continues: "And yesterday morning I had a visit from a reporter for the Sun, who had been sent anonymously a class paper that Hal purportedly wrote two years ago for one of my classes. The paper contained a good portion of a chapter from my new book on Lawrence, and the accusation was that I had plagiarized from Hal's paper. Of course I had the same material in an article I published five years ago in the American Literary Review. I showed a copy of that journal to the reporter, and that put an end to it. But here you have someone concocting this phony paper, and now with this bloody canard delivered to you, I have for some unfathomable reason, also become a target."

John has been speaking mostly to Redding, but Hagen responds with a silky tone. "John, surely you have some notion of who must be behind these accusations."

Glancing at her for a split-second, John addresses Hagen with force. "Surely, I do not, Father. Perhaps you do?" Almost daring the priest, she thinks, to speak Marissa's name.

Hagen looks at Redding, then shakes his head. "No, John, if you can't say, I don't know who can help us."

Redding says, "Lina, you've been very quiet. Please give us your thoughts."

She looks briefly at John, then to Hagen, her gaze finally resting on Redding. "Father, I have only one thing to say, and it is very simple. You will not mistake me. Even if these photographs were absolutely authentic, and even if every word of this accusation were absolutely true, it would be no one's business but our own."

Again Redding and Hagen look at each other, as if trying to communicate telepathically. And again John moves in aggressively on their silence. "Look, Fathers, I have one last thing to say. In my conversation yesterday with Ms. Becca Popp — she's the reporter for the Sun — it was clear that she's been digging into all these afflictions raining down on Prof. Lentini, and now on yours truly as well. She talked about writing a story for the Sun about all this. For the moment at least, I think I managed to dissuade her, but I can tell you, if I find one sliver of evidence that any of this shit..." He paused, as if to let the very smell of that word fill the air, and to tap the photos and the letter in his lap. "If any of it has left this room in any way, shape or form, I'll be back in touch with Ms. Popp in a flash to see what a little publicity might do."

This time Hagen locks eyes with John and in his smooth, slick way, says, "John, you may be taking a bit too seriously the Sun's anti-establishment pose. We've found the publisher to be consistently fair and responsible in cases like this."

John smiles for the first time since they entered this room. The edge to his voice is still aggressive but controlled. "Well, I've found Ms. Popp to be more resourceful and ambitious than you might expect. She's talking about starting a blog on her own website and selling her stuff to national outlets. And, Father, I would not put it past her."

Chapter 24

As if the walls have ears ready to feed their conversation back to Redding's office, he and Lina, each carrying one of the manila envelopes, say nothing as they walk down the echoing hallway. He's thinking about Hagen's response to his threat to go public.

"When you say 'see what a little publicity might do,' what exactly do you mean, John? I fail to see how that might improve matters for anyone, except perhaps the culprits. It certainly wouldn't do you any good, or Lina, who's really taken the brunt of this vendetta, or whatever it is. And it would have only negative consequences for the university. Wouldn't you agree, Lina?"

She looked squarely at Hagen. "Father, I have expressed myself on this. Fully."

Rather than respond, it seemed more effective to simply let his threat dangle there in front of these image-conscious clerics. Besides, he had caught a look from Lina unlike anything he had seen from her before. She was not pleased with this meeting, or with these men of the cloth, or perhaps even with him. But Redding used this silence to venture that it might be time to ask the police to investigate.

Was this a game of double-dare? A way to gauge the sincerity of his outraged response to the contents of these manila envelopes? If there really was nothing to the accusation in those photos and that absurd letter, the priests might figure that he and Lina would have no objection to the police. Yes, it was probably best to take Lina's tack and say nothing. But he couldn't resist calling their bluff.

"Sure, call in the cops, and see what they come up with."

This time Lina's glance was quick and curious. And now as they leave Markham and move into the chilly night air on the quad, he asks, "Are you okay, sweetheart?"

"Yes. And you?"

"I'm fine."

"You were very angry in there."

He stops and says, "Yes, I was, but you were great. You said absolutely nothing more than you had to. And, of course, you're right. It's nobody's business but our own."

"But you felt you needed to deny."

"Yes, I did. Are you unhappy with that?"

She stops a few paces ahead of him. "Unhappy? No, disappointed maybe, that we could not say simply nothing."

Sensing serious undercurrents, he gestures at a nearby bench. "Sweetheart, would you like to sit and talk for a little while?"

"No, we should not. I think there are too many eyes." And as they walk again toward the parking lot, she says, "So anger serves you well, John. You were very resourceful with them."

"But that disappoints you?"

"No, I found it impressive. It revealed a side of you that maybe I did not know. Very tough, very strong. But for me words are wasted when they are neither truthful nor necessary."

"Not necessary?" Again he stops walking, and she does as well. He feels the intensity rising in his voice but tries to keep it soft. "Lina, surely you understand that both of us could not simply say, 'It's none of your business.' To those priests it would have been, without question, a tacit admission of guilt. And then where would we be?"

"I do not know where we would be, but guilt in their eyes is not guilt in fact or truth. With what you said, you admitted their right to judge us."

He breathes deeply. "Darling, I can't believe you're saying these things. Yes, on some clean theoretical plane, where true and fair values hold sway, they have no right to judge. But this is their campus, and we're walking in the same muck they are, and so we have to protect ourselves. To me that means shredding what's in these envelopes in every way I can, and using every ploy I can think of to keep Hagen and Redding from acting on it."

They are walking again, almost to the Saab and the Focus. She says, "Acting how?"

"Look, I've been on this campus for fifteen years. In some ways it's lovely, in others it's small-minded and ugly. You don't really want to know what they might do."

She is silent for much too long, and his stomach is churning. Finally, she unlocks the Focus and says, "Darling, do not call me until I call you. I hate the way I feel now, and I need time to think

145

more carefully about what to do. Please tell me you won't call."

"Lina…"

"Please?"

He shakes his head and feels his mouth go dry. "Yes, I'll wait for your call."

* * *

It was 8:11 pm, according to the Saab's clock, when he turned the ignition. At 12:03 am his cell rings in the office over the garage. The phone says it's Lina. He waits through three, then four rings, nerve-wracked about whether it's good or bad that she's calling so soon…and so late. His gut says it's bad. He clears his throat and gets his voice under control. "Hi, sweetheart."

"Ah, darling, you are up? Can you talk?"

Her voice, warm and filled with deep concern, sounds nothing like the woman who left him bereft in the parking lot four hours ago. So much for his gut.

"Of course, darling. What's going on?"

"John, there was a gunshot here."

"A what?"

"A gunshot. Someone shot through my window and into my wall in the living room."

"My god, Lina, are you okay?"

"Yes, I am fine. I was in the bedroom trying to sleep, which I could not do. I just lay there, thinking about you."

"Yes, darling, all I've done is think about you all night. When did this happen?"

"Maybe 20 minutes ago. At first I was not sure what it was. I heard this crack and something crashed in the living room. I thought it sounded like a gun, but how could that be? I was afraid to go in there to look, but I crawled on my hands and knees and found a way, without raising my head, to turn on the wall switch that lights up the two lamps. Only one of them went on. The other was knocked over on the floor and broken. I could see the hole and a crack in the window, and up on the wall there was a spot. Whoever it was must have shot from the woods. But why do such a thing?"

He says, "I don't know, darling. I suppose it could have been a stray shot."

"Yes? Someone is shooting a gun in the woods at midnight?"

"Not likely."

146

"Then what?"

"Sweetheart, I'm coming over. I need to be with you. You should not be alone."

"No! Absolutely not. Whoever it is could still be out there. You come, and maybe they have something of more interest to shoot."

"I don't think so. Anyway, they probably left quickly, thinking the police would come."

"John, I absolutely do not want you here. I will call the police."

He pauses, then says, "Lina, darling, we've talked about this."

"Yes, this is different now."

He knows she's right but says, "No, we're still facing the same concerns. And this is just one more plague, one more effort to keep us apart. They're trying to scare us, especially you."

"Successfully, I would say."

"Please, Lina, think about this."

"I have, John. I am calling the police."

Chapter 25

Answering the knock on the gatehouse door, he thinks first about the key in the soil of his small potted cactus. Why did he leave it there for the past four weeks? Why not toss it a long time ago? Too late now, with Marlboro and Junior standing there in front of him. His nerves on edge, he can't immediately recall their real names, but the older one, with the eye that never looks at you, helps him out.

"Hey, Stanley, you remember us, right? Detectives Sam Marbow and James Hoekstra, Cedar Hill Police?"

He gathers himself. "Yes, Detectives. To what do I owe this pleasant surprise?"

Marlboro is looking more disheveled than ever, a large spot from soup or salad dressing on his yellow tie, and Junior, with a new haircut, appears even younger than the last time he saw them. Marlboro flicks the smoking butt of his cigarette into the bed of dead flowers next to the door. "Now, Stanley, you can cut that 'pleasant surprise' shit. You're no happier to see us than we are to see you."

Is it possible, after all this time, that these guys actually turned up somebody who saw him leaving Hal's building? Or is it something else? "First of all, it's Stanford. You really should get it right in that little notebook of yours. And second, you tell me what you came all the way out here to talk about, and I'll be happy to invite you in."

Marlboro tells Junior, "What a prince this guy is. Maybe you tell him how this works?"

Junior, with that hyper-sincere look: "Mr. Lyle, we just have a few questions for you, unrelated, we think, to the matter discussed previously. If we could sit down together for a few minutes, I'm sure it would be easier for all of us than if we have to bring you to the station."

So forget the key in the cactus pot. "Well, come in then. I'm all for easier."

He even offers them coffee from the pot he just made, and to his surprise they both accept. From the kitchen where he pours the coffee he sees both of them moving around the living room, scoping everything out, the purpose, he assumes, for their coming to him.

"So what can I do for you gentlemen?" He sits in his leather reading chair, and they finally stop prowling and use the couch.

Marlboro, mug in hand, says, "So, Stanford," getting it right finally, "you know a gal at the university named Professor Lentini."

"Lina? Yes, of course. I was assigned to help her with everything she needed during her stay here at St. Thomas. Started back in late August."

Marlboro's smile is almost a leer. "And how's that been going, would you say?"

"How's that been going? Fine, I guess. Lina, I think, has been pretty comfortable here. At least until recently."

"What happened recently?"

"Well, if you've spoken with her, you probably know that somebody's been harassing her, I guess you'd say, in different ways."

Marlboro says, "What kinda ways?"

"I probably don't know about all of them. Mostly just the ones she's asked me to help her track down and investigate. Of course, I'm not a pro like you guys, so I got basically nowhere. But somebody placed a phony personal ad in the Sun a while back, something saying she'd give guys a massage wearing only lingerie. And another one where somebody left dirty books all over campus with her name in them. Oh, and somebody sent out an email to everyone in the department saying she needed money for an abortion."

Junior says, "Yes, that was from the late Hal Stroheim's computer?"

"Right, so you have spoken with Lina about all this. It's really disgusting, because she's such a refined and brilliant person."

Marlboro again: "What about the one where somebody wrote an obscenity in all the johns, along with her phone number?"

"Right. Well, at least on that one I was able to go to just about every men's room on campus and erase it. Luckily whoever did it used a magic marker that was pretty easy to remove . And then there was the male stripper at George Rolande's retirement party. I don't know if Lina was the target, but I managed to throw a coat over the guy."

"Yeah, she mentioned that." Marlboro sounds less than interested. He turns his one good eye from Junior to him. "So, Stanford, you own a gun?"

"A gun?"

"Yeah, a gun. You know, bang, bang."

"Yeah, Jesus, no, I hate guns. I would never own a gun. Why the question?"

"Because someone with a .22 rifle shot into the professor's apartment last night around midnight."

"Holy Christ, is Lina okay?"

"She's fine. Just shaken up a bit when we talked to her this morning."

"So someone shot into her apartment? What room and from where?"

"The living room," says Marlboro. "And we don't know from where."

"With the living room it must have been from somebody hiding in the woods in front."

Marlboro pulls out his cigarettes. "Hey, that's pretty good. Maybe you'd like to help us with this case? Like tell us where were you last night around midnight?"

"Whoa, you think I had something to do with this?"

The lazy-eyed detective already has a cigarette dangling from his lips, a Bic in hand. "Hey, you don't mind if I smoke, do you?"

"Ah, normally, I don't allow smoking in here."

"Normally." He flicks the Bic, lights up and takes a drag. "You got an ashtray?"

"No, I don't. I told you I don't allow smoking."

"That's okay, I'm done with the coffee. I'll just use this." He holds up the mug.

"Detective, I asked you not to smoke."

"No, technically you did not." He takes another drag and blows smoke at the ceiling. "Anyways, you don't like it, call the cops."

Junior steps in. "He's joking, Mr. Lyle. But we would appreciate your help on this. So where were you last night around midnight?"

He ignores Marlboro and speaks only to Junior. "I was right here. Sitting in this chair reading. But if you're asking me about this, then Lina must think I'm involved, or might be. And I can't believe that.

150

She knows better, especially after all the help I've given her on this."

"You mean on the harassment," says Junior.

"Yes, exactly. She actually said she thought I shot through her window?"

"No," says Junior with a glance at Marlboro puffing away. "She said what you said about helping her in a number of ways. But when we asked Prof. Lentini if there was anyone who might want to cause her trouble, the only name she gave us was yours and said you had expressed a heavy interest in her romantically, even though she had tried to make it clear she wasn't up for it."

"A heavy interest. That's how she put it?"

Junior shifted on the couch and stared at the mug in his partner's fist. "I don't remember exactly how she put it, but it was something like that."

Marlboro took one more deep drag. "Look, pal, let's stop beating around the bushes and cut to chase. How about you let us look around the apartment here a little bit, and maybe that hot-shot little car you got? We find nothing and don't come bothering you again."

He gets out of his chair. "Look, officers, I have absolutely nothing to hide. You come back with a search warrant signed by a judge, and you can look at anything you want. But until then, I'm going to ask you to leave."

"So, sweetie, you really are slow on the uptake. I had given up on you calling. I told myself, 'Self, he said he loved your bod, but maybe he was jiving.'"

He's sitting with Marissa in a booth at Two. The last time he saw her in this place she was snapping photos with her phone. Her vodka and tonic half gone, she seems already buzzed at 1:30 in the afternoon. He didn't see her Volvo in the lot, so maybe she walked here, not wanting to risk more jail time as a two-time loser.

He shakes his head. "No, ma'am. About that I don't jive. I've just been really busy."

"Oh, right, John's a real slave-driver."

"No, it's not John. I'm just really deep into my Levi research, biographical stuff mostly. I hardly come up for air when I'm like this."

"My cute little mad scholar."

They're sitting side-by-side in the booth, and with the dark-haired, sloe-eyed little waitress standing there to take their order, Marissa reaches under the table to squeeze his thigh. He can't remember the last time he actually worked on the dissertation. It's been months. But a woman you've fucked recently invites you to lunch, you've got to come up with some reason why you haven't called. So why lunch...and in this very public place? No doubt she wouldn't mind tongues wagging. Get under her cheating husband's skin just a bit.

He orders an ice tea, and at her suggestion, they get the Greek Salad For Two.

She says, "It's full of aphrodisiacs, isn't it, dear?"

"Oh, for sure," says the waitress with a grin.

On the phone yesterday she said, "So how about Two for lunch? And then we'll see what we feel like doing."

He already knows what he'll feel like doing, and it doesn't include another boring time in the sack. Maybe he'll start calling her "Tross" again, only this time it's *his* neck. Amazing how little interest her body holds for him now, despite her showing major tit, with the plunging v-neck sweater and push-em-up bra. His dick stirred a bit when she grabbed his leg, but it's nice and docile again. Three days since the cops paid their call, but he's curious if his really was the only name Lina supplied. John told him once that Marissa used to hunt with her father and knows how to handle a rifle. So why not give her name to those dick-head detectives? Of course that would bring John into the picture.

He says, "So did you hear about what happened at Prof. Lentini's place?"

"You mean the gun shot?"

"Yeah, so it's all over the neighborhood?"

"No, Loverboy told me. Acted as if they had just run into each other in the cafeteria, and she told him about it. I'm sure he was fishing, trying to see how I'd react, thinking maybe I did it. So I said, 'Yeah, I thought I was a better shot. Next time I'll try the bedroom.'"

"Wow, what'd he say?"

"Nothing. His jaw dropped about to his shoetops. I said, 'Just kidding, Johnboy. But sometimes I wish I still had my trusty old Winchester.'"

"So you still think they're having an affair?"

"Does a bear shit in the woods?"

"I presume they have to do it somewhere."

"You got it, sweetie."

He says, "The cops think maybe I did it."

She draws her head back. "What, that you shot up her place?"

"Yep. The same two knuckle-head detectives who talked to me about Hal's death paid me a call the day after it happened. They were snooping around while they were talking to me, as if I'd be stupid enough to leave my .22 standing around in a corner someplace."

"You own a gun?"

"God, no. But I can't believe the professor gave them my name. I mean, that really pisses me off."

"So what did you do? Did you talk to them?"

"Yeah, I talked, until they finally came to the point and wanted to search the premises… and my car. And I said, 'That's it, fellas. You come back, you better have a search warrant.'"

So did they?"

"Come back? No way. I doubt they'd find a judge who'd sign one, even in this conservative little burg."

She puts her hand on his in clear view of the waitress, back now with their Salad For Two in the restaurant's signature joined double bowls that force you to sit side-by-side. When the girl is gone, she says, "Still, sweetie, you better be sure you've got that .22 buried somewhere."

"I told you I don't own one."

"Sweetie, I can always tell when you're fibbing."

He gives her a thin smile. "Yeah, well, you thought I was fibbing about loving your bod. And you missed on that one."

Coquettish now, she runs her fingers through his hair. Something he can't stand. She says, "So you really like me?"

He takes her hand and brings it down to her lap, then gives her a little feel between the legs. "Of course. What's not to like?"

"Oh, good answer."

"So how are things at home?"

"You mean with John? Terrible. He tells me I'm a crazy drunk. And I say, 'How can you fuck that slutty wop?' You still haven't seen anything between them?"

"I told you, I'm too busy to see much of anything."

"But, sweetie, all work and no play make Stan a very dull boy.

153

How about we finish this and you take me back to your place and we play?"

"Love to, Mrs. Martens, but there's a department meeting this afternoon I can't miss."

She drains the last of her vodka. "In that case, I need another drink."

Chapter 26

Writing, with its focus, concentration and willpower, the one thing that has kept her centered, not scattered, vulnerable and fraught with useless consideration, is now a problem. Ever since the gunshot.

The first, most obvious question is where to work. Unlike others who seem totally oblivious to their surroundings, or somehow find it easier with humanity bustling about to catch the tide and float into that right place in themselves, she has never been good at doing it in public. The spots they seem to love—a coffee shop, an outdoor café, or, on these cold mid-November days, the busy Student Center—are out of the question for her.

Even with the pierced windowpane promptly replaced and new locks on the door, the apartment does not work. Even with the blinds drawn to deflect daylight or to shield the interior from the watchful night, she cannot seem to find the right place in her mind. She needs shades or shutters inside her own head. Ironically, she has been sleeping well, often without dreams, seemingly comfortable only with darkness inside and out. Probably because by day's end, she usually feels totally exhausted with the fruitless effort to find the flow.

The only place she really tries these days is this office in Markham. But even with almost nothing to distract her here, she still finds ways to head in wrong directions. Yesterday she jotted a page of notes on *Exit Ghost*, sitting here at her desk. She felt ready to start in earnest, and then her eye wandered to the old blue spiral notebook shelved just above her head. Before she knew it she was reading through all of her Michigan entries, thinking about what Stan might have thought of this or that as he sat right here in her chair, leafing through her private musings. And when she was finished with those recent posts, she turned back to the things she wrote last spring, mostly about Paolo, that now feel like ancient history.

The fact is it matters not what she tells herself about that gunshot. So, as John said, it was clearly not meant to harm, only to frighten and warn. So the idea was to exert a kind of control over her--something she finds especially odious and enraging. But, yes, it is obviously succeeding in doing exactly what the shooter intended.

Frighten, warn, control. In short, keep her apart from John. Who, at this very moment, might well be down in his office near the building's front door. Over the past four or five days, since the shooting, she has spoken to him only on the phone. First, immediately after the shooting, again the next day after she met with the police, and the third time after she saw them again. Each time he wanted to come to her, and each time she said no. She has not seen him at all, not in the neighborhood, at their favorite grocery, or even in the halls here in Markham. Except for the short distance between campus parking and her office here, she no longer walks anywhere, not to the store and certainly not through the woods. She has become an American, driving everywhere, even though she knows a walk would do her good.

How about a short walk right now? Do the little trek down to his office on the chance he is there waiting for her. She aches to see him, to fold herself in his arms, to feel the touch of his lips on hers, to see those dark blue eyes feast on her, to hear him tell her she is beautiful and brilliant beyond compare, to catch the quick, vital wit, so often comic, in his talk about anything at all, to simply be with him, saying nothing, doing nothing, just simply being with him. But that is just the point. Proximity to her only puts him at greater risk.

Of course, she said nothing about John or Marissa to either of the two sets of police officers. First, the two uniformed youngsters, male and female, who seemed almost like earnest newlyweds, careful, considerate and polite with her and with each other. Then the detectives she saw twice, before and after they "dropped in on" Stan. The older one with the world-weary air, letting her know with a hint or two that he suspected she wasn't giving them all the facts. The younger one said little in either meeting but called later to give her "an update on the investigation." He surprised her with the news that he had spoken briefly "with your colleague Prof. John Martens about the attack on your computer." Just before the phone rang, John's email arrived, forwarding the report from Marcus Bolger in Computer Science.

"Bottom line, there's trace evidence that someone hacked into the computer, but when they were finished messing around, they got out pretty clean. Given that this is a university-owned desktop and was previously in service with someone else, I can't rule out the trace stuff is from back then, or that somebody simply got on this computer and did their dirty work directly."

Young Detective Hoekstra already knew about the report, having also spoken with Bolger, "who works as a consultant with our cyber crimes unit." Hoekstra said he and Detective Marbow had interviewed a number of her colleagues in the department, including Fr. Redding. All of them described her as "a lovely person who has done nothing to merit all this harassment."

A half-dozen neighbors were also interviewed. Two reported hearing what they thought was a gunshot. No one saw a thing. There was no further reference to John, no mention at all of his wife. The young detective actually apologized for not being able to put her "mind at rest," assuring her that they would continue to "follow up on any and all leads, and that certainly includes anything further you can give us on Mr. Lyle."

In her second meeting with the detectives, the day after their visit with Stan, Marbow pressed her for something more on Stan, some reason to connect him with the shooting and convincing enough to persuade a judge to give them a search warrant. But there was nothing more she could give, and she also sensed they knew as well as she that Stan would have taken pains by now to get rid of anything incriminating. Still, they told her they had "put him on notice that we'll keep an eye on him in ways he cannot imagine."

The fact is, for a week now there has not been a new plague. More than ever Stan seems the likely culprit, and perhaps he has been frightened off. And then a knock on the office door comes as if on cue, and somehow, as she swings it open, she guesses Stan will be there.

"Lina," he says, "I'm so glad you're here! I've been so concerned about you. I mean I heard about the gunshot, and that was, what? Several days ago."

"A week."

"Yeah, I've been knocking on this door and leaving phone messages. But I guess I've just been missing you. I'm sure it was scary as hell, and you've been holing up someplace safe."

The police had told her not to have any contact with him. But in that time she has conducted a seminar and given two lectures on le Carre and DeLillo, and to her great surprise he was nowhere to be seen. She moves back to her chair and says, "Would you like to come in?"

"Sure."

When he begins to close the door, she says, "You can just leave it open."

He says, "Oh, sure," and takes the other chair in the office.

She says, "I understand the police talked to you."

"They did."

"I am sorry about that, Stan. I did not mean for them to make trouble for you."

"Oh, it wasn't trouble. I was okay with it. Just a little surprised. That's all."

She stares at him as he moves to get comfortable in the chair. "Yes, of course they asked if I suspected anyone of harassing me, and I said no. So they wanted a list of friends or close acquaintances, and I gave them nearly everyone in the department, including Fr. Redding and a few others I've gotten to know a little, like Fr. Hagen. They asked if I could imagine anyone of these people doing these kinds of things, and I said no. And finally they wondered if there was anyone I had mentioned whom I had ever felt uncomfortable with. I said, 'Uncomfortable how?' And they said, 'Uncomfortable in any way.' And so, frankly, I thought of a couple of moments with you which were definitely awkward and uncomfortable."

"Really, like what?"

"Like the time I found you sitting here going through my personal notebook."

He looked away. "Oh, right, okay."

"And then that night you came over for dinner? And we talked about that 'Loopt' program you put on my phone."

"But, Lina, I told you, that was just an oversight on my part."

"Yes, but the conversation was uncomfortable, and that was what they were asking for."

"Yeah, I guess. But those detectives told me you said I had some kind of big crush on you. I think they called it 'a heavy romantic interest.' And that you rejected me, which, I guess, they figured would be some kind of motive for me to do all those horrible things

158

to you"

His sharp, narrow face has that terribly earnest look etched with a hint of hurt. So deal with this head-on…or attempt to slide around it? "Stan, I certainly never used that language. When your name came up, those detectives recalled they had talked to you about Hal's death. Frankly, they seemed more interested in you because of that. I also told them how helpful you have been, and how you have tried to find who is behind all the harassment."

He smiled finally. "Yes, they did say that. And I want to emphasize again, Lina, that there's nothing more important to me than to please and help you in any way that I can."

"Look, Stan, as I said before, I greatly appreciate your help. But I do not feel good about my own behavior in this. I blame myself for not making it clear from the start that the connection between us could not be personal or romantic. It was unprofessional of me."

The smile again but now with a hopeful, confident air. "Please, Lina, you shouldn't blame yourself. We're all human. We make rules for ourselves, and sometimes we break them. Probably because we never should have made them in the first place. Maybe there's a way for us to start over from the beginning and get it right this time."

The man is so wrong-headed she cannot think of what to say. She begins to shake her head but finally gets to her feet. "Stan, sorry, I am late for an appointment."

Minutes later, glancing back to be sure he has not followed, she stops at John's door. She listens, then knocks and waits for a response that does not come.

Behind the wheel of the Focus in the parking lot, she is about to pull out of the space, when she says aloud, "*Basta.*" Enough. She grabs her mobile and presses her speed-dial number for John, just as she sees the Saab nosing under the lifted gate and into the lot. Through two rings she watches his car moving in the first row, John with the phone to his ear.

His voice is urgent. "Sweetheart, where are you? I need to see you now."

"What's wrong, darling?"

"Nothing, except I haven't seen you in a week. Enough of this. We're letting the assholes win."

"*Si, basta.*"

"So where are you?"

159

"Right here. My car is in the second row." She sees him find her and wave.

"Don't move. I'll be right there." And within seconds he is, though he is still using his phone as he reaches her passenger door. "I've got great news. I've found us a place to be together. Completely private and safe."

"How can that be?"

"It's true." He stops to open the door and slide in next to her. Their kiss is warm, deep, eager and filled with enormous relief. She moans as his mouth leaves hers only to move to her cheek, her eyes and back to her mouth again. She wants to see those sad blue eyes turn bright as they consume her. Finally, he says, "Sweetheart, I've missed you so much."

He has almost taken her breath. "Yes, and I you."

He nods and says, "Six weeks. Nobody will ever find us or know what we're doing."

Glancing for a second past his face, she finds Stan at the edge of the lot, maybe 40 meters away, staring straight at them. She says, "Don't move, John. Stan is watching from the quad."

"So, okay, no problem. Call me tonight, and we'll arrange to visit our new haven."

She smiles and nods. "Who gave us this gift?"

"George Rolande."

"Ah, his closet."

* * *

The house is just as he described, on a tree-less rise, and visible from at least a half-mile away on this empty stretch of rural highway. A small, plain ranch with an attached garage, neatly kept but in no way distinctive, 12 miles from Cedar Hill. Set in such a wide-open space, there is nowhere to hide an observing eye, no way to monitor, unseen, any comings and goings.

"It's perfect," John said that night on the phone. "I mean, he lives out there for a reason. We just pull in the garage, close the door and no one knows we're there."

On his first try at retirement bliss, George Rolande is off on a "research and writing vacation" on Martinique, renting a place on the beach with his friend Louis, a young man getting his Ph.D. at Michigan State. With no classes in this final term and finished with his role as advisor on Sister Martha Cox's dissertation, it's off to the

Caribbean and the favorite isle of two French poets, where he'll work on his book analyzing the influence of island life on their work. Could John perhaps "water the plants just once a week and keep an eye on things?"

No problem at all. Out here three days ago, John confirmed it as their ideal spot. With so much open highway, no one could follow unseen, and with the device FedEx just delivered from spygadget.com, he has made sure the Saab is free of any homing device.

Naked now in George's queen-size four poster, she gently kisses John's eyelids and calls the place, "*La casa d'amore vietato.*" The house of forbidden love. There is a new excitement to their lovemaking, if that is possible. An almost frantic intensity, a kind of desperate edge she ascribes to their long time apart and her feeling during those barren days that this might never happen again. So the pleasure flows deep with a strong sense of gratitude for this new chance, for the joyful glow of a love that more than ever feels unique.

Later as they dress, a ritual, no matter the glow, always tinged with sadness, John says, "So this coming Thursday is Thanksgiving."

"And we will have much to be grateful for."

They are silent until she goes to the window, puts her fingers between the narrow blinds and looks up the road to Cedar Hill. Nothing moves, no one in sight. "So does Stan or Marissa know that George is away?"

"They both probably know. Why?"

"An obsessed person sometimes makes uncanny guesses."

"True enough, but I don't think it matters here."

"I suppose," she says but still feels the prick of unease.

Only late the following morning, Sunday just before 9, does her fear become clear. Before browsing through her newspaper sites, her first check for email shows two new ones. The usual from John sent late last night: "*Buona notte. Ti amo.*" The other says it was sent at 2:34 am from her own address to what looks like everyone in the department, and she knows immediately it means trouble. The subject line is jaunty: "Come to my new MySpace page!" The message is simple: "Please visit my new MySpace page by clicking on the link below. Enjoy!"

The link is lina362436@myspace.com, and she braces for what she will find before she clicks it. Music blares after a few seconds, Dean

Martin's sappy version of "O Sole Mio," The wallpaper is pink on blue, entwined hearts alternating with the male and female symbols, the arrow touching the plus sign. The photos include the same three they found in the manila envelopes, with captions like, "My hot, MARRIED, stud John about to be invited into my boudoir," and "Leaving our favorite little love nest at the Motel 6." There is also her head on someone else's voluptuous bikinied body, and a close up of her smiling face, with a dialogue balloon that says, "Just swallowed John's cum. Delicious!"

Two blocks of printed information add to the page. One is headlined, "What's important about me, Prof. Lina Lentini?"

> The only thing important about me is that I love to fuck my hot, MARRIED, stud, John Martens. We're both professors at St. Thomas University in Cedar Hill, Michigan, and we just hope that everybody on campus is as happy for us as we are when we fuck!

The other block lists "My Favorites."

> Color: The blue of John's studdly eyes!
>
> Food: John's delicious cum!
>
> Pet: John's fantastic Hot Dog!
>
> Body Part: I'll let you guess what part of John I love to suck!
>
> Position: Doggie style!
>
> Book: 'The Joy of Anal Sex.
>
> Activity: Fucking the brains out of my hot, MARRIED, stud, Prof. John Martens.
>
> Gesture: My gift to department head, Fr. Robert Redding—a subscription to Twat Magazine (p.s.: He loved it!).

And near the bottom of the page is a scanned copy of the Sun personal: "Hi, I'm Lina. I'll model lingerie and give you a massage in the privacy of your own home"...complete with her office number. Also a photo of a men's room partition with the scrawl, "Lina loves to suck cock" and her mobile number. And last but not least, an embedded video with the intro line: "In case you missed it on YouTube, here's my favorite video, 'Stripper Does His Thing For Nuns.'"

Chapter 27

Early Monday afternoon he waits in his Markham office for Stan's arrival and Lina's call. This morning he emailed Stan: "It's been awhile since we talked about how the work is coming. How about my office this afternoon, about 2?"

He looks at the reply on his screen: "Sure, 2's good. See you then."

His inbox is jammed with 142 messages since yesterday morning. It feels like a week, but he's been dealing with debris from the MySpace bomb for only a day and a half. It started with voice mail and email he did not pick up until nearly 10 Sunday morning. He slept late, having worked in his garage office until after 2 am, closing down his computer just before the bomb arrived. Turning off the phones, he was quickly asleep in the guest bedroom. Over the past 6 weeks, with things tense and unpleasant in the house, the thought of being in the same bed with Mar has been abhorrent. They are keeping very different hours, he told her, and it was better this way for both of them. She's usually passed out on the sofa or in their bedroom by 10, and he's always working well after midnight. Occasionally at 2 in the morning she might barge into the guest room and wake him to insist she join him in its double bed. Knowing at that point he'll never get back to sleep otherwise, he usually leads her back to the king in their bedroom. At least there he'll have enough bed to make space for himself.

None of this is pleasant, but it's a vast improvement over a year ago, before she spent those two months in the county jail. That stint somehow put a damper on the drunken rages. She's now much less the nasty, violent drunk, sufficiently convincing with a kitchen knife for him to barricade himself in the guest room by inching the dresser in front of the door.

After making coffee, he turned on his cell and found three messages waiting. Lina said only, "John, check your email." Fathers Hagen and Redding offered sympathy and suggested another

164

meeting. When he finally got to his computer and saw the MySpace page, he quickly composed a "reply all" response: "Needless to say to all of you who know me and Prof. Lentini, the referenced MySpace page is a malicious fraud. It is filled with lies, doctored photos and the appalling fantasies of a diseased mind. There is nothing in it akin to the truth."

Lina had already sent her simple response to everyone on the recipient list: "I have never been, nor ever will be a member of MySpace."

Now that he thinks about it, their emails mirror their response to the priests that night in Redding's office.

It didn't help that both of them got to their email late yesterday morning. Incorporating all the previous plagues, except that first box full of religious screeds and souvenirs, whoever was responsible for this vicious attack made sure to send it not only to the entire department but also to Hagen and, most effectively, to about a dozen students taking department courses. At least a few of these young people could apparently not resist the chance to exercise their exhilarating web-world freedom by sending the whole disgusting thing viral. By the time he first opened the bomb, he already had 34 new emails, several from people he didn't know, whose messages ranged from "YOU WILL BURN IN HELL!" to "You dog!" to "Hey, you sound juicy. Let's hook up."

His call to Lina, right after he hit send on his "Needless to say" response, went straight to voice mail. When she called back it was mid-afternoon, and she was on her Nokia. She would no longer use the Sprint phone Stan had set up, or her stthomas.edu email account. When he said that was probably for the best, she said, "No, John, there is no alternative."

Once she sent her one-line response, she emailed MySpace and telephoned until she finally reached someone there on a Sunday morning who promised to see that the page would be "taken down asap." That turned out to be about 2:30 Sunday afternoon, and by then the damage had spread so widely that she had one message from Switzerland and another from India.

She sounded reasonably calm and composed on the phone, but when he suggested a visit to George's that afternoon, she said, "No, darling, I could not deal with that today." How about tomorrow? She said, "John, I have a lot to think about. Let me call you tomorrow."

When he hung up, he felt she was deciding whether to ever see him again. When he called again late that evening, both the Nokia and her apartment phone were off.

To calm his nerves now waiting for her call, he counts up the messages he's received from people he doesn't know. Are their lives so empty they actually get satisfaction from commenting on his? It's up to 67. Astonishing, really. There are also several from friends and colleagues, offering support. One from his workout and running buddy, Bob Bourne: "Hang in there, guy. Don't let the assholes get you down." Another from George Rolande, who's apparently online down on Martinique: "John, this is appalling. I feel so terrible for you and for Lina." But a few, like the one from Sister Gertrude ("John, you are in my prayers."), can certainly be read as ambiguous: Either "You're headed for Hell." Or "Your sad plight deserves God's attention." Or both. Actually, the first to arrive, he notes, at 6:37 am, Sunday, came from Stan and was sent to both of them: "John and Lina, I can't even imagine someone pulling a disgusting stunt like this. You both have my sympathy and support. Best regards, Stan."

When the knock on the door finally comes, Stan enters, not with his usual hip, casual energy, but with a quiet step, closing the door behind softly and moving to the spare chair almost as if he's visiting a patient. "John, how you holding up? This must be such an ordeal for you. And for Lina. Have you talked to her? How's she doing?"

"She's doing fine, thanks, and so am I. This business has gone beyond the beyond. The MySpace thing is so absurd, nobody believes a word of it. Everybody's been great, very supportive." He glances at the computer screen with all those messages. "By the way, thanks for the email yesterday. I think it was the first one I opened."

"Oh, no problem. Glad it helped."

He eyes the guy's face, looking earnest, thoughtful. "Yeah, well, there's been an avalanche ever since, and all of them positive. But tell me something, Stan, just man to man. I mean, yeah, I'm your advisor...and your friend, but just between you and me — honesty is the best policy, cross your heart and hope to die and all that stuff — just tell me, are you the one who perpetrated all this shit?"

Even with the long wind-up before the pitch, Stan seems caught by surprise. His eyes widen, his head dips for a second, then comes up with a strange smile. "You mean..."

John jumps him again. "I mean, yeah, are you the one behind the shit storm that's been ripping through our lives for the past month? Just fucking tell me."

Stan is shaking his head woefully. "I can't believe you." Then he locks John's eyes and says, "No fucking way am I responsible for any of it."

John leans into the younger man's stare. "That's funny, because I can't think of anybody else who could or would do this shit."

Stan swallows and says, "Have you considered your wife? In my experience when she thinks she has a motive, she just might do anything."

"Like sleep with you?"

Again the woeful shaking of his head.

John says, "No, Mar can have her moments, but there's no bloody way she could have pulled off most of these asinine, infantile stunts."

Stan's gaze flicks away for a fraction of a second, then comes back. "John, you are just dead wrong on this."

Was there menace in that almost imperceptible pause between "dead" and "wrong"? His cell goes off on the desk. He looks away from Stan and picks it up. It's Lina.

"Hi, I'm with a student. Can I call you right back?"

"John, it is important that I talk with you." Something in her voice is new.

"I understand. I'll call you right back."

He closes the line and says, "I'm sorry to leave this here. A little domestic crisis that can't wait. I'll drop you a line about when we can pick this up."

Getting to his feet, Stan says, "Hope everything's okay."

"It will be." John nods him toward the door and adds, "Thanks."

Stan walks out without a word.

Alone again with the door closed, he wonders if he should return Lina's call from here. Stan could be lurking right outside to overhear. Slipping on his old brown leather jacket, he takes the phone and heads outside to the quad. Bundled-up figures move with purpose under a low, dark gray sky. The first real snowfall is predicted for tonight; they say up to 3 inches. Stan is nowhere in sight, but, chest pounding and stomach churning, John waits until the path through the woods to call.

She says, "John, I was waiting." Less a rebuke than an urgent statement of fact.

He's still trying to slow down his heart. "I had Stan in my office."

"I thought it might be him."

"Sweetheart, are you okay?"

"I am okay…and not okay."

"What's going on?"

"I spoke with Marissa earlier today."

"She called you?"

"No, I stopped at your house. Almost on impulse. I had to pass your street, and I thought, if she is home, this is meant to be. If not, it is not. Well, she answered the door, and I invited myself in. She sat on the living room sofa, and I sat in what I think is your chair."

"Leather with big arms."

"Yes. So I told her, 'I want you to know I leave for Italy today, and I will not return.'"

"Lina! What are you doing?"

"Please, John, let me finish. I am already a hundred miles away, parked by the side of the highway, because I thought I would crash if I heard your voice. Soon I will be thousands of miles away, and I must say some things to you now, darling."

He says nothing, biting his lower lip until the pain is sharp. He whips around to make sure no one is following. Finally: "So, go ahead. Talk to me."

He tries to picture her in the Focus, pulled off on the shoulder on I-94, probably not far from Metro Airport. Could he get there soon enough, before she's beyond security and irretrievable? Not likely.

"So I told her I was leaving and not returning. And she said, 'Okay, fine. What are you doing here?' I said, ' I want you to answer a question, and I want to tell you something.'"

"She said, 'Let's start with the question.'"

"So, I said, 'Please, Marissa, give me the truth. Are you responsible for all the plagues…the accusations, the harassment, the MySpace page yesterday?'"

He stops on the woodchip path. "What did she say?"

"She asked me if I was really leaving for Italy, and I said at 5:30 this afternoon. I offered to show her my reservation, and she said, 'No, your word is good.' And then she winked, John, she actually winked, and said, 'In that case, I was fully responsible. It was all my doing.'"

Again he looks behind him on the path. "Did you believe her. Was she drinking? Could you tell? I mean, did she sound convincing?"

"Darling, I have no answers. After all this, I have no idea. I just looked at her and said, 'Marissa, your husband is a beautiful and extraordinary man. He's a man of remarkable intellect and heart. He has strength and sensitivity and, whether you know it or not, he is devoted to you. My only hope for you is that you take good and healthy care of yourself. Because that is the best gift you can give him.'"

"Lina…"

"And then I left, and she was standing at the door watching as I drove away."

"Sweetheart, please let me see you at least before you go." A glance at his black Timex says it's 2:32. "I can be there in less than an hour and a half. Ninety minutes at the most, and I could see you at least for awhile before you board."

There's a pause. Is she actually considering it? "No, darling, this is better. To see you would break my heart. And I might not leave."

"Good."

"No, I must leave. And you must understand. I know you understand. This has become completely impossible. It would be foolish and dangerous to continue. And I simply cannot."

"Lina, please…"

"Darling, tell me you understand."

He looks around at the barren trees, and through them now he can glimpse what used to be her apartment. Finally, he says, "Yes, I understand."

"Good. Then we will not say goodbye. Someday…who can know?"

"*Ti amo*, sweetheart."

"*Ti amo*, darling."

And she is gone.

Chapter 28

When the door chime rings she is sitting with her laptop, gazing at the frigid-looking patio beyond the glass doors, snow flurries whirling about the furled umbrella. Mid-December, more than three weeks now, and she finally feels something close to normal.

A minute ago she buzzed in the fellow at the door after hearing him through the intercom's static say, "*Cosegna.*" A delivery, no doubt the hand-carried invitation to Lilli's opening tonight. Of course, if she goes to the gallery, she will not really need the card. Her good friend Lilli is simply trying everything to insure that Lina will come.

Their encounter yesterday was up near San Luca, where Lina had taken one of her long, therapeutic walks. Behind the wheel of her old black Jag, Lilli called to her, then insisted she ride the 3 kilometers with her back to Via San Vitale. Feeling the ache in her thighs after the long climb to the ancient church nearly 1000 feet above the city, Lina accepted. In her black pixie-cut and long leather coat, Lilli had been visiting the studio of the young woman she was showing tomorrow. Having picked up three new paintings to add to the collection, she drove slowly down narrow streets lined with colonnades, and when she asked about the stay in the states, Lina finally let the whole sorry mess come rolling out. Lilli sounded concerned, dropped her near the apartment and said they had "some major catching up to do." She promised the hand-delivered invitation, saying, "I will be hurt beyond words if you don't show."

But now with the door open, the fellow is standing there in a DHL uniform, and one glance at the box he holds tells her it contains the books from what used to be her office in the Markham Building. She signs the slip and asks him to put the box on the kitchen counter.

Who had found this box in her office closet, repacked the books from her shelves, sealed it up and mailed it to her? Probably Stan. From her cluttered utility drawer she pulls a yellow-handled razor knife and slides the blade open. A few quick slits of packaging tape and there are the books. No note. On top is John's on Lawrence. She picks it up gently and opens the front cover. "To Lina from John, with gratitude and affection."

Smiling but feeling as if she has been struck in the stomach, she moves to the sofa, the book to her chest. For the first week back in Bologna she had seen almost no one. This had not been her plan. In fact, on the plane from Detroit she had tried combating depression by thinking about how wonderful it would soon be to surround herself again with old friends and valued colleagues. That was just before she dozed off for a two-hour nap—rare for her on a plane. Sleep was the result of insomnia the night before—also rare for her—as well as a passive defense against the fat American couple sitting next to her in the middle row. Though closed off in her grief, she could tell they were anxious to make their first Italian friend.

"Charles and Margaret Treblehorn, Canton, Ohio," he announced with a hard handshake.

"Marge and Charlie," corrected the woman, also shaking her hand. Yes, this was their first trip to Italy, and even though Bologna was not on their "jam-packed" itinerary, they insisted she give them some tips on what to see there.

How to end this quickly? She tried banality. "Well, certainly do not miss the food."

"Oh," said Marge, actually patting her ample belly, "that won't be a problem."

"And then you must climb to the very top of the Asinelli Tower." This was a bit unkind to a pair who looked unlikely to make it even half-way up, but, forced to interact when all she wanted was to vegetate, she was feeling misanthropic. "It's almost 100 meters tall."

"Wow," exclaimed Charlie, "the length of one of our American football fields."

"Yes, 498 steps to the top, but the view is incomparable. When it was built in the eleven hundreds, there were 180 towers like it in the city. Bologna was like a medieval Manhattan."

"My," said Marge, "why so many?"

"Wealthy and important families built them for protection and prestige."

"Like the Trump Tower," said Charlie. "And are they still there?"

"No, most of them were taken down or they fell down. Both the

Asinelli and the smaller one next to it, the Garisenda, lean a bit."

"Well," said Charlie with a cordial grin, "I guess those old Italians had a problem with their plumb bobs! You know, with Pisa, and now these two."

It was not until their tasteless dinners were consumed that she was able to turn away and fall asleep. And when she woke with the cabin dark over the mid-Atlantic, the Treblehorns were, mercifully, both out cold. So now she could reach into the seatback and pull out McEwan's new one, *On Chesil Beach,* a love story, or, as she already knew, a love *fails* story. But, no, it was not what she needed or wanted now. Not with the ache in her chest.

Really, from early in all that passionate talk and brilliant sex, she had known that what she had with John could somehow change her life. It was the wisdom in his hands, his heart's intuition, the grace of his mind, and it was none of these. The deepest connection was always a mystery, simple and joyful and awful. She had not loved anyone this way before.

The rest of the flight she spent at the mercy of memories. Those calm, remarkable insights enthralling his students, that surprising rage at their meeting with the priests, the deep kindness in his voice when he spoke of poor Hal, his furious "Jesus F Christ!" at the stripper's dance, the way those sad, compelling eyes so often grabbed her, that homely frown when they talked of his terrible wife, and, yes, the superb, energizing way he touched her grateful body.

That last Sunday morning in Cedar Hill she had wakened feeling anxious. Due for her period, she felt the lingering effect of an annoying dream that kept waking her and starting again every time she closed her eyes. Something about living in a strange house where she could not find any of her things — books, clothes, computer. Even after her coffee, she felt unsettled, hardly what she expected after their beautiful afternoon in George's bed the day before. But as her eye began moving down the MySpace page, every word and image told her this was the end. As soon as possible she would leave St. Thomas and return to Bologna.

Still the brave certainty in his voicemail gave her reason to reconsider and gauge regrets. Should they at least meet and talk this through? But later when they actually spoke on the phone, she could hear the anger and the pain beneath what now seemed like sad bravado, and she knew her initial urge was the one to follow. Unable to say the words that it was over, she rattled on about the messages received from perfect strangers overseas.

"Hey, Lina, you sound great," wrote Elizabeth in Mumbai, "just what sexually repressed St. Thomas needs a huge dose of. You go, girl!"

And from Martin in Geneva: "Professor, no doubt this is some kind of horrid prank, but surely you realize you need to leave that hotbed of extreme right-wing, arch-conservative Republican hypocrisy asap."

As she turned off her mobile and closed the email account, she knew if they saw each other again or even spoke on the phone, they would only risk more serious damage. Methodically she moved down her hastily scribbled to-do list, booking her flight online with Northwest (a stop in Amsterdam, then on to Milano), and packing to bring with her only essentials in the smaller suitcase and the carry-on. In the morning, after her unplanned stop at John's house, she parked on a street on the edge of Cedar Hill and called Redding. Elena said he was in Chicago. His brother was in "the final stage."

"Elena, please let him know I decided to return to Italy. I leave today."

"Oh, yes, I'll tell him."

And that was it, except for the painful exchange with John on the shoulder of I-94 as she watched planes climb and descend in the sky nearby.

When she walked into this apartment late the next afternoon, and turned on her computer, two long emails from John were already waiting. They contained exquisitely beautiful expressions of love, support and gratitude, and more than once over the next few days there were tears in her eyes as she wrote back about her own feelings. In those notes back and forth, lengthy and intense, each of them went on about what they might have done differently once the plagues started, about the amusing, absurd, or disgusting reactions that filled their inboxes, about whether to believe Stan's denial or Marissa's admission of guilt. But after awhile it was clear to her—and, she sensed, to John as well—that all this correspondence, all this staying in such close and constant touch, was only making their pain and anguish worse. Yes, words, choosing and sharing them, were deeply, vitally important. And one could think that a passionate literary connection might offer a measure of succor and satisfaction. But she was living with a kind of low-grade anxiety and sleeping only fitfully at night, and when John briefly mentioned Heloise and Abalard, she felt they were both in danger of losing perspective.

On her fourth day back, in another long message she told John, "Darling, I don't know how much more of this I can take." And she finally asked if he would agree "to put this enthralling but impossible experience on pause for a while, at least until after the New Year, to give us both a chance to pull ourselves together." When he responded with only a mild complaint and no real alternative, she was certain it was the right thing to do.

Even so, she was still spending most of her time in the apartment, walking out only for food and other staples. She watched much more TV than normal, telling herself she was just catching up on local happenings. She opened three months worth of mail, mostly overdue bills to be paid. Perusing the periodicals and journals that had piled up, she often lost herself in them, reading in-depth pieces in four different languages, something she had not done since the summer. And she answered a letter from Giuliana, her editor at the publisher waiting for her new manuscript. One of the few people she knew who still eschewed email, Giuliana did not know of the American sojourn. Lina wrote back only that the book had been going reasonably well.

It was the next day in the Piazza Aldrovandi that she acted on impulse and entered her beauty salon. Her usual girl Martina was off, but she sat with Sophia, pointed to an advertising photo in a magazine and asked if she could have that look.

"*Si, certamente!*" said the girl. And in 40 minutes it was done. Did she like the short, chic, shag? She would have to get used to it, but most importantly, it was different.

After a week came the delivery of her large suitcase full of the clothing she had left behind in Cedar Hill. She wondered if Stan had been recruited to take care of the shipping, and if he had first opened and stuck his nose in the bag. Perhaps literally, sniffing her underwear? She would not put it past him.

There were clothes now to wash and have dry-cleaned, closets to re-arrange, swapping summer for winter ware. She took care of several household fix-it chores put off before the Michigan trip—a dripping faucet, a wall that needed painting, a door squeak to quiet. Not until a few days into her second week home did she begin to feel like a hermit.

She had encountered only a few friends on her forays out of the apartment during those first several days. On a trip to the bakery, near the base of the towering Asinelli, the one she had urged on the Treblehorns, she ran into old Prof. D'Antoni, a favorite from her graduate school days. He was retired now, and though he lived in the neighborhood, Lina did not often see him. In their brief chat, there was no mention of her recent stay in the U.S. The same two days later with Wilfrina Po, who was just leaving a café where Lina was headed for an espresso. They kissed and hugged and promised to meet soon and trade updates. She had so much to tell Lina about her six months in Chechnya doing research for her book on the plight of Muslim women.

No, she had finally found relief, not with friends, but in simply walking alone on the porticoed streets of her beloved Bologna. Just walking, moving with a steady, deliberate pace, seemed to help. Movement, she knew, was a recommended way of dealing with depression. But add to that the brisk, cold air of early December; the focused vitality of her fellow Bolognesi, all ages, shapes and sizes filling the street markets and squares; the highly charged intellectual buzz from one of the world's most important universities; the ever-changing angles of light and shadow playing on the ancient buildings and cobblestone streets; the sweet, inviting smells from cafes and shops; the chic, handsome lines and textures in high-fashion windows. All of it was deeply familiar, yet new again, all of it entertained her mind and pleased her senses, reminding her of just how much she had missed this remarkable old city.

With her energy returning, she tried a day trip up to Parma for a Correggio fix. Many of his sensuous and daring frescoes and paintings created back in the 1500s, among her favorites from the old masters, were still housed in his hometown. Her trusty silver VW Golf roared right to life after 4 months in the spot she owned in a private garage a half-kilometer up Via San Vitale, and she soon remembered how much she enjoyed driving it fast. A few days later she drove to Rimini on the coast, just to see and smell the Adriatic and dine on fresh seafood.

Along with the day trips and her afternoon hiking regime, she has lately spent long mornings on line, searching her favorite news sites and blogs for whatever might catch her eye. Yesterday in the NY

Times, she was grabbed by "In a Funk, Italy Sings an Aria of Disappointment," a piece on the malaise of Italians who despair of their country's "fractured politics, uneven growth, organized crime and a tenuous sense of nationhood." She spent much of the morning writing a long post to the Times that ended with: "Do not give up on us Italians just yet, especially the younger generation. My students are energized and engaged. They know what needs to be done, and I think they will do it."

So will she go to the opening tonight? One of Lilli's selling points was that a number of Lina's good friends were likely to be there. And her last words as Lina stepped from the Jaguar were, "Have you heard from Paolo?"

"No," she said waving goodbye and smiling to ensure that her friend understood she had no wish to hear from him. "He is working in Uruguay." That was Lilli for you: the best way to get past a horrid experience with a crazy American was to pick up again with a crazy Italian.

At one point several days ago she had found herself wondering how she would feel if Paolo reappeared now. That was soon answered when a piece in the Corierre della Sera reported he was in Montevideo for the trial of a wealthy Italian exile accused of manslaughter in the death of his girlfriend and of attempting to bribe a government official. Good, she thought. Better he is an ocean away than here to offer unwanted commentary on her mess in Michigan.

It has been clear for a while she has avoided the people closest to her and even the places where she might see them. They would surely ask about her stay in the states, and she would need to answer honestly. And the thought of doing that, of somehow summing up an experience so exhilarating and dreadful, has stopped her cold. She has simply not wanted to talk about it, as if the whole thing carried some kind of terribly complicated shame. Yet yesterday morning when she wrote to the Times about the energy and drive of her students, she knew it was time to rethink her methods of coping. And then in her chance encounter with Lilli, finally letting it all come tumbling out seemed to have a cathartic effect.

She feels better today. Yes, John is out of her life, probably forever. But even if she had finished the term, this is about the time she would have left St. Thomas, and they had always been clear what that would mean. Almost a month now without harassment, cruelty or threat, and at the very least she feels safe, able to sleep through the night, answer the phone, check email and walk the ancient streets of her stimulating Bologna without a trace of anxious concern.

The intercom beeps, and she knows this time it is Lilli's invitation. Next to the door she presses the buzz-in button. Waiting there, she hears the creak and rumble from the old elevator. Oddly, she wonders about her appearance and moves to the mirror with the good light from the patio. With russet-colored slacks she is wearing a cable-knit V-neck sweater in Bologna's dominant tint, the Terra Cotta of most of its buildings. She likes its warmth against her complexion and hair. Good with the green eyes as well. But after living with the cut for two weeks now, does she like the hair? Certainly easier to care for, just wash, blow and a few strokes with the brush. Not as sexy, but now grown out a bit, softer around the lines of her face. Overall, okay, but she has not had short hair since she was a little girl. A few complements have come. Wilfrina: "You changed your hair. I like it." And Lilli yesterday: "Love your hair!" It will still take some getting used to.

Finally, the chime, and she moves quickly to answer it. Turning the deadbolt, she swings open the heavy oak door, and, framed there, in one hand the invitation in a Gallery Azzure envelope with her name in Lilli's beautiful cursive, and in the other a plump lemon he has just picked from the small tree in the large pot next to her entrance, is Stan.

His light hazel eyes, eager as ever, hold her stunned gaze as he raises the fruit a few inches and says, "What a country! Just reach out your front door and pluck a luscious lemon."

She is speechless, struck dumb by his sheer physical presence, but also by her own immediate certainty that this smiling young man was responsible for everything.

Ending the awful silence he says, "So, Lina, you've cut your beautiful hair. But I like it."

Finally, she says, "Stan...*che*...?" But that is all she can manage before her throat closes and her knees so weaken that she fears she will faint.

Chapter 29

Unbidden, he steps in and swings the door closed. She's obviously unsteady, and when her hand reaches to his forearm, he feels her need. As she clutches his black leather jacket, he knows she wants his help. Letting the lemon and the envelope drop to the floor, he takes her in his arms as she sways for a second, then, pressed against his body, seems to find her balance.

So different from the first soft, silvery press of her hand on his in the small piazza that June night in Orta San Giulio, her urgent touch now seems no less extraordinary. Holding her firmly, he says, "God, Lina, I've missed you so much."

She is silent, and his hand moves up to gently cradle the back of her head, feeling the short, feathery red hair in his fingers, waiting for that pliant move of her neck to give him that wonderful face to kiss. Tenderly he touches the top of her neck, but she doesn't move, and he finally bows slightly to give his kiss to the top of her head.

"Darling," he murmurs, "you're so lovely. You know I adore you."

For so long, he's been dying to say that word directly to her heart. Can she really resist? Does any woman not want to be utterly, completely adored? That word has moved him across an ocean to this ancient city and to hold this phenomenal woman in his arms.

When he finally surrendered to it, he was standing in a cold December rain, staring at the old chapel where he had followed her that warm sunny day back in August. He knew he'd soon leave for a city where a 125-year-old church would be nothing special. He talked to no one about where he was going. There was something appealing about just disappearing, but then he thought about possible consequences. He'd be reported as a missing person; the law would put out information, try perhaps to track him down. John might warn Lina that he could be coming. No, it was better to leave with some kind of story. And so in a last-minute email to Redding and

John, he wrote that his "long-lost father" had contacted him "out of the blue, after all these years," and they were going to meet and spend some time together in Mexico City. Was it plausible? Who cared? It was his story. When Bob Daddy's brother finally croaked, most of the department drove west to Chicago for the funeral, and Stan headed thousands of miles in the opposite direction.

He had not been greatly surprised three weeks earlier when the call came from Elena saying Father wanted him to know that Professor Lentini had returned to Italy. Please check his email for the professor's forwarded message about practical things like shipping her large suitcase left in the apartment, the books in her office, and the location of the Focus in the parking structure at Metro Airport. Yes, there was some satisfaction that his plan had finally worked. It had certainly taken much longer than he had thought it would, but now with Lina no longer even on the same continent, he could finally get on with his life.

He was sure the fever had broken, but it all felt strangely anti-climactic. He seemed drained of energy, almost without purpose. Once he took care of those practical requests, there'd be nothing more to do about Lina Lentini. Nothing to wonder, worry, or scheme about.

After a few days he had even called Marissa, suggesting Melody for lunch. Yeah, he wanted to see what things were like between her and John with Lina gone. But he also decided he wanted to fuck Marissa again. So why the change? Maybe he was still pissed off at the arrogant-ass way John had treated him in their last meeting. Maybe he wanted to prove he was really free of Lina. Would another romp with Marissa prove that? Maybe, and he had no doubt she'd be up for it. The woman had come on to him like a bitch in heat at lunch that second time, when he turned her down. She was sexy, attractive, and he had been out of commission for way too long. The plan was Marissa first, then Becca Popp, then the whole damn field.

At Melody, Marissa seemed in high spirits and erotically charged in a tight red sweater and black slacks. She had just taken a new job. "Well, an old job, really. I'm kind of back where I started, doing graphic design for an ad agency." Only this one was the largest in Grand Rapids. Yes, it would be 40 minutes each way, but it was only three days a week. She had applied almost a month ago and told no one, not even John. They had given her a test assignment, and she had passed "with flying colors."

When the subject turned to Lina, she said, "Good riddance,". "You know, I saw her the day she left. She came to the house."

"To the house?"

"Yep, she wanted to ask me if I was responsible for all the harassment and things."

"Really. What'd you say?"

"I said I was behind all of it."

"All of it. Amazing. And that was true?"

"Oh, I had a hand in a couple of things. As for the rest, I suspect only you can say."

"Me?"

"Of course, you, sweetie. Actually, I think we made a very good team, and we finally got rid of the bitch." She winked and did a small fist pump.

He shook his head. Admit nothing, he told himself. "Speaking of a team." He reached across the table to cover her hand. "How about we go back to my place and play a game?"

Her eyes dropped to his hand as she took hers away. "Oh, I'd love to, sweetie, but I'm going to the mall. Really, I need a whole new wardrobe for this job. I mean, this is new." She stuck out her tits to show him the sweater. "But I need a whole lot more. You like?"

"Love 'em. How about tomorrow?"

"Aren't you sweet! But tomorrow I have a physical. And frankly, sweetie, right now I'm thinking I need to do a little repair work with John. I know he's a cad, but I guess he's my cad."

He nodded glumly, and she added, "But if I change my mind, can I ask for a rain check?"

He knew she wouldn't, and by the time he called Becca Popp a week later, his motives had changed. For some reason now he could not stop thinking about Lina. Alone in Bologna. It started the day after he saw Marissa, when he shipped the suitcase. It was probably a mistake, but in the apartment he simply could not resist opening the case, and then with the matching beige lace bra and panties on top, allowing himself one quick sniff of her crotch. All he could smell was the sickening sweet scent of Tide from the box on the kitchen counter.

In the days that followed his mind began spilling images of sparkling red hair and gleaming green eyes, those remarkable tits swelling that generous beige bra and the marvelous line of her sensuous mouth. Unbidden, they would pop into his head, as he drove the quiet two-lane back to the gatehouse, or sprawled in his bed trying vainly to sleep. On campus when he'd pass places where they had been together, her office in Markham or the old chapel, or, it seemed, a hundred others, acutely detailed moments from the past 3 months would flood over him. At times he would feel as if he were choking, as if he were actually going under. When he called Becca's cell, hoping for a life line, he reached her in Chicago where she had started with "a new alternative rag, and I'll be blogging my ass off as soon as my site is up. Watch for it, baby!"

His fucking obsession had obviously been running much deeper than he ever thought. And down in that subterranean trough, he must have planned all along to go to her, once she'd been forced to flee back to Bologna where she'd be away from John, alone and even vulnerable. Able finally to press his advance, he would start over and do it right. This time she would want him. This time he would show her what she really wanted. With certain women there were times, he thought last night, gazing at a table full of Bolognesi coeds at a café near his apartment, when you just had to be firm and give a woman what even she doesn't know she wants.

For months he's been haunted by one moment in that perfect evening when he first brought her to the apartment in Cedar Hill. The warmth of that light streaming through the front window, the flowers, the wine, most of all her surprise hug and kiss at the door, it's all forged forever in his memory. But there is one moment missing, one moment he should have seized but did not, when he should have grabbed her and kissed her back, hard and soft, deep and tender. That kind of kiss would have changed everything, but the moment slipped away. Never again.

As he holds her, that beautiful head remains bowed at the lemon and the envelope on the floor. "Lina!" he calls to her, and when she still doesn't move, he takes her chin with his fingers and lifts it until that lovely mouth is just where he wants it. Her eyes begin to open as he plunges his mouth on hers. He takes her moist upper lip first in his teeth then moves to the lower, and then his tongue is deep in her mouth. His hand drops from her chin to her breast, grabbing its fullness, but only for a second before reaching lower. Now he slips it up under the sweater to grab the front edge of her bra and rip it

181

down until her bare tit fills his hand, the firm, erect nipple between his fingers.

And then he finally feels her moving, slipping slightly away to his left. A second later his face explodes in pain. She has slapped him so hard he blinks.

Her eyes wide with rage, she screams at him, "Get out!" And when he stares and doesn't move, she screams again, louder, "Get out, now!" She sounds strange, like a woman possessed.

She is still only a step away. His urge is to punish, to return the blow so hard her face will break. When he begins to move toward her, she wheels with speed, steps behind the kitchen counter and grabs a phone. "*Polizia!*" she growls softly now, shaking it at him. "*La Polizia!*"

"Lina, " he says finally, his heart pounding hard, "I love you. I've given up everything to come here, to be with you in this beautiful country. Please!"

"Leave!" She's screaming again. "Now!"

He simply stares at her, suddenly feeling strangely calm. He could never have imagined this woman acting so crazy. Shaking his head, he reaches into his pocket to pull out the large switchblade knife he bought last night from a market vendor in the street. He moves his thumb, and the gleaming five-inch blade flies open. Before she can tap the phone, he reaches down to stab the lemon and pick it up. Glancing up at her, he smiles, then stabs again to make an X, then an inch away two more stabs for another X. Then a stab and a curved swipe for the angry mouth. He folds the knife and puts it away. She hasn't said a word since he pulled it out.

He moves to the door, shows her the lemon's sour face and says, "I'll be around, Lina."

Once out the door, he puts the lemon frown up in the pot holding its tree. Then he looks at the old elevator the delivery boy had pointed to after he told the kid he'd be happy to give the message to his friend the professor. The contraption took forever, and he decides to use the stairs.

Chapter 30

She knows she has made a mistake as soon as she approaches the covered entry to Gallery Azzure. Stopping for a moment, she quickly walks away under the portico, wondering if anyone inside glimpsed her through the windows. Two doors down she pretends to look at the bookshop display, waiting to see if anyone comes out of the gallery. She has not been thinking clearly since she found Stan in her doorway, and seeing him again so soon has shaken her.

Obviously she should have assumed he would look at the card in the gallery's envelope and so would know exactly where to find her this evening. So there he was in his sweater and jeans, holding a glass of red wine near the back of the gallery's long, narrow room, chatting with Aldo and Rena, Hans and Marta, the whole group laughing at something he said.

Thus, while she dithered and stalled and fought with herself for more than an hour over whether to leave the apartment and come to Lilli's opening, he has already been here making friends with some of those he met six months ago that closing night of the conference on shores of Lake Orta. No doubt giving all of them his version of the events in Cedar Hill, his view on what it was like for her, his take on their own relationship, his line on why he has come to Bologna. So by giving in to her doubts and anxieties, she has opened the door for him to walk right in and take over, offering his charming, prevaricating words on just about everything.

If she had arrived here first, perhaps she would have urged Lilli to deny him entrance, but now what? Of course she can leave and avoid being in the same room with him, but that would keep him free to continue bending the truth. She can walk in and raise a fuss, asking Lilli to show him out. Or she can avoid a scene, focus on the dear friends she has not seen in so long and ignore him as much as possible. Then later she will make certain that everyone learns the truth.

Walking back to the gallery door, she tries to recall exactly what she told Lilli yesterday. Yes, the whipsaw tale of the love affair and the plagues, but like any capable teller, she had held back details to heighten interest. The Jag had nearly reached Via San Vitale when she finally mentioned that last meeting with Marissa.

"The day I left the States, she claimed she was totally responsible."

"Well, then," said Lilli, "as they say in the procedurals, 'open and shut.'"

"Yes, but there was also a young man, a graduate student, actually one of John's doctoral candidates, who was also assigned to take care of practical things for me. He had an obvious crush, and he was very intrusive."

"How so?" Lilli parked a block from the apartment.

"Well, one day I came back to my office and found him sitting at my desk, reading through my diary."

"Oh, not good!" Lilli glanced at her watch.

"Yes, I tried to keep him at arm's length, but he just kept coming. He seemed fixed in some way, and when the plagues started, John and I both thought he might be involved."

She caught Lilli checking the time again and knew her friend had much to do for the opening. "But to be continued. Thanks for the lift. What a brilliant piece of luck seeing you!"

At the Azzure's window she pauses to take in the show's poster:

GoodEvil

Gemma Roy

New Paintings, 2005-2007

A quick look at the paintings on the walls inside: most of them seem to be pastel gradients slashed with blacks, browns, reds and gunmetal gray. In several the artist seems to have taken a knife to the canvas, producing ragged rips and gouges. The effect she finds disturbing.

She walks in, and a glance to the back across the crowded room finds Stan still holding forth, too busy to see her. Marta is laughing and putting a hand on his arm for a second. Her stomach turns. What could be so funny? She cannot ever recall Stan with a sense of humor. Must she move directly to her friends and the confrontation? No, fortunately Lilli's petite figure in a bold red dress is moving to her, and within seconds they are doing a hug with kisses.

"Darling!" There is relief in Lilli's voice. "I was worried you wouldn't come, but I'm so glad you're here. And I was right, some of your friends are here as well. Even one all the way from Michigan! His name is Stan and he seems very smart and very sweet. And..." She throws up her hands in surprise and triumph. "...he's actually bought a painting!"

"Really." She grabs Lilli's hand and turns so her back is to the group at the rear. With all its hard surfaces the room is noisy, but she leans close. "Lilli, Stan is the one I was telling you about in the car. The one with such a crush that I would call him a stalker."

Lilli's small face loses its smile. "Oh, my god, I didn't catch that! If I had known..."

Lina shakes her head to say, don't worry.

"No, look, I'll ask him to leave straight away. Or should we call the coppers?"

"Oh, no, Lilli, please." She thinks Stan might relish the chance to make a scene. "There is no problem. Nothing dangerous about his being here."

"But I don't want you to be uncomfortable."

"No, I will be fine."

"He said he saw you earlier today and that you invited him here tonight."

Lina pauses. "Well, that is not how it happened."

Lilli's face is full of concern. "Oh, darling, please forgive me!"

Before she can answer, a young woman dressed entirely in black and with thick-rimmed glasses, says, with an accent that matches Lilli's, "So she's trying to rip you off as well?"

Lilli turns quickly to the woman. "Gemma! Lina Lentini meet the artist, Gemma Roy."

Taking her hand, Gemma says, "I thought that was you. Your rep precedes you."

The woman is about 30 and has boldly streaked hair. Lina says, "As does yours. I was anxious to see your work. It has real impact."

With a tilt of the head: "You're so kind to say that. I hope we can chat in a while." Then to Lilli: "Dear, there's another deluded bloke in the back who seems ready to pay good money for one of my so-called works of art."

"Indeed, we need to help him." Lilli gives Lina another quick hug. "Circulate, darling, I'll be back in a flash."

As the women leave, the call comes. "Lina, qui!" Hans with a big smile, his long arm straight in the air, hand waving. Hans, the tallest, sweetest and perhaps brightest, as always in winter with the long brown scarf, his only affectation, wrapped once around that long neck, about which he is so self-conscious. The scarf, of course, only draws attention to it. He is hopelessly sweet on Marta, who naturally will not give him the time of day. Marta, with her pretty, sharp, Romanian features and consistently bad taste in men, clearly has her eye on Stan. He has moved back a bit from the others now.

Edgardo, absurdly handsome but always kind, is suddenly in front of her, and, arms wide, starts the hugs and kisses. His lovely Bella, he says, is with her ailing grandmother in Rome. On to the others. Soft-spoken Aldo, the oldest of the group with his bushy salt-and-pepper hair and beard, and his wife Rena, the vivacious poet who writes so often of her Nigerian father and Italian mother. Hans bends to embrace her and whispers he is working on a paper on *Crime and Punishment*. That is shorthand, she knows, for how grateful he is to her that violent fantasies are no longer a problem for him. Marta gives her an especially long and warm hug, saying they've all missed her so much. And then an embrace from their friend Federico, a singer and songwriter, also, improbably, a chemist, whose family operates a traditional chemist's shop and *farmacia*. He's just had the pleasure of meeting her friend Stan from the States, a chemistry and lit student, who is studying the great Primo Levi, of course also a chemist.

What a coincidence, she says. Then steeling herself, she turns to find Stan, now with a full glass of red in each hand. With an indulgent smile, he says, "Ah, *la bella Lina*," and hands her a glass.

Her own smile feels frozen as she stares him hard in the eye. She says, "*Grazie tante*," takes the glass without touching him and quickly turns back to the group to say they all look fantastic. She has missed them all so much. They counter with about how good she looks, how much they like her hair, and how dead Bologna has been without her. She says, so it is clear they have all turned into liars, and everyone laughs.

Will someone ask why she has been back nearly a month and not called any of them? Instead, Marta wonders what she thinks of painting #23 on the wall nearby.

Guessing that it is Stan's purchase, she gazes at it for few seconds. It has two garish knife slashes. Finally, she says it seems crude, obvious and a bit frightening.

Stan has bought it, says Marta.

Lina says he is a brave man if he hangs it in his home.

A few more laughs and awkward smiles and Aldo says they have all been discussing her post to the Times about the article on the malaise in Italy that everyone in Bologna has been arguing about. As usual, says Hans, Lina's comments are the most cogent and sensible. Edgardo says she would have loved that October rally the writer mentioned in the Piazza Maggiore. Fifty thousand Bolagnesi, intense, energized, angry and determined..

When Federico takes his leave, inviting them all to Cantina Bentivoglio where he will sing with the trio next Saturday evening, she sees Stan head for the gallery's restroom. Enough time now to tell this group how, less than five hours ago, this friendly fellow forced himself on her so violently that he ripped the bra from her breast? Probably not, but a few minutes earlier, she noticed his hand go into his jeans pocket to fondle something, probably the switchblade, and she quickly decided she does not want to walk any part of the way home alone. Is anybody up for a little light supper? she asks. Perhaps the Caffè della Corte in a half-hour or so? As she expects, everyone thinks this is a marvelous idea.

* * *

There are ten around the long narrow table once Lilli arrives with Gemma Roy and Marco, Lilli's new lover, a painter with lots of gray hair, lively eyes and an ascetic physique. Under the coved beige brick of this popular place, Lina is at one end of the table, with Edgardo on her left, and Rena on her right, along with Aldo, Hans and Marta. At the far end sits Stan.

So much for her plan to lose him upon leaving the gallery. She knew it was hopeless the moment she spotted Marta and Stan with their heads together when everyone was leaving. While he was still in the restroom, she had thought about telling them she did not want Stan to come. But then Marta had sidled up close, taken her hand and said with deep concern that Stan had told them all about the terrible experiences she had during her stay in Michigan, all those vicious attacks orchestrated by that deranged woman. It must have been a nightmare.

Yes, unpleasant, she said, as Stan returned to the group, but now back home with all her dear friends, she has left it all behind.

187

Perhaps her first lie since returning to Bologna. How good it has felt to live in a place and in a way that does not force her to avoid the truth.

No, she can hardly blame Marta for simply being polite enough to invite their new friend to come along. Even so, when Rena leans close to say that Marta already seems to have something going with Stan, Lina snaps quietly that of course Marta is famous for bringing home stray dogs from the street.

Rena glances at Stan, then back to Lina. With a serious look, she asks, "*Cara, stai bene?*"

Lina says, yes, she's fine but adds, "*Mi dispiace che lui e qui.*" She is not happy with Stan's presence here.

Rena nods and blinks those large chocolate eyes that seem to miss nothing. She will ask him to leave, she says.

"*No, grazie, Rena, non ora, dopo.*" Not now, later.

With the two Brits and the American more or less conversant in Italian there has not been much English spoken at the table. That changes when Hans, probably the most political of the group, pulls some folded pages from a coat pocket and says he's found a fascinating new piece by the conservative commentator Andrew Sullivan.

"A Brit," says Lilli.

"Yes," says Hans, looking over his big Danish nose at her, "And he has some amazing things to say about Obama." Shuffling pages, he read his "favorite paragraph," ending with, "'If you wanted the crudest but most effective weapon against the demonization of America that fuels Islamist ideology, Obama's face gets close. It proves them wrong about what America is in ways no words can.'"

Marta wants to know what Stan thinks of Obama.

"From what I've seen, I think, as we say, Hillary will eat him for lunch."

And what does Lina think after her stay in the states.?

"Yes, well, it does seem there is something different and admirable about Obama. But it is not clear that he and America are ready yet. Of course, there is nearly a year before the election, and time may prove me wrong."

The table is covered with carafes of wine, baskets of crusty bread, platters with three kinds of succulent ham and marinated chicken, bowls of tasty tortellini, plates of various cheeses and fruit. Hardly a light supper. But after nearly two hours of great food and good talk, she is still pondering the question of how to get home without Stan in tow or following her somewhere under the porticos of Bologna at night.

When the chairs finally scrape back on the red tile floor, she is surprised with the answer that suddenly comes to her.

Chapter 31

Certainly compared to the one he sub-leased two streets over, her apartment is huge. With more than 100,000 university students swelling the population here, he was lucky to find his on-line, some young guy with family problems needing to go home for a while. Yesterday, after driving the Fiat Panda he rented at Malpensa, the Milan airport, to Bologna, he found the small living and sleeping rooms, tiny bathroom and kitchenette barely adequate, but he didn't expect to spend much time there. The best thing: only three blocks from Lina.

Here she has a substantial master bedroom and bath, a second bedroom she uses as an office that is probably as large as his whole place, a second bath, a spacious dining and living room area and a large, well-stocked kitchen, 4 different bottles of olive oil and a major spice rack on the counter, bunches of garlic cloves and peppers tacked up close at hand, pots of basil and oregano under a grow light, expensive and well-used pots and pans hanging from the ceiling.

The kitchen, like all the rooms, is very much a place for everything and everything in its place. But then he had learned that about her months ago from his secret visits to her apartment when she was out. Her office was always meticulous every time he went in there to fool with her computer. The same for her bathroom when he'd go in to pick up the tape from the tiny peep hole camera he had hidden there. It took a while, but he finally got lucky with nearly 20 minutes of footage of this great-looking bitch moving around the bathroom totally nude. He's looked at it now so many times he's got the damn thing memorized, knowing exactly when a great angle was coming up, when you could really see the lines of her tits, the size of her nips and the shape of that pretty little pubic curl.

Here several hours ago he was so focused on Lina, he hardly noticed a thing about this place. Now, escorted by Lilli and along with the two painters, he is taking a tour. He had pegged Lina for traditional furniture, but it is all contemporary, lots of high-fashion leather and glass and dark polished wood. There's a big ficus near the door to the patio and several other large, healthy looking plants that somebody must have taken care of while she was in the States. One whole wall is covered, floor to ceiling, with shelved books, with a rolling ladder to reach the top shelves, but otherwise nearly every available foot of wall space in the apartment is covered with pictures, some photographs, but paintings mostly in a wide variety of subject, style and medium. The place is attractive, warm and tasteful. What else would you expect?

Lilli calls to her, "Darling, I haven't been in here in a while, and I'd forgotten. I think you own more pictures than I do. It feels like a retrospective of all my shows for the past five years. I mean, I see you patronize others as well, particularly Galleria Forni, but I also see you've rather single-handedly kept me in business!"

Lina calls back, "You know it is my one vice, my one true addiction. I see something I like, and I must have it."

"Well, now you need something from Marco and Gemma."

She says yes, of course, and places four bottles of wine on the kitchen counter. As Edgardo opens them, she sets out glasses. The box of books he packed and shipped to her seems in the way, and Stan lifts it off the counter, saying, "Where can I put this for you, Lina?"

She looks up and says, "Just on the floor."

"Really? The floor?"

"There is a closet down the hall next to my office. You could put it there."

There is something in her voice, impatience perhaps. Carrying the box, he moves down the hall to the closet door. Inside the light is dim, but he can see that all the shelves are filled with linens, office supplies and household products. He puts the box on the floor near the back shelves and turns to leave, when his eye catches an old-fashion white apron hanging next to the door jam. The simple fact that she wears this thing makes him take the soft cotton in his hand and move it to his cheek. As he does this, he sees hanging there on a small hook on the jamb, two keys on a ring. He hesitates only a second before lifting the ring off the hook, which is covered again when he releases the cloth. He slips the keys into the right front pocket of his jeans. They settle down there next to his knife.

As he moves back to the group in the living room, he takes a glass of wine from the counter and thinks there has only been one awkward moment. It came just before Lina unlocked the door, and they all walked into the apartment. Standing next to her on the balcony that overlooks the open courtyard at the center of the old building, Marta picked up the lemon he had carved on earlier and stared at it.

"Lina, who would do such a thing to an innocent lemon?"

Turning, Lina had caught his eye for a second. "Someone with a cruel heart, no doubt."

Marta said, "You have a neighbor who would do this?"

"Maybe a visitor." The door was open, and soon everyone was inside, Marta placing the lemon on the kitchen counter for all to see as they moved first to Lina's bedroom to drop their coats and scarves on the bright red comforter covering her queen-sized bed. Only Hans kept his scarf around his neck, a faggy look somehow reminiscent of Hal. Yes, Hans and Hal, there's something in common there.

In any case, he has handled this whole evening very well. In fact it looks like his plan has worked to perfection, with even better results than he could have hoped for. The bottom line is, he has effectively neutralized whatever damage might have been caused by his aggressive come-on earlier today. The key had been to impress and win over all her friends at the gallery. He started with Lilli, saying with a wink he had come all the way from Michigan for her opening. Then he mentioned Lina.

"Brilliant!" said the skinny little gallery owner. "There are several of her friends here tonight. I'd introduce you, but I'm so bloody busy at the moment. Just circulate and you'll find them. And if you're so inclined, have a gander at the art!"

Buying the painting, of course, sealed the deal with her, and charming Lina's friends, who quickly recalled him from the conference, was simple once he learned they knew nothing about what happened in Cedar Hill. At St. Thomas, he told them, Lina had been wonderful, much loved and admired by faculty and students alike. Unfortunately, one "famously unbalanced" woman whose mental affliction and alcoholism were widely known, decided, totally without cause, that Lina was having an affair with her long-suffering husband on the school's literature faculty. And this woman had often made life miserable for Lina at St. Thomas.

He detailed much of the harassment and painted himself as a modest hero, trying to undo the damage and put an end to the attacks. He was in Italy now to do some "first-hand research" for his doctoral thesis on Primo Levi. He had scheduled a brief stay in Bologna to pay his deep respects and make sure Lina was doing okay. But he'd soon be on to Torino, Levi's hometown, and maybe also to Auschwitz where the writer had been held during the last year of the war.

Everyone had seemed suitably impressed, especially hot little Marta, who's been drooling on him ever since. And then he had them all practically wetting their pants with his dead-on imitation of George W. Bush. By the time Lina showed up, they would have invited him anywhere. And with no objection from their world-class professor, it was no surprise they urged him along to supper at the café. Yes, she seemed a bit cold and stand-offish at the gallery, even dismissive with that snide remark about the painting he purchased, but that was probably because the unexpected sight of him at the gallery had re-stoked her face-slapping anger.

But then how to explain her invitation as they were leaving the café? She announced, "You know, I do not want the evening to end just yet. How about a nightcap back at my place?" And when everyone seemed delighted, she added: "Stan, I know you must be feeling jetlagged, but I do hope you are up for joining us."

Really, there is no way to explain that line unless his plan has worked, unless he has so charmed her friends that they've helped her see him through their eyes. His presence here, along with all her old friends, proves he's been right all along. Despite the initial knee-jerk reaction, some part of her really wants him to take her, ravish her, make up her mind for her and show her what she really wants. Sometimes it takes a while for desire to dawn and be accepted. Clearly she wants him now, and he wouldn't be at all surprised if she soon finds a way to get everyone out—she's suddenly exhausted, has to be up early for something in the morning, etc.—but finds a reason for him to stay behind. And then they will really get to it in her big, beautiful bed.

In the living room Aldo and Rena are on the sofa, with Lilli and Marco in the chairs next to it. The black woman with the somber face has been eyeing him for a while and gives him another look he can't quite figure as he heads for the glass doors to the patio. Hans, Marta, Edgardo and Gemma are out there smoking, shoulders hunched against the cold night air, talking with their hands. As the air hits his warm face, he takes in the panoramic rooftop view of the old city, a multitude of serene lights spreading out to the surrounding hills.

"*Che una bella vista!*" he says, and the group turns to him.

"*Si,*" says Hans. "We should ask Stan what he thinks."

The guy is about Hal's height. How about a nickname? Maybe "Goose," for the neck? Would a tough shove in the chest send him over this railing?

"No," says Marta. "We should ask Stan inside. This conversation is chilling enough without the cold out here." They stub out their cigarettes and move inside.

"Ask me what?" says Stan with patio doors closed. Marta sits next to Rena on the sofa, and the others find places on the wood floor near their wine glasses on a low glass table. About to join them, he sees Lina moving from the hallway holding his black leather jacket. She places it on the kitchen counter and walks with a stoic look to a chair on the other side of the group. The sight of his jacket makes him take a nervous sip of red.

Marta says, "We're talking about a friend of Gemma's who is being stalked in London. But you tell it, Gemma."

"Yes, well, she's beautiful, and she met this bloke in a pub. They went on one date, and she blew him off. But he's found where she lives and been hounding her ever since. The usual drill—calls, notes, emails full of declarations of love and adoration. But they gradually turned, and now they're mostly threats to maim and murder. The coppers say, consider the threats serious, and she's taken legal action to restrain, but she's really quite terrified. My question is, how does all this love and adoration turn into the desire to inflict pain and destruction?"

Marta says, "Yes, so Stan, what do you think? Give us your take."

His first thought, prompted by his jacket sitting there on the counter, is that he's been set up, that somehow Lina has quietly clued them all in. But then why the long story about Gemma's friend in London? Why not just tell Lina's story?

He says, "My take is that it's a pretty obvious progression. The guy's in love, then frustrated, then obsessed. And over time the obsession becomes humiliating to him. I mean what's more humiliating than being unable to control the thoughts in your own head? And ultimately the surest way to end that obsession is to annihilate its object."

Marta says, "I think that's brilliant."

He says, "Thanks. So think about O.J. Simpson. He's the best example I can give you. Superstar celebrity, super-stud athlete, movie star, wealthy, handsome, can have just about any woman he wants. But he's fixated, totally stuck on his ex-wife Nicole, the mother of his kids. He's ended it with her more than once, fought with her, reconciled, fought again, divorced her, but he just can't move on. She is frightened of him, has a new boyfriend and has definitely moved on. But Simpson can't. He's obsessed. And for a guy who otherwise has it all, that's totally humiliating. So he does the only thing he can do: he slits her throat, he annihilates the object of his obsession and probably feels damn good. He's finally free, no longer humiliated, no longer obsessed."

"And he gets away with it!" says Lilli. "Goes scot-free!"

"Yeah," he says, "that's great for him. But he'd probably be happier even behind bars."

On the sofa, Rena, with a clouded look, says, "So, Lina, what do *you* think?"

Lina leans forward in her chair, her eyes riveting him. "For me, obsession has nothing to do with love. Otherwise, I think Stan knows whereof he speaks."

It's pretty clear where she's going, but he tries to calm his nerves. "Meaning what?"

"Meaning that you have obviously been dealing with your own obsession almost from the time I arrived in Michigan. And its ultimate expression came earlier today, right here in this room, when you forced yourself on me physically, ripping my bra and stopping only when I struck you as hard as I could in the face."

Lilli, in the chair next to her, reaches to touch her hand." "Oh, darling, I'm so sorry!"

Lina nods and moves her eyes to the others. "I am okay. But, I was stunned to find him here at my door. And I knew immediately he was behind all those heartless attacks on me and on John, my lover. We had suspected Stan, that it was a kind of stalking behavior from someone obsessed, and I gather that you heard tonight about some of it from Stan himself. But it was crude and vicious and unrelenting.

Every day there seemed to be a new attack. A newspaper ad offering my services as an erotic masseuse, men's room graffiti with my phone number, an email plea to fund a fictitious abortion, the deletion of the document files for my new book, a false plagiarism charge that could have ruined John's career, a gunshot through my front window at night. A gunshot! And that is not even the half of it."

Sounds of anger and commiseration come from the others. He says quickly, "Lina, you know John's wife admitted doing all those things."

She gets to her feet, glaring at him. "What I know now is that she could not have done them, because they were all your doing." To the others she says, "No doubt, he has told you that he was my friend, that he tried to fix things and put an end to the attacks. But this is a truly devious man, and at the core of his being, where his heart should be, there is only a black hole."

"Lina…" he starts.

"No!" she screams. And then in a lower voice: "I want you to leave now and never show your face here again!"

There is a shocked, dead silence. Turning his gaze, he finds only dark, hostile faces. He says finally, "I assume no one here wants to know my side of it."

Lina sits back in her chair, and Marta says quietly, "You assume correct."

Hans gets to his feet and says, "Just get out. And don't come back."

Edgardo stands as well, his eyes menacing.

Stan nods, then, shaking his head, puts his hand in the pocket of his jeans and fondles the knife. "Lina," he says, "you've made a big mistake." He gazes at the rest of them. "I leave for Torino tomorrow, so I'll probably not see any of you again."

"Excellent," says Hans.

He gives the guy a look and heads for the door. Feeling a hateful stare from every pair of eyes, his body is stiff and awkward as he grabs his jacket from the counter. Hans is already ahead of him, opening the door.

"See ya, Goose," he tells the long-necked asshole and walks out. He feels the vibration of the door slamming behind him and hears the deadbolt lock slide loudly into place.

196

Chapter 32

At midnight, after fighting with himself for much of the day, he finally decides to write the email. But when he starts, it's not about Stan's possible itinerary, supposedly the point of the message. Instead he begins with Mar and her new job. Maybe later when he covers his concerns about Stan, he'll put that up front. Right now he's catching Lina up on how his wife is driving to a Grand Rapids ad agency three days a week.

"Am I surprised? he writes. "No, shocked is the word. Am I pleased? Of course. Will it last? Almost no chance. Is she still drinking heavily? Yes, but in different patterns. She swears she will never drink and drive to or from work. 'I will kill myself before I ever go back to jail again.' So when she's working the next day, she abstains, and when she's off, she makes up for lost time. On the weekends, forget it. Wine she has always sipped openly, but when she's serious, it's always vodka in secret and huge amounts. Last night I nearly blew up the kitchen when she forgot she'd hidden one of those big Smirnoff jugs in the oven.

"By the second week she was complaining about the job and the uncreative work she's been assigned. So between that and the booze , I'd give her a month before she's sacked or quits.

"As for Mar and me, it's about the same, though I have much less patience. With you gone, she tried to re-establish something, but the alcohol has poisoned both mind and body and the very connective tissue between us. Now what I feel is mostly pity — for her blurred, empty life, the friends lost or driven away, the talents wasted. I fear what seems inevitably ahead for her. I know she's often lonely and depressed, but the basic companionship that used to be there has frayed beyond hope. And sex? As I've said, she only wants me when she's drunk, and that's when she's the last thing in the world I want."

Reading back through this last paragraph, he finds it filled with embarrassing self-pity. So he cuts the whole thing. Stick to news, he thinks, and moves on to the last two days in Chicago. Yes, the drawn-out suffering has ended for Redding's brother, the cancer finally taking the 61-year-old priest. Most of the department drove the three hours plus for the funeral and the memorial service and then returned home. He called his friend Marlon Tish at the

University of Chicago, suggesting dinner that night.

"You'll recall my mentioning Tish, and you've read his one very successful book, *New American Masters*, whose wave he's been riding ever since. We met several years ago at a conference and for some reason hit it off, though I seem to have almost nothing in common with this ebullient rake. We keep a fairly steady correspondence going and see each other occasionally, though more than once he has stood me up for a willing female. He's a star at these events but is lazy about publishing now. His way-too-patient wife, who put him through grad school, finally divorced him a while back, and Tish only upped his shameless tomcatting. I was there a few years ago when a middle-aged gal from some small college stood up during a Q & A and asked flat out how he got away with sleeping with so many young coeds. But then she gave him an out: 'Or is that outlandish reputation of yours more legend than fact?' Ignoring the out, Tish told her, 'Apparently, dear, I've been fortunate enough to engender no complaints. My motto is, Leave 'em pleased, you won't get squeezed.' The crowd tittered, and the woman sat down. Tish told me later he had 'bedded the old gal con gusto' that very evening."

Why is he going on about all this with Lina? Marlon Tish is unscrupulous, unreliable, self-indulgent and facile with unwanted commentary on the foibles and secrets of others. He is both charming and disgusting and the last guy in the world from whom he would ever want advice. And yet he has been musing all day on their conversations over dinner last night and, after sleeping over, with breakfast this morning. And certain that everything said last night would be lost in a boozy mist, he was surprised when Tish garnished their eggs and bacon with a series of thoughts on "your royally fucked-up life."

He started with the talk John had recounted from the memorial service with a fellow named Mixon, a philosophy prof at Creighton and an old friend of Fr. Cary Redding, whose corpse resided in a polished bronze coffin not 20 feet away. According to Mixon, Fr. Cary had lost his calling several years ago and, in fact, lost his faith. He was a priest who did not believe in God, said his friend, and talked seriously about leaving the priesthood. He finally decided to live with his secret and to continue ministering to the folks in a well-to-do parish in Chicago.

"Frankly, Johnny," said Tish, "I sense your own crisis of faith. You no longer believe in your marriage, and yet, like the good father who remained to serve the needs of his parishioners, to feed their delusions of meaning in a meaningless world, you stick it out in your god-awful marriage, feeding your own delusion that you're saving your self-destructive wife. But what you're really doing is making it possible for her to slowly kill herself with booze."

This was a typically inept analogy from Tish, but John said only, "No, what I've been trying to do for at least the past decade is get her to stop drinking herself to death."

"Yes, you've tried to do that, but at the same time, you've made nearly every practical facet of her life with the bottle possible. I mean, without you, how would she make a living, feed herself, keep house, have friends or a social life? No, pal, you make it possible for her to never really take responsibility for her own life. Everything you do helps her keep drinking with impunity. So keep it up, and wait for that final, lethal consequence. And then you'll be able to say, 'Yep, I told her that would happen.'"

About Lina, the message from Tish was simple: "If she is what you say, and you feel about her what you say, why the fuck are you moping around here with an asshole like me and not chasing her brilliant, beautiful tail all over Bologna?"

For that he had no answer and said only, "Why indeed."

Driving back, he recalled Lina also talking about his enabling, and, in fact, he had accused himself with similar thoughts more than once over the past couple of years. Then why the weight of these words now from a self-centered cad whose values and behavior he neither admires nor envies? Whatever, now is not the time to recount all this to Lina.

So get to the point, and talk about Stan. Tell her that despite his apparent closeness to Redding, Stan did not show up in Chicago yesterday. And then came the email about Stan suddenly heading off to Mexico City to meet his long lost father. This story seemed an obvious cover for a visit to Bologna to pursue Lina, and John began the debate with himself over whether to break his promise not to write Lina until after the first of the year. On the road before he reached Cedar Hill early this afternoon, he pretty much decided to give Stan the benefit of the doubt and keep his commitment not to write.

Then he walked in the door and found Mar half in the bag with her vodka and tonic, he told her about the funeral, Stan's absence and the email.

With alcoholic assurance, she said, "Well, that's a crock."

As soon as she said it, he knew it was true. "Why do you say that?"

"Because it's obvious. If he was crazed enough to do all those things to her, where else would he be but Bologna? It's as clear as the fear on your face — that he's there and you're not."

As if this did not deserve a response, he said, "But you claimed *you* did all those things."

"Of course I told her that." A self-satisfied smirk swelled her florid face. "Why not take credit for all the shit that ruined things for a rotten bitch like her? Made me feel great."

"I don't believe you."

"Yeah, well, I talked to that boy. He was kind of hitting on me, but he was consumed with her, and he all but admitted he did it all. Anyway, the next time you write the bitch, ask her if Stan is there. You'll see."

He did not really want to believe Stan was in Bologna. But his initial sense that the guy had gone not to Mexico but to Italy was instinctive, intuitive, and he has learned to trust that kind of response. What harm would there be in writing a note that simply said she might want to be on the look-out for Stan, that he could be headed for Bologna? And that would also give him a chance to exchange words with her, after three painfully silent weeks, to gauge her frame of mind and tell her something about changes in Cedar Hill.

So at his computer desk, in his office over the garage, the night beyond his lone window cold and starless, he starts again, this time with the greeting he was using before their mutually agreed upon silence:

Mia Carissima Lina,

Please forgive that I am breaking my word not to write. You'll see why in a moment. But first, tell me you are well, happy and busy with the book, safe and well-settled back in the amazing old city you've told me so much about, warm in

200

the close embrace of the many friends who love and cherish you. I want only to know that all this is true for you.

Of course, I miss you deeply, painfully, but overall I am fine, busy at the moment reading final papers. I'll spend Christmas in Cleveland with my parents. (I wish they could meet you.) As I say, I feel reasonably well, and this week I have my 6-month check up with my oncologist. As I've told you, this is an important milestone: 5 years since the seed implants.

He adds in the news about Mar's new job and then gets to the point. "I'm writing now because an email arrived yesterday from our friend Stan." Cutting and pasting the lines from Stan's message, he explains his reaction to it, the likelihood, as he sees it, that "you might soon find this unbalanced prick on your doorstep." And then, after taking a few minutes to think it through one more time, he makes his offer.

Look, sweetheart, if Stan is there, or if he shows up, and is causing you any kind of trouble, I will come in an instant to Bologna to give you all the help and support I can. Please don't hesitate. Just tell me to come. Of course, it would be a joy to see you and to be with you for however long, but I want only to be sure you're safe. In any case, please let me know what's happening there, so either I won't need to worry, or I can make plans to be with you asap.

A quick read through the whole thing now, a few word-changes here and there, and then he adds his usual close — I love you in both English and Italian. The clock on his monitor says 12:44 am. With a six-hour difference, unless she is up early on a Sunday morning, she won't pick this up for a while. He marks it high priority, then thinks that's too alarming. Maybe just a return receipt so he'll know quickly if she's up and at her desk. He hits send and wonders yet again this commonplace miracle, his words flying around the world in a matter of seconds.

Waiting to see if the receipt comes back, he reads Dowd and Rich in the Sunday Times, both of them writing about Obama and Clinton in Iowa. He likes the columns. They boost his sense that this campaign has really begun to turn. Still no word from Bologna.

When he opens his eyes five hours later, the spare bedroom is silent and dark. He's wide awake with the thought that he left his computer on, certain that her response will be waiting for him now. Into his sweats and moccasins, he cuts through a frigid wind to the garage. Back in his office, he immediately moves the mouse to bring up his mail. Yes, the receipt notice is there, its arrival listed at 2:32 am. Right below it is her response, sent 25 minutes later. So she got to her computer just after 8:30, wrote back before 9, and it's after noon now in Bologna. There's comfort in these details, but he is nervous as he clicks on her response.

Mio Carissimo John,

Thank you for writing. No need to apologize. You wrote from your heart, and I love you for it. Yes, I am well. It has taken a while, but I am now settled in, and, yes, it is good to be with my friends again. My work on the book has suffered a bit, but I am ready to start again. I am pleased you are well and that you will spend Christmas with your family.

As for Stan, yes, he is here in Bologna. Yesterday he literally appeared, as you say, on my doorstep, and, of course, I was shocked. The moment I saw him standing there, I knew with a certainty that he was the one fully responsible for the plagues at St. Thomas. But to the question of whether you should come here to give me your help and support, I must tell you as clearly as I can, absolutely not.

John, please understand and believe me: your coming here would serve no good purpose. I have dealt with Stan decisively and have put him completely out of my life here. I have told all the friends who are closest to me (and who

202

are very protective of me) everything about Stan—who he is, what he has done, why he is not to be trusted. He said he is leaving Bologna today for Torino to do research on Levi. I believe he will do that, because there is absolutely nothing for him here in Bologna.

Beyond all this, I must say to you, darling, that after a month or so to consider our experience in Michigan, given the fact that we cannot allow ourselves to think about being together because of the situation with your wife, it seems much better for both of us to keep our contact to a minimum. In terms of getting on with our lives, our work and whatever chance either of us might have for a meaningful personal connection, there is no question but that we must keep our distance. I trust you know these words are written with a full appreciation of what we have shared. And I hope you will tell me that you agree.

One last word on the situation with your wife: please understand and accept that I feel very strongly that one must never wish for something for oneself that would entail misfortune for another. This is something my mother said to me many years ago, and I have learned over the course of my life that it is wise and true, so much so that it is one of the central tenets of my life. I wish you all the goodness and happiness that life can offer. I love you.

Ti amo.

Lina

Chapter 33

The Bravo Caffe has been missing from her life for how long now? Three months in Michigan, and then it was one of those places to be avoided in the weeks since. Now she feels grateful for these deep red walls, black furniture, and stylish design cues, even more for the big smiles on familiar faces and friendly greetings from nearly everyone. For years she has made a tradition of Sunday brunch here, the smorgasbord tables covered with Bolognese specialties, soups and pastries, a ritual resumed now as she sits with her newspapers alone at a table with a view of the entrance. Watching for one particular face and hoping not to see it.

She arrived after 1, and the first to stop at her table with warm embraces were Aldo and Rena. Holding her hand, Aldo asked if she had slept well last night. Rena insisted that she come to their place for dinner tonight. It will be something *"semplice ma buono."* Simple but good. Lina said everything she does is good. *"Si,"* said Rena with a sharp smile. *"Allora, questa sera, alle sette e mezzo."* So, their apartment at 7:30. Lina will bring the wine and the expectation of a wonderful evening with two of her dearest friends.

Aldo's reference to last night made her think about Stan again. Despite what she wrote to John this morning, would Stan just quietly leave town? She had told the truth about dispatching Stan with no room to believe he had a chance, and she wanted to be clear that John should not come. But did she really believe that Stan would simply disappear? What if John's email had arrived right after the scene with the ripped bra and the knife? Would she have been more prone to say, "Yes, darling, I want you here with me"? Certainly her least attractive course of action would be to urge John to leave his struggling wife and fly into a mess he could do little or nothing to fix. And yet, what about Stan now? Does he pose some kind of genuine threat? If not, why glance so often at the café's front door?

When she left the apartment, the air cold but the sun already high in a bright blue sky, why stand in front of her building, moving her gaze slowly across all the shadowed porticos where he might be hiding, waiting to follow? And not seeing the slightest hint of his presence, why walk up Via San Vitale a full block out of her way, before doubling back on the chance she might catch a glimpse of him lurking about? Why glance behind her at mid-block and at every corner all the way to Via Mascarella and the entrance to Bravo. Even inside here, with all the good feelings the place engendered, she felt some kind of ill-ease that, given the evidence of her senses, must be paranoia.

Having made her usual online stops this morning at the Times, a couple of political blogs and Juan Cole's site — it still rankles that she never managed to visit him in Ann Arbor — she walked to Titto's stand in the Piazza Aldrovandi where he always holds her Sunday copies of the Corriere della Sera and la Repubblica. Both have stories about the Times' piece on the Italian malaise, and one lifted a quote from her own post to the Times.

Paolo's friend at the University's law school, Vito Zabbini, stopped by her table and mentioned he had seen her quote. But he really wanted to talk about the story of how the CIA had destroyed videotapes of terror suspect interrogations. Mark his word, there will never be prosecutions. Had he heard from Paolo on how his case in Montevideo was coming? Rolling his big brown eyes, Vito said Paolo always thinks he is going to win.

Her friend Stella Ventimiglia, the vivacious professor of political science, is next, sitting down to go on about the car bombs in Algiers that killed 37 this week, half of them UN staffers, one of whom was a friend of Stella's. Wiping a tear, she seems ready to talk for the rest of the afternoon, but understands quickly when Lina says her book is overdue, and she needs to get back to it now.

So braced by friends, a large bowl of white minestrone, freshly baked bread, coffeecake and espresso, she folds the newspapers into her large tote bag and walks back to the apartment. Smiling in the sunshine, she relishes her time in Bravo's style and warmth. And yet she also finds that slight edge of discomfort still with her. Certainly it has to do with Stan, but that nervous, unpleasant feeling is coming from something vague and elusive, perhaps not quite real, almost like a remnant from a dream.

At the entrance to her building, she stops to sweep the street in a slow, careful arc. There are several people in view on this beautiful afternoon, but no one looks like Stan. Once inside she moves past the mailboxes, inserts her key in the access door and pushes through. And then with the keys still in hand, a thought comes to her so suddenly that she stops and looks behind her. As if someone could be there. But now she knows what has been bothering her. Last night, in the kitchen, she was distracted for a moment when he asked where to put her box of books. And she told him the hall closet. Where her spare set of apartment keys always hang on a hook.

As she moves toward the elevator, she tries to slow her heart down with the thought that the keys are inconspicuous there near the door, often not even visible because she hangs her large white apron on a hook above. When she pushes the button, the old elevator opens immediately and gives her an uninterrupted ride to the 4th floor. Paranoia, she tells herself as she uses the apartment key at her door. Inside, walking quickly down the hallway to the closet, she asks silently to please make it paranoia. She pulls the door open, and there next to the jam on her left hangs the old cotton apron she uses when she really gets serious in the kitchen. She lifts the apron, and hanging there is the ring with her two spare keys.

Taking them from their hook, she rubs them between her thumb and forefinger, as if she is feeling for the aura of another's hand. She brings them into the hall, snaps on the overhead and, noting their familiar nicks and scratches, knows they are her keys. "Grazie," she says quietly as she puts them back on the hook and moves the apron to cover them.

Having told Stella that she would be working on her book this afternoon, she feels compelled to sit at her computer and bring up the chapter that includes her discussion of Cormac McCarthy, making several changes, fussing with wording and adding a paragraph with a line of thought that had come to her two days ago on the long hike to San Luca:

> No Country for Old Men wields the power of the unreasoning urge to destroy, the impact of senseless evil. Yes, Chigurh is a narco-operative/hit man, presumably motivated by money. But he moves with a cunning and devotion both fascinating and terrifying, and he also acts out irrational little dramas, at times

206

forcing some unfortunate who crosses his path to flip a coin to decide whether he or she will live or die. It is a story of the human curse of greed — the horrid things men do for cash — but also one of nightmarish and chaotic personal terror.

Her concentration is reasonably solid through the afternoon, but with some frequency she is interrupted by the arrival of email. Each time she expects it to be John's reply, but instead nearly every one of her friends from her little soiree last night wants to know how she feels today, after dealing with "Stan the charlatan," as Hans puts it. All of them express their concern for her and their admiration for how she handled such a shocking and difficult turn of events. Rena, leaving nothing to chance, confirms dinner this evening.

But nothing from John. Was he put off or disappointed? Maybe he read between her lines — something he is good at — and suspected that matters between her and Stan were not simply over and done with. It is tempting, but she does not want to think about that question right now. If she gives into it, continuing to work on her book this afternoon will be a lost cause.

Finally, after 7, when she is in the bedroom getting herself ready to go out, she hears the two-toned call from her office announcing an email arrival. This is probably John, she thinks, moving quickly to her computer. Instead, with a shake of her head, she sees it is Stan. She is loath to open it but knows she will. A click and she sees it is brief:

> Dearest Lina,
>
> It was great seeing you yesterday and meeting your friends. Hey, remember this one from The Police? As always.
>
> Stan

Below is a link to a YouTube video of "Every Breath You Take." She does not have to open the link to know that for the foreseeable future, Sting's haunting line will be even more troubling: "I'll be watching you."

She stands there staring at her large, flat-panel screen, wondering why the message has this mock-friendly tone. And then she thinks that anything he might send her from now on will probably sound like this. He will put nothing in writing that might be viewed as overtly threatening. And this is likely to be as close as he will come to sounding ominous. Before she turns away, the computer calls again, and this time a notice of John's reply does appear. She opens it quickly, and, to her surprise, it too is brief.

> Of course, I will abide by your wishes, though not for a second do I believe he will leave you alone. If you say you need me, I will be there with you as soon as humanly possible. I love you. Ti amo.

Why did it take him so long, more than four hours, to write such a short note? Did he write page after page and then decide against sending them? Did he go back to sleep after reading her email? If she reads between his lines, does he sound hurt perhaps, or depressed? Her questions make her want to pick up a phone and, in a matter of seconds, hear his voice. But that she will not do. It would be, she tells herself, a dangerous thing.

On her way down the elevator, Sting's strange, mournful voice is singing in her head. But as she steps into the light under the colonnade that lines her dark street, closing her long black coat firmly at her throat, she turns in the direction of Via Zamboni without looking around for him at all. Feeling the weight of the bottle of red in her tote, she moves briskly. She has not taken a dozen strides before she glances up and, with her stomach sinking, spots him standing 15 meters ahead, staring at her brazenly, under a portico light on the other side of the street.

The collar of his black leather jacket is up, his hands in its pockets. He smiles, weirdly she thinks, and nods as she passes. She says nothing and looks away, hastening her pace to the corner where she turns past Federico's chemist shop with the familiar green cross that marks it as a *farmacia*. Now she is on the dark, narrow side street that will curve around to the Piazza Verdi. There she will cross Via Zamboni, pass the Teatro Comunale, then hasten two blocks to the building near the Odeon Cinema where Aldo and Rena have their apartment. This is the University District, after all, and the streets, even on a Sunday evening, will be busy with students. There is really no reason to worry, and yet she finds herself moving more quickly.

Her breath is coming more audibly, and when she finally glances behind her at the other side of the street, he is there, 10 meters back, keeping pace.

Chapter 34

On Monday morning he finally feels rested and in good spirits. "Like a new man," he says out loud. Yes, part of him is still surprised he is in Bologna, but yesterday was an interesting experience. The funny thing is, he really meant it when he told the group at Lina's Saturday night that he'd be leaving for Torino the next day. He was feeling jetlagged, humiliated and enraged when he was shown the door, and when he woke late Sunday morning, almost 11:30, he was still feeling that way and still thinking the plan was to get out of Dodge.

Pack his stuff, and maybe have one last look around, climb a tower or find one of those hidden canals so he could say he'd seen the city, and then pull the Fiat out of the spot he'd rented in an old car-park about 6 blocks from the apartment. He'd head off for Torino, or, as it came to him while he was trying to get to sleep at 2 am, perhaps do a little sightseeing first, in Rome, or Florence, or Venice, or all three, and in the process pick up some young, pliant Italian beauty, who, unlike the Bitch, would appreciate his company. Then he remembered the keys.

He thought of three options. He could: 1) toss them into a canal, 2) mail them back to her anonymously, or 3) have copies made. If copies were his choice, he could wait until she went out, then sneak into her apartment, return the originals to their hook in the closet, and maybe snoop around a bit before taking off. Once he thought about that open Door #3, he couldn't close it. She would probably never know the keys had been missing, and he would have access to her place, and to her, anytime he wanted.

It was a Sunday morning, and he had no idea where he could get keys copied in this town. With church-influenced ordinances, most shops were likely to be closed. So he made a bet with himself. If he could not find a place to have copies made by 2 pm, he would drop them in a sewer and leave town. It was silly, with the odds stacked against him, but that was the bet.

Shaved, showered and dressed, he was out the door in less than a half hour. He found the building's eccentric old custodian, Signora Vascone, moving her hunchback strenuously to sweep the street in front of the building's entrance with a worn-out broom. Even with her hump and her scowl, he thought he had charmed the little witch when he moved in last Thursday and so tried his hand again. In Italian he asked how she was doing on this beautiful morning and, getting something akin to a smile, moved on to where he might get keys copied today.

"*Qui*," said the woman, stopping the broom. She was dressed entirely in black.

"Here?" he said, astonished and thinking she must have misunderstood. In Italian he tried again, asking if it really could be done right here.

"*Si*," she said, showing missing teeth and tapping her chest. She would do it for him herself. Inside her ground floor apartment near the entrance, there, sure enough, in one corner of the living room, he saw the machine and the rotating rack filled with blanks. She took Lina's keys from him and nodded, saying these were not the keys she had given him for his apartment. No, he said, they belonged to a friend. Then she got to work, and he sat on her big old sofa covered with lace doilies. This, she said, was a sideline, a service for people in the neighborhood. Her brother had done it for decades, and when he passed away four years ago, she had taken over, the same for his duties with the building. When he asked if it bothered her working on the Sabbath, she said she had no use for a God who would give her this hump.

A half-hour later he was sitting in a small café down the street from the Bitch's building. From his table next to a window he had a clear view of the comings and goings at her entrance. He'd finish this breakfast of paper-thin prosciutto, salami and mortadella, three kinds of cheese, fresh-crusted bread and coffee, and then he would walk up the street to her building and push her call button. If she answered, he'd walk away. If she did not, he'd drop in for a visit. But, engrossed in his food for a time, he finally glanced up to find her walking down Via San Vitale toward her building, slowly looking around. Then as he watched, she moved right past her entrance, turned the corner and headed north into the University District.

In her apartment he figured he had time but quickly returned her keys to the closet. Signora Vascone had done well: the new ones had worked without a hitch. Then he searched through her rooms, looking for he knew not what. In her bedroom a discarded blue sweater and bra were tossed on the red comforter. In the bathroom, he ran a finger over the moist white enamel of her large tub and began to get a hard-on, which really pissed him off. In the kitchen the large stove and oven caught his eye. They were gas, the pilot light visible and flickering in the access on the top. On the counter was a bottle of wine from last night, re-corked with one of those gadgets that sucked out the air. And off to the side, where the books had been, he noticed a sliding razor knife she had probably used to open the box. The living room still felt like rotten humiliation, and he moved through it fast to the patio doors. He wanted fresh air and breathed in deeply as he walked out onto the red tile. The view in the sunshine was amazing, the red rooftops of the whole city laid out around him. At the far end of the patio he leaned on the railing and looked down at the gray stone of the street below, four floors down. Flashing on an image of Hal's pathetic face as he flipped into the night, he turned away and moved inside.

About to leave, he suddenly remembered what he wanted to do with her computer. In her office it was running. Having already done it once in her apartment in Cedar Hill, he took only ten minutes to set up the Trojan. Now he could read her email from a few blocks away.

Which was exactly what he was doing four hours later when Rena's reminder about dinner arrived. Now he knew what he'd be doing at 7:15 or so this evening. But for much of the afternoon, in this warm little room, he was sprawled naked on his bed. Even though he had risen late, he was feeling sleepy. He had not fallen off until after 3 am, and even then his sleep was fitful. So after winning his bet and after his foray into the Bitch's pad, he decided to try a nap. Before long he was playing with himself, casually at first, and then more seriously, telling himself to absolutely not think of the B of B—his new name for her. It stood straight up and then leaned back, as if straining to look him in the eye. And then he knew if he were ever going to nap this afternoon, he would have to beat himself off. He worked fast, then slow, gentle, then hard. Often feeling he was just about to explode, he couldn't finish it off. He tried thinking of Marta, then Lilli, Gemma, even Rena, and finally some nameless Italian beauty. But, of course, not the Bitch, because it angered him royally that she still turned him on. He stopped for a while, and then a surprising question popped into his head. If the B of B walked in right now and began to strip, would he want to fuck her or stab her in the heart? Truth be told, he'd like to do both. And thinking of that and with a few quick strokes applied to the tip, he shot it all over his chest.

Finally he dozed off, but an hour later he was wide-eyed again, his mind awash in violent fantasies. Maybe it was that question about fucking or stabbing that got him revved, but he started with the idea of acquiring a gun. Would a store even sell one to a foreigner? Where in this strange city could he find one that couldn't be traced? He'd try Google, but he'd probably have to explore a bit and ask around. Every city had people who catered to such needs, and even if it was home to Europe's oldest university, surely Bologna was no exception. It wouldn't have to be anything special, not for what he saw so vividly in his mind's eye. Even a little .22 pistol would do when placed to her head.

She'd walk into the apartment, he'd show it to her and kick the door closed. Then to the bedroom, telling her to shed her clothes, and he'd love the fear and despair in those mean, green eyes, the quiver of the lovely lower lip, the quaver in that self-possessed voice and the tremble of that fine-boned hand going to the buttons on her blouse. With her naked in that big red bed, he'd tell her how often he'd seen her like this in the bathroom video he'd made. Maybe he'd tease her snatch with the barrel, see if she could come that way. Ask her if John ever did this for her. If he felt like it, he'd use his dick to tune her up and then plunge it in, all the while holding that little pistol to her temple. Which is where he'd finally do it, literally blow her brains out, maybe fold his hand and the gun in a pillow the way he saw Philip Seymour Hoffman do it in that flick about the brothers who ripped off their parents' jewelry store. Of course, he'd be wearing thin rubber gloves, and he'd make damn sure of all the details well in advance. He'd put the gun in her dead hand, and finally he'd go to her computer and do it right this time, probably write the note the night before, make it pitch-perfect this time.

Or maybe it would be 3 in the morning, he'd waltz in, go directly to her in the bed and, gun in hand, do whatever he wanted. But instead of using it on her, with the messy brains and everything, maybe lead her out onto the patio in the dark and just shove her over the railing. And he'd do the computer thing first, so he could split immediately, lock the door from the outside and leave before anyone could even stir.

Really, he wouldn't even need the gun. Maybe just some chloroform or something that worked like it. He'd have to research that a bit, but just some drops on his handkerchief, then grab her from behind and hold it over her nose and mouth until she was limp in his arms. He'd carry her to the bed, take off her clothes, play a little with those perfect tits, then put her in the half-filled bathtub. Finally, he'd slide that yellow razor knife open to slit her pretty little wrists.

Or maybe just use what was already in the apartment, the gas in the kitchen. Knock her out with those drops and put her on the floor near the stove, and then just blow out the pilot light, turn all the burners on and the oven as well and open its door. Goodnight nurse. Of course his new and improved note would work for any of these scenarios, and he'd be leaving town in the Panda within minutes. No, suicide was definitely the way to go, and no matter how much her friends might suspect him, his meticulous plan would make a connection to him impossible. He could surely come up with more ideas; now it was just a matter of which one he liked the best.

Later on the street near her apartment, on her way to dinner with Aldo and Rena, she looked stricken when she saw him. It was important to show himself to her, to make her feel terrified and humiliated before he ended this. It was why, as a lark, he sent her that song from Sting. And why he openly followed her now on the opposite side of the street, until she reached the Piazza Verdi facing the Teatro Comunale, the big concert hall in town. Then, as she crossed Via Zamboni, the main drag through the student quarter, he stayed with her, only ten yards behind, until she glanced back. As she continued walking, she reached into her big purse and pulled out her cell.

Yeah, so she had screamed "*Polizia*" in the apartment and then never tried to call. Still, he dropped back a bit, keeping her in view but staying behind a few students who sounded like they were heading for a movie. Two minutes later, a half-block from Odeon Cinema, both Aldo and Rena were waiting outside the entrance to what must be their apartment building. So that's who she called. He followed her openly now until she reached them, and all three turned and stared at him. He gave them a smile and a wave and stood there watching as they quickly turned away and moved inside. And then he waited until they appeared in a second-floor window looking out at him as he gazed up at them.

An hour later he was in a cafe on Via Zamboni, finishing a beer and a pizza Margareta. He had struck up a conversation with two girls at the next table who said they were in pre-med and seemed quite taken with him. They couldn't believe he was an American because his Italian was so good. They forced him to speak English to see if he really was from the States, and he fooled with them, putting an obviously phony Italian accent to his English, and when they laughed and insisted again, giving them a British take. Then finally his George W. Bush.

By the time they left together and walked to a small park behind the Teatro Comunale, they were acting like fast friends, the girls flirting, one on each arm, and cute in their matching fur hats. Someday soon, they told him, they would like to give him a tour of the Palazzo Poggi, the large university center, just up Via Zamboni. Four hundred years ago, they said, it was Europe's top scientific institute, and he must not miss the anatomy exhibits, which they described in gory detail. Very sexy, they giggled in English, and when they invited him to join them back at their nearby apartment, he easily imagined a three-some happening after a little too much wine. But he had seen Aldo and the Bitch watching him from that window again, and when the two of them emerged from the building two minutes later, he told the girls he'd love to, but he was really with the CIA and needed to follow someone. He took their names (Marciella and Fauna) and a phone number scribbled on a scrap of paper, kissed each of them twice on the mouth and was on his way.

He trailed Aldo and the Bitch, close enough for them to know he was there, all the way back to her place. There Aldo saw her inside and then turned and stared hard at him as he stood under a portico across the street. He stared back and knew that this guy with the bushy hair under a black tam was fully prepared to stand guard at her door all night. And so he walked back toward his apartment, thinking about Marciella and Fauna and inviting himself over. He pulled out their slip of paper but, feeling exhausted, told himself, next time.

* * *

So now in the morning the new man Stan is feeling good about things, starting with the improbable Signora Vascone's key making yesterday, which was like fate, or destiny, or a coincidence so unlikely that you have to pay it mind. He likes having the Bitch's keys, to her apartment and to her life. He likes feeling so in control, so filled with ideas and options, so ready to improvise on a moment's notice. He likes the feeling he got seeing the fear and confusion in the Bitch's face. He likes those girls who flirted with him last night, and, with its fabulous history and intellectual buzz, he likes Bologna. He'll be staying a while.

He spends an hour with his laptop, googling first How to commit murder and get away with it. Then, odorless colorless tasteless poison. Lots of fascinating stuff he could spend all day on. But once he hits Tetrahydrozoline, he stops and checks his bottle of Visine. The little 30-milliliter plastic squeezer is about three-quarters full, and sure enough, there it is on the label: Tetrahydrozoline HCl 0.05%. So who knew that the colorless liquid he puts in his eyes to get the red out will kill you if you drink it? Today he figures he'll sightsee all over town and stop in stores where he can buy a few bottles, one at a time.

When he walks out, the weather has changed. It does not feel as cold, but the sky is overcast, as if there is rain in store. As he heads for Via San Vitale and the café where he had breakfast and could sit in the window and watch her building, a stray glance picks up someone familiar, moving maybe 30 yards away. A young woman. Marta maybe? A quick glance back and, it is Marta in her bright red coat and purple scarf. A coincidence? It has to be. None of the Bitch's gang knows where he's staying. Without another look back, he negotiates the three blocks to the café and heads inside.

The tables next to the window are all taken. He sits at one close enough to at least check out the street, and to the old guy who waited on him yesterday he says, "*Buon Giorno.*" The fellow rasps the same, giving him a menu. As he opens it, Marta walks in the door. So now he thinks she spotted him on the street, followed him in here and will probably propose that they sit together. The girl has had her eye on him ever since the gallery opening. But instead of greeting him, she takes a table close to the door, sits down facing him and pulls a book from her purse.

216

So now what? Feeling vaguely disoriented, he looks at the menu without really seeing it. When the old guy comes to take his order, he snaps out of it to say just bread, cheese and coffee this morning. The guy grunts, "*Va bene*," takes the menu and moves across the room to Marta, pauses for only a second, then heads for the kitchen.

What is she doing here, and what was she doing on his street? The new Stan will not just sit around wondering. He'll get up, walk over and charm her with how he loves the red and purple against her fair complexion and all that curly dark hair. Then he'll ask her to join him and when she does, he'll find out what gives.

Before he can move, she puts her book down, gets up from her table and walks directly to his.

Chapter 35

She wakes with a vague anger and is still feeling it as she walks out of her building this late Monday morning, determined not to let him frighten or intimidate her out of doing anything she wishes. Moving on Via San Vitale toward the city's center, she looks around freely, telling herself not to worry about being watched or followed. A wave to Federico as he enters the *farmacia*, a *"Ciao, Bella!"* from Titto in his newsstand. Yes, she glances behind a few times and searches the shadows under the gallerias, but something tells her he will not show himself today. For a moment she wonders if that is a good thing or a bad thing. Forget it, and forget him.

Glancing up at the Torre Asinelli, she thinks of the couple on the plane. Do not miss the food, she told them, and today she definitely will not, headed for the Mercato di Mezzo, Bologna's traditional market area for about 2000 years. Probably her favorite place in the city, a maze of streets and alleys full of shops selling everything, but especially fresh produce and food products of every kind. The streets are named for the original artisans and merchants who did business there so many centuries ago, and as she moves onto her favorite, Via Clavature, where locksmiths and key makers had plied their trade, she thinks of something that should have occurred to her yesterday. What if Stan had, in fact, found her spare keys in the closet on Saturday night and then had copies made? He could have returned them to the closet while she was out for brunch on Sunday. She stops in her tracks in front of the place where she buys her fruits and vegetables, a shop called Tartufi. But then, under her breath she says, "Paranoia." Where on a Sunday morning could he have possibly found a place to have keys copied?

Picking out her tomatoes and zucchini, she pays Stefano and slips them into her large cloth shopping bag. From her cheese shop, La Baita in Via Pescherie, she adds parmigiano and ricotta. And then to Via Caprarie to get her prosciutto and meet Lilli at Tamburini, their favorite trattoria for lunch. The place is legendary, a gourmet, self-service deli, and the smiling Signor Tamburini points her to the back where Lilli is already waiting. In one corner she spots the table where she saw Francis Ford Coppola two years ago.

Later over meat ravioli and spinach tortellini, she tells Lilli what happened yesterday evening when she visited Aldo and Rena. There is one point in her story that she is still puzzling over. Just after they sat down to one of Rena's wonderful dinners, Aldo suddenly excused himself, disappeared into his den and closed his door. She could barely hear him in there, speaking on the phone in muted tones. When he returned to the table after several minutes, he exchanged a look with Rena but said nothing about what he had been up to. Lina felt it would be rude to ask him about it, and her only thought now is that Aldo, a professor of practical ethics on the philosophy faculty, who has written papers on the moral dilemmas faced by police officers, may have called someone he knows in the Carabinieri. Perhaps he asked if an officer might come out and deal with Stan. The fact that he said nothing later about the call tells her that what Aldo heard is, of course, what he already knew. The police can do nothing unless a crime has been committed or you have some kind of evidence that one is imminent.

This story has an unexpected effect on Lilli. Sounding genuinely worried, she tells Lina this is exactly what is needed. Go to the police and tell them the whole story. She is certain they will take it seriously and do something, talk to Stan, maybe, warn him he is being watched, anything that might deter a bloke who clearly means Lina no good. Lina resists, repeating more than once that there is nothing the police can or will do in a case like this. But her friend is insistent, and she finally agrees to at least give it serious thought.

Maybe that is the reason why, on impulse, on her way back to the apartment, she stops at a hardware shop and buys a wide-angle door scope. She owns a power drill and thinks she can install it herself, but in all the years she has lived in this apartment, she has never felt unsafe, never even given a thought to the possibility that she might need such a thing.

At five she is sitting in Del Museo, a café near the law school, with Vito Zabbini. She had finally picked up the phone and called him after Lilli's words on going to the police had nagged at her back in the apartment. Yes, she had installed the peephole and felt good about it, but what if she was simply being arrogant about what she thinks she knows? Now as they wait for their wine, there is small talk first. How are Bianca and the boys? They're all so beautiful that when he thinks of them, his heart flips. So how goes Lina's book? Not great lately. Too many distractions and, frankly, worries. Which is really why she called him.

After Stan had left the other night, she had been very open with Lilli and the others at her apartment. She talked about John and what he came to mean to her, and about the role their relationship obviously had in what happened at St. Thomas. But now with Vito, she feels as if she is literally telling him everything that happened over the past four months, the whole sad saga, her affair, the plagues and how it has continued back here in Italy. She tries to be thorough and fair, separating what she knows from what she thinks or feels; describing how her nearly fainting in Stan's arms, from the shock of seeing him at her door, might have led him to misread her feelings, and how quickly he had stopped forcing himself on her once she slapped him. In short, she is honest to a fault, and finished, she tells him with a smile and a hand raised that she has now given him the truth, the whole truth and nothing but the truth.

Paolo always said about his friend Vito that he had certainly been a good prosecutor, but now he was a great professor of law. "He has found his niche," Paolo would say, and there is a deep need for a teacher and mentor with the practical savvy of a prosecutor melded with a devotion to the law and a passion for the constitution. It is one of those basic, vital things every young lawyer-to-be should get from a legal education.

So she knows what to expect from Vito, and she gets it: an erudite yet stirring lecture from a stern leftist perspective on the constitutional issues underlying personal freedom and the rights of the individual. She lets him go well beyond any information she really, practically needs, because she loves to hear this kind of talk, a man speaking, quite brilliantly in fact, from both his mind and his heart. Vito is such a good man, she thinks, as he darts from point to point, his well-manicured hands always moving, dark eyes flashing. He is a dedicated family man, she knows, with a beautiful, accomplished wife, a pediatrician, and two small sons.

Finally, she tells him this is all well and good, but what about the practical reality she is facing here? A fellow who may well have shot a bullet through her front window in Michigan, who is sufficiently obsessed to follow her all the way back to Bologna, who tried to rip off her bra and force himself on her, and now seems to be stalking her and emailing not-so-veiled threats. He, Vito, knows the police, has worked closely with them in the past, and probably still has personal friends in the department. What could or would the police do in a case like this.

"*Niente,*" says Vito, folding his hands. Nothing. Oh, if she looks long and hard, she might find an officer with not enough to do, who'd be willing to meet with this fellow and give him a little talk. Warn him to keep out of her life. Maybe even tell him to get out of Bologna, or he will find himself with more trouble than staying is worth. But frankly, if she chooses to look, he hopes she will not find such a policeman, because Italy will be a better place without him.

In spite of a twinge that feels like fear, she likes his answer. But then she asks, what will Vito say if he hears tomorrow that she has been stabbed to death in her bed? With those warm brown eyes, Vito looks at her and says he will be too completely crushed to speak. He will weep without stopping. But he will not change his mind about what the law should be or what the police should do.

It is nearly 6:30 when she gets back to her building. The street is dark, empty and quiet in front of the entrance. She is at the outer door when she hears a man's voice yelling to her. So startled she does not recognize the voice, she deciphers only her name. And something about dogs? Turning, she looks up Via San Vitale, and there is Stan, charging toward her, running down the portico, about 40 meters away. As she pushes the door open he yells again, his voice ringing in the street's narrow canyon, "*Professore,* call off the dogs!"

In the vestibule, she quickly unlocks the access door, then shoves it shut behind her until the lock clicks. Rushing past the mailboxes, she ignores the elevator and goes to the stairwell. He looked and sounded so nearly out of control that, as she quickly climbs the stairs, she expects to hear him pounding on the door below and yelling at her again. But there is nothing more to hear, and before she reaches the first-floor landing, she feels completely out of breath.

Chapter 36

He can't believe he was actually yelling at her in the street. Her street, where she probably knows everyone. Lucky that when he stepped out from this alley a minute ago and saw her at the entrance, there was no one around to see him make a fool of himself. Of course, someone might have looked out a window to see this crazy American screaming at their illustrious neighbor. And then what? Call *la polizia*? That's all he needs right now.

Yeah, he's been feeling provoked all day, but this was a potentially serious mistake, the kind of impulsive move he must not make. As he walks in the alley, his stomach is clenched. Now what to do and where to go? He certainly doesn't feel like cooping himself up in that crappy little apartment. No, what he needs is a little female diversion to break the hold of this lame fucking obsession. Call those girls? What were their names? Marciella and Fauna. What the hell kind of name is Fauna? From now on they should be Flora and Fauna.

Fishing out their slip of paper, he punches the number into his cell. Flora answers, sounds happy to hear from him and tries out her English: "Ah, *si*, Stan. Did you got the spy?"

He says he can't talk about it and then asks if she and Fauna would like to have dinner.

She says, sorry, they are both "in locked down," studying for exams. And tomorrow the same. But truly, they are thinking now they could not go out with a man who works for the CIA.

He was just kidding about that, he says.

"Yes, we think so. Maybe try the next week again?"

As he walks back onto Via San Vitale, there he is again, standing on the corner under a light: small, dark and bearded, in the green plaid coat. He thought he had lost the little prick when he found a back way out of that café a block over. And here he is now with that stupid fucking eye salute again, right index finger pointed at the right eye and then at him. Just to make sure Stan knows this guy is one of his watchers.

It all started this morning in the café where Marta had followed him and then sat there ignoring him. And then suddenly she was up and moving toward him, her pretty brown eyes holding his gaze. He tried to look surprised, as if he hadn't noticed her, then held out his hand and said, "Marta, what a lovely surprise."

Staring him down, she left his hand dangling. He lowered it, and she said, "Stan, we want you to know that as long as you stay here in Bologna, every step you take, we will be watching."

He heard the echo from Sting, knew it was pointless but asked anyway, "Who's we?"

With a small nod, she said, "If you stay, you will know."

And so he knows. After spending all day traipsing all over this city with his watchers tracking his every move, he certainly knows. "The Bitch Bunch" he calls them. Some he knows, some he doesn't, but they all know him. Or at least believe enough of what the Bitch has told them to consider him a subject worthy of open and non-stop monitoring.

When he left the café this morning, Marta was soon following at a less than discrete distance toward the old town center. At the two towers he decided to test her words: "every step you take." According to his online guide, there were 498 of them to the top of the taller one, the Asinelli. Would she follow him up to watch, literally, every step? Would she wait for him on the piazza until he came back down. Or would she just take off and let him wonder when he returned to earth whether he was still being watched? It would be good to know, and anyway, if she did follow, maybe he could toss her off the top. That would probably put an end to this watching business. Besides, he could use the exercise.

Through a narrow door in the base he headed up a stairway to a landing where he had to pay 3 euros to go further. He waited to see if she was following, but so far she wasn't. So then it was up and around and up, on heavy-duty oak stairs circling the inside of some noble family's 12th century phallic fantasy. His thighs already feeling leaden, he wondered how these crazy towers really provided any refuge in those old medieval days of internecine intrigue and strife. Yeah, enemies could not come up to get you without being picked off one by one, but then you were trapped in the damn place, and it was a kind of idiotic Italian standoff. The quote he liked the most was from Geothe: "Building a tower became both a hobby and a point of honor. In time, perpendicular towers became commonplace, so everyone wanted a leaning one."

Another few minutes of climbing and he was nearly out of breath. At one of the small open windows offering light and air along the way, he stopped and rested, and then he heard above him what sounded like a couple making it. A lot of heavy breathing and several small cries, and when he started up again, he found them on a dark landing, no more than 17 or 18, the guy tugging up his fly and the girl shoving down her skirt. He said, "*Scusi*," and continued up.

At the top, he felt his heart blasting away and his lungs screaming, but on a clear day you were supposed to be able to see forever, at least to the Adriatic on the East and the Alps to the North. With today's overcast sky, no such luck. Still, extraordinary views in every direction, and he tried for a while to find a roof not red. There were only a few. It was why they called this place, "Il Rosso." That and because of its heavy leftist political legacy. He looked down and tried to spot Marta's red coat but couldn't. Maybe she did split. As he was starting down, the lovers arrived, the young guy looking at him boldly, the girl smiling away. The energy of youth. To fuck on the way up these humongous stairs and still finish the climb was indeed impressive.

He took his time going down, and when he finally emerged again on the piazza, Marta was nowhere to be seen. But as he started down Via Rizzoli toward the Piazza Maggiore, he found his next watcher, leaning against a brick column and smoking a cigarette, about 50 feet away. Edgardo looked straight at him and gave him the first of the day's eye salutes.

How long had Marta actually been watching him? Hard to say. It was less than 90 minutes since he walked out of his building this morning, but how long had she been waiting there for him to appear on the street? In any case, she had now passed him on to her friend Edgardo, and it was already clear what was going on here. The Bitch of Bologna had organized her minions and sycophants into an army of watchers, sworn to keep him under constant surveillance. And as he walked into the Piazza Maggiore, Bologna's huge central square, and headed through it to the adjacent, smaller Piazza Nettuno, it came to him finally how they had figured out where he was living.

He had been played last night, gamed by Lina and Aldo. Letting him follow them back to her place, they had arranged to have someone tail him back to his.

The idea was obvious and potentially effective. If they were always watching him, what could he do to her? Eventually, the Bitch assumed, he would tire of this stupid, no-win game and simply leave town. Another kind of Italian standoff. So now what? Maybe he *should* leave town. And then come back when she and they have let down their guard. He needed to think about this more carefully. Clearly, he was being outwitted by the Bitch, and that enraged him. Certainly he was not about to give in, to let them in effect run him out of town. He needed to find a way to move his plans forward no matter what they did. This made it more of a challenge, perhaps, but he was not about to leave the field and simply slip away. He was up for this.

So first, do more of what he was already doing—sightsee and be the tourist. Stay the fuck away from the Bitch, like she was the last thing in the world he was even thinking about. And keep his eye out for ways and places to lose these assholes and purchase what he needed.

Standing in front of the famed Netunno Fontana, he looked up at the giant black-green bronze of King Neptune, surrounded by fat cherubs holding squirting fish and, at the base, his favorite part, a collection of mermaids, squeezing their tits, water streaming in arcs from their nips. Actually the god of the sea looked a bit swishy here, holding the trident in his right hand a tad behind his ass, his left lifted with the fingers spread in a kind of dance move, both his hip and his dick cocked to the left. The guy who posed for this back in the 1550s had an incredible physique but was probably gay. Given his size overall, the dick was definitely less than impressive. What do they say about guys who spend most of their time making themselves big with weights and compounds? Either they're compensating or the stuff they use caused shrinkage. He thought about giving his watcher a dick salute. Point at Neptune's little one and then at the obviously vain Edgardo. But would the guy get it, or just think it was a compliment?

He walked back east across the always-busy Piazza Maggiore and into the area known as the Mercato di Mezzo, a grid of narrow streets that was part of the original Roman settlement. This was where he had found the cutlery fellow who sold him the switchblade, and now as he came upon a *farmacia*, he looked back for his watcher. About 15 yards back, moving intently through a cluster of people. Giving the guy a wave, he pointed at the pharmacy and inside waited to see if the asshole would come in with him. When the guy just stood there and stared in, he found his eye drops and enjoyed buying a bottle of poison right under their noses. He asked the woman at the counter if they had Trichloromethane. Yes, she said, 100 milliliters for 50 euros. He said thank you, that was good to know. He would come back for it another time. Buying chloroform where his watcher might be able to walk in later and find out what the American had just purchased was not a sterling idea. Of course, if he needed to, he could always buy isopropyl alcohol, get chlorine bleach at a supermarket and make his own.

He spent the next 40 minutes or so window shopping and occasionally heading inside to look more closely at clothes, watches, cheese, fruits and vegetables, or at least he pretended to. He passed another *farmacia* but decided that going into two would seem suspicious. He wanted at least three full bottles of Visine, about 100 milliliters, so he'd need to have patience.

This game was pissing him off now, and he decided to lose Edgardo. There had been moments when he thought he might pull it off. Walk in one door and come out another, speed up the pace and put some distance between himself and the watcher trailing behind, then turn a corner and duck into a store or café large enough that he could hide in the back or in the john for a while and not be seen from the street. But what he really needed was a much larger building.

He walked a few blocks to the south to the Palazzo dell'Archiginnasio. Before they opened this complex in 1563, parts of the University were scattered all over old Bologna. Then this place remained the center of things until the early 1800s when everything moved up to the area along Via Zamboni. It was definitely large, with one side featuring a portico that ran for nearly 140 meters. He walked through to a big interior courtyard, then followed the signs up a flight of stairs to the Teatro Anatomico. A dissection theater fashioned entirely from carved wood, it had a white marble table at its center. Four hundred years ago the educational dissection of human cadavers on that table used to be the show here, and it drew big audiences.

Now for an exit from this building that was different from the entrance where he had left Edgardo. But after roaming and exploring for several minutes, he was forced to admit there was only one way in and out. Looking relaxed and patient, Edgardo was waiting for him at the door.

So now he was facing the back end of the Basilica of San Petronio. If he wanted big, this was it. The world's fifth largest church, it reportedly could hold 28,000 people. He noted an exit near the back as he walked around to the front on the Piazza Maggiore. It took several centuries to build this thing but they had never managed to finish the façade. Half way up the marble stopped, and there was only old weathered brick above. Two Caribinieri were eying everyone entering. Last year the cops had foiled an Al-Qaeda plot to blow the place up. Inside was a fresco depicting a scene from Dante's Inferno showing Mohammad in Hell being devoured by demons.

Actually, he found the interior not just vast but quite beautiful. Two rows of massive columns rose to the vaulted ceiling, but he had not come to admire, and he quickly moved behind one. As he peeked around to check out the entrance, Edgardo walked in, and by circling carefully around the column, he avoided the guy's sweeping gaze. Moving with increasing pace while still searching, Edgardo walked all the way through the sanctuary and out the back door.

He'd have to find that fresco with the image of the tortured Mohammad on another visit. Back out the front entrance, past the cops and into the Piazza Maggiore again, he quickly headed across the giant square toward the two towers. And then glancing behind him, he found Rena keeping pace, her dark eyes fixed on him. So was this just happpenstance? He thought so right up to the moment when the black woman, stone-faced, gave him the eye salute.

He kept moving on the edge of the Mercato. So they were sufficiently organized to have, when needed, at least two watchers working in tandem to keep him in view. At the front window of a café, he stopped and pretended to look at the menu taped there. With the light reflecting on the glass, he watched Rena stop about twenty yards behind him, pull out her phone and start texting, thumbs darting on the small keyboard, probably keeping Edgardo in the loop.

Back near the towers again, he found an entrance to the Ghetto Ebraico, the old Jewish quarter, a moody labyrinth of narrow alleys.

For centuries Bologna had welcomed Jews and their contributions to culture and commerce, but in 1555, a paranoid pope ordered them all confined to this place, and within 40 years they had been evicted from the city entirely. Today the Ghetto was supposed to have good restaurants and stylish apartments, but the passageways were still dark and twisting, and he thought this would be a good place to ditch Rena. Instead he kept getting lost, and every time he'd stop for a look at his map, she would find him again.

He wound his way out the Ghetto's north end and finally picked up another eye salute, this one from a tall, gawky gal with a brown knit cap. On his map was a nearby street where you could see one of the hidden canals of Bologna. So why does the idea of secret canals appeal to him? They were originally part of a 12th century system built to bring water from nearby rivers to the old city's center and later played a role in the silk and hemp industries that used to flourish here. Over the past century they had been built over, covered and sealed, but there were still a few access spots. On the Via Piella he found the small, boarded-up bridge with an open window that offered a quaint water view he'd seen online. He stuck his head through and looked down. The water seemed kind of shallow. Maybe not the best place to drop a body.

Heading back to the east, he crossed the outer ring road, a modern boulevard with heavy, fast-moving traffic. Then he spent another hour walking around a quiet, less populated, working- class area and finding another place where you could get right up to a canal. At night, he thought, it was likely to be dark and deserted around here.

In a bar back inside the ring road, he had a beer and a crusty roll and cheese, and when he came out to the street, he'd been passed off to the stocky little guy in the green plaid. For some reason this prick's eye salute seemed so fucking arrogant that the anger he'd been dealing with all day beat up in a big way. The problem was, this was their turf, their city. They knew it, and he didn't. On his way back toward the University District, he began to trot and then to run, and when he looked back, the stumpy little shit was not keeping up.

* * *

Back now on Via Zamboni, with no watcher in sight, he's appalled again by all the grafitti. This ugly stuff is all over the city, on the walls of 16th century palazzos, on handsome wood doors to upscale apartment buildings, even the Bitch's. But here, at the heart of the

228

University, it was the worst, walls for whole blocks covered six, seven feet high with crap. Nothing arty or clever, just empty asshole kids making their pathetic mark on the streets that Dante, Copernicus and Albrecht Durer once walked. The Arabs have it right: chop off a few hands that hold the spray paint cans, and it'll end over night.

In the Café Mancuso where he picked up Flora and Fauna last night, he sips his wine and looks for some nubile coed with no exam prep tonight. No luck yet and still no watcher, at least not here inside. Then after ten minutes, in walk Aldo and the Goose, nodding at him as if they knew he was here. Taking a table with a good view of his, they gesture and smile together and sip their glasses of red. At one point they both look directly at Stan and laugh. After that they ignore him, and Hans with his phone seems to be reading Aldo a series of texts. Probably to and from the watchers. A good thing he hasn't found a gun yet. What he feels like doing now is walking over and capping each of them in the face. Instead, finished with his caprese salad, he gets up and moves to their table with a grin.

"Hey, *buona sera*." They say nothing, their smiles gone as they stare at him. "So do me a favor. Tell *la bella* Lina I had fully intended to leave Bologna, but since she stuck all you assholes on my tail, I decided she needs better company. So I'm definitely sticking around."

The Goose looks down at his backpack on the chair next to him, but Aldo continues to gaze straight at him. He says, "Stan, do yourself a favor and just leave Bologna. It will be better for you, for Lina, and for all of us."

Hans looks up and adds, "Yes, Bologna will be a better place without you."

Stan gives them a shrug. "So which one of you is going to follow me tonight?"

The Goose again: "You will know soon enough."

He shakes his head, silently telling them it's a bad idea, then turns and walks out. On the street the night air is cold. He moves down Via Zamboni, then heads back to the east in the direction of that canal where the area, he thought, would be especially dark and deserted. As he reaches the ring road, he looks back to find, as he figured, Hans hustling after him, craning that long stupid neck wrapped with the dorky brown scarf, and carrying the backpack. He slips his hand into the left front pocket of his jeans and pulls out the switchblade. He wants it in his right hand now and nestled in his jacket's warm right pocket.

Chapter 37

Tuesday, late afternoon, and the first time she actually uses her new peephole scope, the view is surprising. She thought it would be Aldo and Rena coming on some apparently urgent matter that he did not want to discuss on the phone. And now this fish-eye lens is showing her not just the two of them, but also Marta and Bella and behind them, Edgardo. How does this viewer distort? Supposedly a wide-angle look, but all the faces seem long and worried.

There are hugs and kisses with everyone, and a special greeting for Bella, whom she has not seen in several months. The black-haired beauty says her ailing grandmother in Rome is doing better but is very lonely. Moving to the sofa and chairs in the living room, no one accepts her offer of a glass of wine, and she knows this will not be lengthy visit. Sitting in her usual armchair, she moves her gaze across all of them, ending on Aldo, at whom everyone is now looking. "So something is wrong," she says in Italian. "Please talk to me."

She has prepared for something serious. When Aldo's eyes flick at Rena, she thinks maybe they have bad medical news. But then why are the others here? No, more likely it is something about Stan. And her mind makes an awful leap: has Stan done something to himself?

Aldo looks at her steadily and says that Hans has gone missing.

"Stan...?"

"No," says Aldo, "Hans."

Lina says, yes, Hans, and then fights back a feeling so desperate she can hardly breath, She asks if Aldo means "gone missing" in a way that is different from the usual with Hans.

During his more than three years now in Bologna as a valued and cherished member of their circle, Hans has on occasion simply disappeared, just left all of them behind to guess where he went and what he was doing. Usually he turns off his phone, leaves his laptop and returns neither email, voicemail, nor text. On one famous occasion he did send Marta a postcard from Paris with a banal picture of the Eiffel Tower and a message to match: "Wish you were here." But the card arrived after he returned, and they teased him unmercifully about not wanting to be in the same city with the young woman to whom, they all knew, he had completely lost his heart.

When they pressed this normally reliable fellow — always the first to return calls or respond to invitations — about this propensity for disappearing , he said only that there were times when he had a deep need to be alone, to sort the jumble in his head, or, really, just think about nothing at all. And so it might be a hike in the Alps or the Tuscan hills, a few days in his hometown of Amsterdam or a week in the City of Light.

With those grave, dark eyes unwavering, Aldo says it is possible that this is one of those "usual disappearances" they have come to expect from Hans, but they think it is unlikely.

Lina is silent, trying to cling somehow to the word "possible." The last time she saw Hans? Saturday night here with the others. Good spirits, no dark or distant looks. Searching the other faces, she finds no one looking at her, almost as if they share a kind of shame.

Rena tells her husband he needs to give Lina the details of what led up to this. Aldo starts with Sunday night and their deep concern that Stan was following Lina when she came to their place for dinner. When Aldo left the table for his study, he called Hans, and they brainstormed a bit. Knowing the police would do nothing at this point, Hans liked the plan Aldo had begun to shape: a brigade of watchers who would follow Stan wherever he went. Most likely he would soon tire of being watched and end up leaving Bologna. To arrange this they would have to know where Stan was staying. So after dinner, if Stan was still waiting to follow Lina home, Aldo would text Hans. In the meantime, Hans would start putting the brigade together, calling people like Marta and Edgardo and others who could cover a "shift." Aldo said to include Rena and him, and then after dinner, from their living room window, they spotted Stan down in the park. He sent the text, and Hans quickly showed up to secretly follow Stan.

Aldo asks Marta, Edgardo and Rena to describe what occurred yesterday morning and early afternoon, and, as they give their brief reports, Lina feels increasingly impatient and annoyed. She already knows the awful place all this is headed, and she is torn between her love for these dear, caring friends and her anger at what they have

232

kept from her.

As Rena finishes, Lina looks at Aldo and says, "May I ask why was I not consulted?"

Rena answers: "Because we knew you would not permit it. Aldo, who we all know is a fiend about ethics, argued that we should tell you, but he was voted down."

Lina shakes her head.

Rena says, "Actually we said if Stan got close to you, and you noticed us, we would tell you. But, Lina, you know I am right. You would not have allowed it. And we care too much about you to let this crazy man stalk you unhindered."

Lina says, "But this is just the point. He *is* a crazy man, shrewd and clever, and without a trace of scruples. Who knows what he might do?"

Edgardo interjects that no one at any time felt they were threatened. And if they did feel at some kind of risk, it was arranged they should immediately break off and call Hans.

Lina looks at Aldo. "And now you tell me that our beautiful Hans is missing."

Aldo nods and describes what happened last night when he and Hans met at the café where Stan was having dinner. They reviewed the day, and Hans read him some of the texts between the members of the brigade. As the coordinator, Hans was copied on all the texts, and he seemed pleased and proud of everyone. And then Stan came over to their table.

"What did he say?" asks Lina.

"He said to tell you he was going to leave Bologna, but now that we were following him, he would not leave."

"I do not believe that for a second," snaps Marta. She sounds angry and worried.

Aldo says it was his turn to watch Stan, but Hans insisted that he take over and followed Stan out of the café. It was about 8 pm, and that was the last time any of them saw Hans.

"But," says Marta, "I got a text from him at about 9:15 saying Stan was back in his apartment, and another came two hours later to say he was ending the watch and going home."

Lina says, "So by midnight Hans should have been back in his own apartment."

"Yes," says Aldo, "but when Marta arrived at 8 this morning to take up the watch at Stan's building, she sent a text to Hans, and he did not respond."

Marta adds, "And he always responds to my texts, even if it just an 'x,' which is our code for 'got it.' So I called and his phone went right to voicemail. And I am thinking, 'He was up late and turned off his phone to sleep in.' I left a message, but by 10 o'clock, when Edgardo came to relieve me, I was getting worried. I called again, and still straight to voicemail. So I kept calling, every 10 minutes, and nothing. Finally, I went to check out his apartment. I know his super, and she knows we are friends, so she let me in, and nothing. His bed was unmade, but he never makes his bed. His backpack was not there, but Aldo says it was with him last night."

By now Marta's eyes are aimed at the ceiling and near tears. Lina says, gently, "But, Marta, this was just this morning. He could be out anywhere, doing anything."

"No! He always calls me back. Always. And really, he almost never turns his phone off. Unless he is doing one of his stupid disappearing acts."

Lina knows what she is about to say is a stretch, but maybe it will calm Marta, and herself. "Look, we all know that when Hans disappears, all he usually takes is that backpack. And we all know what personal freedom means to him, philosophically and every other way. Maybe the idea — and the reality — of constantly imposing this watch on Stan became too much for him, and he recoiled from it and decided to go off by himself."

Rena stirs on the sofa. "I thought that too. I've always felt Hans has a poet's soul, and we know a poet is like a bird. Sometimes you fly away just to remember how to sing."

Aldo, next to his wife, shakes his head. "No. Part of this idea for watching Stan, came from Hans. He was the most enthusiastic, committed watcher. He would not just abandon this at midstream. We have called all his closest friends and colleagues in both the philosophy and literature departments. No one has seen or heard from him."

The room is thick with gloom. Aldo is right, and they know it. Perhaps just to break the silence, Bella says she was supposed to start this afternoon as a watcher, relieving Rena in the Piazza Maggiore where she was following this fellow Stan, but then they decided to call the whole thing off. Those beautiful eyes glisten, and Edgardo takes her hand. They all love Hans.

* * *

Within a half-hour Lina and Aldo are sitting in a quiet squad room at the Bologna headquarters of the Carabinieri, a short walk from the Piazza Maggiore. They are giving a missing person statement to Detective Pietro Alberri. Young (Lina guesses late twenties), wiry, earnest and formal, Alberri sits at his computer, asking questions and typing answers: Hans Broek, 26, tall and thin, 6'3", perhaps 170 pounds, short sandy hair, fair skin, clean shaven, blue eyes—they will email photos later today—originally from Amsterdam, parents deceased; majored in philosophy at the university, now pursuing a doctorate in comparative literature; last seen—by Aldo, Prof. Signorelli—yesterday evening at about 8 o'clock in the Café Mancuso on Via Zamboni; last communication just before midnight in a text to a friend, Marta Morescou.

So Signor Broek was last heard from late last evening. It is now perhaps seventeen hours later, and they are already concerned about his whereabouts and well-being because...?

Unfortunately, says Lina, this is where this story becomes complicated. As she finishes this line, a good-looking fellow with wavy dark hair and the hint of a swagger in his step, walks in, takes a look at her and nods, then moves to a corner desk and starts up his computer. This detective is probably in his late 30s and seems, she thinks, quite taken with himself.

Complicated how? asks Detective Alberri.

Well, says Lina, for reasons they will soon make clear, last night Hans was following a young American named Stanford Lyle. As she begins what she knows will be a long, convoluted explanation, she sees from the corner of her eye, the detective who just walked in turn from his computer, grab a file folder from his desk and stare directly at her.

"Pietro," he calls to Alberri. "One minute." And then to Lina: "*Signorina*, please forgive the interruption. But the fellow you mentioned just now—Signor Stanford Lyle—he was just in this room not more than two hours ago."

She shoots a glance at Aldo, who looks mystified. "He was here?"

Standing now, the man bows slightly. "Please, permit me, Detective Carlo Ranzone. Pietro, you recall the fellow. Came in here about 2:30 with the flash drive? Very unusual."

235

"Yes, Detective, certainly."

"Hands it to me. I plug it into my computer, and here is a 2-page document, single-spaced." Ranzone holds up two stapled pages from the folder in his hand. Then to Lina: "Allow me to guess, please. Professore Lina Lentini?"

"Yes," she says and sees his eyes dancing. He is pleased with himself,

"Yes, he described you well, and all your misfortunes at the college in Michigan. My sympathies, Professore."

She looks again at Aldo. They are both dumbfounded.

"Yes, all in Italian, and not bad for an American." Ranzone holds up a single sheet. "And also on the flash drive, this list of all the sights he has seen in Bologna and all the people you have asked to follow him wherever he goes. Names or descriptions, places and times."

Lina shakes her head.

Ranzone smiles. "Signor Lyle understood there was nothing we could do about such a complaint, but he wanted us to record this information. If something might happen to him…"

"To him?" says Lina, staring hard at those self-assured eyes. "This is incredible."

Chapter 38

Lately he just keeps surprising himself. After his thing with the Goose last night, he was sure he'd be long gone from Bologna by now, probably from Italy as well. And yet here he is, at nearly 5 in the afternoon, back in the Bitch's apartment. And just as he hoped, there is a re-corked bottle of red on the counter, less than one-third full. Yeah, he's a little surprised he's going with this poison deal, rather than one of the suicide scenarios, but the idea of doing it face-to-face and hands-on had him feeling a little queasy. People do off themselves with poison, but not that often. Anyway, for now this is the best way to do it. Kind of by remote control. He looks at his hands in the surgical gloves and knows there will be no way to tie him to this, no matter what the Bitch Bunch, or the cops, for that matter, might think.

Actually he had a great time a couple of hours ago with that full-of-himself detective, Ranzone. Another piece of luck, having that vain, lady-killer cop to unload his story on. Another surprise: after last night, walking into the Bologna cop shop on his own today and telling them tales. Not tales really, mostly just facts. He woke up this morning thinking the Bitch and her Bunch would be missing the Goose sometime today and probably end up going to the *polizia*. So why not go to the cops first and offer his version of things? And giving them something in writing might be even more convincing. He started with his itinerary yesterday, all the city sights he visited and all the watchers who followed him.

Next he wrote his narrative of the past few months, starting in Michigan with his own assigned role as host/facilitator for Professor Lentini and her lecture series. Unfortunately, her stay had turned unpleasant when she was publicly accused of having an affair with a married professor and then became the target of a vicious series of attacks and harassments. Without success he tried to counter these attacks, and after a time, Professor Lentini became so upset by the harassment that she cut short her lecture series and returned to Bologna. At that point, the wife of the married professor confessed to instigating all the attacks. For confirmation he provided the names and addresses of Frs. Redding and Hagen.

Finally, he described arriving in Italy last week to research his doctoral thesis, stopping first in Bologna to check on the well-being of Professor Lentini, about whom he was deeply concerned. But when he called on the professor, it was clear she had become badly unhinged by her misfortune in Michigan. She accused him of instigating all the attacks on her and of coming to Italy to stalk her. She set her friends and colleagues against him with a number of absurd lies. And now they've been following him all over Bologna as he tries to see the sights in this greatest of all university towns. Frankly, their hostility has made him fear for his own safety.

As a shortcut he used freetranslation.com on both pieces, then spent time refining and enhancing the Italian. Overall, his new friend, Detective Carlo, seemed impressed, raising his thick eyebrows at certain things as he read, almost rolling his dark, knowing eyes at others. It seemed the cop's no doubt vast experience with Italian women inclined him to credit this account. When Stan asked if he could keep the detective posted by email on the latest developments, Ranzone said absolutely.

From headquarters he went straight to the Farmacia Comunale on the Piazza Maggiore, where he bought another bottle of Visine and these surgical gloves. Then it was back to his place to pick up the other two bottles of eye drops. His research had indicated that two and three-quarters bottles, probably 80 milliliters, would be enough, so he slipped the little plastic containers into one pocket and stuffed the rubber gloves in another and headed for his favorite look-out café. Before long he spotted the Bitch leaving her place with Aldo, probably, he guessed, on their way to the Carabinieri to report the disappearance of the Goose. Within 10 minutes he was standing here in the Bitch's apartment, about to pull the rubber cork.

Amazing how his plan, hatched yesterday afternoon when he discovered that quiet canal area beyond the ring road, came off so well. And then how he had free-lanced and improvised when needed. The surprise was how calm he was through the whole damn thing.

After walking last night for close to a half-hour through the damp cold, he finally found the place again. A dark street and then a turn down a darker alley with access to the canal. By now the Goose was using a flashlight he must have had in the backpack. Just as he had thought, the neighborhood was deserted at this hour. There was a smell of rain in the night air.

When he reached the street he began moving quickly, and then in the alley he sprinted for 20 or 30 yards to press himself against the corner of an ancient shed. He took the knife from his pocket, flipped open the blade and moved the handle in his hand so he could hack down and rip. Then the dork's flashlight beam began bouncing ahead on the stones of the alley, sending him a perfect warning of the asshole's approach. Even as the beam shifted back and forth, from right to left to right, it was showing him exactly where the Goose would be looking as he moved past the edge of the shed a few feet away from his hand gripping the switchblade. He had seen it so clearly in his head. With his left hand he would grab that stupid scarf, yank him back off balance and with his right plunge the blade into the right side of that long goosey neck and then rip it back hard to make sure he got the carotid.

And that was exactly how it went. The Goose made a quiet sound, something like, "Ahg." Actually, the loudest noise was the metal flashlight clattering on the old paving stones and rolling right over the edge of the alley and into the canal. As the guy folded to the ground, there were more muted sounds—a choke, a gasp, a gurgle. Maybe he tried to yell but couldn't because of the blood filling his throat. Even in that black, overcast night with no stars or moon, he could see there was already a lot of blood coming from the large wound he had caused, some of it being absorbed by the scarf. He was surprised at how easily the blade had sunk to the hilt and then how much resistance he felt as he ripped back through the chords and tendons. There was blood on the knife and his hand but not all that much. Maybe the scarf had caught the initial surge. Wiping his hand and the blade on the Goose's corduroy coat, he folded the knife.

Then he noticed the cell still clutched in the guy's left hand. He pried it loose and nearly tossed it after the flashlight into the drink. Instead, he slipped it into his jeans pocket. At the edge of the canal he looked for the flashlight. It was still burning but soon died at a depth of maybe 4 feet. This settled his question from earlier in the day about whether the water in these canals would hide a body for long.

He wanted to stow this guy undiscovered for as long as possible. Searching the area in a quick arc, he found no lit windows looking this way from nearby buildings. Time to improvise. He dragged the dying Goose into a narrow space between the shed and an old wall next to it and took off.

On his way back to his building, he moved quickly but did nothing to attract attention. Glancing behind or stopping to feign a look in a store window, he made certain no one was following. He passed no one he recognized, and no one took much note of him. He could not believe how calm he was. Of course his heart had been slamming as he made his move on the Goose, and, yes, the adrenalin was still pumping big time, but he was intensely focused. There was a certainty about him, a strange confidence, like things were just going to break his way.

Rain started falling. He thought, good, come down hard and wash the blood from the alley. Of course, these porticos were perfect for a rainy night. Close to his building he stopped under a light to check for blood on his jacket and jeans. Nothing he could see. Some on his right hand, but he slipped on his black leather gloves and headed for his apartment.

His thought then was just throw everything in his carry-on bag, grab his laptop and leave a note for Signora Vascone, saying he'd been called home. Pull the Panda out of the parking garage, grab the body and dump it somewhere outside the city—he already had an idea for that—and then just keep going. Drive to Milano, turn in the car at Malpensa and catch the first flight available to Detroit. Literally, having blood on his hands and needing to leave Italy would put an end to the fucking obsession. Carving the Goose would carve the Bitch from his life.

In the vestibule of his building he ran into the little hunchback witch coming up from the basement. Instead of something about leaving Bologna, he smiled and said, *"Buono notte, Signora Vascone...alle ventuno e ancora lavora?"* Was she still working at this late hour?

She gave him her version of a smile and said she was always working.

In the apartment he finally remembered the Goose's cell phone. It was a Nokia, similar to the model he was using. He wondered if the guy had sent a text tonight after he had left the café. No, but there was a long list of texts sent and received over the past two days. He found two from last night to Marta. The first, sent about the time Stan returned here after following Aldo and the Bitch, included this building's address and said simply, "S is home." The second, sent about 2 hours later, said only, "Off watch. To home. Good night." Then he thought maybe it was a good thing he had run into the witch just now. If asked, she would say he had come in for the night around 9. And now he could arrange to have the dead Goose confirm to Marta Stan's arrival home as well. So he copied the message from last night, "S is home," and sent it to Marta, knowing, of course, it would have the current time on it.

What if this group had Loopt on their phones to mark each other's locations? Don't take chances. He pried the battery out of the phone, then shoved the pieces back in his pocket.

Yesterday he had seen in a tiny closet a couple of items that would come in handy now. He grabbed the duct tape and a roll of large, heavy-duty trash bags and then spotted a blue plastic rain slicker. He took that as well and started to pack. Then a minute later he stopped. He could send Marta a text from the Goose's phone around midnight saying the Goose was breaking off the watch at Stan's apartment and going home. The dead man would still be texting 4 hours after his demise. Very cool. And, the fact was, if he left Bologna now, suddenly, in the middle of the night, he'd look guilty as sin. Better to dispatch the body as soon as possible, get back here and stick around for a while longer.

Wearing the slicker, the packaging materials in a grocery bag, he moved silently down the one flight of stairs, past the witch's door and back out into the rainy night. Six blocks to the parking garage and there were few on the streets. At the Panda he lowered the rear seats and covered everything with plastic bags, and then he was rolling, back toward the ring road and then the canal. Having made this trip twice now, he found the street quickly and the narrow alley. The little Fiat made it to the shed without a scrape or encountering a soul. The dead Goose was waiting for him next to the shed, and while it was a struggle, he managed to wrestle the body under the lifted hatch and onto the plastic bags. It was still raining hard, but he whipped off the slicker and used it to cover the head and torso, then shoved the stiffening legs far enough in to close the hatch. No panic, but he didn't breath easily until he hit the Via Aurelio Straffi, a main artery out of the city, the one he had come in on just five days ago.

On his way here from Malpensa he had driven for about 90 minutes on the A1, the Autostrada, but south of Modena, wanting to see more of the countryside, he had moved over to Highway 9 into Bologna. About 10 kilometers outside the city, he had noticed a large, dense forest of firs covering a hillside on the west side of the highway. Gleaming in the afternoon sun, its beauty had caught his eye. Now it was of interest for a reason not aesthetic, though on such a dark night would he even be able to find it again? But soon lights from the highway showed it to him, and he found a side road that ran right up into the forest. About half way up the hill a grassy path led off to one side, maybe a hiking or hunters' trail, but just wide enough for the Panda to find its way through the large, thick firs.

He stopped in a small clearing with enough space to turn around. Conveniently the rain had let up, and he hauled the Goose out of the Panda. He was curious about the backpack. In it he found a rolled up yellow poncho, a small thermos of coffee, and a dog-eared and much marked-up copy of *Crime and Punishment* in a Dutch translation. He thumbed through it and stopped on a page where the margin was completely covered with a tight scrawl in English. The guy had told him he was doing all his writing in English these days, needing to improve his facility. Reading it, even at a time like this, was irresistible.

"These pages fill me with guilt. Why? Because of my horrid fantasy of raping Marta and making her like it? Maybe. I adore her, would never touch her with force, yet I am tortured by these ugly, violent thoughts. I would kill myself before I would violate Marta, and yet these awful fantasies and the guilt I feel when I read this book."

He was tempted to take the book because old Dostoyevsky would probably want him to, but he returned it to the backpack. It took about 15 minutes to tape the Goose securely into two plastic bags. And then he dragged the package maybe 40 yards down the hillside to an area that was especially thick with underbrush. He figured it would not be seen from the path above.

Within an hour he retraced his route back to the apartment. He replaced the duct tape and the roll of bags in the closet. He needed to wash blood off the slicker and mud off his sneakers, but after he had sent the "good night" text to Marta, he felt pretty damn good. He showered and slid into bed and thought back over everything, searching for something he had forgotten or slipped up on. He couldn't think of a thing and slept like a guy with no conscience.

Is he really without a conscience? If so, why shrink from staring into those green eyes while he snuffs out her life? Especially now after he's slit a guy's throat. He'll leave those questions for later. Right now he needs to poison this wine and get out of here. With the stopper pulled, he squeezes all three bottles of the clear Visine into the dark red in the bottle of Sangiovese. The label says the grapes are from the Emilia-Romagna region that includes Bologna. Well, now there's another ingredient. He shoves the stopper back in, and in a drawer he finds the vacuum thing. Several pumps and it's back in the drawer. The bottle goes back to its same spot on the counter. And then he stares at it. All the websites listed the same symptoms:

Blurred vision, blue lips and fingernails, change in pupil size, high blood pressure, then low, headache, irritability, nervousness, rapid heartbeat, low body temperature, nausea, vomiting, coma, tremors, seizures, difficulty breathing, or no breathing. He's looking for the last one.

Reminding himself not to be seen leaving, he locks the door behind him and looks at the elevator. The stairwell is the better bet. As he approaches the ground floor, he hears voices he does not recognize in the entry room. He turns on his heel and heads back up as fast as he can without making a sound. On the first landing he waits and listens, ready to go up further if they use the stairs. Instead he hears a welcomed sound, the creaking of the lift.

Chapter 39

Mia Carissima Lina,

So I'm up and writing to you early. Day 3 since you confirmed that Stan was in Bologna. As I said in my last note on Sunday, I don't believe for a second he will leave you alone. Of course, with your silence my mind races. Most often toward dark and violent plots. Please tell me you are okay, and that Stan is not a threat in your life. Frankly, sweetheart, I worry about you almost constantly. I woke a while ago, eyes wide, as if I had spent the last five hours worrying over you in my sleep. I rarely get more than five these days. Okay, enough of this. Just tell me you are safe, your mind peaceful. No sign of Stan in your life. Then I will spend my energy on changing my life. I love you.

Ti amo.

John

The email arrived at 1:32 on Wednesday afternoon, sent at 7:32 am in Cedar Hill. The whole string is here, 4 messages. Glancing through them reminds her of how hopeful she tried to be Sunday and how desperate she feels now. So once again the love they share has put her in a box. She wants to write the truth to him but cannot without risking even more trouble.

Oh, she can say truthful things. And still be deceptive. That she is healthy and has not seen Stan in days, that she went to the Carabinieri, and they have kept an eye on things. She cannot say they are looking at the disappearance of a young man terribly dear to her, and Stan seems almost certainly involved.

244

She wants a glass of wine. She has craved it since walking in the door after she and Aldo spoke with the detectives yesterday afternoon. The first thing she saw was that re-corked bottle of Sangiovese on the counter. She wanted so badly to lift the stopper and pour a glass. And yet she resisted, blaming her depression; the wine, though good going down, would only make it worse. Leaving Aldo, crushed with sadness, on the street, it was all she could do to drag herself up to the apartment. She does not often suffer depression, but this one has been withering, with an almost physical pain. And yet, maybe the real reason she has been holding off on the wine is that she is denying herself, punishing herself for sins real or imagined. The fact is that none of this would have happened—Stan would not be here at all, and Hans would not be missing, or worse—if she had not started up with John. She is to blame. It begins and ends with her, and she has been feeling a dreadful shame. That she rejects the anger she feels toward Aldo, Rena and the others only makes this worse. She knows how it works. Stifled rage turns in on itself.

Actually, with John's note on her screen, she is feeling, if not better, then more energized. At least her mind can work on something other than her own culpability. How to respond to John without making everything even worse? Maybe that glass of wine would help now. Before she can think of another reason not to, she moves to the kitchen, takes the bottle from the counter and forces the stopper out with a pop. She pours the rest of what is left into a large glass and carries it back with her to the computer in her office. She will sip while she puzzles over what to write.

At her keyboard, she drifts back to those two detectives, the young, earnest one, Alberri, and the annoying Ranzone, God's gift to women. They will speak again with "Signor Lyle," but they already have his story on paper, and he will stick to it with shrewdness and tenacity. His account even included their last encounter when he "implored" her to stop having him followed. All she could tell the detectives was that it was not her idea, that she was unaware of what her friends were doing. Ranzone had even scolded Aldo for playing "spy games," as he called it. And when Aldo asked what the police would have done with a request for help, Ranzone had eyed Alberri and said, probably nothing. As for Hans, they said they would "put out notices" and carefully took all the information she and Aldo gave them. But as she left the squad room, she felt certain Ranzone at least was more inclined to credit "Signor Lyle."

Later Aldo asked if she thought Stan was likely to commit a violent, even murderous act. She told him what she had often said before. All of us are capable of violence. Yes, some are more prone, more easily moved by fate or force of circumstance. But other than last Saturday when he forced himself on her—and admittedly stopped quickly when she slapped him—she cannot recall seeing Stan act physically with anyone. Then she recalled the time when he threw his trench coat over a nude male dancer and forcibly escorted him out of the room. At the time, it seemed he had been truly aggressive, but now she thought it more likely a piece of stagecraft.

On Saturday, especially when he pulled that switchblade knife, she did feel threatened by him. But looking back over her months in Michigan, she cannot honestly say he had ever threatened or acted with violence against her.

Aldo asked about the gunshot.

Well, yes, she was sure he had done that, but it was clearly meant to frighten, not harm. The bullet entered at an angle that could not have endangered anyone in that room.

Aldo said, "Lina, I think you let him off too easily."

In her darkened living room, prone on her sofa, she knew Aldo was right. She was being absurdly soft on Stan. Why? Because she did not want to believe what was staring all of them in the face? Something awful had happened to Hans. She wanted to call John, to hear his voice sooth and support her, tell her, as he often had in the past, that everything would be okay. Of course, he had been wrong before, and to call him now would be to court disaster. With John in Bologna, it seemed likely that he and Stan would end up trying to kill each other.

The phone rang and she answered without moving from the sofa. Just checking in, said Lilli. A long, gloomy conversation followed, but it helped to get her through the evening. Learning that Stan had remained very much in the city, Lilli asked question after question about how Lina's loving, loyal friends had responded.

"Why wasn't I called?" Lilli sounded hurt. "I could have helped. And Marco too. Even Gemma. She totally fell in love with you."

"Just be thankful you did not get involved," said Lina, moving on to the rest of the story.

"My god, what chutzpah!" said Lilli about Stan going to the Carabinieri. "But fiendishly clever as well" And now knowing all the sad facts, Lilli wanted to come over immediately.

Lina said, no, she really wanted to be alone. "Anyway, I would be terrible company."

"Not looking for good company, darling. I know you are feeling way below low, and you really should not be there alone. Have you heard from John lately?"

"No," said Lina. She did not want to talk about John, and certainly not with a woman who had demonstrated little ability to be without a man in her life for any length of time.

Lilli said, "Does he know that Stan is in Bologna?"

"Yes," said Lina, now devoted to one-word answers.

She hung up soon thereafter and was grateful at least for the fact that she felt exhausted enough to head for bed. On her way to the bedroom she eyed the bottle on the counter and vowed to come back for it if she could not sleep.

Surprisingly she did sleep, late into the morning, but when she shuffled into the bathroom, she felt just as depressed as she had last night. With the light in this room much too bright, a look in the mirror showed a sleep crease on her cheek, hair spiking in odd directions, and eyes swollen. As if she had been weeping all night.

A half-hour later Lilli called again, sounding bright and determined this morning. How about their favorite lunch at Tamburini? It will do her good to get out. Lina did not even feel up to her usual shopping errands, let alone the bright-lit deli. She said she really needed to stay in and work on the book, trying to sound as if that were not an impossible plan. She promised to call Lilli back later.

"Please do call," said Lilli. "I will worry all day if you don't. And, darling, I've been thinking. You really should let John know what's going on here. It would be great if he could come and be with you. It is exactly what you need."

"Ah, no," said Lina, "that would not be a good thing. Listen, Lilli, I need to ring off. I think there is someone at the door. I promise I will call you later." After she hung up, as if she had actually heard a knock, she walked over to look through her peephole at the empty hall.

* * *

Now, lost in thought, she glances at the old pendulum clock, clicking away on the wall above her desk. She had found it at La Piazzola, the city's ancient flea market, and thought it would be a good reminder of how time, and life, were always slipping away as she sat here trying to write. Often it has worked that way, sometimes not. Right now it says, 2:45, and she still feels stymied in this effort to write back to John. She stares at the glass of red next to her keyboard. She has not touched it yet. Maybe a sip will get her moving, and as she picks it up, she finally has a helpful thought. Maybe she can simply make it more about him and less about her. Yes, it will still need to deceive, but at least about John she will write from the heart. She takes a good sip from the wine glass, puts it down and begins.

Mio Carissimo John,

You worry about me, I worry about you. You do not get enough sleep, and you know that will do you no good. Please, darling, you must not trouble yourself about me. I am fine when I think about you: a beautiful and brilliant man whose love for me feels deeply supportive and selfless. You touch my heart with your concern and buoy my spirit. I think no man has ever loved me quite this way, and I am so grateful. But you must stop worrying about me. As you say, you must concentrate your energies on your own life.

Darling, I can assure you: I am okay. I am safe. I have not seen Stan for two days. I do not know where he is, but he is not in a position to harm me, and many of my closest friends have joined together to keep it that way. If you want to give me something of the greatest value, send me the gift of knowing you are healthy and living well. That will do me more good than anything you might do if you were here with me in Bologna. I love you.

Ti amo.

Lina

She reads it over twice and finally hits send. Another sip of the Sangiovese and then her mobile rings. Where is it? On the kitchen counter. Carrying the glass, she moves quickly to get the call before it goes to voice-mail. Is it Lilli again? Maybe John? And she quickens her step. At the counter she puts the glass down and grabs the phone. It is Wilfrina Po, and she nearly decides not to answer. She and Wilfrina are not especially close, and while their chance meeting in the street a few weeks ago ended with a promise to get together, it has not happened. She is certainly not feeling particularly sociable at the moment. But maybe any distraction in this storm is good.

Wilfrina sounds very up, almost racy, and as she speaks her rapid-fire Italian, Lina can see her—that black hair always up in a clip, the severe black-rimmed glasses, and the only female adornment, garnet studs in her ears. Never one to dally with niceties, Wilfrina quickly says she has just acquired from a nearby shop a bottle of Masi Amarone, 2001.

"You know," she chirps, "that wonderful Valpolicella you served at the dinner you made for the six of us last spring, all us women, Stella, Rena and the others. One hundred euros, Lina! And I won it! In a raffle my department has every month. Each month a different shop donates a bottle, and proceeds this year go to the starving children in Darfur. So I am thinking, Lina, I know this is absurdly last minute, but I thought, I am in your neighborhood, just a few blocks away. I have this beautiful bottle of wine, one of our favorites, and I still owe you for that marvelous dinner. If you are free this afternoon, I could come by, and we could share the wine and catch up. You will talk about your book, and I will talk about mine, and it will be just be a great pleasure to see you again!"

Wilfrina comes up for air, and Lina says, "What a wonderfully tempting offer, Wilfrina," still trying to decide whether to accept.

"Yes, Lina, you must give in to temptation. This is fate!"

And so she says, yes, do come up, it will be a great pleasure to see her. As she ends the call she is already moving down the hall, heading for her bathroom to do something with her face. It would not do to alarm Wilfrina with the look of a mad woman.

Chapter 40

Dearest Friends:

Life has become too painful for me. For many years I have loved my life in Bologna, but lately I have been living with too much guilt, too much shame. I will not elaborate on my pain, because I do not wish to whine and complain about what life has wrought. Also, because, to put it simply, I know all too well that I have brought all of this on myself. Not only am I the author of all my troubles during my recent stay in the U.S. I have also violated my own cherished rules to live by, failing to tell the truth about crucial occurrences. Most important of all, I am fully responsible for the tragic disappearance of our dearest friend, Hans.

I cannot live any longer with the guilt and despair I feel about all of these matters. If you must learn something from what I have done, be sure to understand I have taken the coward's way. The best I can say about my choices in life is that they can tell what not to do, how not to live.

Do not grieve for me. I will soon know and feel nothing. I leave you with my gratitude, admiration and love.

Lina

First in English and then in Italian, he's been fooling with this for two hours, especially the Italian translation. It needs to sound like her, in her native tongue. Now he puts it on his flash drive, ready to be stashed in her computer and left on her screen. Not that he knows for sure he'll need it. For three days he's been waiting and searching, his mood slipping between certainty, dread, annoyance and doubt. It's still not clear if she's dead or alive.

When the knock came at eleven Wednesday morning, he was sure the word was imminent, maybe one or more of her friends there to announce that lovely Lina was no more. Even when he opened to find the cops standing there looking grim, his pal Detective Carlo, and the younger one, Pietro something, he figured they had come with the sad news about Lina. It put a nervous edge to his voice, but they quickly made clear they were there about the Goose.

Non-threatening, even cordial, but he was leery of them. The visit was expected. He had prepared for it, but now that it was really happening, he was a little jumpy. It didn't help that as soon as they said the professor and her friends were deeply concerned about the whereabouts of one of their group, Hans Broek, he suddenly remembered something he should have done after he murdered the guy. He'd gone over everything so many times, and it had never dawned on him that the only physical items that could possibly tie him to the murder were sitting in the tiny closet right behind the chair in which Detective Carlo was now sitting. The rest of those bags and the duct tape should have been pitched in some public trashcan.

No, they were not saying now that the body had been found, but if he was this stupid about the bags and tape, what else might he have fucked up? What they were asking about now seemed easy to deal with, all his movements on Monday, nicely documented in the itinerary and the list of watchers he had given them. They seemed particularly interested in why he had spent so much time in the areas where the canals could be seen. He said he always loved learning about the hidden history of places and was fascinated with the fact that these canals were a kind of secret remnant of the city's ancient past.

Then the conversation zeroed in on that crucial hour between 8 and 9 that night after he left the Café Mancuso, followed by Hans. Keeping his city map clear in his head, he said after dinner he felt like a good, long walk, and so he headed first for the Montagnola public gardens several blocks to the north and west, not knowing that they were closed at night. And then he just kept walking in a wide arc around the old city, south down Via Marconi all the way to

Via Ugo Bassi, and then back east toward the old town center where it turned into Via Rizzoli and ran past the Piazza Maggiore. He walked by the two towers, continued on Via San Vitale and was soon back here in his apartment. Really, he said, offering a look both earnest and sad, the city is so beautiful, it's such a shame that graffiti is such a blight in so many places.

Both cops nodded. Detective Pietro asked what he thought of Signor Broek.

"Hans? I like him." He had almost said "liked" and paused to calm himself. "Of all the folks in Professor Lentini's circle, I think I like him the best. I mean, of course I don't know him well. I've spoken with him only a couple of times, but he seems smart, pleasant, likeable, a good guy. I feel bad that you tell me he's missing, so anything I can do to help, I'm glad to do it."

"So you came back here about 9?" asked Detective Carlo.

Stan was certain they had already talked with Marta and the others and knew all about the texts. Still, he thought it was time to play the little witch card. And so he said it just occurred to him they might want to speak with his building's super, Signora Vascone. She might recall their brief conversation when he came in Monday night and perhaps might even remember the time.

Yes, said the younger Pietro, his eyes boring in, she said it was around 9.

Stan was surprised, but his details were all fitting nicely.

Carlo said she had also told them about the keys. The ones she had made for him a few days ago. She said they were not keys to this apartment but, Stan said, for a friend.

Ah, yes, the keys, he said, more surprised now but not entirely unprepared for this.

So who were they for? asked Pietro.

Stan smiled and tried to look embarrassed. He had thought briefly about this coming up and had sketched for himself the outline of a story. Now he would have to fill it out on the fly.

This was a little awkward, he told them. Last Saturday evening he had socialized with Lina and her friends until she suddenly turned on him and sent him away. He had ended up in an Irish pub, of all things, on Via Zamboni. Full of coeds, and one of them caught his eye. Her name was Regina, and she was just taking a break from her exams. Clearly she wanted an adventure, and he was happy to oblige. They ended up back here in his bed, and she spent the night.

"*Si*," said Carlo, those thick eyebrows arched. "*E le chiavi?*" And the keys?

Oh, sorry, said Stan. And then he flashed on something that almost caused him to lose it. He had just changed his jeans when they had knocked on his door, and the contents of his pockets were sitting on the top of a dresser in the bedroom. Both sets of keys, his and Lina's, out in the open, were certain to be spotted if these guys wanted a look at the scene of his triumph.

Jesus, concentrate, he told himself, smiling again. In the morning the girl said she had a cat and needed someone to come to her apartment to feed it while she was home in Naples for the holidays. He said he was soon leaving for Torino. Well, she needed to study all day, so could he get her keys copied? Then she could give them to a friend who was staying in Bologna. He agreed, and they arranged to meet that night at the same Irish pub. When he showed up with the keys and hoping to get lucky again, she said, no, she had to study all night. She left with the keys and never even offered to pay for them.

And Regina's last name? asked Pietro.

She refused to tell him. Wouldn't say where her apartment was or even give him her phone number. She said anonymity turned her on. He knew this story was a stretch, but they seemed to buy it. Then Carlo was on his feet, moving around the place, pausing at the bedroom door and making Stan's heart jump. Back to the chair, he said on Monday night, had he seen Hans Broek again after he came back here to the apartment at 9?

Only from that window. Stan pointed to his one view of the street in front. For a long time Hans had stood under a light, reading a book and glancing at the building's entrance. It was chilly, and he actually thought about inviting the guy inside. As he said, he likes Hans. But then for a while he disappeared, and he figured he had finally gone home. And then there he was again, out there until about midnight when Stan finally went to bed. In the morning Marta, another of the professor's friends, had picked up the watch.

Then Carlo asked about Stan's earlier encounter with Professor Lentini. She claimed he had sexually attacked her and only stopped when she slapped him. So what really happened?

"Detective," he said, going for a look that mixed hurt with confusion, "I am still trying to figure it out. When I stepped into her apartment, the woman literally fell into my arms. Now maybe I misread her feelings, but at that point I thought she was overcome with emotion. Back in Michigan there was always some sexual tension between us, but I respected her too much to act on it. In any case, this time I kissed her. And she slapped me. Probably not the first time in human history for this kind of misunderstanding."

Carlo nodded solemnly and said the professor claimed Stan had ripped her bra.

He looked the cop in the eye and said maybe he touched the sweater over her breast but never the bra. Amazing what some women convince themselves of in the throes of emotion.

Carlo nodded, emitted a small grunt, and that was about it with the cops. They asked him to stay in touch, and if he thought of anything that might help them with Hans, to please call. He told them again that his plan was to leave for Torino in a couple of days, and he asked if that would be permissible. They said, yes, of course, just let them know when he decided to go.

As soon as they were out the door, he swept the two sets of keys and the switchblade—cleaned of any bloody trace—into a drawer with his socks and underwear. Then he sat on the bed and tried to evaluate his performance. He'd give himself a "C" on most of it. Maybe a little more nervous than he wanted to be, but the one thing he liked was the story about picking up Regina and bedding her here. Not bad for something he partly made up on the go. On that, maybe a "B+". The modest sexual boasting had played well. Of course, he was yet to get laid in a town, where 17-year-old kids were doing it in public in Bologna's most famous phallic symbol.

His main concern over the next three days was learning whether or not he had killed her. Staking out her building was an obvious move, but after that visit from the cops he had to be more careful. On Wednesday he picked up that sappy email exchange with John, who sounded so sweet he wanted to puke, and Lina's flowery shit was just as bad. Those lines about the asshole maybe coming to Bologna made him yell, "Yeah, com'on, man, I'll do you both." But he knew this was false bravado. It would certainly be easier doing them one at a time. Of course, the Bitch might already be done. Email from her stopped after that. So maybe it was over.

Thursday he tried calling her, with his number blocked, four times during the day. No answer. He thought about contacting one of the

Bunch, probably Marta, on some pretext and probing a bit. Not a good idea. Friday he called Santa Orsola-Malpighi, the city's main hospital, and asked if Lina Lentini was a patient there. No luck.

Occasionally he would go for long walks, just to see if the cops, or anyone else, were following him. He pulled all his tricks — using shop windows as mirrors, circling blocks, doubling back, walking through buildings to different exits — but saw no sign of a tail. He even experimented with a disguise, buying himself a ratty brown cloth coat at a flea market, along with an old gray knit cap he pulled low on his forehead, a beige scarf he wrapped over his mouth and some old knit gloves. He hardly recognized himself in a mirror at the pharmacy near the train station where he bought the chloroform. He had decided exactly how he would do it, the whole thing planned out to the last detail. He just needed to find out if she was still alive.

Of course, if she in fact had died, or become seriously ill, he would surely have had another visit from the cops. But the waiting and not-knowing had become a major pain in the ass.

Finally, he gets what might be a break. On this early Saturday afternoon, after he has spent much of the morning on the suicide note, he picks up an email from Federico Aicardi, the singer he met at the gallery last week. A reminder to his friends that he and the trio will perform tonight at Cantina Bentivoglio, and they'll be playing some of Hans' favorites as an expression of love and hope. In their brief conversation about chemistry and Primo Levi, he and the singer had hit it off well enough to exchange email addresses, and so he's been included on the list of recipients, along with the Bitch and her Bunch. Chances are good they will all stop by the jazz café tonight to have some dinner and catch the performance. In his disguise he might be able to hang out unnoticed on the street and perhaps confirm her presence among the living.

And so at 7, more than early enough to catch them coming for dinner, he has found a dark spot about 40 yards up Via Mascarella. Partially hidden behind a portico column on the side that includes the Odeon Cinema, he can keep an eye on the Cantina entrance across the street. In the cold night air he's warm in his flea market duds, but after 40 minutes, the chill is getting to him, and he mutters to himself, "This is crazy." Lately he's been thinking that maybe he really has gone around the bend. This thing has become totally humiliating. And just as he thinks this, the cause of his shame turns a corner, arm-in-arm with Rena and Aldo. She looks beautiful, even at this distance, even with the red hair covered by a scarf, her face unusually pale, and that amazing body lost in a long, heavy coat. Again he wonders which he wants more, to have her, or to kill her?

They enter without looking his way and within five minutes the others arrive, including Marta, Bella and Edgardo and those watchers he doesn't know, the tall blond and the short little prick in the green plaid coat. He wants to go in and sit in a corner and make them all nervous as hell, ruin their evening. Obviously he should not be seen in any proximity to her or them.

Back in his apartment he mopes on the bed and finally decides this will not go on any longer. It will happen tonight, or rather early in the morning. Instead of waiting inside her place for her return, the surest, most efficient way to do this is to let her come home, go to bed and off to sleep, and then make his entrance at, say, 2 or 3 am. He's got her suicide note on his flash drive and enough chloroform in a plastic bottle to soak a thick, very absorbent cloth. Yesterday, after striking out with the hospital, he fooled around with Google and tried "redheads." He turned up a couple of medical articles suggesting that people with red hair are more sensitive to pain than others and are more difficult to anesthetize. Odd ball stuff, but with science behind it. And so he'll have to be careful to use enough chloroform on the cloth he'll hold over her nose and mouth as she sleeps in her bed. And then remember to dose her repeatedly as he fills the bathtub, puts her in it and uses her razor knife to slit her wrist. He'll put the note in her computer, leave it on the screen, and get the hell out. The whole thing should take no more than 15 minutes, 20 tops. And then, with any luck, he'll get back here without encountering anyone he knows.

At some point after 11 he dozes, and when he opens his eyes, it's 12:30. Pretty amazing that he can fall off to sleep for a while before heading out to commit murder.

* * *

The Rolex says 2:24 as he stands just inside her door. He's reached here almost without making a sound, in the stairwell and in the hall, unlocking and coming though the door and closing it behind. His heart is pounding from the climb up the stairs and from being excited. All of this—the scheming, the planning to the last detail, the intense focus he's feeling now—has stirred him, heightened his

256

senses, made him feel so hyper-alive his nerves are almost literally buzzing. He has to admit he likes it. Dressed in his disguise, the chloroformed cloth in the right hand pocket of his coat, he takes off the knit gloves and stuffs them in the left hand pocket. His hands are now incased in thin rubber. Silently he tells himself, "Go! Do this."

He flicks on the small, potent flashlight and moves to the kitchen. He opens the drawer and finds the razor knife. It's quickly in the right front pocket of his jeans. Now he's heading down the hall, past her office, where he'll soon be at her computer. From her open bedroom door there's a soft glow coming from what must be a small plug-in nightlight to the left of the bed. He puts the flashlight away and finally takes one step into the room. And then he notices something different. He's been in here only two or three times, but it's always had a light flowery scent. And now? There's something else. Something musty? Something from damp leather, or maybe from clothes worn for a while. It stops him and makes him look more closely at the bed. The red hair and part of her face are visible above the comforter. She's on her side and facing that dim light on the left. He's holding his breath, and it is so quiet now he can even hear her breathing.

And then he hears something else, a sigh perhaps, or a heavy breath? But it does not come from her. There's a man with her in the bed.

Another step into the room will give him a better look, but he can't make himself move. He strains to see through the soft light but finds only a shock of the guy's hair. His eyes dart wildly around the mostly dark room and stop on a chair to the right. There he can make out a sweater and pants, both in dark tones and draped on the seat. On the back of the chair is a brown leather jacket that he knows is John's.

Chapter 41

"So, the Christmas gift I sent from Cleveland. Sorry, it's a little late."

Three days late, but now on the kitchen counter is the box he shipped DHL the day he left the States. Because she wants to bake him a cake, he's just returned from a quick trip to Federico's farmacia for his family's famed baking powder.

"You are giving me the George Foreman Lean Mean Fat-Reducing Grilling Machine?" She's reading the box, comely in her spotless white apron.

"Well, I know you love to cook." Yes, she suspects something other than a grill in this box, which he didn't wrap, just sealed the edges with plastic tape, so the charming black mauler/salesman would grin at the guy who would scan the box and hopefully see only the grill.

"But unless you bought a Euro model, we cannot even plug it in here." She hands him a razor knife from a drawer.

"True, but it's the thought that counts." And a lot of thought went into this package. Having slit the tape, he pulls out the grill with its styrofoam buffers. When he opens the lid, she can't see inside. "Well, I'll be damned," he says lifting out a lead-sided pouch, still used to protect his dad's Fuji film from airport x-rays. No digital yet for dad. "I missed my calling."

"What calling is that?" Her smile turns puzzled.

"Smuggler maybe, or criminal factotum, or hit man." From the pouch he takes the small Glock 26. "Pre-owned but in perfect shape," said the wizened little guy who sold it to him.

So after all the wasted hours spent online searching for info on shipping a sidearm to Europe, and after staring at the Foreman grill in his mother's kitchen and finding the pouch in his father's den, he improvised. A trip to Sears for the grill, a stop at a suburban gun shop for this sub-compact model made mostly from a nylon-based polymer, and he was ready. He had no idea if this scheme would work. But now, showing her the gun and seeing her suddenly drained face, he certainly knows that thinking she'd admire his ingenuity was a major miscalculation.

"Lina, what's wrong?"

"Darling, what did you think you could possibly do with that here?"

"Protect you?"

"John, possession is illegal here. On your person, in this apartment, anywhere."

"I know, but I was not about to let that deranged prick have another clear shot at you."

"Darling, please promise me you will never take that terrible thing out of this apartment."

And so for the first time since his arrival a week ago they speak to each other in tones that are cross and impatient. Until now they've been on an emotional high that started the moment he and Lilli walked into that large darkened room at the Cantina Bentivoglio. Federico and his trio were performing, and Lina wept in his arms. Tears of joy, she whispered to him.

In Cleveland, his decision on whether to come was fraught with uncertainty. The email from Lilli made it clear she was urging him to come in spite of Lina's stated wish to the contrary. And he had given Lina his word that he would come only if she explicitly asked. But Lilli, one of the few Bologna friends she had mentioned, described in dire terms her visit that day to the apartment on Via San Vitale. No one had seen or heard from Lina for three days, and when she finally opened her door, Lilli said she looked awful. "Can you imagine Lina looking awful?" Physically ill with a stomach virus or food poisoning and seriously depressed, she was blaming herself for the disappearance of one of her favorite students, a young man named Hans, even though she had known nothing of the plan to protect her from Stan that apparently resulted in Hans going missing. "She is literally cowering in her flat, and I have never seen Lina cower from anything. She should not be alone, but she will not allow any of us to stay with her."

Lilli had found his address through the St. Thomas website and made her pitch: "Is there any chance at all that you could come straight away to Bologna to be with your Lina? She desperately needs your strength and support, and most important, love. No matter what she says, I cannot imagine, once you are here, she will turn you away." Deciding was easier once he learned that Lina's friends were convinced that Stan had murdered Hans.

He and Mar had already come to an agreement, of sorts. He had told her he needed some time to himself, and so they should go their separate ways for the holidays. She could spend time with her mom, or drink herself to a stupor. He just wouldn't be there to pick up the mess. He would spend a week with his folks and another in Chicago with Marlon Tish, and then they could see how things looked for 2008. Drunk, she said she would destroy his office in the garage if he left town, even talked of burning the whole thing down, a threat she had used so often in the past he considered it empty. Still he backed up his desktop on his laptop and physically moved certain books and files to his office in Markham. By the next morning, she had decided that time apart actually might be a good idea. Now with his new itinerary, he felt she didn't even need to know.

As for that unexpected spike in his PSA, there was really nothing he could do about it now, except maybe sit and stew. The day before Lilli's email, he had driven to a hospital south of Lansing at 6 in the morning to have the biopsy done, Dr. Soud going up his ass to get at his prostate and doing that little rubber band snap five times to grab bits of tissue to be analyzed and checked for cancer cells. That would have to be done at the U of M lab in Ann Arbor, and with the holidays, there was sure to be a delay in getting the report. Five years ago he had gone through this same drill three times in 16 months before they finally decided he had cancer. Now Soud said a jump to 4.24 was significant; it was quite possible the cancer was back. If the biopsy confirmed it, the next step would be a full body scan to see if it had moved anywhere else. But that wouldn't happen until after New Year's.

Though Soud had his cell number, his phone wouldn't work in Italy. He could call the doc's office later for the results, but what was the difference at this point? He thought, "Make the trip. Who knows how much time you might have?" And he vowed not to tell anyone anything.

Miraculously at this time of the year, both his flights and the train from Milan to Bologna were right on time, and the petite Lilli was waiting on the station platform with a small magic marker sign that said, "John!" In her Jaguar she explained that this was not a festive night out for Lina but more of a memorial for Hans. She gave him a brief version of how the young man had organized a brigade of monitors to follow Stan everywhere and then had mysteriously disappeared. When they walked into the club, Federico was just starting a song called "Non Invento," that dipped into a minor key with echoes of Dylan and Springsteen.

"This was a favorite of Hans, and Lina too," Lilli whispered to him. "About a fellow with a creative block—because of a woman, of course."

And then he was standing next to Lina, the red hair short, as Lilli had warned him to expect. Obviously wrapped in the song, she didn't look up for several seconds, but when she did, the green eyes got large, and she shook her lovely head quickly, as if to say, "No!" But then the tears started, and she was in his arms, her lips eagerly finding his.

Their sex later that night after the concert started slowly, almost tentatively. A bad headache had kept him from sleeping at all on the plane, and for a few minutes he wondered if he might be too exhausted. Might she hold herself back from him, given her obvious anguish over Hans and the inevitably mixed emotions over his surprise arrival? For a while they played softly, adoring each other with delicate touches and tender kisses, everywhere. But soon he could feel it building and knew they would hold nothing back. All those feelings so often bottled over the past several weeks flowed powerfully now. Given the time they had been apart, he knew he would come sooner than usual, but they orgasmed together so intensely that it seemed both exquisitely familiar and astonishingly new.

They had never actually slept together, he realized late in the morning when they finally woke. It was something to treasure now as he held her in his arms for an hour. They talked quietly, catching each other up on what had happened in their lives in both Cedar Hill and Bologna. When they finally pried themselves out of her bed, they showered together, and she said because it was Sunday, the tradition he would share now was brunch at Bravo. Walking out on a sunny afternoon just after 1, he got his first look at Bologna in daylight. With Lina holding firm to his arm, they strolled under the colonnades, stopping for her papers at Titto's stand, then moving

261

past Federico's shop to walk through the center of the University District to the café. Eyes moving in every direction, he was taking it all in and looking for someone they both knew.

"You are searching for him?"

"Of course. So where is this apartment he's sublet?"

"Two streets over."

"I'm going to see him after we eat."

"No!"

He stopped and stared at her. She said, "No, you would be at each other's throats."

He smiled. "Nobody will be at anybody's throat. I'll be perfectly civilized. Look, I want him to know I'm here with you, and the only smart thing for him is to leave."

She shook her head, and they walked on. Bravo turned out to be directly across the street from Cantina Bentivoglio. Inside they found Rena and Aldo. He had quickly hit it off with them last night after Federico had finished singing. Brunching together now, he asked what they thought of his confronting Stan.

"Absolutely," said Rena. "Good idea."

Lina again argued against it. She had forbidden John to come here because his presence would only exacerbate the situation and increase the likelihood of something awful happening.

"But, sweetheart, something awful has already happened."

She looked on the verge of tears, but Aldo came to the rescue with a plan for all of them to go to Stan's place together and talk with him after brunch. Lina was still unhappy but finally agreed, and so an hour later they were standing at Signora Vascone's open door. The young man, she said, had cleared out this morning and left a note saying he was heading for Torino.

On the street, Lina asked if John really thought Stan had left Bologna. Not for a second, he said, and she agreed. Then he asked if she had seen what was in the signora's apartment. She gave him a blank stare; he said there was a key copying machine in there. She makes keys. Lina pressed her face to his shoulder, and to Aldo and Rena he repeated the story he had heard that morning in bed about how she had become so paranoid at one point that she thought Stan might have taken her extra set of house keys and had them copied. Rena pulled out her cell and called a fellow she said would come at any hour to change locks. He would be at Lina's in 30 minutes.

262

The next few days were dominated by food—buying, preparing, eating. He had never known grocery shopping to be a fascinating, sensual delight, but with Lina in the old Mercato area of the city, it was exactly that. The outdoor stalls were full of alluring sights and smells, the visual presentation in the shops, from the front window to the back of the store showed the hand of an artist, with large hunks of Bologna's iconic animal, the pig, hanging from ceiling hooks, stacks of huge black-rind wheels of parmigiano, pastas in a hundred different shapes and hues, breads, rolls and cookies piled high, and arrays of fresh fruits and vegetables, all shiny in their vivid colors. So this was why Bologna was called not only "the Red," but also "the Fat."

Dinner on Christmas Eve was at Aldo and Rena's with Vito, the law professor, his pediatrician wife and their two young sons. On Christmas Day Lina hosted ten, all of whom he had met at the club his first night in Bologna. Both meals were sumptuous, multi-course feasts.

The night after Christmas they wore their gifts to each other, his handsome black belt and her delicate triple-loop gold earrings. In the Mercato each had secretly stolen a few minutes to find something to give. Dinner was at her favorite new restaurant, a place in the old Jewish quarter called Ciacco, in the cellar of a 17th century palazzo. With dual menus, classic Bolognese and Nouvelle Cuisine, he ordered from both. On the way home, she said, "Okay, the next few days we walk off the last few days."

And so they have. She has walked him all over the old center of the city, visiting churches large and small, museums filled with everything from antiquities to contemporary art, libraries jammed with hundreds of thousands of volumes penned by the famed and the obscure, university landmarks, historic public buildings, parks, piazzas, art galleries, even a cooking school—all with a running commentary that soon made him feel he now knows Bologna, its history, culture, politics and social mores, better than his own home town.

Each night in bed—and each morning as well—he cannot keep his hands off her, which, it always seems, is exactly where she wants them. But outside the apartment, on the streets they walk, in the bars and cafes they visit, in all the buildings they tour, they never go for long without careful looks around for a sign or a sense that Stan is

263

near. So far, nothing.

Early on this last Friday afternoon of the year, her freshly baked chocolate cake looks luscious on the counter as they leave the apartment. Outside the day is cold and gray, almost forbidding, but they've decided to walk anyway. She's taking him up to a place where you can see one of the city's old, hidden canals. Aldo told him it was one of the spots Stan had visited with his watchers. Hans is a subject to be avoided, but now she wants to show him the place.

From a small bridge on a narrow street, it's an interesting vista, with old red and brown buildings crowding the canal on both sides, but today at least, it seems neither charming or attractive, the water so low that the flat muddy bottom is exposed. She says, "They cut off the water sometimes. Usually it is a meter or two." As they move on, she takes his arm, something he loves, especially after their spat this morning over the gun. A few minutes later they're in a large open square featuring a huge, ancient-looking gate.

"Porto Galliera," she says, doing her tour-guide thing. "Originally from the 12th century, a gate to the city, reconstructed. On the other side you can see the crumbled walls and openings to another canal that runs underneath." They walk over the gate's wood-plank floor, and on the other side, only a few Bolognesi are moving on the square, going about their business on a frigid day. She takes him to a low wall and points down. "See, more water."

Twenty feet down, in a couple of coffin-sized openings in the green vegetation, dark water ripples. As he looks down at the partly exposed canal, she opens her tote and pulls something out. His glance is almost too late to stop the Glock from dropping into the coffin below. Grabbing her hand, he takes the gun from her. "Jesus! Lina, what are you doing?"

Shoving it into his jacket pocket, he knows he has never touched her with such angry insistence, and when he finds her eyes, they are filled with fear and disappointment.

"Darling," she says, holding her hand out with a slight tremble, "Please let me carry it. It is so much more risky for you."

He takes her hand gently but says, "No, I don't trust you now. Here I think it's in a box in the back of your closet, and you're carrying it in your purse."

"I thought the canal would be a good place for it. You having it with Stan in proximity is a dangerous thing." They're moving again, and she's still holding his arm. The Glock is in the opposite pocket. She says, "Have you ever actually shot a gun?"

"No."

"How do you even know you could do it?"

"It's easy. You point and pull the trigger. The guy who sold it to me showed me how."

He sees a smile curl her lovely mouth, and it breaks some of their tension. She firms her grip on his arm, and after awhile they come upon a large public park that spreads up a hill.

"The Montagnola," she says. "There's something interesting I want to show you here."

They walk up through the tree-lined park, and he can see that kinder weather would make it an attractive place. On this bleak, wintry afternoon, there is almost no one here. They pass a young couple heading down and one emaciated man who looks homeless. Near the back there's a large round pond, dry and desolate now, circled by a path with benches. She stops in front of a large stone sculpture, one of four set behind the benches. This one has two cavorting mermaids.

"Great tits," he says. "Almost as nice as yours. Pretty sexy, actually, for mermaids."

"I have always thought mermaids are probably lesbians."

"Interesting thought." He looks around. "Is this what you wanted me to see?"

"This and the other three. There's another with mermaids over there." Heading for the next sculpture, they move past a large building that looks locked up, empty and unused.

"And now we're on the African plain," he says, stopping in front of a snarling lioness, a dying antelope in her large claws, as she fights a huge python with her chest in its powerful grip.

"Yes, and the male across the way has just brought down a wildebeest."

"'Nature, red in tooth and claw.'"

"Exactly," she says. "What an extraordinary thing that poem is. Tennyson published it a decade before Darwin. And this sculptor, an Italian named Sarti, finished these 30 years later. By then the idea of natural selection and survival of the fittest had turned the world on its head."

Feeling suddenly tired, he says, "How about sitting for a minute?"

She nods, and as they reach the nearest bench, he says, "A pretty strange choice of subject for a pleasant public space." They sit with the deserted building behind them.

"Yes, but that *is* Bologna, always wanting to make you think. Even strolling in a park"

"Ah, Tennyson," he sighs, trying without luck to recall the two lines that lead into the poet's most famous words: "'Tis better to have loved and lost/Than never to have loved at all."

And then there is a crack and a loud metal ping that seems to happen about an inch from his left ear. Lina has flinched on the bench and grabbed his right arm. He wrestles it away to sweep her off the seat to the ground. Another crack, and the bench board next to his left hand splits. Finally, he reaches for the Glock in his pocket and then remembers it has no magazine. He searches wildly across the empty building behind them. The shots seem to have come from there, but he can't find anything moving.

Looking down now, he sees that Lina, cooped on her knees under his shoulder, isn't moving either.

Chapter 42

Paralyzed. Frozen. Even her eyelids cannot blink. She is naked, but no one cares as she lies near them on the hard red tile of her patio. The air is icy, the door to her living room open, but no one in there seems to notice. Somehow she can move among them now, her usual contingent of close friends, including Lilli, Aldo, Rena and Hans, back from wherever he went off to, but also others like Vito and his wife, Wilfrina Po and old Prof. D'Antoni. Even her mother is there, nodding at something that Paolo is saying. They are all speaking in muted tones she cannot decipher, and then she realizes this is a wake, her wake, except that she is not dead and must let them know. She moans loudly, her fear rising. But they do not hear her at all.

This is a nightmare, she tells herself finally and decides to wake up.

When she opens her eyes, she is naked on a bed where the covers have been shoved away. The room is warm, but not familiar. She reaches for John next to her. He is not there. Turning to where he should be, she finds a faint light coming from the room's one window. Now she knows where she is. John closed and latched the shutters on that window after they made love, and now they are cracked slightly. He must be on the balcony.

Out of the bed she moves to the window, pulls the gauzy curtain aside and pushes one of the shutters. Wrapped in the comforter they kicked to the floor, he stands there in front of the moonlit sea. As he turns to her, she says softly, "Darling, what are you doing?"

"Watching for pirates."

"Please come in. I need you to hold me."

Back under the covers, the shutters closed tight again, they lie together, her cheek on his chest. "You could not sleep?" she asks.

"No, I kept thinking about those Turks and Saracens you told me about. Besides it's just so incredibly beautiful out there."

"Darling, it is the Amalfi coast."

At dinner she told him the story she had learned when she first came here in her teens with her mother. This pretty, immaculate little place, the Hotel La Perla in Praiano, just down the coast from Positano, sits above the road called the world's most beautiful drive. Down below, on a rock jutting into the sea, is a small stone tower, and many centuries ago, Turk and Saracen pirates used to prey on the people who lived here, coming ashore to rape the women and steal the children. And so the people built a series of these towers up and down this rugged coast. When someone spotted a pirate ship, they would build a bonfire on the top of their tower, and then fires would appear on the towers to the north and to the south and so on, until everyone had been warned. At which point, they would grab their belongings, and all of them—men, women and children— would flee up into the mountains above the sea.

"Kind of the tactic we're using," he said at dinner with a smile.

They had slipped away from Bologna at midnight, after the shooting in the park. She drove fast through the darkness and sailed her Golf down the A1 in little over an hour to Firenze, where they stayed the night in what is probably her favorite hotel room in all of Italy, a space so amazing that when they walked in, all he could say was, "Holy Christ."

Even prior to John's arrival, she had thought about leaving, just running away. More than once she had told herself, just leave, go anywhere, maybe home to Catania. He will not know where to look, you will be safe and this will be over. But something stopped her, she seemed to lack the energy, the focus or resolve. Now it seemed the only thing to do.

When those gunshots cracked, and she could feel them hit the bench, she was stunned with fear. She ended up in a terrified ball on the ground in front of the bench, rigid, unable to move, until John finally shook her and whispered, "Lina, were you hit?" Finally, she managed to lift her head slightly and say she did not think so.

And then they were running in a crouch, down the wide path toward the front of the park on Via Independenza. As they reached the street, a patrol car turned in with two uniformed Carabinieri. Waving frantically, John flagged them down. Neither man spoke English, and she did most of the talking. In the back seat they rode up to the area around the pond, while the officers called for more cars to search the Montagnola's perimeter and stop anyone leaving. The officers had not heard the shots but were entering the park for their usual sweep, looking for suspicious transactions, mostly involving drugs. The gunshots were probably from a deal gone bad, they said. She and John had just been in the wrong place at the wrong time.

"No," she said. "We know the person who shot at us."

"You saw this person?"

She said no, but they had recently reported the man to detectives Alberri and Ranzone at headquarters. It might be best if she could talk to them as soon as possible. Within minutes officers in two more patrol cars arrived to say they had stopped a few people, none of them a likely suspect. While officers scoured the area based on what little she and John could tell them, one of the cars, sirens blaring, raced them down to headquarters. In the squad room they found the younger one, Alberri. He said Detective Ranzone was "off on assignment."

Alberri carefully recorded their story, taking extensive notes on his computer. Then he assured them that he and his colleagues had taken very seriously the information she and Prof. Signorelli had brought to them ten days ago about Signor Lyle. They had gone to his quarters to interrogate him, had interviewed his building superintendent and spoken with all the so-called brigade members. And then, for three full days, they had staked out his apartment and followed him whenever he left his building. In those three days they had seen nothing unusual or suspicious in any of his movements or activities. Yes, at one point he had worn some different clothing, but that might be explained by the fact that he was concerned about being followed by the professor's friends. In any case, none of his movements had ever brought him any closer than three hundred meters to the professor's apartment.

Finally, two days before Christmas Detective Ranzone received a phone call from Signor Lyle, who said he was leaving Bologna that morning. He would go, as he had planned, to Torino to further his research, although he would probably first spend some time in Milan "to see the sights." He asked about developments in the case of Signor Broek and said to please call him if they felt he could help in any way. They had his mobile number and could reach him at anytime. An hour later, his landlady called to say that Signor Lyle had vacated the apartment and left a note saying he was departing the city. That night he, Alberri, had stayed late to call every hotel and B&B in the city to ask if Signor Lyle was now staying there. In each case the answer was no.

And so, Lina asked, what would they do now that this man had fired two gunshots at them in a public park?

Well, of course, said Alberri, they could not be certain it was Signor Lyle. But they would do another hotel and B&B search and include any rooms listed online. And now he would check to see if the officers on the scene had filed their report yet. With a few keystrokes, he accessed the data entered in their on-car computers, and, yes, they had in fact recovered two .32 caliber slugs not far from the bench but found no signs of forced entry at the empty building from which she thought the shots had come.

She shook her head silently. Alberri said he understood this was traumatic for them. He looked at John. "You know, *si*, shootings is not usual in Bologna?"

"I understand," he said, and then pointed to his chest. "But this was at us."

The young man nodded and said he would get someone to drive them home. Of course, they had her phone numbers, so with any new information, they would call immediately.

Use only her mobile, she said. She and Signor Martens were leaving Bologna.

It was after 6 when they returned to the apartment, and for a while it was as if they were numb. Even though they missed, those gunshots seemed to have taken the life from them. For a long time they just sat on the sofa and held each other. At one point she said quietly, with a mix of anger and relief, "Centimeters."

He nodded. "I know, sweetheart. It'll be better when we leave."

They were not hungry, but she laid out some cheese, proscuitto and bread. They picked at it, sipped wine and finally talked about where they would go. On his two previous trips to Italy, John had never been below Rome, so why not head south? On the way, should they spend time in Florence? She could show him many beautiful things he had not seen there yet. No, it was too close. One lucky guess and they'd be dealing with Stan again. So, just a brief stop tonight in Firenze, then down to Amalfi and on to Taormina in Sicily. They were going to spend precious time together. Why not in two of her favorite places on earth?

She worked on her plan with some energy, calling for reservations at three special hotels. The summer she turned 13, her mother began taking her on trips to different locations across Europe. Business trips, really, related to her successful string of boutique hotels. Unlike with many teen girls, she and her mother adored each other, and there was nothing they loved more than traveling together. Besides, these were trips stamped with her mother's shrewd desire to know and learn from her competition. So at every stop they would stay at least one night at a rival hotel. They would rate the décor, test bed and bath, and sample the food and service. Often mother would ask daughter's opinion. Over the years since, Lina had occasionally returned to these places for both nostalgia and pleasure.

They each packed one bag, filled a smaller one with books and their laptops and watered her trees and plants. From the drawer in her kitchen she put her favorite corkscrew, the box cutter and a small flashlight in a ziplock bag, and at the last minute she grabbed her point-and-shoot Nikon. When she remembered to let Aldo know their plan, it was too late to call, so she sent an email that briefly outlined what had happened. She was not sure how long they would be gone, but if Rena could come in once a week to water, she would be deeply grateful. Their itinerary was not fixed, but within a few days they would be at the Villa Schuler in Taormina.

The Hotel Bretagna fronted the Arno, maybe a few hundred meters from the Ponte Vecchio. But for her that was not one of its attractions. Her favorite room, Camera 2, did not even have a view of the river. "Jesus, this is huge," said John, wandering across the gleaming hardwood floor from one elaborately paneled wall to the other and gazing at the huge mural on the ceiling. "We could play basketball in here."

"That is not really what I had in mind."

"Well, of course, that too."

He paced off the room's dimensions and announced it was 42 feet by 30. The cream-colored paneling edged with gold leaf reached to 9 feet up each wall and then it was another 15 feet at least to the ceiling. On the back wall a huge fireplace with dark carved wood and heavy gilt extended from floor to ceiling and there joined the wide, ornate cornices framing the mural: lovely ladies with their gowns slipping off played with cherubs. The story, she said, was that in the early 1800s Napoleon's brother had purchased this palazzo on the Arno and had it decorated to his taste. Who knew if the tale were true, but it certainly fit this room.

She also told him that from the age of 15, when she first stayed here with her mother, she had dreamed of making love in this room. And when he asked if she ever had, she said no, but held back the details of how two years ago she had arranged a night here with Paolo and then suffered a urinary tract infection just in time to ruin the evening. She was concerned that John might be too exhausted for sex. In the car coming down the Autostrada he had actually dozed off for a several minutes, snoring lightly. But he, and the room, fully realized her teenaged dreams, and afterward, sprawled on the bed, his penis still half hard, he said quietly, "I can't believe it. I forgot to take my pill. And it didn't matter."

They could have easily spent the whole morning in that bed, but she wanted to reach Praiano in daylight, so by 9 they were cruising down the Autostrada again, at a steady 125 kph, while Mercedes, Maseratis and BMWs swept past her little VW. She had always loved this drive through the almost dream-like beauty of the Tuscan hills, even in winter the colors close to surreal, like traveling though one superb landscape painting after another.

They were mostly silent, taking it all in, occasionally one of them pointing to a hill town off in the distance or a large vineyard, and the other nodding and smiling. And the same for lovely Umbria, maybe a bit more pastoral but with its own ethereal, painted charm. At one point he finally found his voice long enough to say, "I thought this was beautiful from the train, but it's even better by car." And then a few minutes later: "I've decided I'm leaving Mar."

After a few seconds, she said, "Well, you will see how things are when you go back."

"No, I've made up my mind. There's no other way."

She changed the subject. So he had that six-month check up. How did it go?

"Fine. The PSA was up a little. I'm okay."

"You never talk about it much. The cancer, I mean."

"I hate talking about it. Not you, but most people only say stupid things. The worst were the idiots who'd say, 'Remember, God doesn't give you a burden you can't carry.'"

They lunched at an AutoGrill just south of Rome, and even here he was amazed at the food. She said, "You know by now it is our national pastime." After lunch she let him drive, and he upped their pace to 140, until they hit the crowded outskirts of Naples. Then in Sorrento she took over again, saying, "From here no one can drive and look. So I drive, and you look."

Two hours later they sat on their balcony at the perfect little La Perla and watched the sun set over the blue Tyrhennian Sea. They were both exhilarated and drained, she from driving, he from looking, as they wound their way down that astonishing, corkscrew road carved into the side of a whole series of craggy mountains, villas perched on rocks that seemed to hang in mid-air and whole Moorish-looking towns somehow glued to steep hillsides all the way down to a beach. Steinbeck, she told him, once described this road as "carefully designed to be a little narrower than two cars side by side." And more than once, this firmly committed atheist cowering next to her exclaimed, "Oh, my god!" as she deftly maneuvered past a huge bus or truck hurtling toward them. They had stopped a couple of times where the road surprisingly permitted a place to park, so they could stand at a cliff's edge, hold onto each other and stare at stunning, dramatic vistas of mountains meeting sea.

They stay two nights in Praiano and over the next day and a half she gives him a kind of artists-and-writers tour of the Amalfi coast. There is Steinbeck's house and some of Capote's and Paul Klee's favorite spots in Positano, and up in gorgeous Ravello, hanging on a mountain a thousand feet above the sea, where Richard Wagner, Gide, Garbo, MC Escher, John Huston and Virginia Woolf had all dallied, she showed him the villa that Gore Vidal owned until recently and the gardens that Lawrence wandered in when he took his breaks from writing *Chatterley*.

Then on the last day of 2007, shortly after noon, later than she wanted, they finally leave the gleaming white La Perla and drive the last southern stretch of switchbacks and hold-your-breath views past the town of Amalfi down to Salerno and hook up again with the Autostrada, the A3 this time. From there it will be nearly 500 kilometers of mountainous highway down through Calabria, all the way to the toe of the boot and the city of Reggio Calabria, where a car ferry will take them across the Straits of Messina to Sicily. They trade off driving, a couple of hours at a time, over, around and through towering green mountains and endless tunnels, with long stretches of road construction confirming the fact that this highway project is so large it will take several more years to complete. This is emblematic she thinks. Poor Calabria has to some extent caught up economically, but it is still well behind the rest of Italy.

When she knows they are close to one of the few cities along the way, she tries the radio, searching through mostly hopeless static for the latest on the death of Benazir Bhutto, shot or blown up, depending on which Pakistani government announcement you believe. It happened the day before they were shot at in Bologna. John says the violent end of the woman who wanted to be prime minister seemed so inevitable. After that suicide bombing nearly killed her back in October, you wonder how she could have had the courage to continue.

Lina says, "It must be a powerful sense of destiny that motivates someone like Bhutto."

"Yes, but where does that come from? It seems so foreign to our own tame little lives."

"Darling," she says, "our lives have not been so tame lately."

At 6:30, it has been dark for quite a while when she turns off at the ferry dock in Reggio Calabria. She has made this crossing many times and knows what to expect. They are fourth in the line of cars waiting, a quiet night so far on this New Year's Eve. Within a half hour they are rolling onto the large ferry.

At the bar inside they decide not to have a glass of wine. It is only a few kilometers across, she tells him; in 15 minutes they will be in Sicily. Outside, as the ferry begins to move, they stand at the rail and gaze silently at the multitude of lights that is Messina. Once they are really underway and leaving the mainland behind, a cold breeze blows, and she tucks herself under his arm. Within a minute, she is about to say she has changed her mind about that wine, and then he says he needs to use a john. She watches him step through the cabin door, then turns and looks down at the dark water sliding past. Unzipping her tote, she finds the gun she took from under the clothes in his suitcase while he showered this morning. Without a pause, she drops it over the rail and watches it make a tiny splash and disappear for good.

Twenty minutes later she is at the wheel of the VW, rolling through bustling downtown Messina. They are only 40 minutes away from Taormina and the Villa Schuler. Lodged in a cup holder next to the gearshift, her mobile trills. She glances at John, who raises his eyebrows at her. She picks it up and tells him, "It's Aldo."

At a red light she pushes talk and says, "Aldo, darling, tell me something good."

His first few words tell her there will be nothing good. "Lina, where are you?"

"Driving in Messina."

"You need to pull over and park."

"What is wrong, Aldo? We are stopped at a red light."

"Please pull over first."

The light changes, and she has the Golf moving again. She says, "Okay, I have parked."

Aldo says, "They have found Hans."

She brakes sharply and stares at John. A loud screech comes from behind them, and in the mirror she sees a fellow giving her the finger. "Aldo, one second."

John points ahead to an open spot at the curb, and she moves into it. Her heart is slamming in her chest, and she looks again at John. "Okay, Aldo, where did they find Hans?"

"In a forest on a hillside off 9, north of Bologna. His throat had been cut, and he was in a plastic bag. Dogs, or animals of some kind, had found the body, and that attracted the attention of a couple out taking a hike."

She drops the phone in John's lap and, with a small cry, buries her face in her hands.

Chapter 43

Four days into the new year and they have found a rhythm in this ancient place. Sleeping until 9, and then middle-aged Anna or the younger Serafina bringing breakfast to this third-floor room and setting it out on their private patio with its stunning views. A 27-room, 3-star hotel, the Villa Schuler is tastefully decorated in pastels and beautifully kept. But as Lina says, it feels like a private home—which it once was—and the service makes it so.

To his eye their balcony offers an unmatched series of vistas, from a jaw-dropping plunge down 700 feet to the glimmering Ionian Sea, to a sweep of the gentle coastline of eastern Sicily, to a climb up the slopes of snow-capped Mt. Etna, blowing off huge white plumes from Europe's largest active volcano, then down from the crater, past the snowline to the dense forests covering Etna's flank, through the dark green hills and valleys below.

From reading online, he knows that 3000 years ago a tribe came from the East to this spot high on Mt. Taurus. A place where they could gaze down that sheer drop to the sea and know that an inaccessible summit had their back. A place where, above all, those first Sicilians could be safe—from inevitable marauders who would come for their town and their lives, and from the monster volcano that would occasionally belch the hell in its bowels all the way to the sea.

Safe for 700 years. But then came the Greeks, the Carthaginians, the Romans, the Saracens, the French and the Spanish, each deciding that Taormina should be theirs. This beautiful place became an irresistible magnet to each of Sicily's serial invaders.

And then came the tourists. Goethe with vivid impressions in his *Journey to Italy*. A young Prussian painter Otto Gelang with his Taormina landscapes, shown in Paris where the word was he had painted fantasized scenes not of this world. No, cried Otto, these places exist, go see for yourselves. And now for 200 years, writers and artists have come to hang out here.

Taormina as safe haven is what he and Lina have come for. But after the news about Hans on New Year's Eve, that first night was tough for her. He only made it tougher when he found the Glock gone from his suitcase. "Lina, for Christ's sake!" he snarled when she explained where the gun was. For the first time since his arrival in Italy they did not make love. They lay in bed, facing away from each other, tense, not touching, not saying a word.

Finally, she apologized. She should not have done that without telling him first. If she had told him, he said, he would not have let her do it. Silence again, and then she said there was no way Stan would find them here. Let's hope, he said. Eventually he had turned and spooned with her in the dark until her breathing told him that sleep had finally arrived. It was after midnight. They hadn't even wished each other Happy New Year.

Subdued in the morning, she finally stirred a bit in the sun on the balcony when he recalled that Aldo had promised a memorial service for Hans would not happen in Bologna until the spring. She talked about how the Schuler family had come here from Germany a hundred years ago, how they had lost this place during each of the world wars and somehow found a way to get it back. Her own family had been coming here three times a year since she was a little girl, usually in the spring and late summer when they loved to ride the cable cars down to the beach and to picnic in the forests on Etna's slope. They would also celebrate New Years here, when the special treat was a long hike, just she and her dad, through some of Etna's giant firs.

Late that morning she showed him the town, walking the length of its main drag, the vehicle-free Corso Umberto, lined with posh shops and restaurants, old stone churches and palazzos around small, charming squares. They had a glass of wine at one of the outdoor tables at the Wunderbar, the favorite hangout of both Tennessee Williams and Truman Capote. In the afternoon they walked again, this time down the Via Roma in front of the hotel to a large public park, again with remarkable views. The last time she was here, about 10 years ago with her mom, after her dad had passed away, the park had been full of cats, lounging in trees, basking in the sun, begging for food. There were only a few now. The town must have finally re-located them, so to speak. The sun's heat, those great vistas and the bitter-sweet pleasure of her memories seemed to warm Lina. That night they made love again with a passion that left her clinging to him and weeping quietly.

After breakfast on the 2nd, they again sat on the balcony gazing at Etna and the sea, and then her mobile rang. It was Detective Ranzone in Bologna. Lina listened and occasionally spoke in Italian. Afterward she filled him in. Ranzone had news on a couple of fronts. First, he was sure that Prof. Signorelli had already informed her of the discovery of Signor Broek's body outside Bologna. An unfortunate case, said the cop, and of course the investigation is on-going. But so far they have found nothing at all that would link Signor Lyle to the murder.

Now as for Signor Lyle's whereabouts, Ranzone had been on holiday since the day before Christmas, and returning to his desk this morning, he found an email from a colleague in Milano that included a personal theft report filed and signed by Signor Lyle. It was dated December 26 and indicated he had been working with his laptop computer that day at the McDonald's ristorante on Via Cordusio in Milano. He stopped briefly to use the men's room, and when he returned, both the laptop and his mobile phone were missing. He had given his residence as the Hotel Zurigo in Milano. And he had also asked that a copy of this report be forwarded to Detective Ranzone with the Carabinieri office in Bologna. Nothing urgent, he said, but he had met with the detective as a witness in a missing person case and wanted him to know why he would not be answering his phone.

Ranzone said when he called the Hotel Zurigo this morning, now one week after the theft report, a clerk told him that Signor Lyle had stayed at the hotel from December 26 to December 31. She remembered him well, she said, a polite American who spoke quite good Italian and, in checking out, had asked about train schedules for Milano to Torino.

"You will note," Ranzone said, "Signor Lyle's stay in Milano included December 28, when the unfortunate shooting occurred in our own Montagnola Gardens."

"Yes," said Lina, "and how long does it take to drive from Milano to Bologna? Two hours? Maybe a little more?"

True, of course, said the detective, but having just read the full report on the Montagnola shooting, he must tell her that, except for the two bullet slugs found at the scene, the person or persons responsible for those gunshots had apparently left without a trace.

After recounting the call, she asked, "So, we are safe? I have told only Aldo and Rena."

"Yes, let's put this out of our heads."

"But how can we know when to return?"

"We'll hear something. We'll know." But he'd been thinking often about that. From Praiano he sent emails to Redding and others, telling them he was in Chicago but had lost his cell and so was a bit out of touch. He had heard from Lina in Bologna that Stan had been stalking her there since mid-December and that the police were involved. His whereabouts were uncertain now, and Lina would be grateful for a confirmation of his presence in Cedar Hill or elsewhere.

As for the issue of his own return, he sent Redding another note, saying he had just received some unpleasant medical news. His cancer was back, and he'd probably need more radiation or maybe surgery this time. In either case, arrangements should be made to cancel or cover his classes.

And Mar? It was over between them, but he cannot go back and make it official until he knows for certain that Lina is safe. Maybe a note also to his wife about cancer and with something vague about a desire to travel while he still can.

Thinking about that made him want to talk with Lina about their future together. He waited until they were walking, after the detective's phone call. She was taking him for a look at the house that Lawrence and Frieda had lived in for two years starting in 1920. They were heading into a heavily built up area on the east side of the town, houses and apartment buildings all jumbled together on twisting streets.

"Think of this whole neighborhood," she said, "as out in the country back then. The Lawrences' villa was built in the 1600s, and there was only one other house on a dirt road that ran though orange and lemon groves. The story goes that Frieda ran naked in those groves with a young Sicilian mule driver, and so *Chatterley* was born. But then you probably know that story."

He nodded and then said almost casually, "So when we're together, where will we live?"

She stopped and looked at him. "John, what has changed between you and your wife that you can ask such a thing?"

"I've told you. The fact is, the bond is beyond repair…"

"But you have known that for years."

"Yes, but now I have simply accepted the fact that I cannot save her. Only she can save herself, and the only thing I can do to help is leave her. So she'll be forced to care for herself. Otherwise she'll drink herself to death."

She nodded but said nothing, and they were walking again. "So here's my fantasy," he said. "I leave St. Thomas. Obviously I'm done there. So in the summer and the fall we'll be in Bologna where you'll teach. In the spring maybe at some university in the states that will accept me part-time, and year-round we will write our books."

"And the winter?"

"The winter we'll spend on some beautiful deserted beach in the Caribbean where we'll run naked, like Frieda."

"Nice fantasy." She smiled but didn't look at him.

"We could do it," he said, hearing defiance in his voice.

She pointed to a large pink home above them and said, "That is Lawrence's house."

Later they climbed back across the town to its architectural highlight, an outdoor theater built by the Greeks in 250 BC. Some of it was in ruins now, but enough remained to imagine what viewing productions must have been like. Wooden benches on the terraces of the amphitheater offered a great view of Etna in the distance above the stage.

"The most amazing thing I've seen here," she said after a while, "was a production of Oedipus Rex. My parents brought me when I was ten, and I think it changed me forever. I was thrilled and terrified and stunned by the power of theater, the power of art."

He shook his head. "I'd love to see something here."

"Maybe we will come back this summer. They do plays, concerts, films."

They had seafood that evening at one of her favorites, Ristorante Granduca, and later she asked the waiter if they had the after-dinner liqueur Strega. He was a pleasant young fellow with round-rimmed glasses framing bright, lively eyes. He said, sorry, they did not have Strega. Probably one of the bars down the way would have it.

She asked if he knew the legend of Strega. He said no, and she explained it was brewed by beautiful witches. Shared by a couple, it would keep them united in love forever.

"Ah, signore, be careful!" he said to John.

"No problem."

"Then I will try to find it for you." And he was off, pulling out his cell. Minutes later he was back with a smile. "I called my friend at Carpe Diem, which is just down the Corso, and they have Strega." Then he placed a full bottle of the golden liquid on the table. "You see, we still have the mafia in Sicily, but now they do good things. My friend brought it for you."

"*Grazie!*" she said, those green eyes smiling. "You have helped change our lives."

"*Prego*," he said and turned to take four small glasses from a good-looking fellow in a chef's hat. The waiter poured and offered a toast. John pronounced the drink delicious.

Walking back up the Corso Umberto toward the Villa Schuler, he asked, "Do you think he's in love with the chef?"

She laughed. "I had not thought of that. Maybe."

"That funny line of his about the mafia made me wonder if, growing up here, you knew any kids whose families were connected"

"With the mafia? Oh, yes. There was one boy in my class all the way through school whose father ran the organization that controlled most of eastern Sicily. I think he liked me. Anyway, he asked me out several times."

"And you went out with him?"

"Never. But actually he was very good looking. I heard about a year ago his father had a stroke, and now my friend is the one in charge."

"I've read they are maybe losing their grip?"

"I see that also, but I doubt it. There have been brave prosecutors and judges and many more arrests and convictions, but the problem still seems enormous. They say 80 percent of business owners in Catania still pay *pizzo*, or protection money. My friend must do all right."

The next morning, after Anna cleared the breakfast dishes, Lina said, "It is time to climb. First the Madonna della Rocca, then the old fort above it, and then all the way up to Castelmola."

All these places were often in view, looming over the town from much farther up. She had pointed out the white cross of the church, the partial walls of the old fort, and the small town sitting proudly on the mountain's rocky summit, floating at times above the clouds. He couldn't imagine climbing all the way up to Castelmola.

On long flights of stairs and a steep walkway with several switchbacks that lead to the church, he watched her move above him and thought he'd follow that gorgeous ass anywhere. But much sooner than he expected, the climbing got to him. His thighs burning, his lungs straining, he stopped on one flight of stairs. And then he must have passed out, because he suddenly found himself sprawled on a landing. Above he could hear Lina speaking to someone in Spanish. When she finally called down to him, he said he was coming, just taking his time.

The sanctuary of the church was the most unusual he'd ever seen, literally hacked out of a huge rock, the ceiling like the roof of a cave. The views in every direction from the old fort were the best yet. But gazing up at Castelmola, still another few kilometers up a winding road, he knew it was out of the question. When he asked, maybe another day? She said of course.

They spent the rest of the afternoon reading on their balcony, she McCarthy's *The Road*, which she was often notating, he an Elmore Leonard crime confection, *Freaky Deaky*, that had some how slipped by him years ago. Vintage Elmore, he thought and then stared into space for a while, wondering if he was really that out of shape, or if the cancer was actually back.

* * *

With the sun in the open sky over the sea lighting a mass of clouds camped over Etna, they are out on their balcony again this morning after breakfast. The air is warm, a balmy 60, not untypical at this time of the year. With her laptop open, she says suddenly, "Darling, you won't believe this. Obama won the Iowa caucuses."

"Jesus. All white Iowa."

"Thirty-eight percent of the delegates. Hillary got 30."

They talk about this for a time, then she asks if he wants to come along to the *farmacia*. She needs a few things. Still feeling less than himself, he says, no, with just 10 pages to go, he'll stay with his book. Once she leaves the room, he thinks about the route she'll take. Down the pretty marble staircase to the ground floor, out the hotel's side door and a few steps right under this balcony to the Via Roma. A few hundred meters to the park and then only a block to the nearest pharmacy. He gets to his feet and looks over the railing just as she walks under.

He loves seeing her move when she's unaware he's watching. In a snug-fitting gray sweater and black jeans, that lithe, lovely body moves with grace on every stride. The sparkling red hair is long enough now to ruffle a bit in the breeze. As she turns into the Via Roma and heads for the park, he leans farther over the railing to follow her progress.

And then his eye catches someone emerging from the side door below. It's a guy in a red Ferrari baseball cap, workout pants and a hooded blue sweatshirt that says "Parma." Pausing at the Via Roma, the guy looks toward Lina, who is striding with pace now 30 yards up the street. Before he slips on shades, the fellow's profile makes John literally bite his tongue.

It's not possible. But it's Stan.

Chapter 44

So how many fucking times is he going to kick himself for not doing it when he had the chance? Probably a better chance than he'll ever have again. It's more than two weeks ago now, and he still sees himself standing in the doorway to the Bitch's bedroom, with the two of them lying there, right where he wanted them, sound asleep. He could have so easily just walked right up and sliced the Boyfriend's carotid and then jumped on her with the cloth full of chloroform and finished the deal in the bathtub. Then just a small alteration to the note he was going to leave on her computer, and it would have all been over and done with. He'd be back in the states getting on with his fucking life, and they'd be just one more tragic couple who did the most common tragic couple thing—murder-suicide.

Instead, he had chickened out, backed away, fled her apartment like a frightened little twit. Just one little wrinkle—that unexpected head on a pillow—and Mr. Cool-and-Collected, Mr. Innovation-on-the-Fly, was running away, almost gagging with his heart in his mouth. He was at her door when he somehow remembered her razor knife in his pocket and returned it to the kitchen drawer. Two nights later, pumped with new resolve, he realized the extent of his mistake when he came back and his key no longer worked. What a sad joke he is.

So now how do you get these lovebirds to another place where you can stage it like they've wrung each other's necks? Maybe it was a bold move to take a room in the same hotel, or maybe it was just foolish. But over the past week, his only remotely workable idea was to somehow get hold of a hotel pass-key, let himself into their room in the middle of the night and do what he should have done two weeks ago. What else is he supposed to do in this popular tourist town—the streets always busy with sightseers and shoppers—just walk up and push them over a railing? Or jump out of the shadows in the hotel garden and stab them both in the throat?

Even if he managed to pull it off, given his history with the Bitch, well-known to the Carabinieri, he would surely be their first "person of interest." Unless he can make it look like something it's not, an accident or the murder-suicide thing, they will knock on his door first.

So he's been working on the maids, the dour Anna and the timid Serafina, who bring his breakfast every morning, and later, usually around 11:30, make up his room. When either of them comes to clean, he doesn't respond to their knock and call, so they need to use that passkey. He quickly learned they keep it in their apron pocket, but his romancing has gotten him almost nowhere with the younger, more attractive Serafina. From their awkward chats, he knows she grew up in the nearby town of Linguaglossa, does not have a boyfriend and actually lives in a small room in the basement of the hotel. His fantasy is that she will come to his room after she is finished with her work, and they will end up in the bed she so meticulously made that morning. Then later, when she's distracted or in the john, he'll lift the key from her apron, or, with pillow talk, he'll learn her routine and what she does with that key when she's done for the day.

No doubt the maids are instructed to be polite with guests but not overly familiar, and skinny Serafina has followed orders. Actually, with the dark-browed Anna, with the look of a woman less than pleased with life, he's made slightly more progress, getting her to smile at him this morning when he asked if her husband was the jealous type who'd be angry if she and Stan had a glass of wine together after work today. No, signore, she said, the corners of her thin mouth turning up a bit, she has no husband. She lives with her invalid mother in a small house in Naxos, and she'd have to ask if she might come home an hour later in order to have that glass of wine. At this rate, he'd be grizzled and gray before getting to first base with either one.

At least the Bitch and the Boyfriend so far have no idea he's with them in Taormina. He wants to keep it that way, but how likely is that in a small hotel in a small town. He nearly blew it yesterday when he opened his door and caught a glimpse of her starting down the staircase. He should have simply shut the door and waited long enough for her to leave, maybe checking at his window to see which way she was headed. But having not seen her since shooting at them in Bologna, he felt his heart jump and reacted by carefully following her down and out of the hotel. She did not stop at the desk to turn in her key, and that told him the Boyfriend was still in their room and likely to stay there until she returned. Behind her on the Via Roma, he thought of the pleasure it would give him to secretly track that sexy ass and do whatever circumstances permitted. Shock her by suddenly appearing in her face, terrify her with a strange smile, or literally stop her breath with his hands on that delicate neck.

And then he stopped himself with the realization that she could glance back at any moment on this open street and, despite his new duds and the wrap-around Raybans, make him. What the hell was he doing, except indulging himself with petty fantasies and in the process increasing the odds in her favor? He ducked between parked cars and out of her line of sight and then quickly made his way back to a walkway and stairs that headed down the mountain.

What the fuck was he thinking? After all the scheming over the past few weeks, after his last minute change of heart at the airline counter at Malpensa, after everything he's been through with this fucking obsession, after following her across an ocean and now down almost the entire length of this bloody country, he nearly shows himself to her just acting on a whim?

How many times has this stupid jig seemed up? How many times has he nearly ended it with one dumb move or another? The day he left the note for Signora Vascone and told the cops he was heading to Torino, he had a strong feeling the Boyfriend would be coming after him. Then he had nearly checked into the Hotel Tulip, just down the way from the Bitch's apartment. He was standing at the front door with his bags when he suddenly realized the clerk would ask for his passport, and all it would take was a call from the scrupulous Detective Alberri to prove he was lying about leaving Bologna.

He ended up at that bar near the Piazza Verdi where he was soon drinking with Fillipo and his two pals, celebrating the end of the term before heading home to mama for Christmas and New Years. He quickly established the thin, bespectacled Fillipo as an impoverished art history major who often indulged in a little pot with his friends. And when it turned out that mama was waiting for him in Cesara, a little town near Orta San Giulio, that gave them something more to talk about. It was all perfect for his purpose, and in less than an hour he had cut a deal to stay in Fillipo's room for 40 euros per night, five nights payment in advance. As an American grad student on an Italian holiday he was looking to explore the treasures of Bologna. Just hang out and enjoy himself a little. Speaking of which, could Fillipo and his friends say where he might score some weed around here?

Laughing, the guys said there's anything you want just up the street in Piazza Verdi. This was not a surprise. He had often seen slacker-types hanging out there, but he wanted a name.

"Look for a North African named Bebe," said Fillipo. "He's Moroccan. He'll fix you up."

And so he did, and not just with the pot. Bebe turned out to be a very dark, stoop-shouldered fellow, almost rakishly handsome if not for the scar that crossed the left side of his mouth and ruined his face. He spoke French-accented Italian but preferred broken English when he learned he was dealing with an American. The pot Stan bought on Sunday night chilled him enough on Monday to return and ask about a handgun. Where dope was sold, guns could be found, he figured, and Bebe didn't blink, saying only, "It will costed you. Five hundred. Two hundred euro in front." His smile lifted that crease on his mouth.

What kind of gun were they talking about?

"The best one. Top in the drawer."

"Okay, it's a deal." He wouldn't know what he was buying until he saw it. "When?"

"This night." But that night Bebe said tomorrow. And Tuesday he couldn't find the guy. He figured his two hundred was gone, but on Wednesday Bebe was back with his weird smile.

"Okay," he said, "Three hundred euro, cash on the barrelhouse."

The weapon was a .32 with a long and no doubt checkered past, a much worked over, sawed-off revolver with every ID mark filed off and a grip wrapped with old electrical tape.

"Five hundred euros for this?" said Stan.

"You not like. I keep."

Along with his two hundred euros. "No, I'll take it."

"You want box bullet? One hundred euro. In armory store they take you name."

Was that true? He decided to spring for the slugs as well. And so he was the not-so-proud owner of a piece-of-shit pistol with which he knew he'd be lucky to hit an outhouse at anything over 10 paces.

287

The only good thing was the size; it was eminently concealable.

Finally, he was on his way to Milano with the plan he had worked on while waiting for Bebe and the gun. He stopped in Parma just long enough to buy the sweatshirt and the hat to give himself a new look and be able to say he'd been there. In Milano he stayed at the hotel he'd found online with a McDonald's and its WiFi nearby, and in the morning he pulled off the phony grab-and-run claim, figuring it would accomplish two good things: establish with his friends at the Carabinieri his presence in Milano and make it no longer possible for them to call his cell and ask for his whereabouts. Then later in the afternoon, he drove into the countryside around Malpensa, found what looked like a deserted farm with a small woods and surprised himself when he tried the gun. Yes, he'd been a good shot as a kid, but he had never fired a sidearm before, nor anything as unreliable-looking as this. Afraid it might blow his hand off, he hit nothing but air with his first shot. But then at thirty paces and holding it in both hands, he put five in a row into a tree trunk about 6 inches in diameter. Way better than expected.

So at 7 the following morning, the do-not-disturb sign in place on his door and the checkout fellow too busy to notice, he left the hotel. He was hardly giving himself a fool-proof alibi, but it was better than nothing. Two-and-a-half hours later he was standing in the portico shadows across Via San Vitale, watching the door to the Bitch's building. With his shades, the hood of his new sweatshirt up over the Ferrari cap and wrapped in the old gray overcoat from a second-hand shop in Milano, he felt reasonably anonymous. When the Boyfriend emerged alone, he was elated. How nice it would be to pick them off one at a time, but in less than a minute the asshole entered Federico's *farmacia* on the corner and was soon headed back to the apartment.

The day was overcast and windy, and it was almost three hours later when the two of them finally emerged together. By then he was cold, tired, hungry and humiliated, wondering how much longer he could wait out here on the street, moving his vantage point frequently, trying several different stratagems to appear not to be doing what he was doing, and not wanting to wait in the café he had used in the past to watch her entrance. He was probably being paranoid, but they knew him in there, and he did not want to show himself to anyone who might remember him on a day he planned to shoot two people dead on the streets of Bologna.

He had moved to the newsstand in the Piazza Aldrovandi, purchased a third newspaper he could read and hide behind and a salami and cheese sandwich from a small shop nearby. Already chomping on the sandwich as he walked out, he spotted them heading into the University district and followed. He was much more familiar with these streets now, so it was easier to follow at a distance without losing them. The Bitch and the Boyfriend paused for a quick look at one of the hidden canals and then, as they moved on, she took his arm in that way that always made him want to puke. Later, beyond one of the city's most elaborate gates, they were looking down over a wall in an area with few people around. A good location, if he had the time to find a decent spot to shoot from, but they were soon moving again.

When he saw them heading into the Montagnola Gardens, he was sure his luck had changed. He knew this park, and if they walked to the back end near the pond, he'd never have a better shot. It was so perfect in fact that he decided to risk losing them by heading around the outside of the park to enter from the back and choose a spot sufficiently hidden to use his little piece. Just wait for them there until they moved to a place where he had a clear shot at both. Bang and bang. Two shots. One for each. That was all he'd allow himself. Two shots and get out. He was not about to risk spending the rest of his life in a locked cell. Not for doing something to these shitty people that could always wait for another day.

He found his spot quickly. Near the building that looked deserted at the back of the pond, there were many trees, and one was a double, two trunks growing together and forming a V starting about four feet up. He could easily conceal himself behind that tree and, when the time was right, aim straight between the V, shoot once and shoot twice, then take off.

That's pretty much how it happened. There was no one else in sight as a frigid wind whipped across the top of the park. They took their sweet time checking out those weird-looking sculptures of wild animals and mermaids. When they finally sat on the park bench, he knew it was time. He fought down a surge of excitement that actually felt good, knowing it was mostly a matter of how calm he could stay. He was taking long, slow, even breaths and using the V to brace his hands while he focused on that red head at a distance, he figured, of about 30 to 40 yards. He squeezed the trigger, felt the crack, heard the ring of metal and flinched. And when he focused again, the Bitch was on the ground with the Boyfriend hovered over her. Despite the ping of the slug hitting metal he was sure she'd been hit, and so he lowered the barrel a hair and squeezed again. This time he saw a piece of wood shatter on the bench, but the Boyfriend's head dropped, and it was more than possible both shots had found their mark.

For a second he considered slamming more shots into them, but his mind was already screaming at him to follow the plan. Get out before anyone could catch a glimpse of him. Seconds later he was racing behind the empty building and out the back end of the park. Then walking at a normal pace, within a few minutes he was in the square in front of the Stazione Centrale, and a minute later, as sirens wailed nearby, he climbed on a bus that would drop him within a block of where he had parked the Fiat. On the bus he felt the gun in his overcoat pocket and knew he needed to get rid of it asap. On the street, and before jumping in the car and getting out of town, he found one of Bologna's large street corners trash bins, lifted the large plastic lid and tossed in that ratty old overcoat with the pistol still in the pocket.

Back in his Milano hotel room, again without being seen by the front desk staff, he did not find the phone message he half-expected from Detective Ranzone. He spent the evening watching TV and tooling through Italian news services on the web, looking for a report of a shooting in Bologna's Montagnola Gardens. He found nothing. He climbed into bed about 11:30 and argued with himself for a while about whether either of his shots had hit its target.

In the morning he found out. Waiting for him on the laptop he had reported stolen was the Bitch's email to Aldo and Rena about the shooting in the park and their plans to head south, eventually ending up in Taormina and the Villa Schuler. It had been so long since he had seen anything useful from the trojan he had slipped onto her desktop, he'd almost forgotten it was there. Yeah, pretty clever, but now what was he going to do?

For the next two days and nights his thoughts and feelings were all over the goddamn place. That his shots had missed the Bitch and the Boyfriend he blamed mostly on Bebe and the piece-of-shit pistol. But that he had set a ridiculously arbitrary limit of two shots only before taking off and so had once again missed his chance to put an end to this absurd comic opera he blamed entirely on his weak-kneed self. How much more risk would he have really incurred had he spent another three or four seconds pumping the rest of the slugs in that little revolver into those two bodies cowering on the ground next to the bench? Once again his nerve had failed, once again he had lacked the fucking balls to pull off what he claimed he wanted to do.

Yes, in his crazy disguise he had followed them across Bologna, and in broad daylight in the middle of a public park he had taken two clear-shot pops at the couple he wanted dead and had gotten away scot-free, without so much as a phone call from the cops who knew where to find him. But the bottom line was that he had failed again, and that forced the question, did he really want to kill these two or was all this just a big-talker's bullshit? Within a few days they would be at the opposite end of the country in a town that, once again, she knew and he did not. Was he going to follow them down there and find a way to do what he had failed miserably at doing three or four times already? He couldn't even think of a decent way of going about it, some plan that did not have the stink of fear and failure all over it. Why not just call it off? He was a free fucking agent. Just put himself on a plane back to the states and be done with it.

And on the morning of New Year's Eve, that's where his head was. He would drive to Malpensa, turn in the Fiat and book himself a flight back to Detroit. Do not start this New Year being ruled by the same old obsession that had ruined his life for the past several months! That was exactly his mind set right up to the moment, late in the morning, when he handed his Visa card to the gal behind the Northwest/KLM counter. She ran it, and, for some reason he will never know, the card was rejected. There was more than enough space on it, and he'd been using it in Italy for weeks. There should have been no problem with that card. But there was, and when he took it back from the older blond woman who looked a little like his mother, and gave her his Mastercard, he said, almost with a kind of shame, "Wait, I've changed my mind."

When his laptop connected with the airport's WiFi, he found a flight from Malpensa to Catania on EasyJet, but the plane had just taken off. There would not be another one until this same time the next day. Maybe he was too depressed to make any kind of move, maybe he was punishing himself for all his stupid fucking indecision, but he just stayed at the airport and pulled a Tom Hanks, living there for the next 24 hours, sleeping in a lounge chair and cleaning up in a men's room. The flight on New Year's Day landed in Sicily 10 minutes early.

He stayed at a hotel near the Catania airport that night rather than go directly to Taormina, vowing not to head for the Villa Schuler until he had a workable plan to kill the Bitch and the Boyfriend. He also told himself he wanted to give them enough time to themselves to feel totally safe in the hotel where he too would take a room. But the fact was his scheming could never seem to move past the idea of somehow getting access to a passkey and doing them in their own room, just as he should have done them in Bologna. And the idea of checking into the same hotel freaked him a bit. What if they walked up to the desk while he was signing in? They could go directly to the Carabinieri and complain that he was stalking them. He would claim it was all a coincidence, that he had no idea they were there, and wasn't this a free country? But then he'd be a marked man, if not followed, then certainly detained and questioned if anything were to happen to either of those two. Or worse, they might just grab their things and go, leave Taormina and head wherever. Anyplace, it would make no difference. He'd never find them. Or was that what he secretly wanted? Totally lose them and have to give up this whole crazy scheme.

He spent another day and night at the hotel in Catania thinking about all these things, about possibilities versus probabilities, taking a long walk in the boring neighborhood around the airport, berating, accusing and second-and-third-guessing himself. Finally he woke up Thursday morning with one idea. Fate. He had done this before, and it had worked out okay. Just go there, and if it were meant to be, the details would work themselves out. If not, not. He called the Villa Schuler and made sure they were still there. Then he called back and reserved a room. Forty minutes on the train, ten minutes in a taxi switch-backing up the mountain, and he was there. No sign of them when he checked in. The first thing he did was something he thought of on the train: an email to Ranzone with his current itinerary. He translated it into Italian and sent it on its way.

So he's been here two days and two nights now. Yesterday, after starting to follow her, he hiked all the way down the mountain to walk the empty beaches by the sea, had lunch at a pizzeria and later dinner at a seafood restaurant down there. It was dark when he climbed all the way back up. Just to see if he could do it, he told himself. Or was he just trying to avoid them? Or was he punishing himself again for the folly of following her? Maybe all of the above.

Now it's late morning. He's reading about the history of this place with the amazing vistas, when there's a knock on his door. His first thought is Anna, maybe with a word about what her mother thinks. When he opens it, standing there looking amused is the Boyfriend.

Chapter 45

Driving up the mountain to Castelmola, they hardly say a word to each other. Two days ago she wanted to hike up here, a good steady climb of about 40 minutes, but with Stan lurking now, it no longer seems a good idea. She figures John is probably also thinking how in the world they have reached the point where they are headed to a meeting with Daniele Sanpietro, her old high school classmate and Catania's boss of the bosses.

The easy answer: John talked her into this. They have been discussing, yes, arguing the question of what to do ever since he found her in the *farmacia* yesterday morning. "Darling, you changed your mind," she said brightly when he entered the shop in his black jogging suit and running shoes. But she knew from his face that something was wrong, some health problem perhaps. There had been hints lately that he was not always feeling well. Last night they had not made love when he complained of feeling "totally exhausted."

Having paid for the tampons and the other items in the white plastic bag, she began moving to the door. He took her arm firmly and said, "Wait. He's here. I've seen him."

"Who is here?" But as he led her out the door, looking in every direction, she knew. They walked quickly a few meters to a small café, sat inside and ordered cappuccino.

He said, "So Stan followed you just now, when you left the hotel."

"How can that possibly be? Are you absolutely certain it was Stan?"

"Absolutely. I was on the balcony watching you leave, and he came out the same side door you used. Right out of our own hotel, Lina."

"I cannot believe this."

"Believe it. He was wearing different clothes, a shirt that said Parma and a red cap. But it was Stan, following you right up Via

294

Roma in front of the hotel. By the time I got my shoes on and ran down to the street, I could see you heading for the pharmacy, but he had disappeared. He must have turned off somewhere. But he was following you. That much I'm sure of."

"So now what do we do?" She reached across the table and took his hand. "Leave?"

"You mean leave Taormina? If he found us here, he could find us anywhere."

"But how could he find us?"

"I don't know. Maybe he put one of those tracking bugs on your car. I wish I'd brought that Spygadget thing, but we probably shouldn't go anywhere until that car has been checked."

"So we go to the Carabinieri here. Tell them the whole story and ask them to contact Detective Alberri."

Silently he takes his hand back, shaking his head no first, then nodding yes. "We need to find out where he's staying."

Back at the hotel, she asked if their friend Stanford Lyle had arrived yet. Gunther Schuler looked over his glasses at her, then down at his computer. Yes, he arrived yesterday. A glance at the box for room 203 found the key. He was not in at the moment. They sat on the balcony and watched for him. After a while, John said, "When he comes back, I'm going to his room."

"Darling, to what end?"

"To let him know that if he stays here, he's the one who will be in danger."

"John!"

"What? You want to sit just here? Just wait for him to do something terrible to you?"

"No, I want to go to the Carabinieri."

"Of course, but let's wait until he comes back. Then we'll tell them exactly where he is."

So they waited for more than two hours, and, with no sign of him, John finally gave in. They walked up to the Carabinieri office off the Piazza Vittorio Emanuele II at the south end of the Corso Umberto. After a wait of 20 minutes, they met with Eleana Stessa, a uniformed officer in her forties who spoke some English. She had a plain face and a no-nonsense manner as she took careful notes in longhand. She eyed John as Lina detailed in Italian their story and emphasized the shooting in the Montagnola. When she produced a card from the detectives in the Bologna office, the woman picked up a phone and made the call. Alberri was out, but she spoke with Ranzone. Lina nodded at John to let him know it was going okay. He looked frustrated with everything in Italian, and when Stessa hung up, Lina asked if she could summarize in English.

"*Certo*," said the officer, looking unhappy. Detective Ranzone had explained that both Signor Lyle and Professore Lentini have made accusations against each other. Both deny the other's accusations, and there is little in the way of evidence that can prove one or the other, although several of the professor's friends and colleagues do back her story. As for the shooting in the Montagnola Gardens, the professor and her friend, the American professor, Signor Martens, seem convinced that Signor Lyle did the shooting, but he was registered at a hotel in Milano for all of that week, and the hotel said he was never seen leaving or returning to his room on 28/12/07, the day of the shooting. Ranzone's view was that the shooting might have been the result of a drug deal gone bad, with, unfortunately, the two of them caught in the line of fire.

And one other thing, said Stessa, tapping her computer keyboard. As they were talking, Ranzone forwarded an email he received yesterday from Signor Lyle. Yes, it was here. She turned her screen to Lina, and said perhaps she would like to read and translate for her friend.

Lina looked at the message for a few seconds and, translating on the fly, read it aloud:

> Detective Ranzone:
>
> A note to let you know that I have delayed my visit to Torino for my research. Instead I am traveling a little, starting in eastern Sicily, which, as I am sure you know, is a fascinating and beautiful place. So far I have been to Siracusa, Catania and now I am in Taormina for a few days, staying at the Hotel Villa Schuler. Since I did not hear from you at the hotel in Milano, I am thinking that, quite understandably, you have lost interest in me. But in any case, you know where to reach me. As you will note, without my laptop, I am using my Hotmail

account and sending from an Internet café here.

My best to you and Detective Alberri.

Stanford Lyle

"His typical M.O.," said John as they left the office. "Go to them first, play nice, look and sound concerned and get them to lean his way."

"Smart," she said as they walked into the shadows on the Corso Umberto.

"Yeah, but I don't understand why they favor this American over someone like you."

"I do not think they have favored him. Ranzone surely seems a sexist, but they have taken what we said about Stan seriously. They interrogated him twice, followed him for three days and checked on whether he truly left Bologna. They have done what is possible under the law."

"Look, cops are the same everywhere. They can do whatever they damn well please and then say they only followed the law. You may be right, but I just think they could cause this dangerous prick so much more trouble than they have."

"Well, yes, but we can hardly complain if they do not break the law for us."

Officer Stessa had said she would take the matter to her superiors in the office and a decision would be made soon as to how they would proceed. John had asked her, "And what should we do in the meantime? Stay off the streets of Taormina because they are not safe?"

She had looked at him for a second and said, "I understand you. I would go careful, in the streets or anyplace. Do not be foolish."

They had skipped lunch and were hungry enough for an early supper. She took him to the Gambero Rosso where they had wine and pizza and tried to decide what to do next. He said, "I've been thinking about your old school friend, the capo in Catania."

"Why?"

"Because, clearly, he could take care of our problem."

"John, what are you talking about?"

"I'm not talking about violence. From what I hear, those guys are great at good old-school intimidation, and that's what we need here."

She stared at him. "I cannot believe you are thinking this way."

297

"Well, you don't want me to do it, so why not get a professional involved?"

"A professional. Darling, the reason they are good at intimidation is because they are great at violence. You start something like this, and you cannot know where it will end."

When they finished the pizza, he tried again, this time using Hans as an example of what Stan might do. For days she had tried hard to keep Hans out of her mind. Now John pressed hard. They knew what this guy was capable of. Hans was gone, had his throat slit, because Stan had been underestimated. Was there any way she could get her old friend's number and ask for a meeting? He'd probably love hearing from her. She said she did not know. Probably.

"All he'd have to do," said John, "Is send a couple of his ugly, dangerous-looking guys to call on Stan and scare the shit out of him. Tell him to get out of Italy now or his life would become problematic. Something cute like that, and it would be all over."

When she hesitated, he said, "I swear, Lina, if you don't at least call this guy, I'm going to see Stan myself. You won't be able to stop me. I'll do it when you're asleep or whatever."

She got Daniele Sanpietro's cell number from her mother's old attorney, Guido Falcone. The careful, white-haired octogenarian still handled the hotel business for Lina. But first Guido asked, "Why in heaven's name would you want to talk to *him*?"

"For a not very interesting reason. So can you get it for me?"

He said he would try, and in ten minutes he was back with the number. "Please tell me it is neither business nor personal."

"It is neither business nor personal."

"Then what is it, Lina?"

"Something in between. Please, Guido, do not worry. I am a big girl."

When she called the number he answered with an impatient "*Si, pronto.*" She said she was not sure he would remember her, but it was Lina Lentini. And after a pause of at least two seconds he said, Not remember? The love of his life for four years? The girl who would never give him the time of day? And after she laughed about how she had been too young for him back then ("Too young! We were the same age!"), she got right to the point. There was a problem she thought he might be able to help her with. She preferred not to speak on the phone, but she was currently in Taormina and wondered if they could meet sometime soon. How about the San Giorgio in Castelmola, he said quickly, tomorrow at 2?

"*Grazie, Dani, grazie mille.*"

"*Sera incredibile ti videre di nuovo.*" It will be incredible to see her again.

When they returned to the Villa Schuler, Stan's key was still in the box. And every time that evening one of them interrupted their reading to walk down to the desk, the key was still there. Once again that night they did not make love. Again he said he was exhausted.

In the morning between breakfast and room clean up, she started her period, and when she came out of the bathroom, John was gone. In 10 minutes he was back with a strange smile.

"What is it?" she asked.

"I talked to him."

"John, you promised!"

"I did not. I said only that I certainly would confront him, if you didn't call Dani boy."

She shook her head and asked what happened.

"Nothing. He was pretty surprised to see me. I'm sure he thought we didn't know he was here. He was almost tongue-tied for a while, and I just kept abusing him, verbally. I told him we knew exactly what he had done both in Cedar Hill and here in Italy. We know he murdered Hans, we know he tried to kill us in the park and we know why he's here."

"What did he say?"

"Not much. At one point he said, 'You know nothing.' It was very lame, and I said, well we had already been to the Carabinieri here and learned they're closing in on him. They're about this close…" He held up a thumb and finger about an inch apart. "…to arresting his ass and trying him for murder."

She pursed her mouth. "And what did he say to that?"

"He told me to go fuck myself. I said if I were him, I'd get out of this country like immediately, before they start watching the airports. And if he didn't believe me, it didn't really matter, because if I don't hear within two days from my friends in Cedar Hill that he's back in Michigan, I'll kill him myself with my bare hands."

She felt her eyes begin to tear. "John, this is my worst nightmare."

"No, sweetheart, your worst nightmare begins if this asshole ever gets his hands on you."

At 1:30, as they left the room for the meeting up in Castelmola, they found a slim young woman in a red sweater and a short black skirt knocking on Stan's door about half way down the hall. A couple of steps closer and Lina was surprised to see that it was actually Serafina, and then even more surprised when his door opened and she darted inside.

* * *

When she pulls the Golf into the small piazza that greets visitors to the little town atop Mt. Taurus, there is a gun-metal gray Maserati sedan parked to the left of the entrance to the San Giorgio Café and Bar. Two well-built young men dressed in dark suits are lounging against the car, smoking and offering occasional, languid gestures to each other.

Lina says, "He's here early."

John turns to look at the car as she parks hers about ten yards away. They are the only two vehicles in the square. "Those are his boys?"

"Yes, for sure."

The young men don't move but watch them walk to the entrance of the tall, thin building perched on the edge of a cliff above Taormina. He had said it would be incredible to see her, and now it clearly is. He is beaming as he gets to his feet from a table for two near a window as she moves through the door of this famous little bar with the region's best almond wine.

In his low, mellow Italian, he says, "Lina, how can it be? You have not changed at all since the last time I saw you, at age 20."

She says also in Italian, "Dani, but you have changed. You are only more handsome."

As he takes her shoulders lightly in his hands, she brushes each of his smooth cheeks with a kiss. He does look good in his expensive beige suit over a white shirt open at the throat. His tanned face is fuller than it was in high school, when he was a little too thin. His thick brown hair is just a bit unruly, the smile shows a good dentist, and the dark, dreamy eyes are locked on her. They have not once looked to John. She introduces her friend, a professor and author, from the states, and while that smile remains as they shake hands, she knows Dani is disappointed. Then he surprises her by speaking decent English as he moves them to a larger table and waves over a bottle of wine. Staying with English she asks how his father is doing.

300

"He is a vegetable," says Dani, the smile gone.

"I am sorry."

"No, *I* am sorry. I know it sounds harsh, maybe heartless. But it is the only way I can deal with it. That is not my father any more in that body. Otherwise, it is too sad."

John says, "Your father had a stroke."

"Yes, a stroke. Strange, is it not, *professore*, that it is the same word we use for the touch of love?" A glance at Lina. "This terrible blow to our brain that can take away our very self."

There is an awkward silence until the wine is delivered and poured. "*Professore*, you will like this. The family who owned this bar invented this almond wine. To life."

They toast, and then he surprises her again. "Lina, I have read all of your book, the one about our Italian novelists. What is it called?"

She teases him: "You have read all of it, and you cannot remember the title?"

"Yes, well, I have a photographic memory for faces. A face I never forget, especially one as beautiful as this!" He gestures at her smile and looks at John. "But words, I am not so good with words. I have to tell you, *professore*..."

"Please call me John."

"Yes, of course, John, I have to tell you, when we were young and in school together, I had such a thing for this woman. That is what you say in America? You have a 'thing?'"

"Yes," said John.

"But such a cold, impersonal word, a 'thing,' for such a warm and loving feeling."

Lina nods. "See, Dani, you say you are not good with words, but it is clear we cannot trust what you say about yourself. As I recall, you did very well in school."

The mafioso sips his wine. "Truly, I loved school. I always regret not going farther."

John asks, "How did you learn English so well?"

"Well, I am not so good. But we learned some in school, and then I spent two years playing around in the states when I was younger, in New York and Miami. And when you play around, you can learn also." The smile is dazzling again.

Lina says, "And now you are married."

"Yes, how do you know?"

"I assumed. And children?"

"Yes, thank God. Three." And out comes a large-screen cell with a photo of an attractive dark-haired wife and two boys and a girl all under seven. "So," he says, putting away the phone, "Tell me the reason for this wonderful chance to see you again."

When she thought earlier about what she would tell him, it seemed that this would be easier if she did not say that she and John are lovers. It also would have been better if John had not come along, but he insisted, and so she said, "I'm going to say only that you are a friend." So now in this version, she was lecturing this past fall at a college in Michigan—where, by the way, she met John and his lovely wife—when she became the victim of a stalker, a young graduate student, who was so obsessed that he followed her back to Italy. In Bologna it was worse. He followed her everywhere, attacked her sexually, and when her friends tried to help, he murdered one of them. Finally, in a city park he used a gun to shoot at her and John.

Unmoving, Dani has been listening to her story with a grave look, occasionally glancing at John, but mostly riveted on her eyes. Now he stirs and says, "And the police?"

She says, "The Carabinieri continue to investigate, but this man, the stalker, is very clever, and so far they do not have the evidence they need."

He turns from her. "And, John, what is your role in this sad story?"

John avoids looking at her. "My role? I'm just a friend concerned about Lina."

"So concerned that you come all the way to Italy for her."

"Well, no. I was on sabbatical doing research here, but then I heard about the trouble in Bologna, and I came to see if I could help." John pauses, but Dani says nothing. "Actually, Stan—the stalker—was one of my students, and I felt a kind of responsibility."

"Ah, si, responsabilità." He looks at her and says, "And so what is it, Lina, you think I can do to help you?" The tone is still mellow, but the soft lines in his face seem firm now.

She hesitates, then says, "Well, I am not certain, but frankly, Dani, Stan is now in Taormina, and I am concerned for our lives."

John adds quickly, "He checked into our hotel, the Villa Schuler."

Dani nods, and no one says a thing. She is hoping her old classmate will suggest something he can do, but the silence is only getting more awkward. Finally, John says, "So we were thinking that maybe you could send someone to talk with this fellow and convince him to go back home to the States."

"*Si*, but convince him how?" asks Dani.

"Well, perhaps tell him that staying in Italy would not be good for his health."

A nod now from Dani, but when he speaks the voice is no longer mellow. "So, you are asking me — I put it with honesty — to break the law. Surely you know that in Italy it is against the law to threaten someone. In the States also, I think?"

Lina tries to stop this. "Dani, we don't want…"

But he cuts her off with a flick of his gold-Rolex-adorned wrist. "No. I must tell you, Lina, I am truly offended that you would ask such a thing, that I should break the law for you, and place in danger someone close to me. This Stan is someone you say has murdered and tried to kill you and this man…" He points a well-manicured finger at John's chest. "…who is either your lover or the police. And that you would do this to an old friend who so much admired you, I find this truly shameful."

He is on his feet quickly with his hand in his pocket. A 50-euro note flutters to the table, and he is out the San Giorgio's front door before she and John can even meet each other's gaze.

Chapter 46

As on the drive up, they say almost nothing on their way down. Until they pass the street where there is parking for the Madonna della Rocca, when John says, "I half expected to see the boys and the Maserati waiting there while Dani visits the church and has a few words with God."

She nods and says, "The mafiosi have a remarkable capacity for compartmentalization."

"Nice word for hypocrisy. We just got lectured on morality and the law by one of the most evil bastards on the planet."

"Darling, it was your idea to enlist his help."

"I'm sorry, sweetheart, I was a fool."

"And so was I. He obviously thought you were the police. Or that we were wired."

"I guess they really are feeling pressured these days."

As she carefully negotiates the tight turns and narrow streets back to the Villa Schuler, he says, "On my own in this town, I'd be lost in about 10 seconds."

"You would soon learn. So now what? Surely the only smart thing to do is leave."

"And where would we go?" He suddenly sounds cross.

"I think Catania. It is a major city compared to this, 300,000 people. We could easily get lost in a way that he could not find us. My attorney friend Guido has a small apartment he rents occasionally. I often stay there when I come for a few days to take care of business with him."

"Lina, Catania would be the most obvious choice. He knows it's your hometown. He'd hardly have to guess. And what if he's bugged this car? He'd be there as soon as we are."

"So where then? We need to leave."

"We need to hear what the Carabinieri are going to say, what they're going to do with him. And if they will do what we asked about, having this car debugged."

"At the hotel I will call Eleana Stessa."

As she parks on the street, she wonders about Serafina's sexy little skirt in Stan's room. John says, "Maybe that's what he needs. Move his mind off us with a little female diversion."

"I doubt it," she says. "In Michigan there were many attractive young women available to him. Remember that sexy girl with the cute name and the tattoos from the newspaper?"

"Becca Popp. With his help she was going write a piece to ruin me."

At the hotel desk, there's a phone note: please call Eleana Stessa. Stan's key is in his box. On the way up the marble staircase, she says, "How good it would be if he checked out."

"I don't know," John says as they pass 203. "I like knowing where to find him."

In their room Lina calls Stessa, who says that Signor Lyle was asked to come in for a meeting. In fact, they called him at 2 this afternoon, and by 2:30 he was sitting in their offices. "Of course, I am at your disposal," he said, "to help in any way I can." She and another officer recounted what she had heard from Detective Ranzone in Bologna and outlined the concerns expressed by Professors Lentini and Martens. And then she asked Signor Lyle what he thought he could do to "defuse" this situation. He said, since the professors' concerns were really "all in their heads," he was not sure what he might do. In any case, this office should be aware of the fact that this very morning Professor Martens had come to his room and threatened to kill him.

That is not true, says Lina quickly. Professor Martens would never make such a threat.

Of course, says Stessa, but it would best if they had no contact at all with Signor Lyle.

"That is exactly what we want, Officer. And so what did you say finally to Signor Lyle?"

"I told him that, given the history of the past months, both in the U.S. and here in Italy, it would be in everyone's interest if he would keep his distance from the two of you and preferably depart from the Villa Schuler and also from Taormina as soon as it was convenient."

"And what did he say?"

"I must say, he responded in a very agreeable way and said he understood that you, professor, have been through a very difficult time, and so he would do his best to not intrude on you. He said it was too late to check out of the hotel without losing his payment for tonight, but he would certainly consider checking out tomorrow and perhaps leaving Taormina. He said, he had not really had enough time to 'see all the sights and sample all the pleasures of this beautiful place.' Perhaps he would stay until at least Monday, if that would be okay.

"I told him we would prefer that he leave immediately, but that we cannot order him to do so. Instead we would record his response here and have it on record. He said he understood and appreciated the manner in which we have handled this situation. Then the meeting ended, and he left about 20 minutes ago. Also, you asked if we might be able to scan your vehicle for the presence of some kind of tracking device? We can certainly do that, but with the weekend, it will have to wait until Monday morning."

When Lina recounts all this to John, he says, "About what I expected."

"Yes. So now the question is, when do we leave? Now or later this evening?"

He inclines his head at her as if he disagrees.

"Darling," she says, "Surely we cannot wait to see what this man decides. If or when he will do what the police have asked him to do. Surely we will not leave these things up to him. So maybe we wait until after dark or very late in the evening, but surely you do not wish to spend another night in the same hotel with this killer."

He nods as if in agreement but then says, "Sweetheart, we need to have a serious talk about all this. And you're not going to like what I have to say."

"Go ahead. I am listening." They have been standing in front of the door to the balcony. Now she sits on the bed, and he continues to stand.

"As I implied a while ago, I think it's smarter to stick around and know where the guy is. If we run, he can always follow, and then we'll never know where he is. He can pop up anywhere, anytime and do something awful to you. And then he is totally controlling our lives."

"And the advantage of knowing where he is?"

"He can be dealt with once and for all."

She feels her body shudder but tries not to let it show. "John, I cannot..."

"No, sweetheart, I said you wouldn't like this, but we have to talk about it. You're right, Stan is a killer. He's killed once, in a gruesome, hands-on way. He murdered Hans, an innocent fellow whose only mistake was getting in his way. He's tried to kill us, and he'll continue to try until either he is successful or we stop him. If we don't, even if he doesn't finally kill us, he will do something terrible to someone else, because, as we've learned over the past several months, the guy has a frozen, heartless core. He has the will to destroy anyone who does not serve his needs. Stan is evil, Lina. I know it and you know it. You've written about this stuff with great intelligence and insight. But this is happening right here and now, in your own life, and there is nothing you can think of, no ideas you can formulate, nothing you can write that can effectively deal with this. There is only one thing to do with someone like Stan. And that's kill him."

His final words hang in the air. She says nothing for a moment, staring at him. Does she really know this man standing so aggressively in front of her? A man of perception, gentleness and love, who has touched her mind, her body and her heart like no other. Now he is talking about killing someone. Finally, she says, "And you think you have the right to do that."

"Yes, *we* have the right. He is intent on killing us, and we need to respond appropriately."

"Appropriately. What about the police, the rule of law?"

"Yes, well, what have they done for us so far? He's been way too shrewd for them, and if we wait until they finally catch up with his cleverness, it is far more than likely we'll both be dead. Lina, sweetheart, I know this goes against everything you think and feel and are. I know for you our every action helps define what a human being is, that we are diminished—that mankind is diminished—unless we live life with truth and beauty. I know how important those lines from Keats are to you, but Keats was a brilliant, inexperienced, hot-house young man to whom much was given before life snatched it all away in a fashion that was unbelievably cruel. Sometimes life is like that, and when it is, we need to fight with all we've got to keep our spirit burning. So when someone like Stan is trying to kill us, we have the right to do whatever is necessary to stop him. Scheme, dissemble, lie, cheat and ultimately, if necessary, kill."

He finally sits in the straight back chair at the small desk and gazes at her as she gets to her feet. She says, "You know, I agree with just about everything you just said."

"Good. If you do, there is no distance between us."

"Perhaps. But this is not about existentialism, or Keats, or life's cruelty, or the right to self-preservation. It is about judgment and the preciousness of the human spirit. The value of a human life. Unless we are absolutely certain our life is at stake, we must look for alternatives."

John slams a hand to his knee. "But we are absolutely certain."

"Darling, I let you lecture. Now let me."

He nods and says, "Sorry."

"For me, we are close to, but not at, the matter of self-defense. We are not in a locked room with someone holding a knife to our throats."

"But, sweetheart, the whole idea is to not let ourselves get locked in that room."

"John, please."

"I'm sorry."

"I feel we do not have the right to extinguish the spirit of another human being just because we know he has been horrid to us, or even because we are relatively certain that he murdered poor Hans and then tried to put bullets into us in Bologna. Yes, we say we know he did these things, but to be absolutely honest, the most we can say is that we are relatively certain. And to me that is not sufficient to justify the most grave and noxious action we can take against another. We may know in our hearts, we may access all the knowledge and intuition we possess about human nature to decide that, yes, he did these awful things. But we still do not know it with the kind of certainty that allows us to take a life in order to preserve our own."

John gazes at her in silence, takes a deep breath and blows it out noisily. "You're right, it is a judgment call. But to me life rarely offers the kind of certainty you're looking for, and the practical reality is that we have to act now to stop him for good. Let me paint one more scenario.

"Say you get your wish, and he leaves Taormina tonight. In a day or two our friends in Cedar Hill say he's back there. We return to Bologna, and you pick up your life again, and everything is as it was before you ever met Stanford Lyle. You know, of course, that in a flash and at any moment, he could be back in Bologna to shove that switchblade knife of his into one of your beautiful green eyes."

She feels herself blink but says, "And *you* know that when we wake each morning, you and I face a day in which a blood vessel may blow in your brain or I may be struck by car, and our lives will be over or terribly diminished."

John gets up from the chair. "We are talking a different order of probability altogether. Sweetheart, I need to take a walk."

"I'll come with you."

"No, I need to think this through more carefully. And your intelligence and beauty are such a distraction. If we decide to leave tonight, I can be packed and ready in 10 minutes."

He is already at the door. She says, "John, he could be out there somewhere with his gun. You are making yourself a nice big target."

"No, I'll be fine. I'll stay in places with other people around."

"So what are you really planning to do?"

"Walk and think. I won't go far, maybe just down to the park. If you're worrying about my doing something to Stan, don't. You absolutely have my word that I won't touch him."

She looks at him with the door open and does not like this. "John, I love you so much. Please stay with me."

"I love you too. You'll be fine. Just don't open this door to anyone. I mean, no one! I'll be back soon." He gives her his sad smile and is gone, the door closed before she can say another word. She wants to go after him and bring him back. At least take his arm and walk with him. But their conversation has worried her. She feels worn out and rooted to the floor, unable to move. She thinks about going to the balcony to watch him leave. Make sure Stan is not following him. But she can't bring herself to do that either. Leave him to his thoughts. If the situation were reversed, it is what she would want him to do for her.

On the desk she spots her copy of *The Road*. Reading Cormac McCarthy on this trip has made her feel good, still connected with her manuscript. She re-read *Blood Meridian*, and then *No Country for Old Men*. The film version had come out in Cedar Hill back in November, just before she left. She had been working on McCarthy after her return to Bologna, when she was finally pulling herself together again and forging ahead with her book. Before Stan's arrival put an end to all that. She sits at the desk and opens the novel. She is nearly finished with it and was jotting notes on a couple of the blank pages at the back of the book. On one she reads:

"*The Road* is the apocalypse shrouded in a nearly suffocating haze, the ultimate end toward which all of his books, from *Blood Meridian* to *No Country for Old Men*, have been headed, the awful culmination of man's rapacious urge to violence and destruction."

She takes the book and moves to a more comfortable chair. Later, darkness has enveloped the balcony as she closes it on her lap and lets the ending wash over her. She wonders, what time is it? And where is John? She finds her cell and lights it up. It's nearly 7, more than an hour and a half since he left. She tells herself that this is not necessarily a long time for a walk, that perhaps he stopped somewhere for a glass of wine and began talking with someone. It is absurd to worry about an absence of a little over 90 minutes. And even as she tells herself these things she feels a kind of dread in her chest.

She walks out onto the balcony, but in the cool night air there is no one to see. Back in the room she finds herself pacing, as if she cannot think clearly without moving. She wants to go to the park to see if he is there. A ridiculous idea. She wants to go to the desk and ask about the last time they saw him there. But he was right about not opening the door for any reason.

Of course, she can call the desk and ask her questions, and so she does. A woman tells her, no, they have not seen Signor Martens since almost two hours ago when he left the hotel. No, Signor Lyle has not returned.

For the next half-hour she becomes increasingly concerned and agitated. She swings wildly from reassuring herself that there is nothing wrong at all, that any minute now he will walk in the door with a totally reasonable explanation for his absence, to torturing herself with hideous images of him stuffed in a dark alley off the Corso with a bullet hole in his head, or his throat slashed. Maybe she should call the Carabinieri office. If Eleana Stessa were off duty, someone could check on any report involving an American named John Martens.

Then there are three discrete raps on the door, and her mind leaps frantically from John at last, to Stan with his knife, to Stessa with terrible news. "Yes," she says, "Who is it?"

"Gunther Schuler, professor. May I speak with you?"

"Yes, of course." She quickly unlocks and opens the door.

He steps in, that friendly, middle-aged face looking serious. "I am sorry to disturb you, professor," he says in Italian, "But I just received a call from a Dr. Notaro at the Ospedale San Vincenzo. She informed me that Signor Martens is there."

Lina feels her throat constrict. She manages to say, "No! But why?"

"Someone found him collapsed in the public park, and they brought him quickly to the hospital. I really know nothing more. Other than the doctor said there were no signs of foul play. He simply collapsed, apparently, and they are doing tests. I gather he either regained consciousness and mentioned the hotel, or they found some information on his person that led them to call here."

"He is conscious now?"

"Sorry, I do not know. But I have called a taxi, and it would be the quickest, easiest way for you to reach the hospital."

* * *

As she waits for Dr. Notaro in an empty lounge, she knows the taxi was a good idea. In her current state she could not have safely negotiated that road down the mountain from the hotel to San Vincenzo. Her thoughts are flipping crazily again, from reassurance to nightmare to self-accusation. If what Gunther Schuler told her is correct, it would seem that Stan's hand is not in this. Then what? A medical problem? That possibility had occurred to her the other day. Some sudden catastrophe, like the stroke she herself mentioned in their argument back at the hotel? Or some condition he has hidden from her. Or from himself?

She does not know this hospital. Thankfully, neither she nor her parents ever had a need for it on their many visits to Taormina over the years. The nurse who brought her to this waiting room took her name and address, her occupation and title, and then asked her relation to the patient. That stopped her for a moment. "We are best friends," she said finally, and the large woman with a pleasant face, simply nodded as she wrote on her clipboard. Lina wanted to learn from the nurse Dr. Notaro's specialty, but she was so addled, she forgot to ask.

Now she hears her name called in a soft but firm female voice. A young woman in white, seemingly too young to be a doctor, is moving toward her. She is on her feet when the woman shakes her hand and says she is Gioia Notaro, assistant chief of oncology.

"Oncology," says Lina, sitting down heavily.

Sitting also, Dr. Notaro, whose dark, intelligent eyes make her look older, delivers an efficient account of what they know of John's condition and how they came to know it. He was unconscious, with no signs of trauma of any kind on his body, when brought to the emergency room. But personnel there reported that he briefly regained consciousness—he was in and out, really—long enough to say, "Please call Lina at the Villa Schuler," and then something that sounded like, "I have cancer...in my wallet." They looked in his wallet and found a slip of paper that said, "In case of medical emergency, call Dr. Ahmed Soud," and a phone number in the U.S. When they finally reached the doctor at home, he expressed surprise that his patient was in Italy. He had been waiting for a call from Professor Martens to let him know that recent tests had indicated a return of his cancer.

At that point Dr. Notaro spoke with Dr. Soud and got the details of the case. Dr. Soud recommended a full body scan to check the possible spread of the cancer from the prostate. Given what he had been told of the professor's condition just now, Dr. Soud thought special attention should be paid to the brain.

Lina asks, so where do things stand right now?

Dr. Notaro says, at the moment the scan is being administered, but the full results will not be known until sometime tomorrow morning.

And what does the doctor expect?

There is no way to know, she says. Then she asks Lina if Professor Martens has family in Italy. Lina says, no, his parents are in Cleveland, and his wife, from whom he is estranged, lives in Michigan. They should probably be notified soon of Professor Martens' condition, says Dr. Notaro. The thought of speaking to Marissa makes Lina feel sick to her stomach. Perhaps those calls could be made after they have the test results? The doctor pauses, looks at her carefully and says, yes, perhaps that would be okay.

Lina nods her gratitude. And once the tests are completed, may she see her friend? Of course, he will be in intensive care, but, yes, she can be with him. Lina says she wants to be right there when he regains consciousness again. She is smiling through her tears.

"*Si*," says the young doctor. "*Speriamo per questo.*" We will hope for this.

Chapter 47

Not exactly the way he expected his Monday to begin. At 9:30, along with his breakfast, Serafina brings a sealed envelope with a familiar-looking cursive: "Stan, Room 203."

The girl is flirting with him again, as she has ever since the Saturday Surprise, but acting very formal, calling him Signor Lyle, while he calls her *la mia gattina*—my little cat—which is what he started calling her in bed. She smiles, spanks his hand and snaps, "*No, signore!*" when he grabs her ass. He asks if he will see her again this afternoon when she is finished with her work. She cocks a hip and says, "*Magari*." Perhaps. Then she's gone.

On the balcony the sun is brilliant again in a mostly clear blue sky. He slips the sterling silver butter knife into the envelope and slits it open. The same handwriting on the same stationery he has in the desk drawer says:

> Dear Stan,
>
> I must talk to you. John is dying, and you are haunting my dreams. Please meet me at the Greek Theater this morning at 11.
>
> Lina

Stunned, not trusting himself, he reads those three short sentences again. And then a third time for that line about how he is "haunting" her dreams. Is this some kind of joke? Is the note serious? Maybe she means that what he is really haunting is not her dreams but her nightmares. Then what does she want to talk about?

He has known the Boyfriend was in the hospital since yesterday morning. Mr. Schuler came out of the office behind the desk to sharply call his name, and he figured the guy was about to tell him to stop fucking the help. Instead, his voice softened to say that "your friend, John Martens in room 210," was in San Vincenzo, the hospital down at the foot of the mountain. Stan expressed shock and concern, but Schuler had no details. From the room he called the hospital and tried to learn more. They told him nothing. Later, after he had spent part of Sunday afternoon in bed with the little cat, he asked if she had heard anything more about *il signore* in 210. "*Niente*," she said, and so later he tried calling the hospital again, this time telling them he was the man's brother. After a long wait, a woman came on to say that unfortunately no information could be released at the moment. Surely the Bitch was behind that.

So how does he feel reading about the Boyfriend dying? A nice surprise, really. After his visit with the Carabinieri on Saturday, during which they were actually quite polite and unthreatening, he knew again what a lying piece of shit the guy was. If he's dying? One thing less to worry and scheme about. The real question is what to think about the Bitch. Is it even possible that her feelings have really changed? That she is suddenly open to him in a way he finally decided would never happen? With the Boyfriend gone, she could be feeling terribly alone and vulnerable, and that presumably could foster a change. But that should also dictate being deeply skeptical about every word that comes from that beautiful mouth. Surely he learned that lesson in Bologna the night she invited him back to her apartment, only to dismiss and humiliate him in front of her friends. Then again, starting with his mother, the one sure thing he's learned about women is that anything is possible.

His Rolex says it's 11 am on the nose as he forks over another 6 euros to enter the Greek Theater. He was here before, on Saturday. He knows right where to go and, he thinks, where to look for her. She'll be sitting in the middle of the amphitheater with none of the tourists close by, so they can speak privately but be observed by everyone at the very center of the largest, most public space in Taormina. Obviously her choice of this spot says she is still frightened of him. But beyond that, he has told himself to have no expectations. Just walk into this with his eyes, ears and mind wide open and decide for himself what it's all about.

As he moves into the sunlight on the stage, he spots her quickly, sitting exactly where he expected. When she sees him, she raises a hand with a wan little wave. He nods. She is wearing a green cable-knit sweater over jeans and sneakers, that red hair glistening in the sun. He climbs up to her row and reminds himself not to be dazzled by her looks. Parse her every fucking word.

She stands when he reaches her row and moves in, and as he approaches, she is looking at him with the ghost of a smile on her sad, drawn face. She extends her hand and says, "Thank you for coming, Stan." Her touch is firmer, more business-like than before.

He says, "Of course, Lina. I'm sorry to hear about John."

She nods and sits, and he sits on the bench as well, not too close, about four feet away.

"What happened?" he asks.

She exhales and doesn't look at him. "The cancer came back to his prostate, and now it is in his liver and his lymph nodes. And in his brain."

The matter-of-fact tone surprises him. He says, "I thought he had beaten it."

"Yes, he did too." She looks off at Etna in the sun, with a plume of white smoke today.

"And how are you, Lina."

Now she turns to him, those sad green eyes finding his gaze. "It is very difficult. I have been living at the hospital, sleeping there. He is in a coma, in intensive care."

"Is that hospital the right place for him? Should he be in a major center somewhere."

"I asked that. They say this is an excellent hospital, as good as anything in Catania."

He is still looking into those eyes. "I'm very sorry for you."

"Thank you," she says, looking away. "It is complicated. Maybe more so than you think."

"Complicated how?"

She is silent for a time, as if choosing her words. Then she says, "I feel betrayed."

"Betrayed by whom?" He steels himself for an answer he doesn't like.

She looks at him again. "By John."

"John?"

"Yes, he knew, Stan. He knew the cancer had returned. He knew he was going to die, or at least that he would be very sick. He knew before he ever left Michigan to come to Bologna."

"How do you know this?"

"I spoke with his doctor in Michigan yesterday. Dr. Soud. John had the tests, and his scores were up, significantly. And they did a biopsy. So he knew, and he came, even at a time when I was telling him, pleading with him, not to come. I said, 'John, what we had was good for as long as it lasted. But it needs to be over now. You are married, and I need to move on with my life and my work.' And out of the blue he is there in Bologna." He shakes his head to look as if he is commiserating. She says, "Stan, I am sorry to be speaking like this. It is not fair to you."

"No, please, don't worry about it. I want to hear whatever you need or want to say."

Her eyes turn to him again. They look sadder than he has ever seen them. "Thank you, Stan. I don't think I have ever felt this alone."

"Yeah, I'm sure. But why would he do that? Come here when he knew he was dying, especially when you were telling him not to come." Recalling those emails he tapped into between them, he knows their tone was passionate, but what she is saying now seems to line up.

"Truly," she says, "I feel so betrayed by a man for whom I had such admiration. I want to grab him and shake him and say, 'How could you do this to me? Cross the ocean and come to me, to die?' To me instead of his own wife, with whom he has been married for fifteen years?"

"Maybe he came because he knew Marissa could never handle something like this. She would completely fall apart. She could never give the loving support he'd need at the end."

"Yes," she says glumly. "The poor man is dying. He is unconscious, but even if he were to open his eyes to me, how could I tell him what I really feel? How betrayed I feel because he has come here to inflict his death on me. I know it is, as you say, understandable that he would do this, but it is also very, very selfish."

"Ultimately uncaring," he says.

She nods, and they say nothing for a time. Finally, she looks at him. "Stan, I know we have had our problems and our differences, but I am grateful that you came today."

"I'm glad you asked me. There have been so many misunderstandings between us."

"Yes, I think so."

He decides this is the time for his most important question. "I want to ask you something about the note you sent to my room this morning."

"Yes, of course."

"What did you mean when you said I've been haunting your dreams?"

* * *

So the afternoon is beginning just as improbably as this morning. He is driving her Golf in the sun toward Etna, his thoughts hidden behind the Raybans, just as he is sure hers are doing their own secret calculations behind the shades she fished out of her tote a few minutes ago. Now she shifts and turns to him in the passenger seat as he urges the car up this 2-lane highway into the dense forests covering the fuming volcano's slope. Her move tells him she wants to talk again, after the silence that has covered most of their trip so far, except for her brief, polite directions. "Now you will take the next exit, to Fiumefreddo."

When they found her car parked on the Via Roma, down from the Villa Schuler, she surprised him again by asking if he would like to drive. "Sure," he said. And taking the wheel, he felt good, actually turned on, his dick stirring, getting stiff, reminding him of the day he turned 15, when his mother first gave him a driving lesson, and he found himself with a raging hard on.

So far, a day of surprises, but none more extraordinary than her answer to his question about haunting her dreams. It was one of those revelations that literally appear to change everything, turn the world upside down, alter your every view and assumption about someone you thought you knew. Actually he can't recall ever encountering something like this in real life. This kind of thing happens only in novels, or maybe in some trashy, super-heated memoir.

As they watched two young girls, 12 or 13, doing an impromptu dance on the Theater stage, she said quietly and almost as if this had all been carefully rehearsed: "You may or may not believe this, Stan, but I have felt drawn to you from the very first moment we met."

He turned and found her looking at him with a calm, bold gaze, as if daring him to disbelieve. He said, "Lina, how can you expect me to swallow something like that? I mean ..."

She interrupted. "Stan, do me one favor. I know what I am saying

318

sounds absurd, but just listen for a moment. Please?"

Absurd was the word he was just about to use. He said, "Okay."

And in a soft and seemingly earnest tone, she explained that, yes, she had wanted him from the very beginning. But she had fought the urge because it was so utterly selfish.

"Selfish?" he managed to ask.

Yes, for a million reasons, she said. Because they should never be together. Because she was nine years older. Because her career was well-established, his just starting. Because she was driven to build her reputation by giving her work everything she had. Because he was brilliant, but a relationship with her would consume, not inspire him, would rob him of the drive and desire to be all he could be — which was someone truly extraordinary. Because what he needed was a special woman who could give him all the love, support and devotion he deserved, who could make him a comfortable home and give him beautiful children. Because what he needed was, in short, everything she was not and could never be.

By now he was thinking maybe there was another reason she chose this ancient theater as the spot for them to meet. It was the perfect place to stage a performance designed to make him think that black was white. "And John?" he asked finally.

She shook her head with a frown. "I found John to be a good man, with a fine intelligence, an interesting man of accomplishment. But John was also convenient, in that he might take my mind off someone else who was so often in my thoughts." For the first time she gave him a small grin. "And frankly, I also thought he might be the perfect way to put you off. Your own advisor, a married man. I thought if I took up with John, I would completely put you off, disillusion and maybe even disgust you, make me, in your eyes, a person unworthy of your care and concern. In that sense, it was all calculated, from beginning to end."

He raised and then lowered his head in a way he thought looked non-committal, but he was thinking again about those emails he had intercepted. They had both sounded like passionate lovers, though he had to admit that John's breathing had definitely been heavier.

"Here is the truth," she said now. "And perhaps I should not tell you this, but what I know, and you do not, is my history with men. Stan, I chew them up, and I spit them out. I use them up and leave them behind, and I have always done that. It is my M.O. Remember when you asked me, last fall, if I had come to St. Thomas because I was running away from a love affair, and I said no? Well, I did not tell the truth. I had just left a passionate fling with Paolo, an attorney in Milano. He adored me, but I was done. That is what I do. It is who I am. And I did not want to inflict that on a beautiful, sensitive man like you."

He remembered references to a Paolo in her notebook—the one she had raged at him for looking at in her office. The one that seemed to have no reference at all to anyone named Stan. If she were in fact longing for him, trying to forget him, wouldn't her notebook at the time reflect that? He said, "So let me ask one more question."

She nodded, and he asked, "Why are you telling me all this now?"

She made a face, as if to say this was a hard question, but fair. "Perhaps because I have been sitting for two days with a man who is dying. It has forced me to think more carefully about what I have done with you, with John, with everything I have told you about, and it has made me feel guilt and confusion and pain. I think now we should have had this conversation back when I first came to Michigan. Certainly I had no right to assume that I knew what was best for you. Deceiving you in order to protect you was arrogant and foolish. I should have told you about my feelings and my history and, of course, let you decide matters for yourself."

She paused, as if thinking through the rest of this. "Stan, I don't know if you could ever forgive me, but I surely would never blame you if you could not."

He was silent for a long time, gazing off at Etna. He was trying to sort through the enormous muddle in his head. Let alone forgive, how could he ever trust this woman? Still, he said, "Lina, what if we tried to make a new start for ourselves? Maybe have dinner later at one of your favorite places in town?"

She smiled at him. "I would like that."

"Good. Then it's a date."

"Let me suggest something else, maybe for this afternoon."

"Okay."

"Would you be interested in a hike up into the lovely forests that cover Etna's flank? They are visible from here." She pointed a pretty finger at the volcano. "You can see the tree line about a third of the way down from the summit. I know some wonderful trails up there."

He wondered where the hell she was going with this. The woman seemed crazy at times. "A hike," he said, "sounds great."

"Good," she said with an even bigger smile and suddenly seeming more relaxed. "When I was a girl, at this time of the year, my parents would always bring me here for a holiday in Taormina. And one of our favorite traditions, certainly my favorite, was a long hike with my father, just the two of us, through one of Etna's forests."

* * *

And now in the car on the way to re-enact that traditional hike with dad, she is half-turned to him and says, apropos of nothing, "So how did you decide to come to Taormina?"

Caught off guard, he starts with, "Well, I don't know. I was traveling, heading up to Torino to do my research, and I just decided, before I got down to work, I wanted to see more of this incredible country. And then I remembered something you said once about this being one of the most beautiful places in the world, and I thought, 'Why not?' So I jumped on EasyJet, and here I am. I didn't even know you and John were here until Saturday, when the Carabinieri called and asked me to come in."

"And they told you they had found Hans' body?"

Caught off guard again. Her voice sounded like she was trying for matter-of-fact, but he caught an edge to it. "Yes, they told me. Very sad. Actually, I really liked the guy. He was really sweet on Marta, wasn't he?"

"Yes, very much. So you picked up on that."

"Yeah, it was pretty obvious. But it seemed like she wouldn't give him the time of day."

"Very true. So you were perceptive about them."

"Well, he and I talked about it a little that night we all had dinner. Walking back to your place, Hans and I were together, and at one point with Marta busy talking to someone else, he leaned over and said, 'You know, sometimes I get so frustrated with her that I have fantasies of raping her and making her like it.' And then he said, 'Of course I would never do such a thing, but often I am tortured by the thought.'"

"Really, he told you that?"

"Yeah, poor guy. I told him, 'Don't worry. It happens to the best of us.'"

Again he drives for a long time in silence, feeling good about pulling off that lie, especially because it was based on his quick read of that note in the margin of the guy's copy of *Crime and Punishment*. That rainy night in those woods outside Bologna. The night he stuffed the book and the backpack and Hans himself into those black plastic bags.

So why would she bring up Hans, except to test him? And now he thinks again about what this woman has put him through, the stuff she's made him do, and how she and her lies have so screwed up his life. And now he's suddenly certain of how this improbable little outing will end. In some lovely forest clearing, where first he will fuck her brains out, and then he will shove his long, trusty switchblade down her pretty, lying throat.

Chapter 48

They continue to climb as the road snakes about two-thirds of the way up the nearly 11,000-foot mountain. At one point the landscape suddenly changes, and he stops the car to gaze out over a huge expanse of deep black volcanic soil. The enormous mounds appear to have rolled down this face of the mountain, wiping out everything in a wide path, including large swaths of forest, leaving only a few bare, bleached and broken trees, sticking out at weird angles on the edges of the lava flow, all of it looking as if it happened not that long ago. The road they've been traveling has been paved right through this huge black field. Above, all he can see is one last stretch of forest, and then sheer rock and the snow that covers Etna's broken crown.

He asks when this happened. Five or six years ago, she says, Etna erupted and wiped out a tourist center and ski station, the restaurant and other buildings buried forever under all this lava. Fortunately, before it boiled up out of the fissure that cracked open above the station, there was sufficient warning, and no one was lost. But over the centuries Etna has taken an untold number of lives, probably the most in the catastrophic eruption of 1669, when a massive river of lava flowed all the way down to the sea, overwhelming a good part of Catania on the way.

They drive past a large, flat area where an attempt is being made to reconstruct the tourist center, nothing much more than a large parking lot and a few small chalets that seem to be open and selling trinkets and souvenirs. She says this used to be a beautiful green meadow in the summer, with lush vegetation cradling the station. Now it is only this huge expanse of black soil.

Twenty minutes later they are walking on that same kind of black volcanic soil, but probably a hundred years older and covered with dead pine needles. This black-and-tan path climbs gently through giant firs with the sun dappling the way. She says of course the trees are of different vintages. You can tell, not just by the size and girth of their trunks, but also by the blackened marks extending a meter or so up some of them. The younger, thinner trees show none of the burn marks. At some point in the past, an Etna eruption had sent a thin stream of lava burning through here, singeing the base of these older trees, before the younger ones were here.

When she directed him to park by the side of the road, she said this was her favorite hiking path, the one she and her father usually took during their sojourns in Taormina between Christmas and New Years. Without thinking, he handed her the car key, which she shoved into the pocket of her short quilted jacket as they entered the woods. Back at the hotel she had said they would need to dress more warmly, since it would be at least 20 degrees cooler up on Etna.

Even with his black leather over the Parma sweatshirt, it's chilly, and he walks with his gloved hands in his jacket pockets. In the right one he fondles the knife. And now he thinks maybe it was a good idea to give her that key. Maybe having it has put her more at ease, made her feel more in control. Exactly how he wants her to feel when he finally makes his move.

For some reason Serafina pops into his head. Despite his surprising sexual progress with her, he has gotten nowhere on the passkey. Now it won't make any difference. On the way here, when they reached the girl's hometown of Linguaglossa, the Bitch noted the strange name. Both parts of it meant "tongue." Lingua in Italian, glossa in Greek. And he thought about how the girl loved to dart her narrow, pointed tongue quickly in and out of his mouth when they were fucking. Now, as if reading his mind, the Bitch starts talking about the maid.

"You know," she says, "I should not tell you, but on Saturday, when I saw Serafina go into your room dressed like a sexy tart in that sweater and little skirt, I felt a twinge of jealousy. I know I have no right to feel such a thing, but I did. So how is this girl? Do you like her?"

"Oh, you saw her?" He's trying to think of what to say. Certainly not that she's already boring him. "Actually she's a sweet girl, rather shy. I always seem to attract the shy ones."

"No, not always." She glances at him as they walk the path together and gives him a provocative smile. "But in bed she is shy?"

He smiles back. "Not really."

And now, because she's being bold, he asks, "So what about John?

324

How was he in bed?"

"We never did it," she says, not looking at him.

"Never?" It seems this woman will say anything.

"No, the poor guy could not. He was impotent. I know that Marissa and everyone she infected with her attacks thought we were doing it, but it was all in her head. She should have known better. He really could not, but she thought he was deceiving her about it. No, John and I had a cerebral affair, platonic really, and while I was getting a bit tired of it by the time I left Michigan, at first and for most of my time there, it was fine. It was actually what I wanted."

"Funny. John told me he had no problem. Very lucky, he said, given what many guys go though after treatment."

"Yes, he felt very bad and would not believe it was okay with me. But in fact, after my relationship with Paolo, I had been thinking of trying something with little or no sex at all. Give it a rest for a while. And so when John came along, it seemed like the perfect chance to try."

He says nothing, and they continue to climb in silence for a time. Finally she says, "But you know, after all this time, I think I am more than ready to start again. I want something that's real and physical and adventurous."

"Sounds good to me," he says. But he's wondering now if what she really wants is his knife in her throat. Why take him all the way out here if what she really wants to do is fuck? There are certain people who want to die but can't bring themselves to do it on their own. They arrange their own suicide with somebody accommodating. Cops see it all the time. One thing is certain: she couldn't be making this any easier.

The path has forked a couple of times, and she seems to know exactly where she wants to lead him. Keeping track of the turns, he's sure he will find his way back without a problem. He feels a tension building now between them. Certainly it's been there the whole time, but since their little sex chat, it's amped up. "You ever see anyone out here?" he asks as they approach a small clearing where the sun is shining more brightly through the firs.

"A fox once," she says, "a porcupine, even a little wild cat when I was a girl, but almost never any people. Only the crazy ones, like me and my father—and now you—come out here at this time of the year. But it is so peaceful and quiet, I love it. I've always loved it."

"I do too. It's beautiful here."

"Good. Here, I want to show you a special place." She points across the clearing to a spot where there's a cluster of small, black boulders, the largest about three feet high. As they approach, she says, "This was my secret discovery, at least my father let me think it was. One day when I was ten, we came out here, and I ran ahead and found this."

At the boulders he can see now a ragged-edged hole or crevice in the forest floor, the opening maybe five feet in diameter. Nearby he can see a few other, smaller openings, all fringed with weeds and dead ferns, the smallest about a foot and a half.

"They are like small craters," she says quietly, but with some kind of excitement. "There are fissures and small caves all over the forests up here. Formed when the lava flows came through, leaving gaps and holes. But some of them are really rents or breaks in the surface that happened when the pressure down below became too much, and it just blew up and out. That is what I think this one is, a small crater. It goes way, way down. Listen."

She picks up a small rock and drops it into the hole. He can hear it bouncing off the walls of the crevice on its way down, for what seems like several seconds. She looks up at him and smiles. He says, "Very cool."

"Yes, my father would hold me close to this big one, and I would put my ear to the edge and say I could hear Etna moaning or singing down there at her core, depending on her mood."

For a second he thinks she might actually ask him to hold her the way her father did, and he could just drop her in. Instead, she says, "And so this is my favorite, secret place." She is hoisting herself now onto the largest of the boulders, with maybe just enough of a flat top to accommodate the two of them. She actually waves her jean-clad legs, like a little girl. "And now I have a request," she says with a demure smile that quickly turns bold.

"What's that?"

"Well, when I would come here as a girl, even into my teens, I would always fantasize that the man of my dreams, the one who would love me forever, would sit with me on this rock and kiss me to seal our love."

"And so how many men have you brought here?"

"You are the first. Other than my father, who obviously doesn't count."

"Hard to believe."

"Yes, surely. But true."

"And you want me to kiss you on that rock."

"I do."

He finds himself moving to her. He thinks she is calculating something here, but says, "How can I deny a beautiful woman's childhood fantasy?" Both of them are smiling as he reaches for the gloved hand she extends, and with an easy move he too is up on the boulder. He takes her in his arms. This is absurd, he thinks, totally unreal, but why not playact the dream for a while and go with it. He draws a deep breath and closes his eyes for just a moment. And now her hand moves between his thighs, and his dick presses hard against his jeans. He kisses her gently, firmly, his tongue easily probing her willing mouth.

Finally, the green eyes open with what, a drugged look? Some deep, distant gaze? A kind of strange passion? He feels doubtful, uncertain. But then she smiles and kisses him back, one hand now high on the back of his head, pressing him to her, the other still on his thigh, her tongue caressing his. Even with the jacket and sweater covering her tit, his hand feels how full and supple it is. She moans and moves in a way that says she loves the hand where it is. But this also reminds him of what happened the last time his hand was there, and he feels an urge to go into his pocket for the knife. No, this is too good to cut short. Just wait...

She pauses, nudging him between his legs, and says, "Somebody is pleased to be here."

"Yes indeed," he says, almost breathless.

"Can you wait just one minute? There is something I need to do." She says this with a twinkle in her eyes, as if this will please him as well.

"Just one minute," he says.

"Good." As he watches carefully, she is off the boulder and removing her gloves. She places them on the ground nearby, and from her left coat pocket she pulls a small, silver digital camera, pushes a button on it and shows it to him.

"I have come prepared," she says with a grin, "to record the moment for posterity. A photo of the man of my dreams on this rock where I fantasized about him for so many years."

327

He shakes his head. "Lina, please, I can't believe you."

"Yes, but it is true. Now give me a smile. Say *formaggio*."

He does, and as she holds the camera to her eye, he can see it's a little Nikon point-and-shoot. Then she lowers it and frowns. "Wait one minute. I have ruffled your hair. But this, of course, must be perfect."

She puts the camera down on top of her gloves, and he tries patting down his hair in the area where her hand held his head. He hates women messing with his hair. "It's too long now," he says. "I need a trim."

Smiling she moves forward. "No, I prefer it longer. Here, let me." With her left hand she lightly brushes and pats his hair, then looks him in the eye and moves her hand with its feathery touch to his cheek. "Now it is perfect!" She kisses his mouth softly, then with what feels like real passion, then gently again.

With his eyes closed, he is lost for a moment in the sweet taste of her, the incredibly delicate touch of her lips on his. And then he thinks of something strange and in some way troubling. If, unknown to him, she had that camera in one of her coat pockets, what else might she have now in the other? But even before he can open his eyes, he knows what it is, and he knows it's too late.

A sudden, searing pain rips across his neck and throat. He screams but hears nothing. And then he sees a razor knife, the very razor knife he so carefully returned to her kitchen drawer the night he found her in bed with John. Covered with blood, his blood, and as it drops from her hand, he sees for one vivid instant its bright yellow handle. He reaches for the switchblade, but the pocket somehow eludes his hand. And now she steps back and away from him, out of his reach. No, now he is the one moving. Falling. She has shoved him, and he is falling. Back and away and off the boulder where they kissed, to that ancient black volcanic soil on this sunlit forest floor.

And then he can see in a blur the bottom of her jeans and her well-worn sneakers moving next to him, and he wants to grab her ankle, and he wants to kick his own leg free as she grips it, but his arms and his legs no longer seem to work, and he feels himself sliding, sliding.

Or is he falling? Yes, falling now into a world of black that he knows, with a certainty beyond all dreams, will be his forever.

Chapter 49

The call from Eleana Stessa in the Carabinieri office comes one month to the day from the afternoon she left Stan in the woods high on Etna's slope. The officer says there has been a development in the case. And Lina thinks first that the body has somehow been found and retrieved from the bowels of that crevice along with the razor knife she had so stupidly kicked in after him, her incriminating fingerprints all over its yellow plastic handle.

It reminds her of how she felt two days after Stan's disappearance when she received a call at the hospital from Officer Stessa, suggesting a meeting with her, either at the hospital or in their offices, whichever she preferred. It was about the disappearance of Signor Lyle. He had not been seen at the hotel since Monday afternoon.

Actually she had expected this call, had prepared for it, but even so, she felt her stomach twist. They sent a car for her, and both Stessa and Detective Gio Florio, a dour little man with a pencil-thin mustache, expressed their sympathy for her friend Professor Martens. Florio took the lead and asked almost immediately about the note found in the missing man's room.

Yes, said Lina, she had sent the note Monday morning. She had hardly slept for two nights, staying up at the hospital, waiting in vain for the moment when John would regain consciousness, and being totally overwrought by this awful turn of events, the shocking news that he might be dying. In the midst of this, she decided to do the one thing she had not done to that point—make a direct, personal plea to Signor Lyle to simply go away and leave her alone.

And her wording in this note, said Florio, looking at the contents of a file folder, particularly this line about how he was "haunting" her dreams?

Her wording had been imprecise. She had meant to write "nightmares," not "dreams." Her mind was not working properly

329

with all the stress. Actually, she should have requested this office to host her meeting with Signor Lyle, but she was simply not thinking clearly. In any case, they did in fact meet at the Greek Theater late on Monday morning. She told him about John's condition and made her plea to be left alone.

It was strange, she said of Stan's reaction to the news about John. "The life seemed to go out of him. That is the only way I can put it. It was as if, being told now that his rival for so long was on his deathbed, he no longer had any interest. As if his obsession with me had snapped or broken. I asked him to please leave me alone, he just looked away and said, 'Of course.'"

Very strange indeed, she repeated, and she wondered if Officer Stessa or Detective Florio had ever seen this kind of reaction before.

No, said the woman, but then she had limited experience with cases of stalking and obsession. The detective simply shrugged as if to say that nothing humans might do would surprise him at this point.

Lina said on their walk back from the theater to the hotel, Stan had continued to seem subdued. She had said goodbye to him there, and maybe it was because of his odd, detached manner, but she remembered thinking it might well be the last time she would ever see him. After getting her jacket from the room, she then tried to clear her head with a long drive in the countryside, making sure she was not followed, and stopping at one point for a glass of wine in one of her favorite places, the little mountain town of Castelione di Sicilia.

Florio said the staff at the Villa Schuler seemed to think they had left together. Lina said no, they had walked out the door together but then went their separate ways.

So that was when she thought she might never see him again?

Yes, she said, thinking, not for the first time lately, what a terrible liar she was. The detective nodded and said along with Stan's other belongings in room 203 they had found the laptop he had reported stolen in Milano. It was being examined by one of their computer experts for what it might tell them about his activities in Italy and for clues to his disappearance.

Good, said Lina, and now there was something she had been meaning to call Stessa about, something that occurred during her conversation with Signor Lyle at the theater. She was quite sure it could not be used in a court of law, but it was something he had said, which, to her at least, incriminated him in the murder of Hans Broek.

Florio said they would certainly want to hear about such a thing. So she recounted their conversation on the way to the forest in which Stan had tried to impress her with his insight concerning Hans and Marta. Stan claimed Hans had told him about being troubled by a rape fantasy involving Marta. But what Stan did not know was that more than four months ago, before she had left Italy for Michigan, she and Hans had a long discussion of that fantasy in connection with Dostoyevsky's *Crime and Punishment*. Reading the novel was making him feel so guilty he could hardly function. And he had become "fixed" on an idea so shameful he could not speak about it to anyone. She told him, surely he could talk with her about anything. No, he could not utter the words. But as they walked the streets of Bologna, Hans said he had written about his feelings in the margins of the passage where Raskolnikov is about to murder the pawnbroker. Finally, she pleaded with him, Hans showed her his book, and she read about the very fantasy that Stan claimed the young man said he was finding so disturbing four months later.

The fact was, during those four months Hans had reassured her more than once that he had moved well past that rape fantasy. Two nights before he disappeared, Hans told her it was so far behind him now that he was even writing a paper on *Crime and Punishment*. But according to Stan, that was the same night Hans had talked to him about how troubling the fantasy was to him. She had no doubt that Stan was lying and simply quoting from those margin notes. Now when Hans worked on a book, he would always carry it around with him. And on the day he disappeared, he probably...

"No," says Florio, "he was definitely carrying the book. I have read the report on the murder, and the book was found in the backpack he was carrying that night."

Lina stared at the little detective. Yes, he said, she was no doubt correct. It would be difficult or impossible to use in court, but it was of definite interest. As she left the Carabinieri office to return to John at San Vincenzo, she wondered to herself again if she would have been able to go through with her plan in the woods, if Stan had not confirmed his guilt to her.

Without question, bringing Stan to the forest on Etna was the most calculated, deceptive thing she had ever done in her life. It was also the craziest, riskiest, most reckless thing by far. So reckless, that she questioned even at the time whether she had really come there to die. Or perhaps there was part of her seeking to gauge how much she really wanted to live.

During those first two nights of sitting with John in the hospital, she had spent much of her time holding conversations with him in her head, mostly on what to do about Stan. The more she sat there, the more persuasive he became. At the theater she simply told as much of the truth as possible, bending it slightly or substantially whenever necessary. She really had little idea of how she was doing until he agreed to join her on the hike. And even then, had she actually convinced him of anything she was saying, or was she simply handing him a perfect opportunity to dispose of her forever? On the way up, as they approached the tourist center, she sensed that he was not at all deceived and that what she was doing bordered on the insane, or the self-destructive, or both. But as they started on the hike, the sweet, sad, thoughtful face of Hans came to her almost as a presence, and she told herself to concentrate with everything she had only on him. Not on John, not on herself. Simply and intensely on Hans. That morning she had even practiced pulling the razor knife out of her jacket pocket with as little wasted motion as possible. Then thumbing the blade open even as she moved it up to his neck. But afterward she knew it was not the practice, all the repetitions, but only the thought of Hans that helped her do it.

She had always thought of herself as a terrible liar. A catch or thinness in the voice, a gaze wandering or too intense, a slackness in the lines of the face in the effort to appear calm were all dead give-aways with her. She had never performed on a stage, even as a girl in school. Yes, she had read about theories of acting and could imagine how it was done, but actually performing as an actress, someone capable of sustained make-believe, some fantasized construct or deception, had always seemed totally beyond her. Until that walk in the woods with Stan.

There was only one time she thought of John. When the moment came to kiss, and to kiss back. She needed John then, and he was there. But the biggest shock was how precise and powerful she felt at the crucial moment when it had to be done. Yes, she had dropped the razor knife and later thoughtlessly kicked it in, but by then it was really all over. He was finished, and she surprised herself again with a strength beyond anything she thought she possessed, dragging him by an ankle to that waiting, gaping crevice. And when his head had reached the hole's edge and was about to drop forever, their eyes locked for one long second, his with uncomprehending shock Or complete recognition? She was not sure. But there was no doubt what her eyes held for him. The deep, grave satisfaction of a grim task completed.

There was blood on her hands, blood on her jacket, blood even on the camera. But at the Golf she found a small towel left in the hatch from some long-forgotten outing, and she used it to wipe most of the blood away. Later when she stopped for the Carabinieri's benefit at the little bar in Castelione di Sicilia, she left the jacket in the car and used the restroom to do a better clean up. The old woman who served her the wine seemed to notice nothing, and they chatted a bit, Lina telling her that a dear friend was dying, and she had gone for a drive to be alone with her thoughts. Yes, said the woman, and now she must stop at the church just down the street to say a few words so God will know how she is feeling. It will help.

That night, concerned that someone at San Vincenzo would overhear something she might say in her sleep, she stayed not at the hospital but in the room at the Villa Schuler. Surprisingly she slept soundly at the hotel and did so for the next three nights, only feeling nerves a bit in the mornings when Serafina came in and seemed to be giving her strange looks.

After her meeting with the Carabinieri, Gunther Schuler helped her find a small apartment to rent near the hospital, and for almost a month she has made the short walk each morning to be with John in his room. Now it is on that walk, her mobile in hand, that she is talking with Officer Stessa. There is nothing new on Signor Lyle's whereabouts, but the report on his laptop computer has finally been completed. Lina breathes again. Sounding almost apologetic, the woman says examining the laptop took so long because they needed their best person in the Catania office to comb through it, to make sure they missed nothing. The results turned up no help in solving the mystery of Signor Lyle's disappearance. But the search found something interesting they thought Lina would want to know. Signore Lyle had apparently found a way to intercept messages to and from her email account.

"Intercept," says Lina.

Yes, says Stessa, emails not intended to be sent or copied to his address. He was somehow picking them up. Stessa affirms she is no technical expert, but as she understands it, this probably means that Signor Lyle had, at some point, gained access to Lina's computer in Bologna and surreptitiously placed some kind of program on it to allow the intercept.

Lina shakes her head. "That means he got into my apartment without my knowing it."

"A frightening man," says Stessa, her first words not strictly professional.

Over the past month with calls, emails and even a visit, she has heard words of sympathy and support from all her closest friends in Bologna. Aldo and Rena have written often and at length, and about halfway through this painful vigil with John, Lilli and Marta arrived to be with her for a few days. About Stan Lina has told all of them only what she told the Carabinieri.

Marta said, "I hope someone dropped him into Etna's crater. It's where he belongs." Her face drawn, she was heartsick about Hans and still finding it difficult to deal with his murder.

Ever the staunch friend, Lilli had closed her gallery for a week to be with her. She was feeling especially bad because she had prevailed on John to come to Italy in spite of Lina's wishes to the contrary. "What about his wife?" she asked.

Lina explained that she had called Marissa after talking with Dr. Soud on Monday evening, two days after John's collapse in the park. Early afternoon in Michigan, six hours earlier there, she was at least sober. Of course, she said, she knew John was in Italy with Lina. Where else would he be? And she had some notion of her husband's condition, because Soud had called her when he had failed to reach John with the news that the cancer was back. The woman seemed to be speaking with a half-controlled fury. "Call me if he comes to and asks for me," she said and rang off before Lina could say another word.

John's parents were not entirely in the dark, because Marissa had called them looking for John. From her they heard their son had "gone off the deep end with some young Italian sexpot, and he was riddled with cancer again."

"We've been worried sick and not sure what to do," said his mother Tamela, who made it clear within the call's first two minutes that she and her husband Bob had little use for their son's wife.

"Thank you so much for calling, dear." The woman's voice sounded clear and firm. Lina knew they were both in their late 70's. "This must be so difficult for you. We'll be there asap." Within an hour she had called back to say they had booked their flights and would be in Catania by 4 pm the following day. Her husband, John's dad, was "a bit under the weather. He was one of those physicians who always took good care of everyone but himself, and his diabetes has been flaring up lately. Still, he absolutely insists on coming."

They were at the Villa Schuler for a week, and four days into their stay John finally came out of his coma. It was late afternoon, and Dr. Martens was back at the hotel resting. Lina and Tammie—the woman had quickly insisted it was what everyone called her—were in chairs on each side of the bed in the private room he had been moved to after three days in intensive care. A number of times over the past few days those deep blue eyes had fluttered and blinked and even remained open for several seconds. The first time this happened, Lina, feeling her heart surge with hope, had said quickly, "Oh, John, darling, there you are! I am here with you!" And then she realized that he was completely unaware of his surroundings, including her presence, those beautiful eyes unseeing, or uncomprehending, or what?

"The brain has mysteries it is loathe to reveal," said Dr. Notaro when Lina told her about the episode. "We have learned so much, and there is so much more to learn." The young doctor urged her to read to him even if he seemed not to respond, and in a Taormina bookstore Lina found a British edition of *Chatterley*. Somehow she felt soothed, even hopeful, as she read it to him for hours on end. John's mother also thought it was a great idea, and she was the one reading this time when he opened his eyes again.

"Tammie, look!" said Lina. John, with his week-old salt-and-pepper beard, moved his head slightly to Lina as she rose from her chair to look into his eyes and gently take his hand.

"Oh, good, good!" said the petite, white-haired woman also getting to her feet. This time Lina thought there was something different about his gaze, a measure of recognition.

Then he said in a voice barely above a whisper, "Lina, sweetheart, where have you been."

It was a kind of admonition, but caressing his head, she too spoke softly, "John, darling, I have been right here. And look, your mother

335

is here as well." The older woman had already moved around the bed and, hugging Lina, said, "Yes, Johnny, I'm here, and your father too. He'll be so pleased." Lina stepped back so his mother could move closer, covering his hand and touching his check, then bending to kiss his forehead, saying, "Oh, my poor Johnny."

Lina's eyes were welling. John's were locked on his mother. "Mom, why are you here?" And then his gaze found Lina again. "Where is Stan?" Tammie's eyes, tearful, turned to her.

Lina told him, "Darling, do not worry. Stan is gone forever."

"Gone?"

"Forever." Trying with one word to tell him everything. He closed his eyes for a while.

Lina thought they had lost him again. But then he said, "He's gone. You're certain."

"Absolutely certain, darling."

That evening she called Marissa again, explaining that John had come out of his coma earlier that day and had spoken with her and with his mother. Yes, his parents had come four days ago. And did he ask for her, Marissa wanted to know. No, frankly, he had not, but then he had been conscious for only a short time, and even before his father had been able to come from the hotel, John had drifted off again. How long do they say he has? asked Marissa.

"They do not say. They do not know."

"Look," said his wife, not sounding as angry now, "I've thought about this long and hard, and I've decided he's with the woman he wants. And I'm going to keep it that way."

"Marissa, I think you should come. It would be good for him and good for you."

The woman said, "You have no idea what is good for me," and hung up on her again.

John was in and out over the next couple of days, but even in, he often seemed not entirely clear on where he was or what was happening to him. The day after Lina's second call to Marissa, his father had a good talk with him for close to twenty minutes. Walking slowly with a cane, the old man was clearly frail and infirm. He had seemed a bit flinty at first but had warmed quickly to her. With John he was deeply loving, not at all the detached physician he had been in his lengthy talk that first day with Dr. Notaro.

Lina had not been entirely truthful with Marissa about John's prognosis. She had followed closely Dr. Martens' conversation with Dr. Notaro, and while it was highly technical at times, the basics were clear. They had been clear as soon as those test results had come back. The cancer was extremely aggressive, it was now lodged in a part of the brain that was inoperable, and they did not expect that he could last for very long. Weeks or perhaps months but probably not many months. It was then that Dr. Martens had hobbled off to sit in the room with his son, and she and Tammie had stayed in the lounge to weep together for a long time.

In rambling talks over the dinners they usually had together, in their lunchtime chats in the hospital cafeteria, in the long hours of reading together or simply sharing the silence in John's room, Lina drew very close to Bob and Tammie Martens. With several installments she told them the full story of what had happened in Cedar Hill between Stan, John, Marissa and herself and then moved on to the events in Italy. In turn they told tales of their loving only child, and she came to know their warmth, wit and intelligence. They were, after all, John's parents.

On their seventh morning at the Villa Schuler, Dr. Martens could not get out of bed. His wife came to San Vincenzo and told Lina there was no way she could face the prospect of the two men in her life, the two great loves of her life, both dying in this same hospital. Bob needed to be with his doctor at the Cleveland Clinic, and she was going to book the next flight back. They had known from the start that moving John was out of the question, so the choice was excruciating, but she must return with her husband and leave her son in Lina's loving hands. She would be back again as soon as Bob had been stabilized and his doctor said she could safely leave him for a time. Not at all certain that it would happen, Lina held the woman in her arms and said with assurance that she and John would see her again soon.

It was a week later that Lilli and Marta had come for their visit, and it was Lilli who suggested the room be re-arranged, a small table brought in so Lina could work there, the bed moved so that John had a better look out the one window and on a clear day could actually see Etna smoking in the distance. At Lina's request, Rena boxed up several books from Lina's apartment and sent them to her, so she could try working on the manuscript again right there in his room. And to her surprise, this actually began to work. She spent much of her time reading aloud to John, passages both from the novels she was writing about and from the manuscript, and she did so whether or not he really seemed to be with her and comprehending.

Word of John's plight had filtered back to St. Thomas. She received emails and a few calls from Fr. Redding and others in the department, all of them solicitous and supportive. The most moving were notes from Bob Bourne, John's old "running buddy," whom she had never really gotten to know, and from George Rolande who said he and his friend were planning a trip to Taormina very soon. Even John's old friend Marlon Tish at the University of Chicago finally heard and somehow got her email address. "Apparently I was John's beard," he wrote. "He told people he was visiting me when in fact he was coming to you, something I had strongly urged him to do the last time we talked. So at least there is one thing I can feel proud of in this heartbreaking story."

* * *

Now after finishing her call with Eleana Stessa, she is in the hall outside John's room and encounters Donatella, the nurse with the perpetual smile. They begin the ritual that has repeated itself for weeks. Lina asks how he is, and the nurse replies, about the same. They have him resting comfortably. Lina enters the room and kisses John on the forehead and then on the mouth. After several seconds he opens his eyes and seems to attempt a smile. She holds his hand and caresses his face. He says finally, "You're sure, he's...?"

She says, "Gone. Forever."

After a long pause, he opens his eyes and struggles to say: "You must..."

She gives him a chance to finish but finally says, "And I'm here with you forever."

Moving to the window she gazes at the blue sky over Mt. Etna. Something is different about this morning. Maybe it is the phone talk she just had with Stessa, or maybe it is the ache in her heart that feels deeper, more ragged today. For whatever reason, she turns back to this man she loves beyond words, knowing she must tell him the truth. She sits in the chair next to the foot of his bed, the place where she reads to him and where he can see her with Etna behind.

And speaking softly but firmly, she tells him, with every detail she can muster, exactly what happened the day she brought Stanford Lyle to the place on that mountain she will never visit again.

###

From T.V. LoCicero:

Word-of-mouth
It's vital to any author. If you enjoyed this book, please consider leaving a review at Amazon. It may be only a line or two, but it could make a big difference and would be deeply appreciated.

Be the First to Learn of a New Release
If you'd like to receive an auto email when the next book is released, please sign up at: http://eepurl.com/z26Vv

Your email address will never be shared, and you can unsubscribe at any time.

Say Hello
My website (http//www.tvlocicero) offers info, thoughts, photos, videos and much more. I'd love it if you come by and say hello. You can also get in touch on Facebook, or send me an email: tvloc1@netscape.net

An excerpt from Vol. Two of The Truth Beauty
Trilogy

THE DISAPPEARANCE

By T. V. LoCicero

TLC Media

Chapter 1

Clara knows this is not exactly a whim. Over the past several weeks she has thought about doing this more times than she cares to remember. But tonight? Certainly she has not thought about doing it tonight.

Until now. Even though over lunch on Monday she listened to her new dear friend Lina reading aloud from Clara's old e-mails to and from Marc — all those words flying back and forth across the Atlantic that neither of them could understand without the idiot translation machine — and she suddenly knew without question that if she and her lover were genuinely hopeful about their future, one or both would have made the requisite effort to learn the other's language. It was time to end it.

Until now. Even though Marc's e-mail this morning on her office computer strained as usual for upbeat, disguising despair about somehow finding a free-lance job that would send him to Europe so he could be with her for at least a few precious days. She could have done it this morning, a quick, cold note meant to set them both free. But she was busy and bothered, and it was worse in the afternoon, and then she had to leave early to pick up those matching little sailor suits the twins ended up loving and their mother hated. She would wait until tomorrow to write back.

Until now. Even though at the twins' fifth birthday party this evening, her two adorable grandsons began chanting, for no discernable reason, "*Le folie de Grandmaman! Le folie de Grandmaman!*" Grandma's folly. Honore, their mother, who has no doubt uttered the phrase about Marc so often that the boys picked it up, tried with a

i

cross look to shush them, while Vera, who seems as flighty lately as her older sister is predictable, simply laughed. Clara's two daughters have been impossible lately. Only Louis came to her rescue, telling his sons with a smile and a wink, "Yes, you two scamps are definitely Grandma's folly."

But on the way back into Geneva from their home in Carouge her eye glimpsed the little Italian place where she and Marc had their last dinner together way back in March, eight months ago now, and that started a train of thought to which she has finally surrendered.

She parks her four-year-old red Opel Astra near the front of the Banque Privee Morneau on the rue de Hollande, the heart of the financial district quiet at this hour on a Thursday evening. A wave and a smile through the glass of the front entrance, and Marcel, the former policeman at the night desk in the lobby, buzzes her in. Walking across the sparkling, high-ceilinged space, she digs in her large purse and pulls out her badge. Just one of the many changes she has seen over the past three decades in this proudly unchanging institution. In the old days, coming at this hour, she would have needed to sign in and out and notate the times.

Now as she says brightly, "*Bonsoir*, Marcel," he simply scans the bar code on her badge and punches a key on his computer. She glances at the large gold clock above his head: 9:32.

"Forget something?" he asks in his clipped French. As usual he looks morose.

"No, I just need to answer an e-mail I neglected this afternoon. I won't be long."

"Monsieur Lyon is up there."

This stops her, and she nearly turns to leave. With Julian in the office does she really want to sit there writing an e-mail ending it with Marc? Her boss has been obnoxious about her lover lately. "Your American Casanova," he calls him. But if Julian is actually working at this late hour, maybe he'll be so engrossed he won't bother her. Or maybe he'll finish soon and leave. In any case, she's determined to do this tonight. Get it over with, this one of too many things in her life she cannot control. At least she'll be out from under this one.

"So," she says finally, "our man burns the midnight oil." She heads for the lift. "*Merci*, Marcel."

On the second floor when she opens the door to the suite and walks in, Julian's office door stands wide open, the lights inside glowing. Not to startle him, she calls softly, "Julian? *Bonsoir*." There is only dead silence. She puts her purse on her desk and moves a few steps to rap twice on the jam and look in. His chair is pushed back away from the desk, and his computer screens are bright. But no Julian. She walks in, a slow step at a time, feeling somehow drawn. And then she stops, telling herself not to do this, not to be in here without him. His firm rule (only one of the things she finds annoying about him) was established from the beginning: Do not enter this office unless your presence is requested. He could walk in any time, in the next second or two, from wherever he went — the men's room maybe, or chatting with Giles, if the chairman has also stayed late? And yet, feeling strangely compelled, she moves slowly to the desk and around its edge.

Now she has a good look at the two large flat panel screens angled together to one side of the glass top desk. At first glance the pages they display seem familiar. Certainly the one on the left has digits in a configuration she has seen many times before on the client account printouts she has delivered to Cecile every quarter for much of the past five years. Except — and now she is moving closer to the screen on the left — there are differences here, rows of numbers that vary markedly from what she has seen before. But then, of course, this must be someone else's account. Except — and now she moves even closer — Cecile Eaton's name is exactly where it always is in the upper left corner. And in the upper right the quarter listed is not from some decade or two past but is in fact the most recent, completed 30, September, 2009.

With her stomach beginning to twist, she moves her gaze to the screen on the right, and scans slowly, steadily, back and forth across its lines and totals. Then she looks again at that familiar screen on the left, and with one more long look at the screen on the right, she knows with a certainty that lands like a terrible blow to the chest that her life has just changed forever.

She feels dazed, stunned for several seconds, until the perfect silence in this office is cut with the distant rush of a flush from the men's room down the hall. And suddenly she feels her heart slamming. If the fastidious Julian stops to wash his hands, she will have maybe 30 seconds to flee unseen.

Moving quickly now, she pauses for a second at her desk,

wondering if she should just sit there and start her computer. No, she grabs her purse and, feeling her mouth quiver, heads for the hall. Pulling the door open, she looks up the corridor to the men's room entrance, then slips off her heels and shoves them in her bag. Go, go! Silently she closes the door behind her and, with a soundless dash that feels like forever, she reaches the near end of the hallway and turns the corner just as she hears the soft creak of the men's room door opening. Pressing herself against the wall next to the lift, she stares at the door to the stairwell. As she listens to his footsteps coming closer, she wonders if he caught a glimpse of her rounding the corner. If so, would he have called, or simply continued to follow her down here? But the footsteps stop, and the sound of the door opening to their suite brings her some relief. Finally when it clicks shut, she breathes.

On the landing heading down the stairs, she slips on her shoes, and when she reaches the lobby door, she stops, shakes her hair into place, takes one deep breath and practices the smile she will give Marcel as he again scans her badge and she wishes him "*Bonsoir.*"

For more information on this and other works by T.V. LoCicero please visit:

www.tvlocicero.com

www.ingramcontent.com/pod-product-compliance
Lightning Source LLC
Chambersburg PA
CBHW032135190626
46814CB00005BA/1711